D1711187

CENTRAL ARKANSAS LIBRARY SYSTEM
SOUTHWEST
BRANCH LIBRARY
LITTLE ROCK, ARKANSAS

JAN 2 5 1990

DARK HARVEST
Arlington Hts., Illinois ·1989

Night Visions 7

Edited by Stanley Wiater

· all original stories by ·

Richard Laymon

Chet Williamson

Gary Brandner

illustrated by

Charles Lang

Trade Hardcover Edition ISBN-0-913165-50-6

NIGHT VISIONS 7 Copyright ©1989 by Dark Harvest, Inc.
Introduction and AfterWords Copyright ©1989 by Stanley Wiater
Illustrations Copyright ©1989 by Charles and Wendy Lang

These stories are works of fiction. Names, characters, places and
incidents are either the product of the authors imaginations or are
used fictitiously. Any resemblance to actual events or locales, or
persons, living or dead, is entirely coincidental.

"Mop Up" Copyright ©1989 by Richard Laymon.
"Wishbone" Copyright ©1989 by Richard Laymon.
"Bad News" Copyright ©1989 by Richard Laymon.
"Madman Stan" Copyright ©1989 by Richard Laymon.

"Blue Notes" Copyright ©1989 by Chet Williamson.
"Confessions of St. James" Copyright ©1989 by Chet Williamson.
"Assurances of the Self-Extinction of Man" Copyright ©1989 by
    Chet Williamson.

"Damntown" Copyright ©1989 by Gary Brandner.

All Rights Reserved.

Manufactured in the United States of America.

FIRST EDITION

Dark Harvest / P.O. Box 941 / Arlington Heights, IL / 60006

DEDICATION

To Iris, who allows me to avoid the real
horrors lurking just beyond this book . . .

CENTRAL ARKANSAS LIBRARY SYSTEM
SOUTHWEST BRANCH
LITTLE ROCK, ARKANSAS

The Publishers would like to express their gratitude to the following people. Thank you: Ann Cameron Williams, Kathy Jo Camacho, Dawn Austin, Stan and Phyllis Mikol, Dr. Stan Gurnick PhD, Wayne Sommers, Tony Hodes, Bertha Curl, Kurt Scharrer, Gary Fronk, Linda Solar, Ken Morris, The People of the All American Print Center, Raymond and Teresa and Mark Stadalsky, Tom Pas, Dean R. Koontz, Ken and Lynda Fotos, Joe R. Lansdale, John Farris, and Stephen Gallagher.

And, of course, special thanks go to the most important people to this book. Without them NIGHT VISIONS 7 would not exist: Richard Laymon, Chet Williamson, Gary Brandner, Stanley Wiater, and Charles and Wendy Lang.

STANLEY WIATER

RICHARD LAYMON

CHET WILLIAMSON

GARY BRANDNER

Introduction

One of the most popular yet troublesome questions asked a writer is the age-old *"Where do you get your ideas?"*

In spite of their protests to the contrary, most creative people know exactly when and where the flash of inspiration occurred. Unfortunately, by the time this question is eventually asked, the writer has usually moved on to several other major projects. Naturally, each new idea has since taken precedent in the storage banks of his imagination over whatever title a fan has just now happened to inquire about. Indeed, most of us can't recall how many cups of coffee we had this morning, let alone have the ability to remember the moment of inspiration for a story or novel which may have been published months, if not years, ago.

For example, the stories you are about to read—though written expressly for this volume—are already nearly a year old from their conception. So who could be there to ask the classic question while the ideas were still freshly percolating through the writer's brain?

Which is all by way of saying that when I was invited to edit a volume of NIGHT VISIONS, it was primarily because the publishers knew me by reputation. Not as an author (though I have published horror fiction), but as someone who has been interviewing other writers and filmmakers in the field since 1974.

Simply stated, I was given the unique opportunity to confer with three fabulous writers, and torture them if necessary to try and pry loose that age-old secret from them. *Where do you get your ideas?* is still what everyone wants to know, though few fans are brave or naive enough to openly inquire in public anymore. Hopefully, the "After-words" conducted at the end of each writer's—and artist's—contribution will shed some light on how and why these particular night visions came to be.

So turn down the lights and welcome to NIGHT VISIONS 7.

Stanley Wiater
Holyoke, Massachusetts
March 1989

Richard Laymon

Flophouse Droolers

A live one came after Mike Phipps when he shouldered open the door of 214. This kind of thing had happened plenty of times before, but it still turned his stomach to warm jelly.

The drooler hadn't been missed by the main force when it moved through. He'd been hit by something, all right. In the shimmering red fire glow from the tenement window, Mike could see that he was holding a bundle of his guts with one hand as he lurched past the end of the bed, raising a butcher knife that looked as if it had already been used on someone. "Commmme to papa," the guy said, foam spraying from his mouth.

Mike groaned.

God, he hated this.

He gave the drooler a squirt.

The blast of fire from his flame thrower filled the room with light. The drooler, ablaze from head to toe, shrieked and staggered backward, dropping his knife, dropping his guts. His intestines spilled toward the floor, sizzling and snapping like sausage on a skillet. The end of the bed knocked his legs out from under him. He flopped onto the mattress.

By the light of the burning man, Mike scanned the room. Over near the open closet was sprawled a naked woman. She'd been head

15

shot, probably by the main force. From the looks of her, the live one hadn't been so far gone that he'd lost his appetite.

Mike gave her a squirt, shrouding her with flames.

He looked back at the bed. The fiery body seemed to be sinking into the mattress.

Backing into the corridor, he did a quick pivot to make sure there were no other live ones around. The smoky hallway fluttered with firelight from the doorways of the three other rooms where he'd already torched bodies. He ran past them, crouching low, eyes watering, the smoke bitter in his nostrils, dry in his throat.

His heart gave a sickening lurch as he started down the stairs and stepped on a drooler. He'd forgotten about this one. He'd passed it coming up, and planned to light it on the way out. But the damned thing had slipped his mind. When his boot came down on its shoulder, the body flipped onto its side, hurling Mike at the banister. The rail creaked and wobbled as his hip slammed against it. For a moment, he thought he was going over the top. But he rebounded off the banister and stumbled down several stairs, some-how missing the drooler's legs, grunting each time the fuel tank pounded his back. With a quick grab of the rail, he managed to stop himself.

When he had his breath again, he turned around and gave the corpse a quick burst.

He trotted to the bottom of the stairs. He was tempted to skip the ground floor rooms. The last thing he needed was a run-in with another live one. Besides, the fire would take care of any leftovers down here.

You can't be sure of that, he told himself. One could get buried under the rubble and never be touched by the flames. Might pass it on to somebody sooner or later.

Nobody would ever know it was Mike's fault, but he didn't want something like that on his conscience.

So he rushed down the dark, narrow corridor to its far end. Then he began working his way back toward the foyer, throwing open doors, stepping carefully into rooms, checking inside closets and bathrooms, behind furniture and under beds, finding plenty of dead droolers and torching each of them.

After the last room, he paused in the foyer. The top half of the stairway was a bright pyre. Its flames had already joined the con-flagration at the opening to the second floor hallway.

Feeling shaky but relieved, Mike pushed open the front door. He rushed out into the night.

Sarge, Ray and Stinger, already done with their buildings, stood by the Land Rover in the middle of the street. Only Stinger still carried his flame thrower. He was busy taking the tank off his back as Mike approached.

Sarge was lighting a cigar.

Ray was using the front of his open fatigue shirt to wipe the grime and sweat off his face.

Doug was missing.

Mike turned around slowly as he pulled the straps off his shoulders. The street, flanked by burning shops and flophouses, was a junkyard of charred cars, broken glass and rubble blasted from buildings. Several bodies were scattered around—black, misshapen heaps on the pavement, some still smouldering. Mike had fired a couple of them, himself, during the Exterior Mop Up Phase.

But he saw nobody moving about.

No sign of Doug.

He eased his flame thrower down, stretched, and rubbed his shoulders.

"Having fun yet?" Stinger asked.

"Take a leap," Mike said.

Stinger's lean face grinned. "Got me a couple of livies over at the pawn shop."

"Made his day," Ray muttered. Ray, a baby-faced kid of nineteen, didn't care for Stinger any more than the rest of them did.

"Yessir. They was both packin' heat. Not as much as me, though." Chuckling, he nudged his flame thrower with a boot. "Took out the fella, first. Gals can't shoot worth shit, anyhow. Shoulda seen the tits on this one. Out to here, y'know? Gazoombas. She's coming at me, butt naked, poppin' caps, missing by a mile, these big old headlights bobbin' around. So I let her have it, y'know? Zip zip. A dash here, a dash there. She starts floppin' around with her tits on fire."

"Shut up, huh?" Mike said. "I'm getting pretty sick and tired . . ."

"Hey man, hang on, haven't got to the good part yet. So then I lay one right in her face."

"Knock it off, Stinger," Sarge said.

"Her fuckin' head explodes. *Explodes!* Can you dig it? Got some on me." He wiped his hand across a gob of goo on his shirt and swept it at Mike's face.

17

Mike swatted the hand away.

"I *said* knock it off!" Sarge snapped.

Stinger laughed, shook his head, and rubbed off the mess on a leg of his fatigue pants.

"You're having such a high old time," Sarge told him, "suppose *you* go look for Doug."

"Fuck that. Dickhead's a pain in the ass."

Sarge scowled at Stinger, squinting through gray shreds of cigar smoke. Then he took a final suck on the stub, plucked it from his mouth, tapped off a load of ash, and shot the cigar at Stinger's face. Red sparks flew as the glowing tip shattered against the soldier's cheekbone.

"Hey! Ow! Shit!" Stinger cried out, slapping away the embers and ash.

"Do what I tell you," Sarge said.

"Jesus! I was *gonna*. Jesus!"

"On the double."

"Yessir!" Stinger hefted his fuel tank, swinging it onto his back and shoving his arms through the straps. Crouching, he snatched up the squirter. "Which way'd he go?"

"He took the Carlton Hotel."

"Well no wonder he ain't back yet," Stinger whined. "Look at that place!" The hotel, at the end of the block, was a square brick structure with four stories.

Mike scanned its upper windows. He saw no trace of fire. Doug would've started at the top and worked his way down. That was s.o.p. If he'd made it to the fourth floor, he must've found no droolers to torch.

But maybe Doug hadn't made it that far.

Mike didn't like Doug. But he liked even less the way the squad was getting whittled down. If they lost Doug, they'd be down to four men. Scuttlebut had it that they wouldn't be getting any replacements.

"Okay if I go with him?" he asked Sarge as Stinger headed for the distant street corner.

"Yeah. Go on. It'll hurry things along."

Mike picked up his weapon.

"While you're in there, do the place."

"Right."

"Be careful," Ray said.

18

"Bet on it." He slapped the kid on the shoulder, then hurried to catch up with Stinger.

He joined the lanky soldier and walked beside him.

"Just don't fuck with me, Phipps. Goddamn candy-ass pussy."

"I may kill you, pal, but I'll never fuck with you."

Stinger laughed.

Mike followed him into the lobby of the hotel.

Sissy Suit

"Krugman!" Stinger yelled up the dark stairway. "Krugman, you shit, answer up!"

"He isn't going to hear you," Mike said.

"Oh, yeah. Worse pussy than you are."

They turned on flashlights and started climbing the stairs.

Doug Krugman, an effete jerk who acted as if every other guy in the squad was no more endearing than an after-birth, had a fear of contagion that prompted him to continue wearing his sissy suit long after everyone else had tossed theirs. Mike had kept his longer than anyone except Doug. He didn't consider the protective garments to be sissy suits, but they were just too bulky and confining. And the head covering knocked out most of your vision. He'd decided he would rather take his chances with the virus than get himself blind-sided by a live one. Or fall down a flight of stairs.

Which I nearly did anyhow, he thought, remembering the last place.

Stopping at the second floor landing, Stinger again yelled, "Krugman!"

"Knock it off."

"He mighta tooken off the headgear, dipshit."

"Not Doug. So hold it down."

"Scared I'll wake the dead?"

"It's not the dead I'm worried about."

Mike heard a soft, nasal snort. "Wouldn't be no fun, we didn't run into some livies now 'n then. Know what I mean, sweetums?"

Mike didn't bother to answer.

As they climbed toward the third floor, Stinger said, "Booger at twelve o'clock."

"Hold fire."

"Yeah yeah."

They reached the landing and hit the drooler with their flashlight beams. He was a kid, maybe sixteen, slumped against the wall with an axe across his legs. He wore his Fruit of the Looms, and nothing else. Someone had stitched him with an M-16, poking a trail straight up his front groin to forehead. As if for the fun ot it, his eyes had been shot out.

Stinger laughed softly. "Guess what? I'm not the only guy with a sense of humor."

"Let's split up," Mike said. "You take this floor, I'll take the top."

"Don't like my company?"

"Just don't go torching anyone till I'm down."

"Can't make no promises. I run into a livie . . ."

"Use your pistol."

"Where's the fun in that?"

"All depends where you shoot 'em," Mike said.

"Ha! Good one. Hope for you yet, dickhead."

Mike stepped over the outstretched legs of the drooler, and shined his flashlight up the last flight of stairs. The area looked clear. He started to climb.

He felt a little guilty about his last remark to Stinger. Like stooping to the creep's level. Better that, though, than to leave him down there thinking it might be amusing to set the place on fire.

The bastard might do it, anyway.

Probably fire escapes up here someplace, Mike told himself.

Stinger'd better pray he doesn't make me use one.

Nearing the top of the stairs, Mike switched off his flashlight. He climbed the final steps, crept across the landing, and leaned through a doorway. As he'd expected, the corridor glowed faintly—light from the burning neighborhood that came in through the room windows. Several doors had been left open by the soldiers of the main force, so that patches of murky, rust-colored light trembled in the hallway. Not much, but enough to see by.

Mike clipped the flashlight to his web belt, glad he wouldn't need to use it.

He stepped into the hallway, took a shaky breath, and tried to decide whether to start here or at the far end. There were points in favor of both methods. If you torched them in the rooms as you went along, you took a chance of fire spreading into the corridor and blocking your escape. That was its down-side. Its up-side was that it pretty much removed the chance of a live one getting you from the rear.

The first order of business is finding Doug, he reminded himself.

So he made up his mind to check each room as he went along, hold off on squirting any droolers he might find, and take care of them on the way back.

Where the hell *is* that guy?

He stepped into the first room. A female drooler lay spread-eagled on the floor at the foot of the bed, her face shot away.

Like most of them, she was naked.

All they wanted to do, once the virus nailed them, was fuck and kill and eat each other.

The damn germ must've been invented by a guy like Stinger, Mike thought.

Stingerovski.

Huffing out a soft laugh at his crummy joke, Mike stepped past the sprawled body. He used his flashlight to check the bathroom and under the bed. No other droolers. No Doug.

As he headed for the door, glancing all around, the pale beam of his light swept across the body and his heart gave a kick when something moved down there. He whirled. He gazed at the corpse.

It *couldn't* have moved. The poor gal was as dead as dead can be. What he'd seen must've been a shadow cast by her body as the light passed over it.

Nothing more.

But he stared at her chest, half expecting it to rise and fall with her breathing.

If she sits up, he thought, I'm gonna throw a heart attack.

But her chest appeared motionless.

She had a small freckle above her left nipple.

The same as Merideth.

She *looked* like Merideth.

Feeling hot and sick, Mike realized that the dead woman appeared to be in her early twenties. Her hair, spread out against the floor, was long and blond. She had Merideth's slim build, small breasts . . . and that freckle.

With the face demolished, there was no way . . .

It's not her, Mike told himself. Impossible. She was in Sacramento when Black Widow hit.

But she's just as dead as this woman. Probably sprawled out naked and shot in her apartment . . .

He knew that. She'd had no more chance than anyone else who didn't have protective gear when the strike took place. He'd been living with the knowledge, trying to do his job, trying to keep her death hidden in a back corner of his mind.

He wished he hadn't come into this room.

He wished he hadn't taken a closer look at this corpse.

His throat tightened. The body blurred as tears filled his eyes. Switching off his flashlight, he backed away. His shoulder bumped the doorframe. He staggered into the corridor, turned away and flinched as a dark shape moved through the shadows down the hallway.

He brought up his flame thrower.

Suddenly he realized the vague figure was a man in a sissy suit. "Doug!"

A gloved hand waved a greeting at him.

"Jeez, man, what've you been doing up here? We figured they must've gotten you."

Doug didn't answer. The lenses of his headgear shimmered golden for a moment as he strode past the doorway of the next room down. The glow of distant firelight fluttered on the camouflage pattern of his suit.

He had no flame thrower. His gunbelt was gone.

"Where're your weapons?" Mike asked. "What's going on?"

A muffled sound of laughter came from him.

Mike felt a chill spread up his back.

"Take that thing off and talk to me," he said.

More laughter.

"Doug, stop being an asshole and . . ."

In a voice that sounded as if it came from inside a tight box, Doug said, "Okay, okay." A stride away from Mike, he halted. With gloved hands, he reached up and tore at the seal of his mask.

He lifted the hood off his head.

He grinned and laughed, slobber flowing down his chin.

22

Mike thought, *Quit kidding around.*

Then he thought, *He's turned into a drooler.*

Then he knew, *It's not Doug.*

A live one who just bore a vague resemblance to the guy.

He thought, *Oh shit!* and tried to swing up the muzzle of his flame thrower as the laughing drooler rammed the headgear into his face and shoved him. He stumbled backward. He crashed to the floor, the tank slamming into his spine. The drooler kicked the weapon from his hands. It tumbled across the hallway until the fuel hose jerked it to a stop and it dropped. Mike tried to sit up, saw a kick coming at his face, and turned his head so the blow only clipped his cheek. It was enough to knock him back.

The drooler stomped on his belly. His breath blasted out.

The infected man flopped down on him, straddling his hips, ripping open his fatigue shirt. Mike went for his pistol, but a knee blocked his way. He landed a punch that snapped the drooler's head sideways. The guy didn't seem bothered, though. Chuckling softly, he rubbed and slobbered on Mike's chest. Then he clutched Mike's shoulders and lunged toward his face, the germ-rich saliva splashing a trail up his chest and throat and chin. Clamping his lips tight, Mike punched both thumbs into the man's eyes.

The eyeballs popped, splashing warm fluid down his thumbs and wrists.

The drooler shrieked.

Thumbs deep inside the sockets, Mike clutched the sides of the drooler's face and hurled him sideways. Scrambling to his knees, he jerked out his Beretta and put three 9 mm. slugs into the man's head.

Hot Split

Mike tried not to panic. Keeping his mouth shut and panting through his nose, he threw off the straps of the fuel tank and yanked his shirt off. With the back of his shirt, he scrubbed the foamy

23

spittle off his mouth and cheeks, his chin, his neck and chest. He wiped spit and blood and viscous fluid off his hands and forearms.

I'll be okay, he told himself.

He didn't think he had any breaks in his skin.

If the stuff doesn't get into your bloodstream . . . What do they know? Maybe it only has to get in your mouth. Nobody knows shit.

Snatching up his sidearm, Mike glanced through the doorway at the body of the woman who looked like Meredith. He didn't want to go in there. So he ran to the next room. He fumbled the flashlight off his belt, switched it on and rushed in.

Looked empty.

He raced to the bathroom door and threw it open. A skinny, naked drooler lay sprawled over the side of the tub—feet on the floor, butt on the edge of the tub, back bent, shoulders and head resting on the bloody enamel of the tub's bottom. His arms were flung out, and a straight razor lay near his right hand. He'd been hit in the chest with something better than an M-16. Probably an assault shotgun.

Crouching beside the body, Mike twisted a faucet handle. Water splashed from the spout.

Works!

He grabbed the drooler by the ankles and yanked him out of the tub. The head made a nasty thump when it struck the floor. Mike dragged him from the bathroom, rushed back inside, and slammed the door. It bumped open. The doorframe was splintered, the latch plate hanging by one screw. Soldiers from the main force must've bashed the door open, coming for that guy.

Big deal, Mike thought. So you can't lock it. The bastard slobbered *all over you!*

He set his flashlight on the edge of the sink so its beam lit the partly open door. Bending over the tub, he turned the water on full force. No hot, but he didn't care. Lucky to have any water at all. He plucked up the shower knob. In seconds, a hard spray was rushing from the nozzle. He let it run to wash the drooler's blood down the drain. While he waited, he picked up the straight razor and tossed it into the sink. Then he hurled his shirt into the tub and climbed in.

The water felt icy on his hot skin. It splattered his face, sent cold rivulets flowing down his body, soaked through his pants and made them heavy and clinging.

With a bar of soap from the dish beside the tub, he lathered his body.

24

He left the shower curtain open. He kept the automatic in his right hand. He watched the lighted door. He wondered if the soap and water would do any good.

Or was he already a walking dead man?

Yesterday, a live one bit Rogers. The little guy had kept it quiet, explaining his torn and bloody sleeve away by claiming he'd been cut on a broken window. They went about their business. Two hours later, when he didn't come out of a liquor store, Ray had gone in after him. Ray returned looking as if the blood had been drained from his usually rosy cheeks. He'd found Rogers in the back room, humping a drooler. When he shouted, Rogers had turned his head and grinned, the tell-tale foam gushing from his mouth. One squirt took care of Rogers and the girl.

After Ray finished telling his story, Stinger had said, "You get all the luck, Raygun."

I'll blow my brains out, Mike told himself, before I end up like Rogers.

I'll know one way or the other in a couple hours.

Thinking about that, heat seemed to pulse through his body and he had a hard time catching a breath.

I'm probably all right.

Jesus, what if I've got it?

He rinsed off the suds. Watching the door, he soaped himself again.

How do you know if you've got it? he wondered. All of a sudden, you just start feeling horny for no good reason?

When Stinger starts looking good to me . . .

He heard himself laugh. It sounded a bit mad.

Maybe it's when you start laughing at shit that isn't funny.

God, he thought, I'll be like one of *them*. When it hits, maybe I'll *like* it. Maybe I won't want to kill myself, just everyone else.

Mike let the spray wash the soap off his face, then turned his back to the shower. He raised his Beretta in front of his face. He could barely see it.

Go ahead, he thought.

But what if I'm not infected?

What if you are? You want to risk it? What if it hits you and you take out Sarge or Ray?

He tipped the barrel downward to make sure it had no water in it.

What, scared it'll blow up in your hand?

He opened his mouth wide. He inserted the muzzle. He clamped it between his teeth.

Oh shit, he thought. I don't want to do this.

Merideth's dead. And Mom and Dad. The whole country's fucked. Maybe the whole world, by now. Or pretty soon. Nobody around but droolers and soldiers. Even if you get out of this mess in one piece, what's left?

Come on, find one good reason not to blow your head off. Better make it a good one.

Okay. What about Sarge and Ray? Stinger can take a leap as far as I care. But what about Sarge and Ray? They're my friends. How're they going to feel, I go AWOL on them? What if they run into some bad shit and need me?

I'll go back out there. Tell them what happened. Tell them to drop me if I turn haywire.

Mike eased the pistol out of his mouth. He slipped it into his holster and sagged beneath the cold spray, shivering and gasping for air.

Hider

Dropping to a crouch, Mike drew his sidearm, pivoted and swung the gun toward the bathroom doorway where Stinger stood in the bright beam of the flashlight.

"It's only me from across the sea, dickbrain."

"Jesus."

"How'd you guess?"

Mike stood up. He put away his gun and bent under the spray to shut the water off.

"What the fuck are you doing in here?" Stinger asked.

"I got drooled on. Did you see the guy in the hallway?"

"Doug?"

"That's not Doug."

27

"Could've fooled me. Course, there wasn't much face to go by."

"Must've killed Doug and taken his suit." Mike bent to pick up his shirt, then decided against it.

"And he gotcha, huh?"

"He didn't *get* me. It's not like Rogers. He just yucked me up, so I showered off."

"Yeah?"

As Mike climbed out of the tub, Stinger unclipped his own flashlight and stepped the rest of the way into the bathroom.

The beam hit Mike's face. He squinted and turned away.

"Don't mind if I check you out, do you?"

"For what? Bite marks?"

"That. Broken skin."

"What if you find something? You going to torch me?"

"Yep." The beam swept slowly down Mike's body. "Turn around."

He did.

"Drop your pants."

"Not for you, pal." He turned around slowly and squinted against the glare of Stinger's light. The muzzle of the flame thrower was pointing at his chest. "Maybe the guy did get me with his spit. I don't know. I guess there's a chance of it. So how about you keep an eye on me? If I start acting weird, take me down."

"Maybe I oughta just do it now." In the glow of the flashlight on the sink, Mike saw a grin tilt the corners of Stinger's mouth.

"Maybe you should," he said. "No replacements coming, though. It'll just be you, Sarge and Ray. You three and the droolers."

For a few moments, Stinger didn't move. Then he lowered the muzzle of the flame thrower. "I can wait," he said. He backed through the doorway.

Mike rinsed off his flashlight at the sink, dried it on a leg of his pants, and followed Stinger to the corridor. They made their way toward the far end, Mike checking the rooms on the left, Stinger taking those on the right.

Mike found plenty of dead droolers, but no Doug. He had two rooms to go when Stinger called, "Got him."

He rushed across the hallway. Stinger was standing over the body.

Doug lay on his back between the bed and an open closet. The top of his head was caved in. His shirt had been ripped open. His pants were down around his knees. Here and there, his skin was caked with white glop. Strips of his flesh had been torn off. Chunks of him were gone.

"Who says this ain't a picnic?" Stinger said.

"Shut up."

Doug's flame thrower and gun belt were a few yards to the right of the body. They looked as if they'd been in the drooler's way, and he'd flung them.

Mike stepped over to the cast-off gear. With his flashlight, he checked for drool. Then he hefted the flame thrower, slung its tank onto his bare back, and worked his arms through the straps. He fastened Doug's web belt around his waist, just above his own belt, then slid the buckle to the rear so that the holster rested against his left hip.

"You're takin' all that stuff, go on and help yourself to his dog tags."

"Why don't you."

"I'm not touchin' that fucker. Be glad to torch him, though."

"I'll do it," Mike muttered. Stepping close to the body, he shined his light down. The dog tags were embedded in the bloody mess that was left of Doug's neck. Mike put his flashlight away and shifted the flame thrower to his left hand. Crouching, he took out his knife. He cut off a patch of Doug's shirt, sheathed the knife, and wrapped his hand in the fabric.

"What a pussy."

With his covered hand, he fished the dog tags out of the gore and yanked, breaking the chain. He left them wrapped in the square of shirt. He shoved them into his pocket.

As he backed away, Stinger sent a stream of fire into Doug's bloody groin.

"You rotten . . ."

Laughing, Stinger hit the body with a full dose that wrapped it in flame. "Happy trails, asshole."

Mike, staggering backward, had his pistol halfway out of the holster when he thought, I can't shoot him for being a maggot.

He wondered if his urge to kill the son of a bitch was an early symptom. Jamming the pistol back down tight into the holster, he turned away and rushed from the room.

Seconds later, Stinger joined him in the hallway. "You got a problem?"

Mike glared at him.

"Okay, let's move it. We got us four stories worth of droolers need squirting."

They took care of the rooms at the end of the corridor, then made their way back toward the stairs, racing from room to room, entering those they'd already checked and torching the corpses. Mike came to the one with the body that looked like Merideth. He didn't focus on her, just fired a quick stream through the doorway.

He grabbed a strap of the flame thrower he'd discarded after nailing the drooler in the sissy suit. Hefting it beside him, he watched Stinger torch the guy. Then they rushed down the stairs.

At the third floor landing, he dropped the spare weapon beside the dead drooler who had the axe. He raced down the hallway after Stinger. They split up and charged through the rooms, leaving fiery bodies behind. Mike lugged the extra flame thrower down the stairs to the second floor. He left it on the landing, and picked it up again after they'd flamed every body on that level of the hotel. He lugged it down to the first floor and left it near the foot of the stairs.

"You take care of the hall," Stinger gasped. "I'll see what we've got in the lobby."

Mike didn't like that idea. Alone, it would take him twice as long to hit each room. Twice as long, with three stories of hotel above him. Ten to fifteen fires on each story. All of them growing.

But the lobby needed to be done. There was an area behind the registration desk. There were at least two doors that he could see at a glance. Maybe more, off in the shadows.

"Okay," he said, and dashed for the end of the corridor.

Don't worry about the fire, he told himself. Right. Probably an inferno up there, by now.

But it won't spread downward all that fast.

You hope.

I'm on the ground floor, he reminded himself. I can always bail out through a window.

And the door at the end of the hall was probably an emergency exit.

He stopped short of that one, and shouldered a room door hard so it slapped the wall behind it. Satisfied nobody was behind it, he entered. Nobody on the bed or floor. He pulled his flashlight and rushed to the bathroom. Clear. He dropped and shined the light under the bed. Clear.

He rushed across the hall and hit the next door. Male drooler slumped against the wall, one arm blown off, a pulpy chasm in the middle of his chest. Mike searched for others. None. He splashed the corpse with fire, and rushed out.

Ran to the next door. Hit it. Charged in. A pair on the bed. Still at it, obviously, when the troopers nailed them. An automatic had poked a large S into the guy's bare rump and back. Mike couldn't see much of the woman. Just her spread legs on each side of the guy and one arm stretched across the mattress.

The floor around the bed looked clear. He checked the closet and bathroom. No one. No need to check under the bed. If a drooler was down there, it would go up when he torched these two.

Mike wondered about the woman, though. If she'd been under this guy when the troopers barged in, where was she hit?

Stepping closer to the side of the bed, he checked her with his flashlight. Her head was turned the other way, the guy's face resting on top of it. She had blond hair, very short. No head was visible. Mike began to wonder if she might be a male, after all. But he saw that her armpit was shaved. A woman, all right. Not much of her showed, the way she was mashed between the body and the mattress. Just her bare side. Still, he saw no evidence of wounds.

Her skin, glowing softly in the firelight from the window, looked warm and smooth.

He considered throwing the guy off her.

You want to see how she got it? he thought. Or you just want to check her out?

Come off it! She's a drooler. She's dead.

He realized he *did* want to look at her. There was a tight, growing heat in his groin.

It's kicking in, he thought. Oh, shit! The bastard got me, all right. I'm a dead man.

All of a sudden, he didn't feel horny anymore.

He felt as if his genitals were shriveling with cold.

Maybe there's hope?

He heard himself let out a weird laugh.

He raised the flame thrower.

Someone made a faint, high whimper.

Mike gasped as the man's head lifted.

A live one!

Before he could fire, he realized that the man hadn't moved his

31

head. The head beneath it was already facing his way.

Wisps of golden hair across the brow. Big, terrified eyes. A bruised cheekbone. Lips pressed tight together. Chin trembling.

The mouth opened. No foam spilled out.

"What're you gonna do with that thing?" she asked in a tight, shaky voice.

She looked no older than twenty. She looked beautiful. She didn't look like a drooler.

"You're alive?" Mike muttered.

"So far. No thanks to the goddamn army."

"Sorry. I . . ."

"You gonna kill me?"

"How can you be alive?"

"I'm a good hider." She shoved the dead man. Mike stepped back fast as the corpse tumbled off the bed and hit the floor at his feet. He watched the woman sit up and swing her legs toward him. She had a slender body. One of her breasts had a smear of dried blood on the side. There was another stain on her belly, just above the gleaming curls of her pubic hair. Another on her left thigh. Mike watched the way her breasts jiggled slightly as she stood up. She pushed his flashlight aside. "You don't have to *inspect* me, do you?"

"Sorry," he muttered.

Crouching, she rolled the body away from the side of the bed. She got down on her knees and reached under the bed.

Mike gazed at the sleek curves of her back and rump.

He felt a hot swelling in his groin. This time, it didn't throw him into a panic. It's not Black Widow, he thought. Just healthy lust. Besides, it's too soon. With Roger, it took a couple of hours.

The young woman dragged a small pile of clothing out from under the bed, got up and sat on the mattress. As she drew pink panties up her legs, she looked at Mike. "Come on, do you mind?"

He suddenly remembered something.

"Oh shit, we've gotta get out of here! The whole damn building's going up in smoke."

R.I.P.

He grabbed her arm and yanked her off the bed. She came up clutching some clothes to her belly. "Take it easy!" she blurted. She jerked her arm, and Mike let go. Crouching, she snatched a pair of sneakers off the floor.

Mike raced to the door. The corridor was bright with fire from the rooms to the right. Some smoke, but not much. Should be no problem making it to the lobby.

He looked back. The woman, just behind him, was bent over and pulling her shoes on.

"Come *on!*"

She rushed up to him. He gave her a shove to help her through the doorway, then took a stride toward the corpse on the floor.

A *good hider,* he thought. Christ, how could anyone do that? Play dead under a drooler. Both of you in the raw.

He squirted the body, then turned to the doorway.

She was in the corridor, glimmering with firelight, a skirt or something clamped between her knees while she stretched up both arms and worked a T-shirt down over her head. Her face popped through the neck hole. "What're we waiting for?" she asked, lowering the shirt. It was bloody, torn, and much too large for her. It hung off one shoulder. It draped her thighs like a short skirt.

Mike shook his head. He rushed past her, crossed to the next room and bashed its door open.

"I thought we were getting out of here."

"I've got a job to do. Stay put." He entered, checked the room, found no droolers, and returned to the hallway. Now, the woman had a skirt on. It looked like denim. Only a bit of it showed below her draping T-shirt.

She stayed beside him as he hurried to the next room. She waited while he went in. One drooler. He torched it. When he came out, flames were lapping out of the doorways down the hall.

"Shouldn't we get going?" she asked. "I don't exactly look forward to getting cooked."

"We'll be okay." He left her and did the next room. Empty.

When he came out, the woman was gone.

He snapped his head to the left.

Spotted the faint white of her Tshirt. She was running. Almost to the lobby.

"Stop!" Mike shouted.

She kept running.

He raced after her.

So I let her have it, y'know? Zip, zip. A dash here, a dash there. She starts floppin' around with her tits on fire.

Mike ran as hard as he could, hands squeezing the flame thrower, tank pounding his back, lungs aching as he gulped the smoky air, eyes watering.

"No!" he yelled, and wondered if she could hear him over the noise of the roaring, snapping flames. "Stop!"

Blinking his eyes clear, he saw the woman halt and turn around.

Not soon enough.

She was already beyond the start of the corridor, standing in the foyer.

Good as dead, Mike thought. If Stinger's there.

Dashing closer, he expected a burst of fire to squirt out of the darkness and engulf her.

"STINGER!" he shouted. "DON'T HIT HER!"

Probably can't hear me, anyway.

But the woman heard. She looked away from Mike for a moment, then hurried toward him.

They met in front of the last room before the lobby.

"I told you to wait!"

"I'm sorry. But the fire . . ."

"I know, I know."

"There's somebody else?"

"Yeah, a trigger-happy jerk. He'd zap you in a flash and enjoy it."

"Oh." She bared her teeth. A grimace as if she knew she'd done something stupid and wanted to kick herself for it.

"Get behind me and stay close."

She nodded. She followed him into the lobby.

There was no sign of fire except for the glow behind them and brightness near the top of the stairs. The lobby looked just the same as when Mike had left Stinger there. Except for a door behind the registration counter. It had been shut. Now, it stood open.

"Stinger!" Mike yelled.

No answer. He heard only the roar of the fire at their backs and above them.

"Maybe he went outside," the woman said.

Or ran into trouble, Mike thought. Doug's kind of trouble.

Then a dim shape filled the upper part of the doorway that was visible beyond the counter. Fire bloomed. In its light, Mike saw Stinger back out of the room and turn around.

He wondered what Stinger had been doing in there before torching someone just now. Must've spent at it a long time. Better if I don't know, he thought.

"It's me," he announced. "I've got a survivor with me, so take it easy."

"You *what?*" The lean soldier braced a hand on the counter, swung himself up, scuttled across the top and leaped to the floor. He raised his flame thrower.

"She's okay. She's not a drooler."

"Step aside."

"I told you, she's okay."

"I'm not infected," she said from behind Mike.

"Then you're the only one, babe." Striding closer, he said, "Let's see ya."

"Don't even think about torching her, man."

"Shut your face. Over here, hon." He gestured with the muzzle of his flame thrower.

The woman stepped out from behind Mike and stood beside him. Her arms were raised high as if she knew how to behave like a prisoner.

Stinger blew through his pursed lips. Holding his flame thrower on the woman with his right hand, he used his left to unclip his flashlight.

From somewhere above them came a wrenching crash. Mike felt the floor shake under his boots. "The place is coming down," he said. "Let's get out to the street and . . ."

"Go on and get, dickhead. She stays." The beam of his flashlight roamed up the woman's body. She squinted and turned her head away when it hit her eyes. "A real cutie. Open up, cutie."

She opened her mouth wide.

"Say 'ahhh.'"

"For Godsake, Stinger! You wanta play doctor, wait'll we're outa here."

"And let Sarge spoil the fun?"

"You bastard."

35

"What's your name, hon?"

"Karen."

Fire began to lap around the doorframe behind the registration counter.

"She doesn't *look* like a drooler," Stinger said. He sounded amused. Stepping close to her, he slipped his flashlight under the bottom of her T-shirt. Its beam seaped through the thin fabric. He moved the flashlight upward, lifting her shirt.

"Leave her alone!" Mike snapped.

"Stay out of it, pussy."

He could see Karen trembling as the bastard raised her shirt above her breasts. She made quiet gasping sounds.

"Just checking for open wounds," Stinger said.

With the rim of the flashlight, he rubbed her right nipple.

Karen swept her arm down. She knocked the flashlight aside.

Stinger smashed her jaw with it.

Crying out, she stumbled backward. She fell to the floor.

Stinger pointed the muzzle of his flame thrower at her.

Mike put a bullet in his head.

The 9 mm. slug came from Doug's Beretta, held low in Mike's left hand. It punched through Stinger just above his right ear, kicked his head sideways and came out the top throwing up a tuft of hair, gobs of brain, chunks of bone, and a thick spray of blood. Stinger stood there while the mess rained down. Then his legs folded. His rump hit the floor. He flopped onto his side.

Mike gazed at him, stunned.

My God, he thought.

I didn't have any choice. He was going to torch Karen.

I killed one of our own.

He realized Karen was holding him, pressing her warm body tight against his, pushing her face against the side of his neck. He could feel her harsh shaking. And the racing of her heart.

"You okay?" he asked.

He felt her head nod.

Am I? he wondered.

He flinched as he saw a fiery beam crash down at the top of the stairway. With a shower of sparks, it slammed against the banister. The railing shook, but held. The heavy beam, weirdly balanced, rode it down, lopped the knob off the top of the newel post, and dropped to the lobby floor.

On top of Mike's discarded flame thrower.

He yelled, "CHRIST!" He shoved Karen back, holstered Doug's gun to free his hand, grabbed her wrist, and ran. They raced past the beam's burning end. He threw open the front door, tugged Karen outside, and dashed with her into the street.

At the far curb was the charred husk of a station wagon.

Behind its rear fender, Mike clutched the back of Karen's neck and forced her down flat against the pavement. He sprawled on top of her.

"What're you doing?"

He didn't have the breath to answer.

"You're mashing me."

An explosion pounded the night. A few seconds later, debris started coming down. Mike lifted his face off the back of Karen's head and saw splinters of wood and glass striking the pavement alongside the car. A few bits of something clinked against the tank on his back. But he felt no jabs.

He felt Karen shaking and flinching beneath him. Soon, the flinching stopped. But she continued to tremble.

Through the ringing in his ears, he heard her say, "Holy cow."

"Yeah."

"Can we get up?"

"Not just . . ."

A second explosion boomed in his ears. That would be Stinger's fuel tank. Not as close to the front of the hotel. The blast wasn't quite so deafening, and none of the debris came down anywhere near Mike and Karen.

"Okay," he said. He crawled off her, lifted his flame thrower by its forestock, and got to his feet.

Karen stood up.

He rested a hand low on her back.

Side by side, they gazed over the roof of the car at the blazing hotel. The brick walls were still intact. Fire flapped and fluttered from the demolished doorway and most of the windows.

"I'm sorry about your friend," Karen said.

"He was no friend."

"I'm sorry anyhow."

He rubbed her back, and she leaned against him.

He looked up the street. The Land Rover was gone. Sarge and Ray were nowhere in sight.

RICHARD LAYMON

The Survivor

Mike led Karen out to the middle of the street—a canyon walled by burning buildings. The squad had been working its way through the slum from west to east. Maybe Sarge and Ray had gone on ahead to the next block. Nothing beyond the cross-street appeared to be on fire, though. Mike couldn't see the Land Rover, but it might be there, blocked from sight by the numerous abandoned vehicles.

"I was with two other guys," he said.

Karen looked at him.

"Don't worry, they're not like Stinger."

"Where are they?"

"Must've moved on. I don't know." He took off his flame thrower. Crouching, he checked the tank's fuel gauge.

Still has some juice, he thought. But not much.

He stood up and faced Karen. "About what happened back there."

"I'll back up whatever you say," she told him.

"Thanks. A drooler got Stinger, that's all. We didn't see it happen, just found the body."

Gazing at him with solemn eyes, she nodded.

Mike reached behind his back and unhooked Doug's web belt. "Put this on."

She took the belt from him. She swung it around her waist and fastened it in front, the holster low against her right hip. Mike saw how the belt pulled the T-shirt taut over her breasts and how the wide neck hole, stretched shapeless, drooped off her right shoulder. The shirt was smudged with grime and dry blood, torn here and there. A small flap hung down, showing the smooth skin just below her collar bone. Her belly showed through a sagging rip that looked like a big, grinning mouth.

She finished adjusting the belt, and looked up at Mike. "Not much," she said, "but at least I've got one."

"Huh?"

A smile crooking her mouth, she reached out and patted his chest. "A shirt."

"Mine got wrecked," he said.

Her smile vanished. "Mine got taken. This one's borrowed."

He nodded. "Do you know how to use the pistol?"

"I'll manage. What's your name?"

He was surprised she didn't already know it. He felt as if they'd been together for a long time. "Mike," he said. "Mike Phipps."

"Karen Hadley." She offered her hand, and he shook it.

This is strange, he thought as he said, "Nice to meet you."

"Same here." Her smile returned. "Boy, is *that* the truth. An honest-to-God human being who doesn't want to rape, murder and gobble me up."

"I just wanted to burn you."

"Well, you didn't. And you saved my life."

"Glad to be of service, ma'am." He looked over his shoulder. "I guess we'd better try and find the others."

Karen stepped up beside him, and they started walking up the middle of the street. "You're not taking your flame thrower?"

"It's almost empty," he said. "And there are some extras in the Land Rover. If we can find it."

"Think the guys ran off and left you?"

"Probably just on the next block. We were in there a long time."

"*I* was in there for days."

Mike wrinkled his nose, and couldn't look at her. "Under that guy?"

"Lord, no." She took hold of his hand. "Ten minutes, maybe. When I heard you guys, I . . . *Ugh!* I don't like to think about it."

"Must've been gross."

"I've been through worse."

"Can't imagine that."

"Then you're lucky."

He looked at her. She turned her face toward him. Her jaw was slightly swollen where Stinger had struck her with the flashlight. Her eyes glimmered in the firelight. Somehow, they looked both vulnerable and tough.

"Want to tell me about it?" Mike asked.

"Not much."

"That's okay. I know it must've been pretty bad."

"Yeah. If it wasn't the sickies, it was the soldiers. It's a miracle I'm still alive."

"Why *are* you still alive?"

"Darn good at playing dead, for one thing. As you saw."

"But the Black Widow?"

"Is that what they're calling it?"

"It's what *we* call it, anyway. Because of how it makes people act."

"The Russians do it to us?"

"That's what we've been told. Who knows. They tell us whatever they want. But I haven't heard of any other survivors. I mean, as far as I know, the thing nailed everyone who was exposed to it. We were told there *weren't* any civilian survivors."

Karen looked up at him with something of a smirk, her head tilted to one side. "That's 'cause they didn't know about me."

"You weren't exposed to it?"

"Oh, you've got to be kidding." She turned her face away and peered straight ahead, her eyes narrow. "For starters, the strike caught me outside. So I got . . . what do they call it? 'Primary exposure.' After that . . . I had some intimate contact with sickies. A *lot* of it." She glanced at him, a fierce hurt look in her eyes, then lowered her head.

"I'm sorry, Karen."

She squeezed his hand. "Anyway, I've probably had enough of that virus in me to kill off the planet."

"But you're okay?"

"Peachy," she muttered. "But I don't have the foaming crazies, if that's what you mean."

"Why? It doesn't make sense."

"It's 'cause I'm pure of heart."

Mike felt a smile stretch his face. "Maybe that's it."

"Either that," she said, "or I've got some kind of a natural immunity."

They stepped around the charred heap of a body. He saw Karen turn her face aside.

"If you're immune, there might be others." He thought of Merideth. Maybe she . . .

"Won't be," Karen said, "by the time the army's done. They're dropping everyone in sight."

"God," Mike muttered. Survivors being cut down by the military. Maybe only a few here and there. But if Karen was immune, there almost had to be others. "They think everyone's a drooler," he said. "We've got to let someone know . . ."

"Sure. Phone the White House."

"The Land Rover has a transmitter. We can radio a message to . . ."

"But where is it?"

Mike halted, and Karen stopped beside him. They were in the middle of the intersection. On the block ahead, no fire seemed to be coming from any of the buildings. But there was plenty of light from the burning block at Mike's back to reveal corpses littering the street. Most were naked. None had yet been torched. There were some abandoned vehicles: a taxi at the curb, its windshield shot up; an overturned clunker with a body hanging out the driver's window; a bullet-riddled VW bug resting crooked on the center line, doors on both sides open; a few others. Halfway down the block, faint but visible in the ruddy glow, was an RTD bus that had crashed into a parked car. The bus, angled sideways, blocked out a lot of Mike's view.

He didn't see the Land Rover. He didn't see Sarge or Ray.

"Hope nothing's happened to them," he muttered.

"Maybe they're behind the bus," Karen said.

"Could be." He glanced to the right and left. The cross-street didn't catch as much firelight as the area straight ahead. Not far beyond the intersection, the glow faded to moonlit darkness. From what Mike could see, however, it was no different from every other street in this section of the city. It looked desolate. He saw the dim shapes of scattered bodies. Trashed vehicles. Debris he couldn't recognize.

Nothing moved out there.

He saw no Land Rover. No Sarge or Ray.

"Let's go straight," he said. "I don't know why they'd take off, but that's the way we were heading."

They started walking again. Karen held his hand tightly. They cast shadows on the reddish pavement in front of them.

Even though the night was warm, he felt a chill on his sweaty back as they left the fires behind.

Twin bright lights suddenly broke through the darkness beyond the rear of the distant bus.

Headlights!

He grinned. "We're in business."

He heard the faint, familiar sound of the Land Rover's engine turning over.

The headlights started to move, pushing their pale beams through the night.

41

"I guess they've seen us," Karen said. She sounded a little nervous.

"Don't worry," Mike told her. "These guy's are okay."

The vehicle picked up speed. It swerved to dodge the VW, but didn't bother to miss a body. A front tire bumped over the corpse, tipping the headlight up for a moment.

Somebody let out a merry whoop.

Mike said, "Uh-oh."

He drew his automatic.

The Charge of the Night Brigade

"Your guys?" Karen asked.

"Can't be them."

Then the vehicle was close enough for Mike to make out the shapes of people above the glare of the headlights. A woman rode the hood, feet on the bumper, bare skin dusky in the fire glow, hair blowing, arm waving a K-bar as if she were leading a cavalry charge. A man behind the windshield. Someone in the passenger seat, mostly blocked by the gal on the hood. Two or three in cargo bed, one standing.

The standing one, a bald man with a beard, raised a handgun as the Rover bore down.

Mike put two rounds through the windshield. One of them caught the driver's face. The vehicle swerved, throwing out the drooler with the gun. It sped by, fishtailing, tires screaming, and spun around. The one who'd fallen out stopped flipping over and lay motionless. Mike heard the engine die and watched the Rover skid until it came to rest near the far curb, some fifty feet down the street, headbeams pouring through the remains of a shop's display window.

He and Karen opened fire. Droolers leaped and scurried from the vehicle, ducked behind it. Someone shot back at them. A bullet whined off the pavement a yard to the left of Karen.

Mike slapped her arm. She looked at him. "Come on!" He whirled around.

Side by side, hunching low and weaving, they dashed across the pavement. Behind them, gunshots crashed. They leaped the curb, crunched across the glass-littered sidewalk, and lunged through a dark doorway. They crouched and leaned against the front wall. Karen was huffing loudly.

"You okay?" Mike gasped.

"Peachy."

"Christ."

"At least . . . you got two of them."

He duck-walked past Karen, and she followed him toward the display window.

"How many more?" he asked. "Did you see?"

"Four, maybe. I don't know."

"Where'd *they* come from?" The damn troops, Mike thought, were supposed to nail these fuckers. How in hell did they miss so many? And how come these droolers had bunched together instead of going at each other?

He wondered if they'd killed Sarge and Ray.

Likely.

But there were other mop-up squads around the city. The Land Rover could've been taken from one of them.

Then where's ours?

Stopping at the edge of the smashed window, Mike leaned sideways until he could see out.

Nobody coming.

There were some droolers behind the Rover, keeping low, heads backlighted by the fires on the next block.

They all there? he wondered.

"Do you see them?" Karen asked.

"They're still at the Land Rover."

"What're we going to do?"

"Take 'em out."

"You're not into hiding?"

He laughed softly. "Not when I have a choice. Besides, I want to get my hands on that radio."

"We could sneak out the back," she said. "There must be a rear exit."

Karen's comment reminded him of the store at their backs.

43

He'd been too concerned about the droolers in the street to worry about others. Unclipping his flashlight, he turned away from the window. "Keep an eye on 'em," he whispered.

Karen crept past him, squatted beneath the window and peered out.

Mike swept his beam across the room.

They seemed to be in a small grocery market. A checkout counter to the left of the door. Beyond that was a refrigeration unit, probably the meat section. In the middle of the room stood three rows of shelves, the floor cluttered with fallen cans and packages. Over to the right was a liquor section. There, the shelves he could see were almost bare. Some broken bottles on the floor, but he supposed that most of the booze had been taken by looters—droolers, or soldiers from the main force.

He saw no bodies.

He saw no live ones.

Karen was right, though. There had to be a delivery door at the rear.

"Mike?" she whispered.

Stowing the flashlight, he twisted around and looked out the window.

The droolers were inside the Land Rover again. Its lights had been shut off, and it was slowly backing away from the curb. It came across the street at an angle, rear first, swerving slightly from side to side but making steady progress toward the market. And picking up speed.

One drooler was driving. Two seemed to be watching, their faces pale blurs just above the tail gate.

"We got trouble," Mike muttered. "Tail gate's armored."

"Does that mean we can't shoot them?"

"Not unless you're Annie Oakley. Let's try for the driver."

Mike shuffled sideways until his shoulder met Karen's. Then they opened up, their automatics roaring, jumping in their hands, spent cartridges flying. The moment the shooting started, the droolers in back dropped out of sight. Bullets sparked off the tail gate. Others slammed through the windshield. The driver slumped out of sight.

The Rover kept coming. Faster and faster.

Karen's gun went silent.

Mike fired his last round. He jerked Karen's sleeve. "Let's go!"

he shouted as the vehicle sped across the center line.

They lurched up and staggered away from the window.

Mike expected the Rover to keep on coming and try to ram through.

But it skidded to a halt at the curb, and the two faces rose above the tail gate. A third drooler stood up behind them.

Time seemed to slow down as that one came to her feet in the cargo bed, as Mike rushed backward with Karen, as his hand worked fast to release the empty magazine.

She was the one he'd seen riding on the hood when the vehicle first came at them. Her right side caught the distant firelight, and her left side was dark. She looked magnificent standing there—tall and slim, her shoulders broad, her right breast glowing like polished gold, pubic curls glistening. Magnificent and awful. She had the K-bar clamped in her teeth. Slobber flowed down her chin. The shoulder Mike could see bore the dark strap of the fuel tank she wore on her back. Clamped between her arm and ribcage was the stock of the flame thrower. Its muzzle swung up toward the store window.

Mike hurled himself sideways, slamming against Karen. They hit the floor rolling as a gust of fire rushed by. He kept tumbling until he saw Karen scamper up. He thrust himself off the floor and followed her. Glancing back, he saw a path of fire that led from the window sill, across the floor to the first section of standing shelves.

The woman came through the display window like a hurdler.

Before she landed, shelving blocked Mike's view. He kept his eyes on Karen's back. She was a few strides ahead of him, her shirt a pale, jolting blur.

As he ran, he shoved a full magazine up the butt of his pistol. He slapped it home. He jacked a cartridge into the chamber.

Karen still had an empty gun. He wondered if she knew how to reload. Probably not.

They were almost to the rear of the store. He glanced back. The drooler'd had time to reach their aisle, but she wasn't there. Probably in a different aisle, planning to get them as they cut across the back. He was about to warn Karen, but she let out a small yelp and lurched to a halt. Mike dodged, missed her, and stopped.

Just in front of them was a refrigerator unit that ran along the back wall. It had sliding glass doors. Instead of soft drinks and beer, it held a drooler. Mike couldn't see much. But he saw plenty. The naked guy was spread-eagled so tight against the glass that it pressed his skin flat. His nose and erection looked mashed. He was writhing, licking the glass, gazing out at them.

One arm stretched out farther. He hooked a rim of the door with his fingertips and the glass started to slide.

Mike put a bullet in his forehead.

He stepped around Karen, holding a hand up to keep her still, and leaned past the end of the shelves. In the fluttering red light from the fire, he could see that the back aisle was clear. The rear exit ought to be just beyond the end of the refrigeration unit.

If they went for it, they'd be exposed to anyone lurking between the next two rows of shelves.

Though he heard nothing except the crackle and snap of the fire, he knew that the gal with the flame thrower had to be nearby. And the other two or three droolers were probably in the store by now, sneaking through the aisles. One of them, at least, had a gun.

He didn't want to go out there.

Maybe sneak back to the front and try to . . .?

He heard a quiet skidding sound—the sound that a door of the cold drink compartment might make, sliding open. The skin on his back crawled. He snapped his head around.

The body of the drooler toppled out as Karen, gripping the handle, leaped out of the way.

"What're you doing?" Mike whispered.

She didn't answer. Crouching over the feet of the body, she reached forward with both hands, lifted up on a wire shelf rack inside the refrigerator and shoved it. Mike heard a few cans tumble and roll. The rack clamored, apparently dropping to the floor behind the unit. Karen raised and pushed the next shelf up. More falling cans. Another clatter.

Mike checked the rear aisle. Still clear. He scooted backward and glanced around the way they'd come. Okay there.

Where are the fucking droolers!

As another rack rang against the floor, he crawled past the end of the shelving for a glance down the next aisle. He eased his face around the corner and looked straight at the belly of a drooler. A skinny old thing. A woman. Squatting there, grinning and slobbering. "Hi-ya, honey," she whispered.

Mike was on his hands and knees, his automatic pressed against the floor. As he started to bring it up, the hag dropped toward him, grabbed his hair with both hands and twisted his head, flipping him onto his back. He clamped his mouth shut tight.

Foam spilling onto his lips and chin.

Just like last time.

If the other time didn't infect me, he thought, this won't either.

Her tits slapped the side of his chest. Her hair draped his face. He jammed the muzzle of his automatic against her ribs. Her open mouth was inches above his face when a sneaker shot in from the side, caught her in the eye, knocked her head sideways and Mike pulled his trigger three times.

He shoved the drooler. She tumbled off him. Karen grabbed the wrist of his gunhand and pulled as he staggered to his feet. She kept his wrist. Crouching, she led him toward the open refrigerator. He stumbled as he stepped on the rump of the drooler who'd been in there. He fell to one knee between the guy's legs.

Something to the left.

He snapped his head that way and jerked his hand from Karen's grip as she ducked into the compartment.

Beyond the last section of shelves stood the gal with the flame thrower.

K-bar still in her teeth. Tawny skin shimmering. Thick suds of drool flopping off her chin and flowing like lava down between her breasts.

Mike triggered four rounds at her. The first seemed to miss. The next pounded her hip. One got her square in the chest, making her breasts shake and splashing out a thick spray of drool and blood. One punched her under the nose. She flinched as each bullet struck her. As she staggered backward, Mike knew she was dead on her feet. He back hit the far wall. She dropped to her knees. And flame bloomed from the muzzle of her weapon. Straight at Mike.

He sprang for the darkness. His hip scraped the edge of the sliding door. The back of his head struck a wire rack. Cans above him bounced and clinked. He landed belly first on the floor of the refrigerator compartment, sliding, kicking up his feet. Karen grabbed him under the armpits and dragged him the rest of the way through.

He looked behind him. His boots weren't on fire, but the aisle back there was ablaze.

He stood up, Karen holding him steady as cans and wire racks teetered under him. They were in a storeroom stacked with cartons.

Apparently, the stock people loaded the shelves from back here. Karen must've known that.

It looked like the looters had missed this place.

"You okay?" she whispered.

"You're a genius," he said.

"That's me. Used to work in a 7-Eleven."

Things Can Only Get Better

Mike wanted to hug her, but he realized his face was still wet with the slobber of the drooler.

No shower handy, this time.

"What happened out there?" Karen asked.

"I bagged the babe with the squirter."

"All *right!*"

"Gotta clean my face," he muttered.

Karen put a hand on his shoulder. "Bend down," she whispered. "You think we got them all?"

"One or two left, maybe."

When he was squatting in front of her, she tugged her Tshirt free of her belt, put a hand inside it, and lifted the fabric toward his face.

"You don't want to get this on you."

"I'm immune, remember?"

With the front of her shirt, Karen rubbed the saliva off his cheeks and lips and chin.

"Thanks," he muttered. He straightened up. "Give me your pistol."

She handed it to him.

"Over here." He stepped around a stack of cartons, and she followed. They crouched down.

"Do you think we hit the driver?" Karen asked.

Mike dropped the empty magazine into his hand. "I don't know."

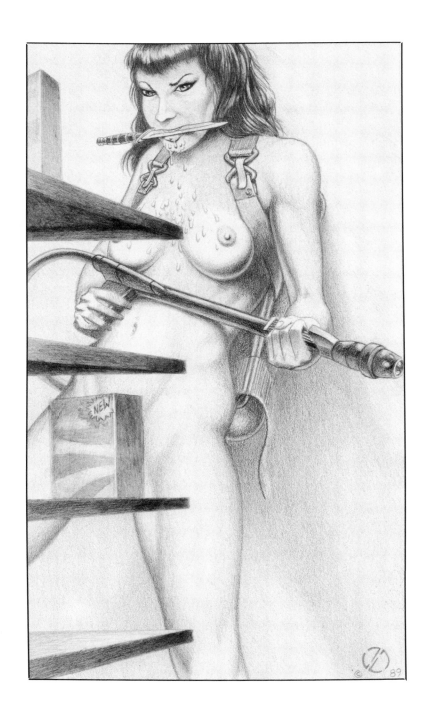

"Me either."

"There ought to be one more, plus the driver if we didn't get him." He took a fresh magazine from the pouch on his belt, slammed it up the pistol butt, and worked the slide. "Maybe they can't get back here," he said, giving the weapon back to her. "That gal laid a path right across the rear. They'd have to come through it."

"So you think we're safe?"

"Well, we might burn up."

He heard a soft laugh come from Karen.

After reloading his own Beretta, he said, "What we'll do is take the back way out. Work our way around to the front and get back to the Land Rover. Then head for battalion."

"What about your friends?"

"I don't think they're alive anymore. These creeps must've taken 'em out."

Mike stood up and turned around. Most of the storeroom was in shadows. Here and there, firelight shimmered on the sides of stacked boxes. He saw no one. "Looks okay," he said, holstering his sidearm as Karen rose beside him.

He ripped open the top of a carton, reached in and pulled out a can. In the gloom, he couldn't see what it was.

"Thirsty?" he asked.

"You bet."

He popped the can open and gave it to Karen. As she drank, he took out another, and shook it hard.

"Hey, that'll . . ."

"I know," he said. Tipping the can toward his closed mouth, he flipped its tab. With a *whish*, warm soda sprayed his face. Some went up his nose, but most of the liquid splashed his lips and cheeks. It spilled down his chin, ran down his neck and chest. He rubbed it around with his left hand.

"That's a crazy way to drink Pepsi," Karen said.

"I can't stand having that stuff on me. I know it's not supposed to give you the Black Widow, but . . ."

"No harm being careful." Karen set her can on the box. She pulled off her T-shirt, turned it around, and used its back to mop the soda off Mike. "You're going to be sticky."

"You too, now."

"I'll survive," she muttered.

He wanted to reach out and touch her, slide his hands up her smooth sides. But one hand was wet and the other held the Pepsi can. Besides, she might not appreciate it. God knows what had been done to her by droolers before he came along.

Thinking about the feel of her, knowing that she was bare to the waist, Mike felt a hot tightness start to spread through his groin.

She finished drying him, shook open her shirt, and lifted it overhead to put it on. He watched her small breasts rise slightly. The ruddy light trembled on them. Her nipples were dark and jutting. Then they were out of sight beneath the filthy, torn shirt.

She picked up her can, and drank some more.

Mike rubbed his wet hand on a leg of his fatigues. He shifted the can to that hand, and drew his pistol. He took a few swallows of the Pepsi. He wished it were beer. He wished it were cold. But it tasted sweet and good. He finished off the can, and set it down inside the carton.

"Maybe we can latch onto some food," Karen said.

"When was the last time you ate?"

"I don't know. The army came through here this afternoon. Yesterday, I . . ." She shook her head. "Must've been day before yesterday. Didn't get much, though. I got into the kitchen of some diner, but then a couple of sickies came after me. The whole place was crawling with them before the soldiers showed up." She made that "Ugh" sound again.

"Come on," Mike said. "Let's see what we can find. But we'd better hurry." Though the fire hadn't yet penetrated the storeroom, smoke was coming in and the temperature seemed to be rising fast. "Keep your eyes sharp," he said.

Karen took another swig of Pepsi, then set the can aside.

They made their way across the floor. They passed the double doors that led into the shopping area. Tongues of flame were lapping through the crack at the bottom. Rushing by, they came to more stacks of boxes. Karen started ripping them open while Mike stood guard.

"Chicken soup," she muttered. She tore open another box. Mayo. Darn."

"Hurry."

She ripped into another. "Ah-ha! Oreos! Do you like Oreos?"

"Fine."

"Double-stuffed, too." She hugged them to her belly. "All set."

"That's all you want?"

51

"It'll do for now."

He led the way to a large metal door at the back of the storeroom and shouldered it open. "Wait a second," he said. He stepped out.

An alley.

He checked both ways. Dark back here. Walled in by brick buildings. To the left, the alley stretched into darkness that seemed to have no end. To the right, the distant opening at the cross street glowed from the block that Mike and the others had left burning. He saw trash bins here and there along the walls. Most of the buildings had rear doors. Some had loading docks. He saw no droolers.

"Looks okay," he said.

He braced the door wide with his back and Karen came out, followed by a few shreds of smoke. He stepped away. The door swung shut with a heavy clank.

Side by side, they walked down the middle of the alley toward the ruddy light. The plastic wrapper crackled, and Mike watched Karen take out a cookie. "Open up," she said. He did. She pushed the cookie into his mouth. As he chewed, he peered past her at a loading dock to the right. The bay door beyond the platform was open.

We could go straight through to the street, he thought. We'd come out by the Land Rover.

But the area beyond the door looked black.

God knows what might be in there.

Here in the alley, at least he could see what was coming.

Karen used her lower teeth to pry her cookie in half. She chewed, then scraped off the white filling with her teeth and moaned softly as she savored it.

Mike switched the pistol to his left hand. He put his right hand low on Karen's back. Her shirt was damp. He thought about drooler germs, but told himself that the real slobber was on the front of her shirt. This was mostly Pepsi. So he caressed her back through the moist fabric.

She turned her head and smiled at him, the bottm half of the Oreo wedged between her teeth.

Looking at her, Mike felt warm and achy in his chest. He smiled. "You're something else," he said.

Karen crunched the cookie.

He moved his hand higher on her back. Up between her

shoulder blades, the shirt was dry. He slid it against the smoothness of her skin.

"I came real close to blowing my brains out, earlier tonight."

"I'm sure glad you didn't," she said.

"I thought I might be infected," he explained. "And there didn't seem to be much point in going on, anyway. Everything's . . . gone."

"Not everything. There's still Oreos."

Mike laughed softly. "Yeah. And there's you."

Karen shifted the package of cookies to her other arm and eased closer. Her hip touched the side of his leg. Her arm went around his back and she caressed his side. "I'm awfully glad we found each other," she said. "Things were looking pretty bleak, all right. Not that I ever considered suicide, but . . ."

"You're a survivor."

"I just like things, you know? Food . . ."

"I noticed."

"Sunsets, baths, friends, lovers."

Mike curled his hand over her bare shoulder.

"You name it. There's always enough good stuff to make up for everything that's rotten. Besides, I figured things could only get better, you know? Turns out, I was right." She squeezed his side.

Mike realized they were nearing the cross street. And he realized he'd forgotten about their peril. He quickly looked over his shoulder. In the shadows behind them, nothing stirred.

We're doing just fine, he told himself.

But there's got to be droolers around. Don't let your guard down again.

At the mouth of the alley, he glanced from side to side. There was good light from a blazing tenement at the corner across the street. He saw debris, bodies, abandoned cars. Nobody moving.

He turned Karen toward the right, took a few steps, then stopped and faced her.

She looked up at him.

"I don't want to lose you," he said.

She nodded slightly.

"If we join up with the main force . . . I'll be in it all again. They'll probably ship you off somewhere."

"I wouldn't like that," she murmured. She caught her lower lip between her teeth. She had a cookie crumb at the corner of her mouth.

53

"When we get to the Land Rover . . . How would you feel about heading west? I don't know what we'll find. Just dead people and ruins, probably. But there won't be any troops. We'll be on our own."

"That sounds good to me."

"I can radio battalion headquarters from the Rover to pass on the word that there are survivors. Then we'll just head the other way."

"You'll be a deserter, Mike."

"They'll just think I'm a casualty. Hell, our whole squad's bit the dust. I'll just be one more guy the droolers got."

"Are you sure you want to do this?"

"Do you?"

"You bet your ass. Let's get to that Land Rover and head for the coast." Breaking away from him, she hurried up the sidewalk. She had a bounce in her step. Her short hair shimmered golden in the firelight. The tail of her T-shirt, rounded over her small buttocks, shifted and swayed with each step. She looked over her shoulder and smiled at Mike.

His bowels seemed to freeze.

The naked drooler that lurched around the corner of the building twenty feet in front of Karen was a fat bald man with a hard-on and an automatic.

"NO!" Mike shrieked.

The drooler fired.

Gunplay

Karen's head jerked as the slug hit her. She twirled like a clumsy ballerina, her arms swinging out, cookies flying from their package as it tumbled through the night, her legs doing a weird jig until she stumbled off the curb, tripped over her own ankles, and flopped onto the street.

Mike watched. Numb.

A bullet zipped past his ear, and he focused his mind long

enough to empty his Beretta into the drooler.

He staggered toward Karen's body. She was sprawled on the pavement, her face turned away from him. One of her sneakers had come off. The bottom of her bare foot looked clean and pale. Her foot seemed very small, almost like that of a child.

Mike sank to his knees beside her.

The tail of her T-shirt had come up. It lay rumpled and crooked against the seat of her denim skirt. He holstered his pistol. Leaning forward, he rested a hand on the back of her shirt. It was still a little damp from when she'd used it to dry the Pepsi off him in the storeroom.

A sob wrenched Mike's chest. He hunched over and clutched his face with both hands and cried.

"I'm not dead yet," Karen muttered. "No thanks to you, Quickdraw."

"Oh God!" He wiped his eyes and tried to stop crying as she rolled slowly onto her back.

The right side of her face was torn and bloody. She kept that eye shut, but it didn't look damaged. There was a pulpy furrow just in front of her ear. Her cheekbone was laid bare. A corner had been knocked off the tip of her nose.

"Won't win any more beauty contests, huh?"

Mike sniffed and wiped his nose. "You will if I'm the judge," he murmured. "Does it hurt much?"

"I've hurt worse."

He unsnapped a satchel at the side of his belt and took out his first aid kit. As he opened it, he checked around. The area looked clear.

He remembered that he'd emptied his pistol into the drooler.

He lifted the front of Karen's T-shirt above her waist and pulled Doug's pistol from the holster. He set it down on her belly.

For the next few minutes, he worked on her face. She flinched and gritted her teeth as he fingered the wound, gently prodding some torn flesh back where it seemed to belong. The bullet had carried plenty off with it, but enough remained to fill in some of the gouge and cover most of her cheekbone. When Mike figured he could do no more to improve the situation, he took a small canister of spray disinfectant from the first aid kit and squirted the area. Karen arched her back and hissed through her teeth as he sprayed. Then she settled down again. He bandaged her, taping down the gauze pads as firmly as he dared.

"That should hold you," he said, "till I can get you to a field hospital."

"Field hospital?"

"You need real doctors."

"We're going west, remember?"

"I can't take the chance. The wound might get infected. You could die."

"Not me. I'm the survivor, remember?"

"Pure of heart."

"Damn right. We're heading west, just like we planned."

"I don't know."

"I do." She started to sit up, and groaned.

"I'd better carry you," Mike said.

"Yeah, you'd better. I'll ride shotgun." She reached down to her belly and picked up the pistol. She raised its barrel toward the reddish sky, made a little curlicue with it, and said, "Let's go."

Mike pushed one arm under her back. He slipped the other behind her knees.

"I think I'm missing a sneaker."

"Okay." He left her for a moment. He picked up the small shoe. She wiggled her toes as he started to put it on her. He felt his throat thicken.

"You don't have to tie it," she said when he was done.

"Thanks." He returned to her side, squatted low, and lifted her.

Instead of taking Karen to the sidewalk, he made his way to the middle of the street.

No more surprises, he told himself.

It felt wonderful to be holding her. To feel her warmth and movement as he walked.

He stepped past the corner, continued to the center of the intersection, and turned to the right. Some distance up the street, the Land Rover was just where he'd last seen it—stopped a few yards from the front of the market. The store was blazing. Though flames were gusting up from the display window, none reached as far as the Rover.

Karen's head was turned. She was looking, too. The pistol, tight in her grip, rested on her belly with its muzzle pointed that way.

"Spot any sickies," she told him, "just say the word."

"If I spot any, I'll put you down and take the gun."

"Don't trust me?"

"I've never seen you hit anything," he said.

"Doesn't mean I can't."

Mike smiled down at her.

She was cradled against his chest, the bandaged side of her face upward as she watched the area ahead. Her right arm was pressed against him. It was bent at the elbow, forearm angled across her belly, the barrel of the pistol resting on her left wrist as if ready for whatever might come at them from the front.

Her left hand lay curled between her upraised legs. The denim skirt, bunched around her hips, left her thighs bare. They gleamed in the ruddy firelight.

Mike knew he should be watching for droolers, not admiring Karen.

But she was keeping watch.

So he looked at her breasts. They were just below his face, very close, The loose T-shirt hung lightly over them. It took on their shape. He could see the way her nipples made the fabric rise. The motion of his walking made her breasts shake and tremble just a bit.

She's so beautiful, he thought.

If he lifted her higher, he would be able to kiss her right breast. He imagined the turgid, springy feel of the nipple in his mouth. The shirt would be in the way. It would taste dry.

"Looks like we got him," Karen said.

Mike raised his eyes, then halted. They were only a few strides from the Land Rover. The driver was slumped forward, head against the steering wheel. The exiting bullet had splashed gore against the pocked and webby remains of the windshield.

Mike carried Karen closer to the Land Rover. A single flame thrower remained in the cargo bed. No droolers.

He leaned over the side and started to lower her.

"Hey, I want to ride up front with you."

"You should be lying down," he said. Gently, he set her on the floor of the bed.

"No, I mean it. I don't want to be back here, Mike."

He pulled his arms out from under her. She started to sit up. With a hand on her bare right shoulder, he eased her down.

She strained against it for a moment, then seemed to relax. As if giving up, she let her legs go out straight.

"How am I going to ride shotgun for you if I'm back here?" she asked.

57

"Won't be for long," he said.

"Promise?"

"Yeah." He slid his hand away from her shoulder. He curled it over her breast. Through the shirt, he felt the heat of her skin, the push of her stiff nipple. Karen covered his hand and pressed it down more tightly.

Mike's heart raced. He had to swallow, but his throat felt tight. His penis felt like a hot iron bar jamming into the front of his fatigues.

He freed his hand.

He climbed over the side of the Rover, and Karen scooted sideways to make room for him.

"Mike," she said softly. "I don't know."

"It'll be all right." He crawled onto her, knelt above her.

"My face . . ."

"I know, but . . ." Shaking his head, he lifted the T-shirt above her breasts. The nearby fire felt hot and good on his back, but he wished his shadow wasn't in the way. He caressed her breasts. So smooth. They felt even more wonderful than he had imagined.

Karen writhed a little. In a low, husky voice, she said, "We'll be in an awful fix if some sickies show up. Shouldn't we wait?"

"I can't."

"Okay. I want you, too, but . . . Okay."

As he gently explored her breasts, Karen set down the pistol. With both hands, she unhooked Doug's belt and spread it away from her waist. She unbuttoned her skirt, lowered the zipper.

Mike crawled backward, pulling the skirt down her legs. He slipped trembling fingers under the elastic of her panties. As he drew the flimsy garment over her sneakers, Karen sat up slightly. She crossed her arms and lifted the T-shirt over her head.

Kneeling beside her feet, Mike no longer blocked the firelight. Karen's naked body was bathed in the russet glow. As he gazed at her, she lifted a foot, gently rubbed his thigh with the sole of her sneaker, then swung her leg past him.

She was sprawled before him, open, waiting.

Mike unhooked his fatigue belt and tossed it aside.

"Come here," she said.

He crawled forward. Her thighs felt like warm satin under his open, fluttering hands. Between them, she was hot and slick.

Karen guided his hands to her breasts. And while he caressed them, she opened his fatigue pants. She tugged them down his thighs. She drew the band of his shorts away from his belly. She dragged the shorts down.

Suddenly free of the confining garments, he let out a shuddering breath.

He had never known such desire. His penis felt solid, huge, monstrous.

Karen's fingers slipped around it. They guided downward.

Gasping, he squeezed her breasts. She whimpered quietly, squirmed, but didn't tighten her grip. She slid her hand slowly upward.

And then it was gone. Mike sank onto her. He kissed one of her breasts. He tongued the nipple. He filled his mouth with the breast, and sucked. Hard enough to make her cry out softly and flinch.

He wondered how it would be to bite in.

Karen clutched his hair with one hand. She gave it a sharp yank.

She can't take any more, either, he thought.

He scurried up her body. He licked drying blood from her lips, savoring its coppery taste, then thrust his tongue into her mouth. He pushed his erection slowly into her slippery, tight warmth.

Karen writhed under him. She raised her legs, and he felt himself sink in more deeply.

He felt buried in her.

Then he felt a cool steel ring against his temple.

He pulled his tongue from Karen's mouth. He raised his face, but the muzzle stayed tight at his head. He stared down into her eyes.

"I hope to God you don't have it, Mike."

"Huh?"

"But I think you might."

"No!" he blurted, panting for air. "It's just you! I haven't got the Widow!" A string of saliva spilled from his lips and dribbled onto Karen's chin. He swallowed hard. "It's just . . . I want you so bad!"

"I'm sorry," she said. "God, I'm sorry."

His shouted "DON'T!" sprayed her, and a hot blast kicked through the side of Mike's head.

Wishbone

"Some honeymoon," Diane muttered, stepping to the side of the trail. She squatted until a boulder took the weight of her backpack.

Scott, farther up the trail, stopped and turned around. "What's the matter now?"

"What isn't?"

He came toward her, shaking his head. Diane knew that his pack was even heavier than hers, but he seemed just as energetic as when they had started out this morning.

She took off her hat and sunglasses. Squinting against the brightness, she unknotted her neckerchief and used it to mop her sweaty face.

"We'd better keep moving," Scott said. "We've only got a couple more hours before sunset."

"Why don't we just camp here?"

"You're kidding."

"I mean it. I'm wiped out."

"There's no water here, for one thing."

"Well, I'm not moving another inch."

"For Godsake . . ."

"We've got plenty of water for one night."

"There's supposed to be a lake just on the other side of the pass."

"Well, fine. *You* go to the lake. I'm staying."

"Diannnnne."

"I mean it. My blisters have blisters. Every bone in my body aches. Besides that, I've got a headache."

"But this place really sucks."

"I wanted to stop by that stream, remember? But no. 'Oh, we can make it over the pass,'" she mimicked him. "'No sweat, sweetheart.' You want to see sweat?" She raised her red bandanna toward Scott, balled it up with one hand, and squeezed. Sweat spilled out, fell between her boots and made dark spots on the trail dust.

"Just think how nice the lake'll be," Scott said. "These are glacial lakes up here. Ice cold. You can take a dip while I set up camp."

"I'm not budging."

"All right. Suit yourself." He turned away and started hiking up the trail. His boots scuffed up pale puffs behind him. The gear on his backpack and belt creaked and clanked.

He isn't really going to leave me here, Diane told herself.

The bandanna felt a little chilly when she tied it around her hot neck. She slipped out of her pack straps, made sure the bundle was steady on the boulder, and stood up. Her feet felt cramped and burning. But she enjoyed the feel of standing without the awful weight of the pack. The breeze cooled the sweat on her back.

Scott was still walking away.

"I know you're just bluffing!" she called.

He acted as if he didn't hear her.

He passed a bend in the trail and disappeared behind a cluster of blocky granite.

He's just going to stop there and wait for me, Diane thought. It'll be a long wait.

Groaning, she rubbed her sore neck. She peeled the sodden shirt away from her back and fluttered it. Shoving a hand down the seat of her jeans, she plucked her wet panties out from between her buttocks.

"Scott?" she called.

He didn't answer.

"Stop playing games, okay? Come on back here."

She heard only the wind.

What if he didn't stop?

Diane felt a squirmy coldness in her bowels.

He wouldn't leave me here. He just wouldn't.

She left her pack on the boulder, and strode up the trail.

Scott wasn't behind the outcropping. The trail ahead slanted upward, bordered by blocks and slabs of rock. About a hundred feet ahead, it bent out of sight.

She saw Scott nowhere.

Either he'd hidden, or he'd kept on going.

"You shit!" Diane yelled.

Then she hurried back to the place where she'd left her pack. She put on her hat and sunglasses. She slipped her arms through the straps, leaned forward, and felt like weeping as the weight came down on her shoulders like the hands of a giant trying to shove her into the ground.

She began trudging up the trail.

How could he go off and leave me? I'm his wife.

Shouldn't have married him, she thought. She'd known he could act like a real bastard. But that side of him had always been directed at other people, not at her.

If I'd known he might treat *me* like this . . .

What if I can't find him?

*   *   *

She found him nearly two hours later atop a high boulder beside the trail, perched up there in the last rays of sunlight, a corncob pipe in his teeth and a flask of rum resting on his knee. He smiled down at her. "What took you so long, sweetheart?"

Diane gave him the finger. Staggering past the boulder, she saw their campsite surrounded by a stand of trees. The tent was already up. Pale smoke curled and drifted above a campfire. Beyond the encampment was the lake, dark blue in the shadow cast by the bleak wall of granite along its far side.

She almost made it to the tent, then yanked the straps from her shoulders and let her pack drop. She sank down in front of it. Struggling for breath, she unlaced her boots and tugged at them. Her feet made sucking sounds when they came out. Her white cotton socks were filthy and drenched. They were dappled at the heels and toes with rusty bloodstains. She peeled them off. She slumped back against her pack, gasping and trembling.

Scott loomed over her.

"I knew you could make it," he said.

63

"Go to hell."

"I'll tell you what. Why don't you just relax. Camp's already up, and I'll take care of tonight's supper."

He walked away.

Diane remained where she was, her back braced up by the pack, her rump on the ground, her legs stretched out. Soon, her breathing was almost normal. But the wind was stronger now, and colder. Though the sky remained pale blue, the sun was below the ridge and gave her no heat. Something on the ground was digging into her left buttock. Her skin felt itchy because of the damp clothes.

She felt miserable, but she couldn't force herself to move.

She wished she had the strength to get up and change her clothes. Put on something warm and dry. She wished she had socks on. Warm, dry socks.

I'll never be able to move again, she thought.

They'll find me up here someday, frozen like that leopard on the western summit of Kilimanjaro. And they'll wonder what I was doing up here.

Killed by an asshole.

Who strolled by, just then, and took the corncob out of his mouth long enough to say, "You shouldn't just lie there. You'll get hypothermia, or something."

"Thanks for the warning," she muttered.

"Want me to get you something?"

"Yeah. An annulment."

He chuckled. "I think I'll do a little exploring around the lake before I start cooking. You want to come along?"

"Gee, I don't imagine so."

He wandered off.

Diane was glad to be rid of him. After a few minutes, she managed to sit up. She crawled to the other side of her pack. Kneeling there, she opened it. She tossed her rolled sleeping bag toward the tent, took out her coat and spread it on the ground. Soon, she managed to dig out a fresh pair of socks, sweatpants and a hooded sweatshirt.

She pulled the socks over her tender, wounded feet. Then she stood on the coat. She looked all around. No sign of Scott. Shivering, she stripped off her cold, damp clothes. She stooped, picked up her sweatpants, lowered one foot into the waist hole, lifted her foot off

64

the ground as she sought the opening at the ankle of the pants, and lost her balance. She stumbled backward, fighting to stay up.

She landed on her back, feet in the air.

The ground felt moist and cold. Twigs and rocks dug into her bare skin.

"Great," she muttered through her tight throat. "Just great."

Then she saw someone high in the branches of a nearby tree, staring down at her.

Not *someone*, exactly.

Not *staring*, exactly.

The skeleton of someone. It had a skull with empty sockets.

It seemed to be sitting up there, the gray bones of its legs straddling a limb, its back resting against the trunk, its skull tipped downward as if watching her.

Diane felt icy fingers squeezing her insides.

She thrust both feet through the sweatpants and scurried up. She brushed damp debris off her buttocks, then tugged the pants around her waist.

"Scott!" she yelled. "Scott, get back here!"

She heard only the wind.

It's just a skeleton, she told herself. Nothing to be afraid of.

Shivering, she swung the sweatshirt behind her back. She held it by the sleeves and swept it from side to side a few times. Then she put it on. She brushed some dirt and bits of leaves and twigs off the front. She pulled up the hood. She hugged herself, clutching her breasts through the soft fabric.

Shoulders hunched, legs tight together, she stood there trembling and gazed at the skeleton.

It really did seem to be staring down at her.

Just a heap of bones, she told herself. It isn't watching me. It's dead. It's got no eyes, no brain. Nothing but bones. It's no more alive than a rock.

It doesn't even know I exist.

We've gotta get out of here.

Kneeling on her coat, Diane searched her backpack until she found her sneakers. She put them on fast, got up wincing, snatched up her coat and hobbled toward the lake.

She stepped out onto a flat shelf of rock that jutted into the water. From there, she spotted Scott roaming among the jumbled granite beyond the lake's northern tip. She shouted his name. He turned his head and waved, then gestured for her to join him.

"Come here!" she yelled. "Quick!"

With a shrug, he started to come back.

＊   ＊   ＊

"What's the matter now?" he asked, obviously annoyed that Diane had interrupted his exploration.

"We've got a visitor," she said.

Scott raised his eyebrows, looked toward the campsite, and shook his head. "What're you talking about?"

She pointed toward the high branches of the tree.

"I don't see anything."

All that Diane could see was one bony foot. The rest of the skeleton was hidden behind limbs and leaves.

"What is it, an owl or something?"

"You'll see." She led the way, and stopped beside her pack where she'd changed her clothes. From there, the entire skeleton was in plain sight. She pointed up at it. "That's no owl," she said.

She watched Scott. When he saw the thing, his eyes opened wide and his jaw dropped. After a few moments, he rearranged his face into a smile. He met Diane's eyes. "Big deal," he said. "A skeleton."

"*I'll* say it's a big deal. I'm not spending the night here. No way. Not a chance."

Scott smirked at her.

"I mean it."

"Don't be ridiculous."

"It's a *dead* person, for Christsake!"

"So? It won't hurt anything."

"Damn it, Scott."

His smirk twisted into a scowl. "You've been dragging your ass all day, belly-aching about how fucking *tired* you are, and now that we're finally here and the camp's all set up, you wanta get everything alllll packed up again and go looking for someplace *else*, just 'cause of some crummy skeleton? Right. Sure thing. Every day and twice on Sunday. Has it ever occurred to you that maybe *I'm* tired, too? I spent a fucking *hour* putting up the tent all by myself and fixing the place up for you while you're taking your sweet time back

66

on the trail somewhere and now you wanta just keep going? Well, fuck that!"

"Fuck *you!*" she yelled.

"Fuck *me?*" He slapped her, smacking her face sideways.

Diane twisted away from him, held her cheeks and hunched over, crying.

"You don't like Ol' Bony up there, go and hide in the fucking tent. Go on, get." He swatted the back of her head.

Whirling around, Diane smashed her fist into Scott's jaw. For a moment, he looked stunned. Then he chuckled.

Diane grabbed her sleeping bag and rushed for the tent.

* * *

She was snug inside the down-filled mummy bag when she heard the rustle of the tent flap.

"You'll come out to eat, won't you?" Scott asked. He sounded calm and caring.

Diane raised her face off her crossed arms. She looked over her shoulder. Scott was crawling over the floor of the tent. The tent was dark inside. Behind Scott, she saw the glow of the campfire, the gloomy hues of dusk.

"What can I say?" he said. "I'm sorry. I don't know what got into me. I can't believe I really hit you."

"Twice," she murmured, and sniffed.

Reaching out, he gently stroked her hair.

"Are you okay?" he asked.

"What do you think?"

"I told you I'm sorry."

"That's a big help."

"Don't be that way, honey. I love you. I just lost my head. Come on. Why don't you get up and come out by the campfire? You'll feel much better once you've got some good hot food inside you."

"All right."

"That's my girl." He patted her back.

After he was gone, Dianne struggled free of her mummy bag. She put on her coat and sneakers, then crawled from the tent and stood up. She peered into the tree. The skeleton, way up there, looked as if its gray bones were melting into the darkness.

"You oughta stop worrying about that thing," Scott told her.

"Sure." She moved in close to the fire and sat down on a rock. The surface was rough, but fairly flat. Cold seeped through the seat of her sweatpants.

Scott, bending over the fire, ladled stew out of the pot. He filled a tin plate, added a fork, and brought it to her.

"I just wonder what Ol' Bony's doing up there," he said.

"Watching us," Diane muttered.

Scott laughed.

She set the plate on her thighs. It felt nice and hot. Steam rose off the stew.

"I mean, I find it intriguing. What's he doing up there, you know? Who was he? How'd he get there?" Scott filled a plate for himself and stood at the other side of the fire as he started to eat. "Maybe he fell out of an airplane. You know? Could've been a mid-air collision. Or maybe he parachuted. Hey, maybe he's D.B. Cooper."

"Cooper didn't even jump in this state," Diane pointed out. "Besides, where's the parachute?" She took a bite of the stew meat. It was stringy and tough, but hot. It tasted good. "For that matter, where are his clothes?"

"Probably the same place as his skin and eyes."

"Oh, very clever."

Scott laughed, and ate some more. "I've got it!" He pointed his fork toward the skeleton. "Jimmy Hoffa. No, I've got it! Judge Crater!"

Diane smiled.

"All right! She's perking up!"

"That's just because God's gonna strike you dead, any second now, for being such a wiseass."

"You'd find that amusing, would you?"

"It'd serve you right for making fun of dead people."

"Ol' Bony doesn't mind." Scott turned toward the tree and tipped his head back. "Yo! Up there! Wishbone! Yeah, you!"

"Don't," Diane said. "Come on."

Laughing, ignoring her, Scott cupped a hand to the side of his mouth and called, "You got any problem up there with what I been saying? Are you . . . taking offense at my remarks?"

"Would you shut up!" Diane snapped.

He looked at her. Grinning, he said, "What's the matter, afraid he might answer?"

"It's just not right. Okay? That was a person once."

"Whoop-dee-doo."

"God, why don't you grow up."

"Oooo, the little woman's getting testy. Again."

She hunched low over her stew and forked some into her mouth.

"Yo, up there! Now look what you've done! You've got my bride all upset! How dare you!"

Diane kept her head down and kept on eating.

What's *wrong* with him? Maybe it's marriage. Now that he's got me, he thinks he can start dumping all over me. Now he can treat me like shit, the way he treats everyone else.

Maybe it's just being in the mountains. Maybe roughing it brings out all this nasty macho shit.

"You're really fucking up our honeymoon, Bonebrain!"

Diane raised her head.

Crouching, Scott set down his plate. He picked up a stone, and cocked back his arm to hurl it at the skeleton.

"No!"

He threw it.

The pale chunk of rock flew high and vanished into the darkness. For a moment, Diane heard only the crackle and pop of the campfire, the distant howl of the wind. Then came a faint thud as if the rock had struck the tree. Or the skeleton.

"Did I getcha?" Scott yelled. "Huh? Want me to try again?" He squatted and searched the ground for another rock.

Diane flung her plate down. She leaped to her feet. "Damn it, don't you dare!"

"Oh, dry up." He found a rock. He stood up. He tossed it under-hand, caught it, and grinned at Diane.

Oh shit, she thought. *This one's for me.*

But she never found out for sure.

Out of the corner of her eye, she saw something sailing down from the tree. She jerked her head that way and squinted.

A big, pale rock was curving down through the darkness at Scott.

Not a *rock,* exactly.

A skull.

Just as Scott turned toward the tree, the skull crashed against his forehead. It didn't shatter. It didn't bounce off. Its teeth clamped,

69

biting into his scalp and eyebrow. It stayed there, hanging on as Scott staggered backward and dropped his rock and fell to the ground beside the fire.

Diane stood frozen, staring and dazed.

That didn't happen, she told herself. Impossible.

This isn't happening, either, she told herself when she looked toward the tree and saw the headless skeleton on its way down.

It seemed very agile for a pile of bones.

It shinnied down the trunk to the bottom branch, some ten or twelve feet above the ground. It sat on the branch. Then it pushed itself off, dropped, and landed standing up.

It seemed to have a bounce in its step as it walked toward Scott.

Bending over him, it grabbed its skull with both hands and tugged. Its teeth ripped free of Scott's face.

He groaned.

Through the disbelief that fogged her mind, Diane realized he was still alive. He'd been knocked unconscious by the skull. Now, he was coming to. His face was bleeding horribly.

The skeleton, holding the skull in one hand, seemed to examine it for a moment. Then a fingertip of bone flicked a scrap of Scott's flesh off one of its upper teeth. With that accomplished, it raised the head and planted it atop its spinal column.

Scott, eyes still shut, squirmed a little bit.

The skeleton placed a foot on his chest. It rubbed its hands together.

Then its head slowly swiveled until its eyeless sockets seemed to fix on Diane. It raised an arm and waved.

Waving goodbye? Wants me to leave?

This can't be happening, Diane thought.

But just in case it is . . .

She staggered backward a few steps, then swung around and ran.

*   *   *

Diane didn't sleep.

She spent that night huddled in a crevice, hiding from the skeleton and the wind, shivering, wondering what had happened.

When dawn came, she climbed onto a boulder. From there, she

could see the northern end of the lake at the bottom of the slope. But not the campsite. Outcroppings along the shore hid that from her view. She was glad.

Soon, the sun appeared above the eastern ridge. Its rays slanted down across the valley, warming her. She took off her coat and sat on it for a while, savoring the feel of the heat.

She didn't want to return to the camp. But she knew it had to be done.

And so, with shaky legs and a sick lump of dread in her stomach, she made her way down the slope and along the lakeshore.

The campsite was just as she had left it.

But the fire was dead. And Scott no longer lay sprawled on the ground beside it.

His clothes were there. Shredded and bloody.

Diane gritted her teeth to stop them from chattering. She wrapped her arms tightly across her chest. She turned toward the tree and raised her eyes.

Scott was straddling a high limb. The skeleton, braced between his body and the tree trunk, appeared to be sitting on his lap. His face rested against its skull, his lips mashed to its teeth. His bare legs dangled. Diane could see one arm of bone wrapped around his back, one fleshless leg against his side like the thigh of an eager lover squeezing him.

Some honeymoon, she thought.

She started to giggle.

Bad News

The morning was sunny and quiet. Leaving the door ajar, Paul crossed the flagstones to his driveway. He sidestepped alongside his Granada, being careful neither to tread on the dewy grass nor to let his robe rub against the grimy side of the car.

As he cleared the rear bumper, he spotted the *Messenger.*

Good. Nobody had beaten him to it.

Every so often, especially on weekends, somebody swiped the thing. Not this morning, though. Getting up early had paid off. The newspaper, rolled into a thick bundle and bound by a rubber band, lay on the grass just beyond the edge of Paul's driveway.

On Joe Applegate's lawn.

Crouching to pick it up, Paul glanced at his neighbor's driveway and yard and front stoop.

There was no sign of Applegate's paper.

Probably already took it inside, Paul thought. Unless somebody snatched it.

Hope the damn redneck doesn't think *this* is his.

Paul straightened up, tucked the paper under one arm, and made his way up the narrow strip of pavement between his car and the grass.

Inside the house, he locked the front door. He tossed the newspaper onto the coffee table, started away, and thought he saw the paper wobble.

He looked down at it.

The *Messenger* lay motionless on the glass top of the coffee table.

It was rolled into the shape of a rather thick, lopsided tube. The wobble he'd noticed out of the corner of his eye must've been the paper settling from the toss he'd given it.

It shimmied.

Paul flinched.

A rat-like, snouted face poked out of the middle of the folds. Furless, with white skin that looked oily. It gazed up at him with pink eyes. It bared its teeth.

"Jesus!" Paul gasped as the thing scurried out, rocking the paper, and rushed straight toward him, claws clicking on the table top, teeth snapping at the air.

Paul staggered backward.

What the fuck is it!

The creature left a slime trail on the glass. It didn't stop at the edge of the table. It tumbled off, hit the carpeted floor with a soft thump, and sped toward Paul's feet.

He leaped out of its path. The thing abruptly changed course and kept coming.

Paul hurled himself sideways, lurched a few steps to his easy chair and jumped up onto the seat. His feet sank into the springy cushion. He teetered up there, prancing for balance as he turned around, then dropped a knee onto the chair's padded arm.

He watched the thing rush toward him.

Not a rat, at all. It had a rodent-like head, all right, but beyond its thin neck was a body shaped like a bullet: a fleshy, glistening white cylinder about five inches long, rounded at the shoulders, ending just beyond its hind legs without tapering at all as if its rear was a flat disk. It had no tail.

At the foot of the chair, it dug its claws into the fabric and started to climb.

Paul tore a moccasin off his foot. A flimsy weapon, but better than nothing. He swept it down at the beast. The limp leather sole slapped against the thing's flank, but didn't dislodge it. It kept coming up the front of the chair, eyes on Paul, its small teeth clicking.

He stuffed his hand into the moccasin and shoved at the thing. Its snout burst through the bottom, a patch of leather gripped in its teeth. He jerked his hand free, losing the moccasin, and sprang from the chair. Glancing back as he rushed away, he saw the creature and moccasin drop to the floor.

At the fireplace, he grabbed a pointed, wrought-iron poker. He whirled to face the beast. It worked the rest of its body through the hole in the slipper and charged him. He raised the poker.

Something brushed against Paul's ankle. A furry blur shot by. Jack the cat.

Jack slept in Timmy's room, curled on its special rug beside the boy's bed. The commotion out here must've caught its attention.

"Don't!" Paul blurted.

The tabby leaped like a miniature lion and pounced on the creature.

Stupid cat! It's not a mouse!

Paul's view was blocked by Jack. He bent sideways, trying for a better angle, and saw the blunt rear and tiny legs of the thing hanging out the side of Jack's mouth.

"Nail the bastard!" he gasped.

Jack worked his jaw, biting down. His tail switched.

"Paul? What's going on out there?" Joan's groggy, distant voice.

Before he could answer, the cat squawled and leaped straight up, back hunching.

"PAUL!" Now alarmed.

Jack went silent. All four paws hit the floor at once. The cat stood motionless for a moment, then keeled over onto its side. Its anus bulged. The bloody head of the beast squeezed out.

Paul stared, numb with shock, as the thing slid free of Jack's body. It came at him, a tube of red-brown mush flowing out its stubby rear.

"Christ!" he gasped, stumbling backward. "Joan! Don't come in here! Get Timmy! Get the hell out of the house!"

*   *   *

"What's going . . .?" The next word died in Joan's throat as she stepped past the dining room table. She saw Paul in his robe dropping to a crouch and whacking the floor with the fireplace poker. The hooked end of the rod nearly hit a yucky thing that she thought for a moment was a rat. It scooted out of the way.

It wasn't like any rat that Joan had ever seen.

She saw the cat, the carpet dark with gore near its rump.

"Oh dear God," she murmured.

Paul gasped and leaped aside as the creature darted toward his foot. It chased him across the carpet.

Joan took a step forward, wanting to rush in and help him. But she stopped abruptly. She had no weapon. She was barefoot, wearing only her nightgown.

"Shit!" Paul jumped onto the sofa, twisted around and backstepped, the poker raised overhead. The thing scurried up the upholstery. "Do like I said! Get Timmy out of here. Get help, for Godsake! Call the cops!"

The little beast suddenly halted.

It looked back at Joan.

Ice flowed up her back.

She whirled around and ran. Straight to Timmy's room. The boy woke up as she scooped him out of bed. "Mommy?" He sounded frightened.

"It's okay," she said, rushing out of the room with Timmy clutched to her chest. Hanging onto him with one arm, she snatched her purse off the dining room table. She raced into the kitchen, put him down while she opened the back door, then hoisted him again and ran outside.

"What's wrong, Mommy?" he asked. "Where's Daddy?"

"Everything's fine," she said, easing him down beside the Granada. "A little problem in the house. Daddy's taking care of it." She fumbled inside her purse, found the car keys, unlocked the driver's door and opened it. "You just wait here," she said, lifting Timmy onto the seat. "Don't come out. I'll be back pretty soon." She slammed the door.

And stood there at the edge of the driveway.

What'll I do?

Go back inside and help him?

He's got the poker. What am I gonna do, go after the thing with a carving knife?

She cut off its tail with a carving knife.

That was no damn mouse.

He said to call the cops. Oh, right. Tell them a *thing* is chasing my husband around the house. And then when they get here in ten or fifteen minutes . . .

Joan snapped her head toward Applegate's house.

Applegate, the red-neck gun nut.

She crouched and looked through the car window at Timmy. The boy wasn't stupid. He knew that, somewhere in the house, shit was hitting the fan in a big way. His eyes looked huge and scared and lonely. Joan felt her throat go tight.

At least you're safe, honey, she thought.

She managed a smile for him, then whirled around and rammed herself into the thick hedge beside the driveway. Applegate's bushes raked her skin, snagged her nightgown. But she plunged straight through and dashed across his yard.

She leaped onto his front stoop.

The plastic sign on Applegate's door read: THIS HOUSE INSURED BY SMITH & WESSON.

What an asshole, she thought.

Hoping he was home, she thumbed the doorbell button.

From inside came the faint sound of ringing chimes.

Joan looked down at herself and shook her head. The nightie had been a Valentine's Day present from Paul. There wasn't much of it, and you could see through what there was.

Applegate's gonna love this, she thought. Shit!

Where *is* he?

"Come on, come on," she muttered. She jabbed the doorbell a few more times, then pounded the door with her fist. "Joe!" she yelled.

No answer came. She heard no footsteps from inside the house.

"Damn it all," she muttered. Being careful not to slip again, she hurried to the edge of the concrete slab. She stepped down, took a few strides across the dewy grass, then made her way into the flower bed at the front of Applegate's house. He must be home and up, she thought; his curtains are open. He always kept them shut at night and whenever he was away.

Joan pushed between a couple of camelias, leaned close to his picture window and cupped her hands around her eyes.

She peered into the sunlit living room.

Applegate was home, all right. But not up. He lay sprawled on the floor in his robe and a swamp of blood.

*　　*　　*

Paul leaped off the end of the couch. He landed beside the front door.

Get the hell out! he thought.

Sure. And leave the thing in here? You come back and can't even find it.

I've gotta kill the bastard.

He lurched sideways as the creature sprang off the arm of the couch. He was almost fast enough. But he felt a sudden small tug on his robe, and yelped. The thing was hanging by its claws near the bottom of the robe, starting to climb. Paul threw open his cloth belt. He twirled to swing the beast away from his body, and jerked the robe off his shoulders. It dropped down his arms.

He let go of the poker so his sleeve wouldn't hang up on it. The poker thumped against the carpet. With one hand, he gave the robe a small fling. It fell to a heap, covering the beast.

He snatched up the poker. For just an instant, he considered beating the robe with the iron bar. But the rod was so thin, he'd be lucky to hit the beast.

Squealing "SHIT!" he sprang onto the cloth bundle with both feet. He jumped up and down on it. Shivers scurried up his legs. He felt as if cold fingers were tickling his scrotum. The skin on his back prickled. He thought he could feel the hair rising on the nape of his neck. But he stayed on the robe, dancing on it, driving his heels at the floor.

Until his right heel struck a bulge.

He screeched, "Yaaaah!" and leaped off.

He whirled around, poker high, and bent down ready to strike.

The robe was too thick, too rumbled, for Paul to locate the lump he'd just stomped.

Gotta be dead, he thought. *I smashed it. Smashed it good.*

Then he realized he hadn't actually felt it squish.

He whacked the robe with his poker. Stared at it. The rod had left a long, straight dent across the heap. Nothing moved. He struck again. The second blow puffed up the old dent and pounded a new one close to where it'd been. He struck a few more times, but never felt the rod hit anything except the robe and the floor.

Paul stepped a little farther away, then leaned forward and stretched out his arm. He slipped the tip of the poker under a lapel, jostled it until a heavy flap of the robe was hooked, then slowly lifted.

The blanketed area of carpet shrank as he raised the robe higher.

No creature.

Then the end of the robe was swaying above the carpet, covering nothing at all.

Still no creature.

It came scurrying down the slim rod of the poker toward his hand.

Paul screamed.

He hurled the weapon and ran.

*   *   *

Racing up the Applegate's driveway toward the rear of his house, Joan wondered if she should try next door. An older couple lived there. She didn't actually know them. Besides, they might be dead, same as Applegate.

And what if they didn't have a gun?

Applegate had plenty. That, she knew. She and Paul had been in his house just once—enough to find out that he was not their kind of person. A Republican, for godsake! A beer-swilling reactionary with the mean, narrow mind of his ilk. Anti-abortion, anti-women's rights, big on capital punishment and the nuclear deterrent. Everything that she and Paul despised.

But he did have guns. His home was an arsenal.

Dashing around the corner of his house, Joan spotted a rake on the back lawn. It had been left carelessly on the grass, tines upward. She ran into the yard and grabbed it up, then swung around and rushed across the concrete patio.

She skidded to a halt at the sliding glass door. With the handle of the rake, she punched through the glass. Shards burst inward, fell and clinked to the floor, leaving a sharp-edged hole the size of a fist. Reaching through the hole, she unlatched the door. When she pulled her hand out, a fang of glass ripped the back of it.

She muttered, "Fuck."

Not much more than a scratch, really. But blood started welling out.

I'm ruining myself, she thought. But then she remembered how Applegate had looked, remembered Paul scampering over the couch with that little monster on his heels.

He could end up like Joe if I don't hurry, she told herself.

Why doesn't *he* get the fuck out of the house?

Deciding to ignore her bleeding hand, Joan wrenched open the door. It rumbled on its runners. She swept it wide, and entered Applegate's den to the left of the broken glass.

There was the gun rack on the other side of the room. She hurried toward it, holding the rake ready and watching the floor.

What if Applegate hadn't been killed by one of those horrible *things?* Just because we've got one . . . Maybe he was murdered and the killer's still . . .

One of those horrible *things* scurried out from under a chair and darted straight for Joan's feet.

She whipped the rake down.

Got it!

The tines didn't pierce its slimy flesh, but the monster seemed to be trapped between two of the iron teeth.

Joan dropped the rake.

She rushed to the gun rack. A ghastly thing with the weapons resting on what appeared to be the hooves of deer or stags. Wrinkling her nose, she grabbed the bottom weapon. A double-barreled shotgun?

She whirled around with it just as the monster slithered free of the rake tines.

Clamping the stock against her side, she swung the muzzle toward the thing, thumbed back one of the hammers, and pulled the front trigger.

The blast crashed in her ears.

The shotgun lurched as if it wanted to rip her hands off.

The middle of the rake handle exploded.

So did the monster. It blew apart in a gust of red and splashed across the hardwood floor.

"Jesus H. Christ," Joan muttered.

Then, she smiled.

*   *   *

Paul slammed the bathroom door. He thumbed in the lock button.

An instant later, he flinched as the thing struck the other side of the door.

Just let it try and get me now, he thought.

Then came quiet, crunching sounds. Splintering sounds.

"Bastard!" he yelled, and kicked the bottom of the door.

He pictured the beast on the other side, its tiny teeth ripping out slivers of wood.

If only he hadn't lost the poker, he could crush its head when it came through.

Rushing to the cabinet, he searched for a weapon. His Schick took injector blades. They'd be no use at all. He grabbed a pair of toenail scissors. Better than nothing. But he knew he couldn't bring himself to kneel down and ambush the thing. Not with scissors four inches long.

If only he had a gun.

If only the cops would show up.

He wondered whether Joan had managed to call them yet. She'd had plenty of time to reach a neighbor's phone. Applegate himself might come charging over with one of his guns, if she went to his place.

The door rattled quietly in its frame as the creature continued to burrow through.

There must be something useful in here!

The waste basket! Trap the thing under it!

Paul crouched for waste basket. Wicker. Shit! They'd had a heavy plastic one until a couple of weeks ago when Joan saw this at Pier One. The bastard would chomp its way out in about a second.

He looked at the bottom of the door, and two tiny splits appeared. A bit of wood the width of a Popsicle stick bulged, cracked at the top, and started to rise.

He heard a faint boom like a car backfiring in the distance.

The flap of wood broke and fell off. The snout of the beast poked out.

Paul whirled. He rushed to the bathtub and climbed over the ledge. The bathmat draped the side of the tub. He flipped it to the floor.

The shower curtain was bunched at the far end, hanging inside.

With no rug or shower curtain to climb, the thing couldn't get at him.

He hoped.

81

I don't care how good it is, he thought, it can't climb the outside of the tub.

"Just try," he muttered as the thing scurried across the tile floor. It stopped on the bathmat and looked up at him. It seemed to grin. It sprang and Paul yelped. But the leap was short. The beast thumped against the side inches from the top. Its forelegs raced, claws clittering against the enamel for a moment. Then it dropped. Its rump thumped the mat. As it keeled backward, it flipped over and landed on its feet.

Paul bit down on the scissors. He crouched. With both hands, he twisted the faucets. Water gushed from the spout. As it splashed around his feet, he stoppered the drain. He took the scissors from his mouth, stood up straight and looked at the floor beside the tub.

The beast was gone.

Where . . .?

The waste basket tipped over, spilling out wads of pink tissue. It began rolling toward the tub.

"Think you're smart, huh?" Paul said. He let out a laugh. He pumped his legs, splashing water up around his shins and calves. "BUT CAN YOU SWIM? HUH? HOW'S YOUR BACKSTROKE, YOU LITTLE SHIT?"

The waste basket was a foot from the tub when the beast darted up from the far side. It landed atop the rolling wicker. Paul threw the scissors at it. They missed. The creature leaped.

He staggered backward as it flew at the tub. It landed on the ledge, slid across on its belly, and flopped into the water. It splashed. Then it sank.

"GOTCHA!" Paul yelled.

He jumped out of the tub. Bending over, he gazed at the beast. It was still on the bottom, walking along slowly under a few inches of water.

He jerked the shower curtain over the ledge so it hung outside.

The beast came to the surface, glanced this way and that, then spotted Paul and started swimming toward him.

"Come on and drown," he muttered.

It reached the wall of the tub. Its forepaws scampered against the enamel. Though it couldn't climb the smooth wall, it didn't seem ready to drown, either.

Paul backed away from the tub.

On the counter beside the sink was Timmy's Smurf toothbrush

standing upright in its plastic holder. He rushed over to it and snatched it from the Smurf's hand.

He knelt beside the tub.

The beast was still trying to climb up.

Paul poked at it. The end of the toothbrush jabbed the top of its head and submerged it. But the thing squirmed free. It started to come up. Before its snout could break the surface, Paul prodded it down again.

"How long can you hold your breath, asshole?"

It started to rise. He poked it down again and laughed.

"Gotcha now."

Again, the beast escaped from under the toothbrush and headed for the surface.

Paul jabbed down at it. His fist struck the water, throwing a splash into his face. As he blinked his eyes clear, something stung his knuckles.

He jerked his hand up.

He brought the creature with it.

Screaming, he lurched away from the tub and shook his arm as the thing scampered over his wrist. It held fast, claws digging in.

He swiped at it with his other hand. It came loose, ripping flesh from his forearm, and raced up *that* hand.

Raced up his left arm, leaving a trail of pinpoint tracks.

Swinging around, he bashed his arm against a wall. But the beast merely scampered to its underside. Upside-down, it scooted toward his armpit.

*　　*　　*

"PAUL!"

Joan twisted the knob. The bathroom door was locked. From beyond it came a horrible scream.

She aimed at the knob and pulled the trigger.

As the explosion roared in her ears and the shotgun jumped, a hole the size of a fist appeared beside the knob. The door flew open.

Paul, in his underpants, stood beside the bathtub shrieking. His left arm was sheathed with blood. In what remained of his right hand, he held the monster.

He saw her. A wild look came to his eyes.

"Shoot it!" he yelled, and thrust his fist toward the ceiling. Blood streamed down his arm.

"Your hand!"

"I don't care!"

She thumbed back one of the twin hammers, took a bead on her husband's upraised bleeding hand, and pulled a trigger. The hammer clanked.

"My God! Shoot it!"

She cocked the other hammer, aimed, jerked the other trigger. The hammer snapped down. The shotgun didn't fire.

"RELOAD. FOR GODSAKE RELOAD!"

"With *what?*" she shrieked back at him.

"IDIOT!" He jammed the monster into his mouth, chomped down on it, yanked, then threw the decapitated body at her. It left a streamer of blood in the air. It slapped against Joan's shoulder and bounced off, leaving a red smear on her skin.

Paul spat out the thing's head. Then he dropped to his knees and buried it in vomit.

*　　*　　*

In the living room, he put on his robe. They hurried outside together.

Timmy was still in the car, his face pressed to the passenger window, staring at the woman in curlers and a pink nightgown who was sprawled on the sidewalk, writhing and screaming.

From all around the neighborhood came the muffled sounds of shouts, shrieks and gunshots. Paul heard sirens. A great many sirens. They all seemed far away.

"My God," he muttered.

He scanned the ground while Joan opened the car door and lifted Timmy out. She kneed the door shut. She carried the boy around the rear of the car.

"Where're you going?" Paul asked.

"Applegate's. Come on. We'll be safer there."

"Yeah," he said. "Maybe." And he followed her toward the home of their neighbor.

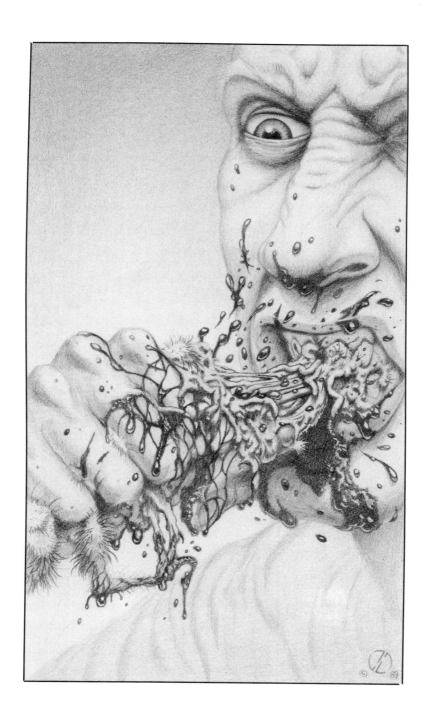

Madman Stan

The TV screen went blank.

Billy, sitting on the floor in front of it, felt his mouth sag open. He twisted his head around. Agnes gave him a mean smile from the couch. She had the remote control in her hand, aimed like a gun at the television. "Hey, that's no fair," he said. "The show wasn't even over."

"It is, now," Agnes said. "Time for beddy-bye, children."

Billy turned his eyes to Rich, looking for help.

The boy's arms were folded across his plaid robe. He was frowning. "We're allowed to stay up until eleven on Saturday nights," he informed the woman. "It isn't even ten yet."

Billy nodded, proud of his older brother.

"Children your age belong in bed at a decent hour," Agnes said.

"If I may speak my mind," said Rich, "that really bites."

Agnes smiled at him. "Aren't you the little darling?"

"Well, it does. And Mom and Dad are going to hear about this. *They* let us stay up. So does Linda."

"Linda isn't here," Agnes said in her sweet, nasty voice. "And frankly, I'm more than a little sick of hearing about that twit."

"Linda isn't a twit," Billy said, gaining courage from his brother's stand against this dumpy old creep. "She's a lot nicer than you are. And besides, you don't even know her."

Agnes peered at her wristwatch. "I'm losing my patience, children. It's off to bed with you, now."

"You're really a rotten babysitter," Rich said.

"Why, thank you. And you, my dear, are really a rotten child."

Rich's face turned red. He stood up. "Come on, Billy. Let's get out of here."

"Yeah." He got to his feet.

"Don't go away mad," Agnes said, and chuckled.

They headed for the other end of the living room, glancing at each other. Rich looked steamed.

"No, I mean it," Agnes called after them. "Come back here. I've got a little surprise for you. Something to cheer you up."

They turned to face her. "What?" Rich asked.

The lamplight gleamed on Agnes's glasses. Her chubby face widened with a grin. "A bedtime story. A *scary* one."

Billy felt a quick flutter in his stomach.

He looked at Rich. Rich looked at him.

"I'll just wager your precious Linda never tells you spooky stories."

"Sure she does," Rich said, and Billy nodded.

"Not as spooky as mine."

That wouldn't be too hard, Billy thought. Linda was great, but her stories were just okay. Billy figured *he* could tell scarier stories than Linda.

"You want to hear it, don't you?"

Billy blurted, "Sure."

Rich shrugged. "Yeah, I guess so."

"Should I . . . ?" Billy stopped himself.

"Should you what?" Agnes asked.

"Nothing," he muttered.

He had almost said "turn off the lights." That's what they did when Linda told stories. Made the living room dark and sat on the couch, Linda between them. Even if her stories weren't so hot, it was wonderful. She would put her arms around them. Even in winter, she always seemed to smell like suntan oil.

"Why don't we turn off the lights?" Agnes suggested.

Rich shook his head. "Billy's afraid of the dark."

You lying sack, Billy thought, and nodded and tried to look worried.

He wasn't afraid of the dark. Not usually, anyhow. But he certainly did not want to be in a dark room with Agnes.

"Leave the lights on, then." She patted the cushion on each of her.

Billy pretended not to see that. He sat down on the carpet, facing her, and crossed his legs. Rich sank to the floor beside him.

Agnes laughed softly and shook her head. Her cheeks wobbled. "You're not frightened of *me*, are you?" she asked.

"Huh-uh." That was the truth, too. He wasn't frightened of Agnes. Not much, anyhow. But the idea of sitting close to her on the couch was revolting. The woman was not only fat and ugly, but she had some kind of sour smell like a washcloth that had sat around damp too long.

For the zillionth time, Billy wished Linda didn't have that date tonight. He sure liked sitting up there with her.

"This is how we always sit," Rich lied again.

"I didn't relish the idea myself," she said, "of you two darlings up here with me."

"Are you going to tell us the story?" Rich asked. He sounded good and impatient.

"Are you ready for it? Maybe you need to wee-wee first."

"We'll urinate later," Rich told her.

Billy almost laughed, but held it in. He didn't want to make Agnes mad, or she might call off the story.

The woman scooted back on the couch. She grunted softly as she brought her legs up and crossed them on the cushion. Billy was surprised she *could* cross them, they were so thick. He was also surprised her pink sweatpants didn't split open. The way they bulged, they looked as if they might burst at any second and let Agnes's flesh flop out all over the couch.

She folded her arms across the front of her sweatshirt in a way that made her look like she was trying to hide a couple of footballs and sneak them past the defensive line.

The idea of that made Billy smile.

"Would you like to tell us what you find amusing, young man?"

He felt his face go hot. "Nothing. Huh-uh. I was just daydreaming, that's all."

"Don't daydream during my story."

"We're both going to fall asleep if you don't get on with it," Rich said.

"All right." She cleared her throat. She squirmed a little as if trying to work her fat rump deeper into the cushion. "This is the story of why nobody goes to bed at night without making sure to lock the house up tight."

"I know, I know," Rich said. "So the boogeyman can't get in."

"Save your sarcasm for that Linda twat. And don't interrupt me, or I won't let you hear the story."

"C'mon, Rich," Billy said. "Don't interrupt."

Rich made a quiet huff.

"In some towns," Agnes said, "people don't lock their doors at night. But we always do, here in Oakwood. There's a very good reason for that. It's because of the madman." Agnes bobbed her round head. "Madman Stan," she said, her voice lower, almost a whisper. "Nobody knows where he comes from. But I've heard it said he hangs around the cemetery, especially on hot summer nights when he likes to take off all his clothes and get up against the tombstones. They're cool, you know. They feel good when it's so hot at night you can't sleep. Remember that, come summer."

Rich glanced at Billy and rolled his eyes upward.

But Agnes didn't seem to notice. She was gazing straight ahead, swaying gently back and forth.

"Myself," she said in that same low voice, "I've never seen him in among the graves. But I've been told by others. I've been told that's where he takes his victims. Nobody'll even whisper what he does with 'em. But I've got my own ideas on that."

"What?" Rich whispered.

Agnes stopped swaying. She stared down at him. "You don't want to know."

"You're just making this up, anyway," he muttered.

She smiled. "The Madman Stan will settle for men and women. And he likes little girls very much. But more than anything else in the whole wide world, he likes little boys. They're his favorite."

"Sure," Rich said.

Billy nudged him with an elbow. Rich elbowed him back, harder.

"Like I told you, I don't know what the madman does with them. But they're never seen again. Ever. Folks who live over by the graveyard say they hear screams, sometimes. Horrible screams. And sometimes, they hear digging sounds out there."

"Like fun," Rich muttered.

"Not much fun for those he snatches," Agnes said. "Not much fun at all, I should think. That's why we all lock our doors up tight, here in Oakwood. Like I told you, I've never seen Madman Stan over by the graveyard. But I've seen him other places. Plenty of times. Always late at night. I'll be looking out a window at the street, or I'll be walking home after a sitting job, and I'll see him. I've even seen him right here on Fifth Street. Do you know what he's doing?"

Rich didn't make any crack. Billy felt a little breathless and sick.

"The madman is walking from block to block, from house to house, going up to each and every door and trying the knob. He's looking for a door that isn't locked. And when he finds one, in he goes. And that's the last of someone." Agnes nodded and grinned. "Off to bed, children."

"That's all?" Rich asked. "That's no story."

"That's my story. Now, to bed with you. I want you to go straight to sleep, children." Her grin suddenly grew so large that her cheeks pushed against the bottom of her glasses and the round lenses drifted upward. "If I hear so much as a peep out of either one of you . . ." Unfolding her arms, she pointed past the end of the couch toward the front door of the house. "I'll unlock it."

*   *   *

"Rich?"

"Shut up," Rich whispered.

Billy braced himself up on his elbows and squinted through the darkness. His brother's bed, just on the other side of the night table, was a dim blur. He thought maybe the small pale area near the headboard might be Rich's face. "It wasn't true, was it?" he asked.

Low on the pale area, a dark spot moved when Rich said, "Don't be a dork."

Billy was seeing Rich's face, all right. That was a relief. He said, "It kind of sounded like it might be, you know?"

"She was just trying to scare us."

"Are you sure?"

"There's no madman going around trying doorknobs. Are you kidding? The cops'd be all over a guy like that."

"Yeah, I guess."

"And we'd of heard about it if people were disappearing around here."

"Yeah. I guess."

"So forget about it and . . ."

The bedroom door flew open, slamming the wall. Billy flinched.

He jerked his head toward the light.

Agnes filled the doorway, fists on her hips. "What did I tell you children about talking?"

"We weren't," Rich argued.

"I'm not deaf, sweetie-pie. I told you what I'd do, didn't I? You bet I did! And that's just what I aim to do."

She jerked the door shut, cutting out the light.

Billy clutched his pillow to his face. He clamped his lower lip between his teeth. He tried not to cry.

He listened.

Listened for the quiet sniffing, gasping sounds. They came from the other bed.

"Rich?" he whispered.

"Shut up."

"Are you crying?"

"None of your business. It's all your fault, you little crud." He made a wet, slurpy sniffle. "Why'd you have to go and open your big mouth?"

"I'm sorry."

"Now she's gone and unlocked the door."

"You said you didn't believe in Madman Stan."

"I don't."

"Then what are you crying about?"

"I'm not. It's just she's such a bitch." Another loud sniff. "How could Mom and Dad leave us with a bitch like that?"

Billy shrugged, even though he knew Rich couldn't see it. "Linda had that date."

"Hope she had a rotten time."

"Don't say that, Rich."

"She should've been with us."

"You're telling me."

"Shut up before *she* comes back."

"Okay." Billy rested his head against the pillow and shut his eyes.

He heard soft, muffled sobbing.

Jeez, he thought. Rich is even more scared than me, and he doesn't even believe it about the madman.

Bet he *does* believe it.

"Mom and Dad'll be home pretty soon," he whispered.

"Oh, sure. Pretty soon. Like two or three hours."

"I bet she didn't unlock the door, anyway."

"Like fun she didn't. Shut up, huh?"

"Okay."

Billy rolled onto his back. He stared at the ceiling. He listened to his brother cry.

After a while, the crying stopped.

"Rich?" he whispered.

No answer.

"You asleep?"

It seemed impossible. How could *anyone* fall asleep with the front door unlocked and everything?

Soon, Rich started to snore.

Billy felt deserted. It wasn't fair. Rich shouldn't leave him alone like this.

He wished *he* could fall asleep. But his eyes felt locked open.

My bed's closest to the door, he thought. When Madman Stan comes, he'll get me first.

He had an urge to watch the door. But fear stopped him. What if he turned his head to look and just then the madman smashed the door open?

So he kept on staring at the ceiling.

He wished Rich would wake up.

I could wake him up, he thought. We could sneak out the window and get out of here.

If we do that, we'll be outside where *he* is.

Billy considered hiding under his bed.

That's probably the first place a madman would look.

Besides, what if I hide and he gets Rich instead of me?

For a while, he wondered how things would be without his brother around. Rich teased him a lot and started fights. But sometimes he was okay. Billy sure didn't want the madman to get him and take him to the graveyard and do things to him that even a rotten bag like Agnes wouldn't talk about.

Rich called her a bitch.

He'd get in trouble if Mom or Dad found out.

Well, she *is* a bitch.

Billy suddenly had a thought that made him smile.

If Madman Stan comes to the house and the door is unlocked and he comes in . . . won't he get Agnes first?

Doesn't she know that?

Is she a stupe, or what?

Billy had another nice thought.

The bitch didn't unlock the door, at all.

*   *   *

He knew positively that Agnes had lied about unlocking the door.

He just wished he could be sure.

*   *   *

Heart slamming, Billy eased open the bedroom door until a strip of light came in. He peered through the crack. The coast was clear.

He slipped into the hallway. Getting down on his hands and knees, he made his way to the dining room. He crawled between a chair and a table leg.

What'll I do if she sees me? he wondered.

Sometimes, Mom and dad caught him under the table. But plenty of times they hadn't. He and Rich had both gotten away with watching late TV shows from under here while their parents watched from the couch, just out of sight because the edge of the doorway blocked them out.

Billy halted when he could see the television. It wasn't on.

What's she doing anyhow? he wondered.

Maybe reading a magazine, or something.

If she was reading, he might be able to sneak by and get to the front door.

He crawled slowly toward the far end of the table, turning his head and gazing out through the bars of chair and table legs. Finally, the bottom of the couch came into view. He inched upward. leaned forward, and peered around a chair back that was in the way.

Agnes was lying down on the couch.

A big mound of pink, hands folded on the hill of her stomach.

Her eyes were shut. She didn't have her glasses on.

Billy spotted her glasses on the lamp table between the end of the couch and the front door.

94

Okay, he thought.

He didn't *feel* okay. He could hardly catch his breath and his heart was thundering and he felt like he needed to use the bathroom bad.

But this was his chance.

He crept out from under the table. Staying on his hands and knees, keeping his eyes fixed on Agnes, he crawled into the living room.

Wait'll I tell Rich, he thought.

"You what?" Rich would say.

"Yeah, I just crawled over to the door and made sure it was locked."

"And Agnes was there?"

"Yeah, right on the couch."

"Wow, Billy. I didn't know you had that kind of guts."

"Wasn't any big deal."

"How did you sneak by without her seeing you?"

"Indian style."

"Was she asleep or something?"

"I don't know. She could've been playing possum."

Billy's fantasy fell apart. *What if she is playing possum?*

He halted and stared at Agnes.

Her eyes were still shut. Her mouth hung open. Her chin looked like a golf ball someone had shoved into a pile of raw dough that was heaped up where her neck was supposed to be. The front of her sweatshirt slowly rose and fell.

She *is* asleep, Billy told himself.

But he wasn't sure of that, any more than he was sure she had lied about unlocking the door.

If only she would snore.

Billy forced himself to start crawling again. He was halfway to the door when a floorboard creaked under his knee. He cringed. A hand slid down the slope of Agnes's stomach. It fell off the edge of the couch, taking her arm with it. Billy scurried forward, knowing she would wake up, praying he could get past the head of the couch before she opened her eyes.

His spine froze as she mumbled something.

Her eyes stayed shut.

At last, the stuffed arm of the couch blocked Billy's view of her head. He slowed down, and crept past the lamp table. When he was even with the front door, he turned to the right and crawled toward it.

Staring at the lock.

It had an oblong brass gizmo that you turned between your thumb and forefinger. It was straight up and down. But it always was. By looking, you couldn't tell whether or not the door was locked.

Billy would have to try the knob.

Bracing himself up with his left arm, he raised his right hand toward the knob.

What if Madman Stan's right outside? he thought.

What if he's reaching for the knob right now?

Billy's fingers fluttered as if he were having a spaz attack. He closed them around the doorknob. The knob rattled. He heard a soft whimper slip out of his throat.

Holding his breath, he turned the knob.

He pulled.

The door wouldn't budge.

The dirty pig hadn't unlocked it, after all.

* * *

Behind the dining room table again, Billy got to his feet. He pressed a hand against his chest. His heart was kicking like a wildman.

I did it, he told himself.

I did it and she didn't catch me.

He stared at Agnes, still sleeping on the couch.

He felt a smile stretch his mouth.

Then he tiptoed toward the bedroom, hoping Rich might be awake so he could tell him all about it.

* * *

Billy woke up in the dark, terrified, hot urine shooting down his leg as something bashed the bedroom door again and again and Rich shrieked, *Yaaaaaaaah!"*

More bashing. The door opened wider with each bash as the

96

straight-backed chair under its knob scooted a bit more on the carpet.

"Boys!" Dad shouted.

Billy had never heard him sound so scared.

"Boys! What's going on!"

Billy hurled himself out of bed. He rushed toward the door, wet pajama pants sticking to his groin and left leg. He pulled the chair out from under the knob and backed away.

Dad came in. He hit the light switch. He was out of breath, eyes bulging as he looked quickly from Billy to Rich. "They're okay!" he called over his shoulder.

"Oh, thank God." Mom lurched through the doorway, weeping.

"What's been going on around here?" Dad asked. "Jesus! Where's the babysitter? Why was the door blocked? What's going on?"

Rich had stopped screaming a few seconds ago. Now, he was sitting up in bed, crying and shaking his head.

"Agnes was *horrible*," Billy blurted.

"Well where is she? How could she go off and leave you guys? What the hell . . .?"

Mom, Billy noticed, was holding Agnes's glasses down by her side.

"We come home," Dad went on, "and the goddamn babysitter's gone and the front door's standing wide open! What the hell happened?"

"Madman Stan got her," Rich whimpered through his sobs. "Oh geez! She unlocked the door so he'd get *us*, but . . ." Then, he was crying too hard to say more.

Billy looked up at his parents and shook his head. He decided not to tell who unlocked the door really.

After-Words

Richard Laymon, for a reason no one can yet provide an answer, is presently better known in England than he is in his native America. Born in Chicago, he currently resides in southern California, where he often socializes with fellow authors Dean R. Koontz and Gary Brandner. He has published 16 novels to date, and close to 50 short stories. The novels include *The Cellar, Tread Softly, Night Show, Out Are The Lights* and *Flesh*. At least one major publisher of horror fiction has rejected his work as being too graphic for the average reader. However, one aspect of his style which has been recognized both here and overseas is his capacity to strip his stories down to the bone, leaving only the central characters—and the horror. In the words of one critic, to make "the readers turn the pages so fast they leave burn marks on the paper." Another aspect that the critics have missed is that Laymon was writing in the "splatterpunk" mode long before the term was even coined. Using a word processor, he works often seven days a week to make it bloody right.

* * *

SW: Explain the basic genesis of "Mop Up."
RL: I had a vision of a young, scared soldier in the ruins of a city, who, with a few buddies, were getting their asses ripped by these vile creatures in this post-apocalyptic world, and then meet this nice young lady survivor somewhere along the way. I thought of the general situation a long time ago, but couldn't figure out how to make a novel out of it. Then I realized this would be my opportunity to flesh it out. It took me about three weeks to do it.
SW: The setting seems like something out of a Italian zombie movie, with its non-stop action and gore. We know you're a big fan of horror movies.

AFTER-WORDS

RL: It was inspired in part by George Romero's movies—*Night of the Living Dead; The Crazies*. And I think maybe a little of John Carpenter's *Assault on Precinct 13*, and some of the movies that have been spawned by Richard Matheson's *I Am Legend*.

SW: You mentioned in a letter that the origin of "Wishbone" has a rather interesting history. At the time, you were stuck with a final story to contribute.

RL: All of the stories were written for NIGHT VISIONS at the same time, and I knew I still had to come up with one more story. I got the idea when I went with my family and some friends to Death Valley, and we went to this ghost town. We were wandering through this building, which seemed to have been abandoned fairly recently, judging by the pictures on the wall. We had wandered out back, which was pretty much like a junkyard. Then our wives found something, and began yelling, "Come here! Get here quick!" I figured at first someone had tripped or gotten hurt. But actually they had found a skeleton in one of the rooms that we had earlier overlooked. It was in a black coffin with a glass lid. It had a whiskey bottle resting against its shoulder, which I imagine was somebody's idea of a joke. So I figured when we got back that I just had to write a story about people coming across a skeleton, and "Wishbone" came out of that.

SW: Your stories and novels rarely possess many "happy endings." Is there any reason why your stories in NIGHT VISIONS are so particularly grim? Or do you always just think that way?

RL: No, that's just the way they turned out! [laughs] My first novel, *The Cellar*, had a real downbeat ending, and a lot of people were upset by that. But I think an ending where things don't turn out rosy is pretty appropriate to a horror story. I'm not obsessed with downbeat endings, but I do have a real appreciation for endings that deal with a sort of poetic justice.

SW: Where did the bizarre inspiration for the enigmatic "Bad News" originate?

RL: Well, I go out every other morning and pick up our newspaper, because if it sits out there very long, somebody swipes it. [laughs] So very early, I go out and grab it before somebody else does! And on occasion it's occurred to me that something might be inside the newspaper . . . I'd like to say that this is probably the most political story I've ever written, and people can read it a lot of different ways.

SW: How long did it take to write?

RL: Both "Bad News" and "Madman Stan" took me two to three days to write. They were done in fact while I was working on "Mop Up." If I got tired with "Mop Up" in the morning, I would work on one of the shorter stories instead. At a Bouchercon once, Gary Brandner and I were sitting around drinking with Robert L. Fish, who told us, "If you spend more than two days on a short story you're wasting your time." I do think that knowing I was writing for NIGHT VISIONS, and what the audience expects, made my work easier. It was actually inspiring. These things had been simmering in the back of my mind, and I was glad for the opportunity.

SW: In spite of your reputation, the violence in ''Madman Stan'' is noticeably ''softer'' than in the previous tales.

RL: It's true the others have a lot of hard-core action, and with this one I wanted something a little more subtle. I came up with the idea for the "Madman" long before there ever was a story. As I recall, my daughter Kelly left the front door unlocked one night. And to break her of the habit, I told her there was a guy who wandered the neighborhood at night, trying all the doors, looking for the one that wasn't locked. While I was making that up, it occurred to me that it even scared *me*. Months later, she had a friend staying over for the night, and I told them both the story. The girl started crying, and then called up her mother to have her take her home! [laughs]

When it came the time to make it into a story for NIGHT VISIONS, I thought up the angle of the babysitter telling the tale to give it a structure. I did have some trouble giving the madman a name. I remember a movie where a guy told a spooky story around a campfire, though I can't remember the name of it. But in early drafts I called the character "Madman Mars" after the character in the movie. Then I simply called him "Madman."

SW: Do you think anyone will ever learn how you settled on the final choice of a name?

RL: Well, Stan is such a nice name for someone who's a total lunatic. [laughs] It just sounds so All-American.

Chet Williamson

Blue Notes

We were always arguing about them, about blue notes. Hell, we had ever since we were kids. I guess it was to be expected. Even though we played together in the same band in high school, we came from two different musical worlds. Todd was headbanging 4/4 straight-ahead rock and roll, as dependable (and to me as dull) as clockwork. Jazz was where I came from, and it was as boring to Todd as his music was to me. Jesus, he could play that guitar, though. I have to give him that.

Or maybe I should say *had* to give him that. I just hope wherever he is he got his right hand back.

But blue notes. I love them and use them like a carpenter uses a hammer and nails. You play jazz, you have to, you want it to *sound* like jazz. But Todd thought they were bullshit.

"Man, a note's a note, Lute. I mean, you got C, you got C sharp, there's *nothin'* in between there." And he hummed a note and went up a half step: "Da-*dah.* See? Nothin' in the cracks of the piano keys except dust. And no magic invisible frets on my Rickenbacker either, you know?"

And I explained to him again about the notes, slightly flatted, called blue notes, told him one more time about the tribal singers in Africa who can sing eight different tones between a C and a C sharp, told him how his own sweet rock sprang from the blues, and that the blues were called the blues because . . .

"Okay, spare me the adventures in good music," he said. "We're living in America, man, not Africa. Land of the free, home of the brave. Rock and roll heaven. We descend from European musical ideas, not from your African ancestors, no slur intended."

"None taken." Say what you would for the heavy metal thickness of Todd's skull, there wasn't a racist bone in his body. He had kicked a lot of white boys' asses while we were growing up to save me from getting mine kicked.

"Now I'm not saying they don't exist. I mean, I know about quarter-tones and all that crap. But what I *am* sayin' is that nobody gives a shit. You go up to your average rock fan and start layin' quarter tones on him, you see how long he stays around to listen. It'll just sound flat to him, like get it in *tune*, y'know? Sure, I bend a note now and then, but big fuckin' deal. You make it sound like blue notes are God's own truth or something."

"It *is* God's own truth that there's always something between," I said. "It's not just black and white."

"Yeah? Look at us."

I grinned. "I've got lots of white blood in me, Todd. And maybe there's a drop of Africa in you."

"In the eyes of the world, ole bud, it's still black and white. Like everything else."

Like everything else. That was the way life was for Todd. One-two-three-four, rock steady. I signalled to Tamara to get us two more beers and looked at my watch. I had another five minutes until the next set. "How do you like the new drummer?" I asked Todd.

He swung his leonine head around, the long blond hair following a millisecond later, and looked toward the bandstand at the lustrous black Yamaha Power Series drums surrounded by the gleaming Zildjian cymbals, then back at me. "He's okay, but there's sure no strong beat there. Does all those little riffs between the beats, don't know how the hell you can follow him."

"It's jazz, Todd," I said patiently. "I don't know why the hell you come here if you don't like it."

"Shit, you know why," he said, taking his fresh beer from Tamara's tray as she set mine in front of me. "You're my ole bud, and I like to hear you play. You blow like nobody else, man. I just wish I could get you out of this jazz crap and over into rock." His face lit up with the boyish glow that had lasted into his late twenties. "With you behind me, I could be the new Boss, you could be my Big Man—"

"It's been done." I took a sip of beer. "Besides, I'm not big enough to be any Big Man." It was true. Todd was only medium height and was taller than me by half a head. "Besides, you're doing well enough without me."

"Yeah, sure. You know where my album's stuck at on the Billboard charts?"

I nodded. "The low sixties. You told me."

"The past fuckin' month. Hit with a bullet, then goes from sixty-one to sixty-five, then to sixty-eight, and this week it's at sixty-nine."

"Erogenous number," I said. "Maybe some people'll buy it because of that."

Todd shook his head and drank half his beer. "Shit."

"What are you 'shit'ing for? At least you're *on* the charts." Five months before I had recorded an album with myself on alto and EWI, Fives Markham on keyboards, Tommy Aleet on bass, and Tweet Lewis on drums. The four of us had put up most of the money, and the album sank like a stone. The distributors treated it like musical AIDS, and as far as I know, the only place you can get it is the NMDS catalog. It didn't get one review, good or bad. "Maybe I should change my name to Kenny G," I told Todd.

"Number sixty-nine don't mean dick," he said. "If you're not in the top ten—hell, if you're not number *one,* you're nothing."

"No blue notes," I said.

"Huh?"

"No in-between. All or nothing."

"You got it."

"It's all black or white, up or down, huh?"

"That's right. No in-between."

"How about good and bad?"

"That too."

"And what are you, Todd?"

He thought for only a second. "Bad."

"Bull."

"I'm a Savage, man. We scare little boys and threaten little girls. Tipper Gore wants to stick labels on our albums and our crotches." He was grinning. I could see he was really into it, just the way he psyched himself up with the other Savages on stage. "We sing about blood and death and guns and knives and pain and—"

"And you get past the phony image, you're a Boy Scout."

The grin hung there on his face for another moment, then melted down into a soft, sad smile. "No, man. I think I *am* bad. The Savage stuff is image, sure, but goddam it, Lute, I'd sell my mother to Libyans if I could hit number one. You know I'm not much for loyalty . . ."

"You keep coming to hear me in dumps like this."

"I like dumps like this." His face twisted in the little-boy sneer that had gotten him a quarter cover on TIGER BEAT. "It makes the dumps I play in look good."

"Thanks."

"No, really, I'm not a good person, ole bud. I'm really really selfish."

"And because you're selfish, that makes you all bad."

"Basically."

"That's stupid. I'm not all bad, and I'm not all good. I'm in between, like everybody else."

"Nah. You're good. You're a sweet little chocolate bunny who's true to his ideals, and who won't . . ." He thought about the words, finally came up with them. ". . . compromise his art."

How fucking wrong you are, my friend, I thought. But I didn't say it. "Well, I won't give up my blue notes," and went back to the tiny stage, where Chip, the drummer, was warming up with his brushes.

As I took my alto off its stand, I felt the need inside me, and I wondered if good guys did blow. Christ knows I never wanted to get hooked on the shit, but people had offered, I had taken, and before too long people weren't offering as much as I wanted to take. Maybe the desire was more psychological than physical—I don't know, I never looked it up—but I couldn't play without it.

Couldn't play without it and couldn't live with it.

I was in hock to my balls for the stuff. I had two grams left of the twenty I had bought at the beginning of the month, and owed Mickey three thousand dollars. The grams had sat untouched now for four days, the same four day grace period Mickey had given me to come up with the money, come up with it or go down the tubes, over the bridge a block from the club, into the water of the bay.

I didn't have three grand. I didn't even have a hundred bucks, and I wouldn't until Saturday night, which was payday. Jim, the owner of the Purbright Jazz Club, wouldn't give me another advance, and I had already borrowed more from my friends than they could afford. I'd never borrowed anything from Todd, though. I could never bring myself to ask him. It was weird, but it seemed like Todd came to hear me play to recharge his batteries with our youth. Shit, neither of us was a kid any more—he was 29 and I was only a year younger. But he still had this image of me as the shy little black boy who played the hot sax, and somehow I didn't want to destroy that. It sounds stupid and probably was, since I'm sure Todd did his share of toot along with a helluva lot of other goodies, and wouldn't have held it against me, at least not overtly. But I was always afraid that it would disappoint him.

Of course, the alternative was disappointing Mickey, and that was the one thing I didn't want to do. Mickey was in his early forties, a veteran of at least a quarter century of mayhem and scuffling that had made him cocaine king of the section around the bay. The flake he handled was excellent, and the price was commensurate with its quality. Apparently people who Mickey offered credit to had been sticking him lately, and Mickey didn't like that at all. In fact, he told me when he gave me the four day ultimatum, "It's high fucking time I made an example out of somebody. Like, see, people know you've been buying from me, and they know you haven't been paying on time, and so if you were found somewhere dead in an alley, or washed up at the docks with your balls sewn in your mouth, then other people who owe me might begin to pay on time, you see what I mean?"

I saw all too well, and had been around long enough to know that Mickey didn't make idle threats. He wasn't a big guy—even I was taller than him—but he could move as fast as the lightning and hit as hard. He must have had money out his ass, but he looked as poor as dirt with his long, greasy hair and the faded jeans and worn cowboy boots he dressed in. He had rat eyes, and a mouth whose lip always lifted to show yellow teeth. It looked like a harelip, but I don't think it was. I think it was just a fucking mean mouth.

After the last set was over, I sat down again with Todd and told him about Mickey. I was right about his being disappointed.

"I never had you pegged for a cokehead, ole bud," he said, smiling to make me think he wasn't taking it too hard.

"I'm going to kick it. I have to. I just can't afford it. And it's doing shit to my breath control."

He nodded. "Didn't think some of those rides of yours were as long as usual. Where you meetin' this guy tonight?"

"The bridge. Middle of the goddam bridge. That way if I don't have the money, he puts me over."

"Well, you won't have the money tonight, but I can get it for you." I didn't understand him. "Tomorrow, I mean. Shit, I can't lay my hands on three grand tonight, banks got hours, y'know. But tomorrow."

"I don't know if Mickey'll wait till tomorrow."

I had running on my mind. I knew I couldn't run forever, but at least it would keep me alive a little longer. But if I ran, then Mickey would do for me automatically. There would be no explaining, no pleas for an extension. If I stayed, there was a slim chance I'd live, but a better one that I'd die tonight. If I ran, death was certain, if more distant. The situation sucked.

"The sonuvabitch'll have to wait, man," Todd said. "Hey, Lute, he doesn't want your ass, he'd much rather have your money. The guy's a businessman, right?"

"Right. And businessmen can't afford to extend credit indefinitely."

"What indefinitely? Tomorrow morning when the bank opens." He looked at his watch. "Eight hours away, he can't wait that long?"

"I guess I'll have to ask him."

"No no," he said quickly, "I'll ask him."

"*You'll* ask him," I said. "Todd, Mickey would eat you. He would take one look at you, see everything he hates, and fucking eat you."

"Hey, I'm no pushover."

"Mickey is never alone, man. He has friends—two big ugly friends that go everywhere with him. They will kill and cook you before Mickey eats you."

"Look, if you go they'll eat *you*, because you don't have the money, and all the blue notes all the boogies in Africa sing won't do you an ant's fart worth of good. But if *I* go, I can tell him who I am, tell him you just told me about this little problem, and that I can take care of it if he'll be so kind as to wait till morning." Todd paused for a second. "You think he's heard of the Savages?"

"Mickey doesn't give a crap for music. I doubt he's heard of the Beatles."

"Well, no sweat. I'll just tell him I'm on the Billboard charts."

"He'll be thrilled. Probably ask for your autograph. Look, Todd,

I appreciate the offer, and if Mickey lets me live I'll take you up on it, but I can't let you face *my* executioner."

"Will you relax? I can handle this, I've handled drug guys before —been a long time since school, ole bud. Believe me, the guys I've owed money to would make your Mickey look like Mickey Mouse."

"Todd . . ."

"Now get your ass home and into your nice warm bed and let me keep your appointment on the bridge. The voice of reason, music hath charms, all that other shit, okay? Mickey will fucking *love* me. Meet me at Chemical Bank on 14th tomorrow at ten, and everything will be copesetic, right?" He smiled boozily at me.

The thing is, even now I know why I said yes. I can't rationalize it. I said yes because I was afraid that Mickey would kill me. If Todd had been a little less drunk, he might have realized that the better way would have been for us both to go meet Mickey. Hell, I thought of it, but I didn't suggest it because I didn't *want* to meet Mickey. So I nodded, I agreed, I sent my scapegoat, the guy who was willing to put it on the line for me—his money or his life.

The sons of bitches took the latter.

I tried to call Todd beginning at four in the morning to ask him what happened, but there was no answer. I called every ten minutes until six o'clock, then got dressed and went back out on the street. I walked the seventeen blocks to the bridge and got there just as it was getting light.

There was no one on the bridge, and no one nearby, so I walked out on the cement sidewalk toward the middle. A few cars passed, but none slowed to look at me. The bloodstain was on the other side, so I didn't see it until I was almost past it, and wouldn't have noticed it all if a gull hadn't flown close to my head, so that I turned to watch it. The stain was partway up the four-foot wall. It looked like a patch of rust, but I knew that cement doesn't rust.

I also knew that the blood must have come from where Mickey and his friends cut off Todd's right hand. The stump must have spurted like a hose. There were droplets of dried blood everywhere. And I knew it was his *right* hand because it was lying there in the gutter.

I didn't go over to it right away. I just stood and looked for a while—at the dry blood, at the gray hunk of flesh with the rings still on the fingers—and I thought, those bastards weren't interested in the money at all. Jesus Christ, they didn't even take the rings. Or maybe they left them on the fingers so I'd be sure it was Todd. At any rate, they didn't want the money, they wanted blood, and they got it, and if I had gone it would have been mine.

I wished it would have been. I still do. I don't like living with a friend's blood on my hands, especially after he gave it up to save my worthless ass.

Finally I went over to the hand and knelt next to it. Most of the blood had drained out, and it took me a moment to convince myself that it was real and not some Taiwanese novelty. But as I looked closer I knew damn well it was Todd's. It was just too perfect to be fake. Hairs, pores, all that crosshatching on the knuckles, it wasn't a fucking joke at all.

Go to the police? It crossed my mind for only a minute. What was the point? There was no proof, no definite link between Mickey and Todd. And even if there were some sort of proof, Mickey had friends.

I felt totally lost, completely powerless. I felt like a dead man. Like Todd.

The hand was cool and dry when I picked it up, not at all like what I expected to feel. It made a small splash when it hit the water, and sank right away. The heavy rings must have pulled it down. "Bye, Todd," I whispered to the expanding circles of water, and watched until I couldn't see them any more. Then I walked back to my place, thinking about Todd.

Todd had said he was bad. The old black and white routine. He wasn't bad any more than Jesus was bad, and I thought—and think —about Todd and about Jesus and about the Southern Baptist church my parents took me to, and about the preacher talking about laying down your life for your friends.

Thank you, Todd, and thank you Jesus. Thank you and thank you again. And thank you for making me live the rest of my life in guilt.

But back then, on that morning, it was the kind of guilt I couldn't live with, and I was almost relieved when Mickey called me at noon. He didn't identify himself, but I knew it was him.

"Stupid," was the first thing he said. "Very very stupid, Luther. Sending your faggot friend in your place—that way two assholes get killed instead of one. That guy really play guitar in a rock group?"

"Y . . . yes," I managed to get out.

"Well, he's gonna have a rough time playin' now. Like, he can

110

use those fret-things, but he ain't gonna strum for shit."

Mickey was using present-tense, and something hot ran through me. I had assumed they had killed Todd—Mickey had said *killed*—but maybe . . . "Mickey . . ." I said.

"Who's Mickey?" Just in case, he figured. Just in case the phone was tapped.

"He's dead?"

"Playin' guitar for the fish." He laughed. "Like in *The Godfather*, you know? You see that? Part about sleepin' with the fish? Only this is playin' *guitar* for the fish, huh?"

I didn't know what to say, so I didn't say anything.

"What's the matter, *ole bud?*" he said, and the words cut me like a knife made of ice. "Cat got your tongue? Or maybe a fish, huh? A fish with those sharp little teeth you can hardly see, but shit you sure can feel, those little teeth nibblin' away on the soft parts, like your tongue and your eyeballs and your ball-balls? How much you think they've chewed off your long-haired buddy right now? Or maybe I oughta ask how much you think is *left?*"

He started chuckling then, and I blinked hard to get rid of both the tears and the pictures I was seeing. "What now?" I finally said.

"Now you pay," he answered, the humor gone from his voice. "*You* pay, Luther. Your *ole bud* was one day's interest, that's all. One day's interest on three grand. But I don't want anymore meat unless it's yours, see? No more babies you send to be butchered. Uh-uh. I want you. You or your money. You be on the bridge tonight. At midnight. Then we'll see what you got."

Absurdly, the first thought that went through my head was that I didn't get off from the club until two. It's amazing how the tyrannical details of everyday life intrude at the most inappropriate times. Fortunately, I didn't say it. I just said, "All right. Midnight," and hung up.

I expected to die. I wanted to. I couldn't pay the bastard any more today than I could have the night before, and I didn't want to run. I was tired and sad and beaten. I would meet him at midnight and he could do whatever the hell he wanted to. I didn't even have the energy to kill myself. Or maybe there was just too much of that Southern Baptist stuff left in me to do that. Mickey could do the dirty work and send my soul to heaven. Maybe I'd see Todd there. Maybe he'd be willing to play blue notes then.

I played damn fine that night. My solos were clean and sweet as

111

a baby's ass. When you know that death's waiting, I guess you want to leave something behind, even if it's only the memory of some beautiful sounds. The wailing was full of blue notes, and a couple of times it threw Max, the piano player, who asked me at the first break what the fuck key I was playing *Tenderly* in.

Midnight came partway through the second set, and I nodded to Max to take a solo and walked off the stage out of sight with my horn. It wasn't a surprise to him—we did it from time to time when we wanted to take a leak or when Buddy, the bass man, wanted a line.

But I didn't go to the john. Instead I walked out the back door into the alley, my sax still in my hands. I wanted to take it with me. I guess I was thinking about Sonny Rollins, about the sax on the bridge. Besides, it was the only thing I had. It was my tool, what I made my living with. If I was going to go, I was damned if I was going to leave my horn behind.

With that slim piece of metal in my hand, I felt a little like a gunslinger going out to take on the Clanton gang. But it wasn't a gun, it was just an alto sax, and I would much rather have faced the Clantons than Mickey and his boys.

There was a light fog hanging in the air, just enough so that the street lamps that lined the bridge were haloed. There was hardly any traffic, and as I neared the middle of the bridge I saw that I had beaten Mickey there. I was alone in the night as I walked up to where the bloodstain was, the place where I had tossed the hand over the side, and where Mickey had tossed the rest of Todd. I leaned back against the wall, hugged my horn to me, and shut my eyes.

Ole bud . . .

It sounded like Todd's voice, but faint and faraway. Still, it seemed real enough that I opened my eyes and looked around. No one was there.

Although I should have been spooked, I wasn't. Instead I felt suddenly calm. I'd been nervous as hell walking out on the bridge, but now that I was here I felt a lot better. Maybe, after it was all over, I really would meet Todd.

A rough laugh ripped through the mist, and I looked toward the city. There were three of them, a short one flanked by two giants, and they were coming toward me. When they were fifty yards away, I started to play.

It was bravado, no doubt about it, that made me bring my horn to my lips and blow, bravado and maybe that voice that I thought I heard, the voice that said *Blow it, ole bud. Play them blue notes . . .*

I did, and I didn't stop then to wonder why the hell that voice I thought was Todd's should be telling me to blow the blue notes. I just played. I played blue notes between blue notes between blue notes, and I was sorry that the only people there to hear it were three shitbrains who wouldn't know good sounds if the muses came down and sat on their heads.

"Hey!" No voice inside my head. This one was real. "*Hey*, asshole," Mickey repeated. "Knock that shit off, enough to wake the fuckin' dead . . ."

I didn't listen to him. I just kept playing. They were twenty feet away now, and had slowed down. Mickey put his hands over his ears, made a face, and stopped.

"You oughta get that thing in tune, Luther."

"He must think music hath charms, Mickey," said one of Mickey's helpers. From the puzzled and pissed way Mickey looked at him, I could see that Mickey had never even heard the old saying before. Then Mickey turned back to me.

"You got the money, Luther?"

I just kept playing.

"Goddammit, cut that shit out!" Fast as a thought, Mickey moved to my side, knocked the sax out of my hands, and swatted me on the side of the head. I went down hard, feeling hot warmth on my lips where the mouthpiece had ripped them. Then everything seemed to swim around me, and when I looked up at Mickey and his goons, I was looking through water.

I don't mean that metaphorically—I mean it *literally*. The whole picture shimmered, rippled, and I could have sworn I was not lying on the sidewalk, but underwater, at the edge of a pool, looking up at Mickey like some crocodile eying its prey. And *that* isn't metaphorical either.

What happened next didn't take very long. All of a sudden someone else was there on the bridge with us, someone who grabbed Mickey's boys and shook them like a dog with a rat. Their heads began to shake more than heads should, and then something wet struck me in the face. When I wiped it away I saw that the stranger had Mickey, and was carrying him with one hand to the wall. They both tipped over and I lost them, but I heard Mickey scream for a

113

long time. I hadn't realized before just how high the bridge really was.

The sensation of looking through water was gone now, and I could see that the wetness on my hands and face was blood. When I looked at Mickey's boys lying next to me I saw where it came from.

Mickey was nowhere to be seen, and I staggered to my feet, walked to the wall, and looked over, down to the bay below, through the mist to the water lit dimly by the street lamp so far above.

I saw Todd. He was floating face-down, but I recognized him by his clothes, by the long blond hair that lay fan-like on the surface of the water, and by something else—the rings sparkling on his right hand, the same right hand I had thrown into the water the night before. I didn't see Mickey anywhere at all.

It was time to leave this place, to find a phone and call the police and tell them there was a body floating in the bay beneath the bridge. That was what was important, to get Todd out of the water. They could find Mickey's boys on their own. And I didn't give a shit if they ever found Mickey.

My sax was lying where it had fallen. There was a big dent in the bell, and the neck was bent, but the keys all worked. I thought about playing it again, playing one last farewell, and maybe thank-you to Todd, but I decided not to. What if this time the blue notes brought back Mickey?

Because it was the blue notes that did it, whatever it was. Maybe life and death is like everything else—with an infinite number of spaces in between, a spectrum of grays between the black and white, a symphony of blue notes between C and C sharp. And what if certain needs, certain sympathies, empathies, memories, voices—even the blue notes themselves—can bring those *spiritual* blue notes back, just long enough to do . . . what happened on the bridge that night?

Blue notes. It's the right name for them. Because all I know is that whatever I saw in those few seconds, whether it was Todd or some part of me, when I blinked away the red, it was blue, a deep blue, the deep dark blue you hardly ever find in nature, not in the nature that most of us know. It was the blue that lies between the brightness of the sky at noon and the blackness of that same sky at night. Somewhere in between those. That dark, sad, somber blue.

The blue note of blue.

The Confessions of St. James

"Except ye eat the flesh of the Son of Man, and drink his blood, ye have no life in you . . . He that eateth my flesh, and drinketh my blood, dwelleth in me, and I in him."

—John 7: 53, 56

* * *

It is this that is so shocking, and I shall say it at once, that in the eating of human flesh I feel God's love.

It is so difficult to write that. I never have before. I have never written it or spoke it aloud to anyone, even to myself. My *thoughts* have been full of that knowledge for years, of course, for it was necessary that I be able to rationalize my actions to myself, else I could not continue as a pastor. And I have, I think, done it successfully in my eyes, hopefully in the Lord's, but most assuredly not in Mankind's, not yet. What I do and have done is crime, not sin. Even the most recent actions that prompt the writing of this testament, if you will (unseen and unknown reader—perhaps policeman, prosecutor, judge, or beneficiary), are the same, for the commandment states "Thou shalt not murder," in the strictest sense of the translation. What I have done is no more murder than when Gideon executed the kings of Midian, or Samuel put to death Agag, King of the Amalekites. Though I would do nothing differently, and if my actions are misunderstood and I am taken, may these words, written at leisure and in the coolness of my spirit, speak for me.

The flesh, first of all, for it is my belief and joy in that which caused much of what was to follow.

It is difficult to know how to describe it to someone who has never tasted it. The salt is naturally the strongest flavor, since that is what preserves it. But in time the palate educates itself, seeks beneath the salt to the true taste. As you hold it in your mouth, thinking of its meaning, the saliva softens it and the salt slowly fades away, leaving only the delicate, wafer-thin flesh, like a coating over the tongue. And then, very slowly, as the now moist and tender morsel dissolves, the ineffable flavor of God's spirit and love comes upon you like the presence of the dove at Christ's baptism.

There is no sin in it, not even that of gluttony, for my taking of this mystical communion occurs only twice a month, and the piece is always small, smaller and thinner than the cubes of white bread I have distributed at my church's legal and not at all shocking communion. Indeed, these bits of flesh look far more like the pale and fragile wafers the Roman Catholics serve than the dotless dice of Methodist dough offered up on our wooden plates.

Take, eat; this is my body, which is broken for you: this do in remembrance of me.

I do love God—Father, Son, and Holy Spirit—and if you were to say that I blaspheme, I would tell you that I do not. I have never intended, in word nor deed, to go against the will of God. The only Biblical laws that I have broken are those of diet and health as pronounced by the Pentateuch, and Protestantism has blithely ignored most of those for centuries anyway. My conscience is clear. God knows.

God knows and God has blessed me. He has given me a wonderful community in which to live, good health, a lovely church steeped in history, an old and stately parish house, and access to the fruits of my unique mode of worship. The only thing I have not been granted that the rest of the world sees as necessary is my own family. This omission has been by personal preference, for reasons that I will set down at some more opportune time.

But into every Eden a serpent may come, and so it is with Hempstead. God blessed this area of the state with dark rich soil which lured the Amish and Mennonite farmers from the fields of Germany. They settled here on their farms, and around them the small towns sprang up, towns with names like Myersburg, Paradise, Purity, Hempstead.

Hempstead, named for the growing of hemp which, until the late 1800's, was as highly prized a crop in this area as tobacco, which still flourishes. It is still a small town, the town itself, that is. But now, along with the assortment of stores that seemed to have been here since the thirties if not before—the grocery, the dry goods, sporting goods, drug store—have been added two video rental stores, a computer store, a games arcade, a beer distributor who carries domestic but specializes in imports, and a "New Age" shop that peddles herbs and books, among other things.

The town changed because times and people change, but the town changed mostly due to the influx of people from Philadelphia, for the county is slowly becoming a suburb of that large city. The population of our own county seat has already grown to overflowing, and now the new folks are spilling out into developments that surround the small towns like barbarians around the walls of Rome. Farms are sold to developers for as much as $20,000 an acre, and the Amish are moving upstate, far from the madding crowd who are more concerned with widening the highways to ease their drive into Philadelphia than they are with easing their souls by preserving the agricultural heritage that has nourished the county for so many years.

These people are different. They are outsiders—or insiders, depending on your point of view. Most of them regard the natives as impossibly backward, even amusing. You see it most clearly when they are confronted by an Old Order Amishman. The two cultures are so far apart. One, it seems, belongs to God, and the other does not.

They have no time for religion. Oh, some make an effort for their children's sakes perhaps, for this past year my church has welcomed four new families, all of whom were originally from the Philadelphia area. Now only three remain. They sit in the stern, wooden pews on Sunday morning, not even trying to hide the fact that they are bored. When my congregation—my *native* congregation—begins to lapse into that catatonic condition caused by a too-hot Sunday morning, they fix a look of placid contemplation on their broad, well fed faces, some of them adding to it a gentle smile, as if to say yes indeed, pastor, you are so right, I understand perfectly, so you and the Lord will forgive me if my mind wanders just a bit to cooler and less loquacious climes.

I understand, and I forgive, and sometimes I speed the sermon along, or try to make it a bit more dramatic in order to win them back again. But the Holts, and the three other families who still remain, were and are irretrievable. Sadly and, in the case of the Holts, tragically irretrievable.

There was a sense of wrongness about the Holts. I have read in several books recently of the uncomfortable and unmistakable feeling one gets when one is in the presence of people who are truly evil. This was the feeling I had when I first met the Holt family, at least the three older members. Kimberly, the six-year-old, seemed too young to be tainted by the bland corruption I smelled in the father, and the silky superiority worn by the mother, which, I feared, had blended together into a potent and heady malignance that simply exuded from every pore of fifteen-year-old Keith. His parents wore masks that were but feeble attempts to hide their true personalities, but the fact that they knew the masks were needed and thus recognized the evil in themselves said something for the possibility of their eventual return to normal humanity.

But the boy wore no mask at all. He smiled when I first set eyes on him from the pulpit, but it was a wolfish smile. With such a smile must Satan have tempted Christ to cast himself from the roof of the temple, a smile that said to Christ, there is pride in you, for what God cannot be proud? and in that pride will come your fall, as did mine.

In weeks to come, I began to see more in that smile. I began, to my horror, to see knowledge in it. I began, even as I continued to mouth the words of my sermon and to chant the litany of the well-known scriptures, to hear his thoughts. This is what he said, what he said with that smile—

You are an Eater of Man-Flesh.

I see you. I can see all the way inside you.

I can see the flesh inside your mouth.

That is what his smile cried to my guilty mind, my mind that, after so many years, retained no self-guilt, no guilt in the eyes of God, but still lived in fear of discovery by those who did not understand, by which I mean, of course, the world. Even now I do not know whether or not what his smile spoke to me was true or not.

After all, he did not really find out until later. Still, all in all, he knew. In a way, somehow he knew. And I felt guilty.

I say that I have banished the guilt, and I have, except for every now and then, when the teachings of society come thundering into my brain and displace the teachings of God. It was much the same, I have no doubt, for Jimmy Swaggart. Though I have no sympathy for the unkind politics he espouses under the name of religion, I have nothing *but* sympathy for his weakness of the flesh that made him seek the company of prostitutes. Society has said for the past twenty years that sex is fine, sex is all right, sex is open and free and natural. Sex is sold in every movie, every novel, every advertisement that we and our children see in newspapers and magazines and on television. And finally it becomes too much and the man—a man of God—goes out and sins and sins and sins some more. Crimes? Only partially. But sins? Yes, most emphatically.

I know the pressures of society all too well, pressures that have a hundred times nearly made me stop my communion with God. But His law is the higher one, and it is in this way that He has allowed me to draw so near to Him and know His love.

It *is* His will, I believe, His guidance. For a long time I attempted to look for a human reason, to psychoanalyze myself, always a dangerous occupation. And if I am discovered, I am sure that someone else will try and do the same. It may be a combination of both God and man, for I do not claim full knowledge of how God works. I only know that what brought me into the ministry also brought me to the partaking of flesh—

My mother. Rather one should say the *absence* of my mother. That, and blisters.

It sounds quite absurd, and it is funny when you come to think of it. I can just see myself on Phil Donahue—

And what turned you into a slavering ghoul, Pastor St. James? (for ghoul is what I would surely be called)

Oh, I suppose it must have been nibbling blisters, Phil. (and Phil says)

And we'll be back with Pastor Brandon St. James, the Ghoul of Dunbarton Church, right after these words from Chapstick.

Morton Downey Jr. would be even less kind.

But in truth it was blisters, the blisters that sprouted on the palms of my hands just below the finger joints when I was eleven years old and began to mow the lawn for the first time. We had a

119

push mower, for our yard was small and my family far from being wealthy enough to afford a power mower. And that spring night, when I lay in bed waiting for sleep, I rubbed my fingertips over those blisters and began to pick at the dead flesh that covered them, and slowly they came off, one by one.

I held them for a long time, marveling at the whole idea of it—this was my *skin*, my actual flesh. It was almost as though I was a soldier wounded in battle, and these thin strips—not strips, really, more like soft, tiny coins—were evidence of my courage under fire. Then I examined them in the dim light of the luminously painted ceramic moon over my bed. It glowed for hours after the bulb was turned off, and gave just enough radiance so that I could look through the epidermal discs and see the lines that the motion of my hands over the years had impressed in my flesh. I sniffed at the pieces, but they gave off no smell but the scent of the soap I had used to wash with that evening. Then I put one of the tiny fragments on my tongue.

At first it was tasteless, but slowly I became aware of the most delicate flavor I had ever known, a sweetness that was almost not to be borne. It was then that I had my first erection, and it so alarmed me that I pressed down on it immediately, and spat the piece of flesh from my mouth into the darkness.

I lay there trembling for a long time as the tumescence subsided, and finally felt over the sheets for the two other bits of skin that had been lost when I panicked in my pre-pubescent terror. In a few moments I located them both. The temptation was strong to taste them as well, but instead I rose from my bed, tiptoed to the other side of the room, brushed them off my sweating fingers into the waste basket, and returned to bed, where, that night, I had my first nocturnal emission, the result of a dream, which I remember even today, about my mother's breasts.

That was the beginning, and even then I felt the presence of something holy in the partaking of flesh. Perhaps I equated it with the communion service in which my parents would not allow me to share. The grape juice was never what tempted me in those services. It was rather the bits of bread that were chewed so slowly and solemnly. The body of Jesus! How I wanted to taste that bread! When I learned, a few years before my experience with the blisters, that it was nothing but white Holsum Bread, the same kind we ate at home, I immediately cut a slice into squares and placed the pieces, one at a time, in my mouth, whispering *Take, eat, this is my body.* It was a huge disappointment. There was no sense of spiritual fulfillment, none of the sacred sense of purpose I always saw in the gently masticating jaws of the recipients of communion. It was nothing but Holsum Bread in cubes, the same as Aunt Lily used in her Christmas stuffing, but without the added gustatory inducements of saffron and celery. I did not play at communion again.

It was that desire, however, to share in communion that first made me think of life in religious service, and that sensation of exaltation upon tasting my own flesh that night in my room that gave me the idea that man could, in some distant and unfathomable way, commune with God. On such small things are our futures determined. On such things was forged my link to God.

I wonder, and have wondered long, on what things was Keith Holt's link forged to that other.

He was the one who chose my church, I think, probably because it was old, it was isolated, and it had a graveyard. The crematory, I believe, had little or nothing to do with his choice. It was not ashes he was after. When did his obsession with darkness begin? At the same age as my own with light? Or before? Did he, as a mere toddler, ignorant of speech, read the evil in his father's words, his mother's glances? And did he let them fester inside of him, grow into that malignancy with which he hoped to blight everyone he met?

Perhaps I imagine too much. It may be that he was merely a thrill-seeking child who went too far. It *may* be that, but I think not. How could anyone with any amount of goodness in them do what Keith Holt did? And at Dunbarton Church, *that* was the worm that gnawed as much as anything. It was selfish, I know, but I cannot help but admit that a great deal of my initial wrath came from the defilement of what I think of, with hubris of which I am ashamed even as I am powerless to dismiss it, as *my* church.

God's, of course. First and always God's. But mine as well. It was mine from the moment I lay eyes on it. I have been here for many years and hope to remain for many more. It was my first church and will be, I trust, my last. So many young pastors see a rural church as merely a stepping stone to some massive pink-bricked suburban edifice, or a wealthy and imposing Gothic church in the city, but for me Dunbarton United Methodist was perfect. I realized that from the first, but could not know at the time just *how* perfect it would prove to be.

121

The nearest village, Hempstead, is two miles to the east. Dunbarton Church, founded in 1829, sits in its own verdant grove, an oasis of green amidst the farms. The grounds comprise four acres, an eighth of that occupied by the cemetery. The church itself stands, as it has for over a century and a half, on the long north side of the cemetery wall. The exterior is plaster, and always bears a fresh coat of whitewash. It is not a large church. The sanctuary, which might seat five hundred parishioners should all choose to come at once, naturally takes up the greater part of the building. It is painted white, with dark brown trim on the timbers and the ornaments and hard wooden seats of the pews. The windows are white and translucent, with borders of colored glass around the edges. Pulpits stand on either side of the altar, all as old as the church itself. Two pews are behind the righthand pulpit, for the choir to occupy, and the organ is behind the lefthand pulpit. The ceiling is lower than that in most modern churches, and there is no balcony nor choir loft. A small wing adjacent to the sanctuary holds the pastor's office, two Sunday school rooms, rest rooms, and robing rooms for the choir. A social hall and kitchen were added in the 1930's by excavating underneath the sanctuary. A horse's skull was discovered buried there. No explanation was ever found, and it was reinterred beneath the basement floor.

The thing that impresses visitors most about Dunbarton Methodist is its cleanliness. The whiteness of its spartan and colonial interior makes it appear Bauhausian, and it is always a pleasant and fresh surprise for those used to dark, gothic arches, or the soft pastels of surburban churches.

This lightness, however, is undercut by the presence of the cemetery, although adjoining cemeteries are quite common, indeed the norm, in churches of this area. The cemetery is noted more for its history than its practicality, for the last interment took place here several years before my tenure began. The family plots are all filled, and no new burials will occur, due to lack of space.

But what people find more oppressive than the cemetery is the small crematory that crouches at the cemetery's western wall. Needless to say, crematories are *not* the norm in this area. The crematory was built in 1912, when Pastor Fletcher came into residence. He was British, part of an exchange program between the American Methodists and the Brits. Cremation was all the rage in England just then, and Fletcher brought this pet to America, persuaded the congregation that the church should have its own crematory (a motion that passed by the narrowest of margins, some say due to the hypnotic effect the young, single, and goodlooking Fletcher had over the distaff members of the congregation), and supervised the building himself. A local undertaker, who was also a member of the congregation, was trained to run the operation along with his more cosmetic duties in Hempstead, a state of affairs that still exists today, though the undertaker in now known as the funeral director.

There were several dozen cremations from 1912 through 1915, a tribute to Pastor Fletcher's persuasive powers. But when he returned to England at the advent of the Great War, the craze died down and the crematory went totally unused for forty years. From time to time the suggestion was made by the lay committee to dismantle the building (for no one wanted to renovate it into a meeting place), but, since no profit nor good could come of its razing, it remained, a monument to Pastor Fletcher, who had died a chaplain at Mons. Then, in the late 60's, cremation once more became a viable and rather trendy method of disposal, and the Dunbarton Methodist crematory began to hum once more. The unattractive and conspicuous oil tank at the side of the building was removed, and the furnace was converted to electricity. As the only crematory at that time in the county, it got a great deal of use, and until another and larger crematory was finally built in 1974 at the Peace Haven Memorial Park in the southern end of the county, scarcely a week went by without a cremation. At present, our crematory averages from six to eight creamations a year. It is enough.

The crematory's external design is similar to that of the church, though the whitewashing of the smaller building occurs far more frequently, since even the hint of soot is disquieting when one is aware of the building's purpose. Fortunately the system is arranged so that the smoke is recirculated through heat chambers, so that hardly any is visible coming from the chimney. The building is surprisingly small, but it needs to be no larger. Within is a tiny chapel capable of seating only twenty people, for crowds are never great at cremations. In fact, most of the time none of the bereaved are there at all. There are only Jim Meinhart, the funeral director, and the witness appointed by the family, generally me, which makes it very convenient.

Jim is an excellent funeral director, one of the many with whom I have come into contact who takes his job very seriously. I have always felt that death really does sadden Jim, that he sees every one of his charges as a rose cut down in the prime of youth, be they two weeks or ninety years old. Some funeral directors wear a mask of piety around me, but I can see through it easily enough. If their look could speak it would say, "Enough meditating, pastor, let's shut that lid and get on with it." But not Jim Meinhart. I think that's why he does such a good business—people believe him.

He does, however, find cremation somewhat distasteful. It springs not from religious beliefs, however, but from an aesthetic sense. For all his piety, Jim takes great satisfaction in a cosmetic job well done. He loves to create what funeral directors call a memory portrait, which is simply putting the best face possible on the deceased. Cremations are done most often as not with closed caskets, which gives Jim no possible opportunity for his make-up miracles, and, even in the few cases where the body is viewed beforehand, his handiwork is reduced to ash before the day is through. For Jim, who takes deep delight in knowing that his work will last, unseen, for many years, this is as hard as a child watching the sand castle that has taken all day to build be destroyed by the tide in minutes.

That image makes me think of him again, of Keith Holt, that child who was not a child, but something older than even Amos Goss, who sits in the back row every early service, singing or not depending on whether he remembered to put in his teeth that morning. Keith Holt, older even than Christ. But not older than God. And certainly not stronger.

I began to truly realize what Keith Holt was that first Sunday evening when he came to Youth Fellowship in the social hall beneath the church. I don't usually attend YF, leaving that to Randy Kronhauser, the director of Youth Ministries, but it was September, the beginning of the school year, and I knew that there would be a number of first-timers there that evening, sons and daughters of some of the new people who had as yet made no new church affiliation, and some, like Keith Holt, who had attended services with his parents for several weeks, and I thought my presence might warm even further the welcome they were sure to get from Randy and the other students.

After the opening prayer, Randy started a discussion with the previous attendees, while I took the six new children into a corner, told them a little bit about the church, and asked if they had any questions before they rejoined the group. As is the way of teen-agers, they shrugged or shook their heads gently, except for Keith Holt, who narrowed his reptilian eyes, and asked me, "And what's the church's position on cults?"

"Cults?" I said. "What kind? There are a lot of them."

The boy shrugged. "How about Satanism, for instance?"

What I should have done was answered politely, reasonably, gone off on a speech about the church's disapproval of anything that detracted or stood in opposition to God and his works, talked about youthful follies and the importance of returning to the company of believers when questing indiscretions had ended. But I did not. I felt something from the boy, something evil, and I looked at him sharply, as an inquisition judge would no doubt have eyed an heretic, and said, "What do you think?"

He looked back with undisguised hatred. "I think the church is probably as narrowminded when it comes to that as it is to everything else."

The reaction from the other students was not unexpected. It was one of embarrassed amusement, as if they were pleased to see the quaint country parson squelched, but were afraid to laugh out loud at him.

"You believe the church is narrowminded then?" I asked, trying to keep the anger buried. It was not that I objected to difficult questions, for I have been answering them ever since I entered the seminary (indeed, the theological questions that I proposed to myself were far more perplexing than any asked by my parishioners). It was rather the boy's attitude of smug superiority, the feeling that whatever I might reply, even to the point of giving actual physical proof of the existence of God and the divinity of Christ, his words and looks would mock me—and God, and Christ—just the same. And in that moment, and long after, I hated him with a fiery and implacable hate that I prayed the Lord to banish from my soul, but to no avail.

The further conversation was chilling to me. He said that yes, he thought the church, *most* churches, were narrowminded, and that do what you want to should be everyone's creed. To which I added, as long as you don't hurt anyone else? thinking of that tired old humanist saw. But he said not necessarily, and that made me think of Crowley, that pitiful, fraudulent, English wizard, and I said, recalling the words from a workshop on cults I had participated in,

Do what thou wilt, that shall be the whole of the law. Is that what you mean?

From the smile of recognition he gave, I knew that he was no stranger to the quotation, and I remember thinking, oh God (asking Him, not giving an oath), what kind of world is this in which children read and accept the work of self-deluded devil-worshippers rather than the Scriptures? But God did not answer me. Not then.

Keith Holt answered, though. He said yes, that the world in which we live today is not the world of desert-wandering tribes nor Galilean shepherds and fishermen. And carpenters, he added dryly. And that the first law of Satanism—do what thou wilt—made much more sense for this world and this time. "'Do unto others as you would have them do unto you'" the boy went on, "is only going to get you f . . ." The foul word was nearly out of his mouth, but he pulled it back in time, in counterfeited consideration of his surroundings. ". . . messed over," he finished. "Today's world is built on greed, Reverend. You know the saying about the guy who has the most stuff when he dies wins? That's all there is to it."

"That's what you *think*," I said. "But you may not always think that way. There's more to life than money."

"Sure there is. Power's nice too."

"Power," I said, trying to smile. "How old are you, Keith?"

"Fifteen."

"And what would a fifteen-year-old young man want with power?"

"The same thing anyone else would, Reverend. It's a rush. It makes you feel good. Feel strong."

"There are other ways to feel good."

"What, you mean sex?" One of the boys snickered, and the sole girl giggled, averting her eyes. "Or drugs?"

"I mean by *doing* good."

"That's just *your* way of getting off. Hey, the only reason people do good things is that it makes them feel good, you just said so yourself. But most of the time they won't admit that's why they do it. And that's hypocritical. At least satanists are honest about what they want."

"Honest? Then why is Satan called the Father of Lies?"

"Don't ask me—I never called him that. That's the name the Christians give him." He said *Christians* as though he was saying *cockroaches*.

Now when most children ask questions like these, it is born out of natural curiosity, the desire to question authority. I have answered, time and again, such queries as where did Cain's wife come from, and how did the sun stand still in the heavens without wrecking the earth, and isn't it possible that Jesus wasn't *really* dead when they took him off of the cross, and dozens more. But Keith did not have the almost apologetic tone the others had, the sense of, "Gee, Pastor, I'm sorry to destroy the faith you've followed for so many years, but did you ever realize that . . ." He was savage. He wanted to destroy not only my faith, but me personally.

I won't go on any further. I think that anyone can see by reading this that Keith Holt was sick, troubled, even evil. I had met his parents, so I wasn't surprised. I think the only thing that would have saved the boy is if he had been taken away from his parents when he was his sister Kimberly's age, or perhaps even earlier. This is terribly ironic coming from me, for all my life I have endeavored to keep families together. Indeed, that was one of my prime motivation in entering the ministry—to keep families together.

It was the breakup of my own family, I suppose, that caused my concern with the families of others. I saw what it did to my father, and of course I know firsthand the effects it had on me, being a bachelor to this day, and being something even more—what word shall I use? Alien? Enigmatic? Different? All of those, certainly. Ghoulish? Fiendish? Bestial? I most assuredly pray not, for I do not feel as if I am those things, and after I explain all, I pray that whoever reads this will no longer feel that way as well.

My mother then. Back to my mother, back to my family, back to the communion of flesh. I should have explained this all before, pages back when I talked about the blisters on my hands. But one thing leads into another, and I stray. That is a major flaw of my sermons, I fear. I have my outline, rigorously gone over several times before Sunday morning, but once I begin to speak, to actually address my congregation, I think of other things that I *must* tell them, that are *essential* for them to know, and I extrapolate, expound, until I have wandered so far from my starting place that I must strike some sort of verbal bell, be it gold or brass, and hope for the resonances to vibrate long enough to let me retrace my steps, lead myself, blindered, down my previous path, and finally race ahead on it so that my listeners may arrive home before their roasts and chickens burn.

And I have done it again. From my mother and the flesh to my sermons and the succulent flesh of Sunday dinners. I must concentrate on the subject at hand and not digress.

My mother then. She was a large-boned but soft woman, nice for a little boy to hug. She always smelled of flowers (her perfume, I suppose), and she left our house when I was twelve, a year after I first devoured my own dead skin. I blamed myself for her departure, as children will, but finally understood that it was not my fault that she had run away with one of my father's friends, a man with whom my father and I used to drive to Philadelphia to see the Phillies play once or twice a year. He had a son too. I don't know if he ever saw his son again after he went away with my mother. I know I only saw my mother one time after that, and that was after she died.

It sounds like an old story, but my father began to drink after my mother left. Not much, though. I don't think he was really what one would call an alcoholic, though my memory may be wrong, and I know I wanted to imagine him less drunk than he many times was. He retained his job, he never abused me, and he was supportive when I told him, in my senior year of high school, that I wanted to study for the ministry.

He had been farsighted enough to save some money for my college education, and that, combined with my part-time job in the college dining hall, was enough to enable me to graduate with a liberal arts degree from a small, state-owned university. I purposely chose to study for that degree, since I wanted to get as wide a background as possible, feeling that if four years of liberal arts could not dissuade me from my goal of service to God, then nothing could. Once I entered a seminary there would be three long years to concentrate on religion.

My broken home and my father's drinking and loneliness combined to create in me that desire which I have previously expressed —to help to hold families together through the countless emotional storms with which they can be rocked. So as an undergraduate I took a number of courses in psychology, and later, in seminary, concentrated on social services.

It was in my senior year of college that I rediscovered the penchant for flesh that had intrigued me years before as a boy. This is a section of my confessions that I am most loathe to write, for it was not only crime but sin that I committed, the sin of assault.

At college I had a small circle of friends. Some were music

majors, there were a few English majors, and the majority majored in psychology, with an eye to guidance in schools. Although I had my share of dates, I remained a virgin, due to my feeling that religious service demanded purity in thought and deed, a tenet to which I still hold. I did drink before I was of the proper age, but only infrequently. When I became twenty-one in the spring of my senior year, I imbibed without guilt, though never to excess. The week before graduation, however, I attended a party at a house which several students (all of them now seniors) rented. It was proposed to be the biggest party of the year, celebrating the fact that we had all made it through the four years. There were two kegs of beer to quench the thirsts of the nearly one hundred people there, as well as punch bowls filled with some crimson and questionable fluids. I drank beer until I felt slightly woozy, then decided that the time was ripe to switch to something non-alcoholic, and asked one of the hosts if there was any unspiked punch. He pointed to one of the bowls, from which I began to drink cupful after cupful. It was only much later I found out that particular punch was laced quite strongly with devastating and tasteless vodka.

I felt no effect for some time, during which I fell into a conversation with a sophomore music major named Sally. I had gone out with Sally twice, but when she had become too aggressive in her movements in the back seat of a friend's car, I had not asked her out again. This particular evening she seemed merely friendly, talking about professors and classes and the future that awaited me after graduation. When I told her I had been accepted in seminary, her interest seemed to be piqued, and she put her arm around my waist.

For some reason that I know now to be the effects of the alcohol, I felt no urge to disengage myself from her sisterly embrace, and put my own arm (the one not holding a cup of punch) around her as well. In another few moments she kissed me and I reciprocated, feeling her tongue lick my lips, part them, and slip into my mouth. I felt a sexual stirring, as who would not, and when the kiss broke, Sally smiled and said that we should go upstairs, that one of the students who lived there had a great record collection in his bedroom.

I followed willingly, knowing what would happen and wanting it all the same, the vodka lowering my defenses to such sinful snares, telling me that this might be my only chance for such a sudden and clandestine affair, one which I really *should* have before

I entered the seminary and such joys were closed to me save in marriage, to which, for my wife's sake, I really should not come without some knowledge of carnal things. So my drunken mind rationalized (at the time, I felt) brilliantly, as Sally's hand—and my semi-erect organ—led the way up the steps.

In the bedroom, she closed the door, embraced me, kissed me, rubbed her lips against mine, and we toppled onto the bed. When my body reached the horizontal position, I knew the whole thing was a tremendous mistake. My head started to swim, and the room began to whirl. Sally told me to close my eyes, which I did gladly. Then I felt her hands unbuttoning my shirt, undoing my khakis, tugging my clothes down and off my body. Still I kept my eyes shut tightly, hoping that the sickness rising in me would subside.

When I next opened my eyes, it was because I felt Sally's hand on my organ—I should write penis, I suppose—in the context of a pastor and a church, organ has too amusing a connotation. My penis, then was only partly erect, its hesitancy due not at all to Sally's deft ministrations, which, in due course, brought it to a degree of tumescence firm enough for her to straddle me and press it within her.

She rode atop me for a while, but I confess I felt little sensation beyond the pure visual excitement of seeing a naked woman perched over me. At some point I decided that I should be the aggressor (or that I could bear her weight on my sickly stomach no longer), and, being careful to remain within her, rolled over so that she was next to me. She completed the action by moving beneath me and grasping my hips, sliding me back and forth so as to put more pressure on her mons.

The motion did nothing to stimulate me, as it was now my pubic bone rather than my penis that was receiving the friction, a fact that did nothing to quell my rising nausea, and I slowly felt my penis losing whatever firmness it had acquired. In embarrassment at my oncoming impotence, and in the fear that my expression must appear ghastly to the grunting girl under me, I hid my face by burying it in the fleshy pouch between her neck and shoulder, and, in so doing, my lips were forced against the jutting, curved section of her clavicle, and my tongue was pressed against the soft, warm salt of her skin.

Had I been sober I never should have done it. Had I been sober, of course, I never should have been in that position in the first place. But I was not sober, and when I tasted her skin—the first skin except my own that my tongue (o wondrous organ of sense) had ever come in contact with—I felt as though my body was no longer in that place, that soiled, rutting bed, but that I was somewhere above and beyond, where the angels sang and where Christ sat in glory, and I *wanted* that flesh, wanted to make it part of me, to consume it and so be consumed by my God.

And I bit down.

My teeth tore through her skin, and for an instant, before her blood entered my mouth, there was total clarity, absence of alcoholic haze and nausea, and in that infinitesimal space of time I felt the love of Christ and saw his face as clearly as if peering through the purest water of the most holy font in the City of God.

But then the water of the font grew dark, as crimson as her sour, salty blood, and the music of the spheres was obliterated by her scream, a sound as harsh and shocking as the feeling in my teeth when they scraped against her bone. The sound and the blood taste were too much for me, and I threw myself off of her with the little strength I had left, so that I rolled off the bed, onto the floor, and immediately vomited up a copious quantity of fluid mixed with bile. The girl screamed once more, but it seemed less shrill, covered as it was by the sounds of my own violent retching.

When at last I got up from my hands and knees, I saw Sally in the bed, her right hand pressed against her left shoulder. Blood was oozing through the spaces between her fingers. She was panting raggedly, and looking at me as if I were a monster, and I suppose she was right. The beast in me had escaped, and I decided in that moment that it never would again, that never again would I sink my teeth into living flesh. And I never have.

It would do no good to chronicle in detail what happened next —her revulsion, her threats, my attempts to calm her, my early departure from the party. She told no one about the details of what happened in that bedroom, as far I could ascertain, except to suggest that, as one of my friends later told me, I was a whole lot kinkier, as she had put it, than I let on. Such a rumor was galling to me, as everyone who knew me knew of my aspirations to the ministry, but she could have said far worse.

Fighting the urge toward self-analysis, I still must voice my suspicion that my attack on that poor girl had something to do with the absence of my mother, as if by actually ingesting part of a woman for whom I felt love (or in Sally's case, I blush to admit, lust), I would be able to keep her with me always, and so retain my mother's love. I am not a Freudian, but there may be more than a grain of truth in this theory.

At any rate, from that day to this I have never permitted myself to become involved with any woman, except for a few social dates, and I am a teetotaler, save for an occasional glass of wine at a more formal dinner, when to refuse would be impolite. I fear that, even if I were married, the presence in my bed of a fellow creature with flesh might arouse me to the point that it did with that young woman back in college, and I would not want that for the world. So, although I have been sexually drawn toward women, I tell anyone who is curious enough to ask (suspecting, perhaps, that I am a latent homosexual) that, although I am a great admirer of the fairer sex, my work keeps me too busy for a wife and family. It is a response that has put me in the uncomfortable position of celibate priest to some members of my congregation, and some of the single or widowed women seem to look on it as a challenge. As a result of these unwanted attentions, I have had to develop a self-effacing and humorous manner to ward off light flirtations before they can proceed to the point where real insult might be felt by my necessary rejections.

It is ironic that I, who have such a deep respect for the sanctity of family, cannot have one of my own. Still, it is a sacrafice I gladly make. And Mrs. Bunn is enough of a family for me, I suppose. She is my housekeeper, an extraordinarily gifted cook, kind to a fault, black as night, with more jokes than one can laugh at in an entire evening. Where she gets them from I shall never know, although she receives at least two letters a day from relatives in Baltimore, her home town. Perhaps one of them subscribes to one of the joke services whose flyers we ministers are constantly receiving, as though religion is a thing best made palatable by as much humor as possible.

Mrs. Bunn takes splendid care of both me and the parsonage, a small building across the cemetery from the church. The house was built not long after the church itself, and is similarly plaster on brick. The downstairs consists of an entry, living room, library, dining room, and kitchen (in that order from west to east), while the upstairs contains my bedroom and bath, a bed, bath, and sitting room for Mrs. Bunn, and a guest bedroom. There is also a cellar, used for storage. Mrs. Bunn hardly ever goes down there.

When her hearing aid is removed, Mrs. Bunn is as deaf as the dead that sleep in the cemetery overlooked by her sitting room window. This handicap of hers has proven to be of great convenience to me on those nights when I wish to work alone and unobserved, and I am sure that not seeing what took place in Dunbarton Church Cemetery has saved Mrs. Bunn a great deal of anguish over the past few months.

The first episode came on the Wednesday night after the Youth Fellowship meeting of which I have written. I was sleeping only fitfully that night, having stayed up past midnight working on a brief tribute to a member of the church who was celebrating his one hundredth birthday. The difficulty was that there was very little of a positive nature to say about the man. A party in his honor was being given by his grandson, whose respect for his grandfather's life well lived was purely delusional. The man had worked two wives to death, had browbeaten his children mercilessly, and had been a brutal drunk until the age of seventy-eight, when, under the influence, he fell down a flight of stairs and was placed in a rest home, where he suffered several weeks' worth of delirium tremors. He then fooled everyone by living twenty-two years as an embittered resident, given to soiling his bed at every opportunity (on purpose, it was felt). I had finally come up with some feeble musings on longevity and the Lord working in mysterious ways, comments that would let me walk that fine line between hypocrisy and honesty without offending those few people who still might harbor good thoughts toward the old sinner, and lay wearily down.

But sleep came hard, and I was awakened out of whatever light slumber I had attained by the sound of a car engine starting, and tires chattering on the loose stones of the church parking lot. I got up and looked out the side window, only to see a pair of red tail lights fading away toward the road. What, I wondered, would young people be doing back here at this hour? If they wanted to park, it could have been done much more easily nearer the road, rather than driving the full quarter mile down the lane to the church. Unless, the thought occurred to me, they were doing something that could be done only *at* the church.

I pulled on trousers and a shirt, slipped on some shoes, and went outside. The moon was bright, so I needed no flashlight to see if the church had been broken into. It had not. All the windows and doors were secured. I then checked the door of the crematory, which was locked (it has no windows), and finally I examined the cemetery, though I expected to find nothing amiss, since the last case of vandalism had taken place long before my arrival at Dunbarton Methodist.

It is easy to forget the original purpose of a picturesque old cemetery, steeped in tradition. I was brutally reminded of it by the open grave only a few feet away from me, just inside the cemetery's western wall. What was left of the coffin was sitting next to the hole. The corpse, nothing but a skeleton that appeared dull gray in the moonlight, was lying half-in, half-out of the split and rotted casket. Its clothes had long since deteriorated, so that only a few scraps clung to the bones. The skull was nowhere to be seen.

I must confess that my first thought, once I had quelled the horror the act produced in my mind, was to rebury the mortal debris in an attempt to forestall the inevitable questions and consternation that would ensue. As I have mentioned, I fear the judgment of the police far more than the judgment of God, for God is more merciful. A moment's contemplation, however, told me that any such cover-up would be impossible. People would surely notice that the sod had been broken, the ground had been disturbed. Better then to call the police and cooperate in every way possible. After all, I wanted to find the perpetrators of this deed as much as they.

I went into the parsonage and made the call, and a police car arrived in less than a half hour with two officers inside it, neither of whom I knew. They were young, scarcely more than teenagers themselves, but they were pleasant and efficient, taking photographs and samples of this and that, and looking at things that had made no impression on me. After they were finished, they helped me reinter the body and pieces of coffin, and bade me goodnight. When I went back into the parsonage at 3:30 in the morning, I discovered that Mrs. Bunn, the good soul, had slept through the entire incident, and I was glad of it.

I must confess myself rather nervous when the two young policemen were there, as I could not help but imagine their presence under quite different circumstances, questioning me about certain matters—

And did you see anyone else in the vicinity who might have disfigured the body? . . .

Do you mean to say that no one was in the crematory in that

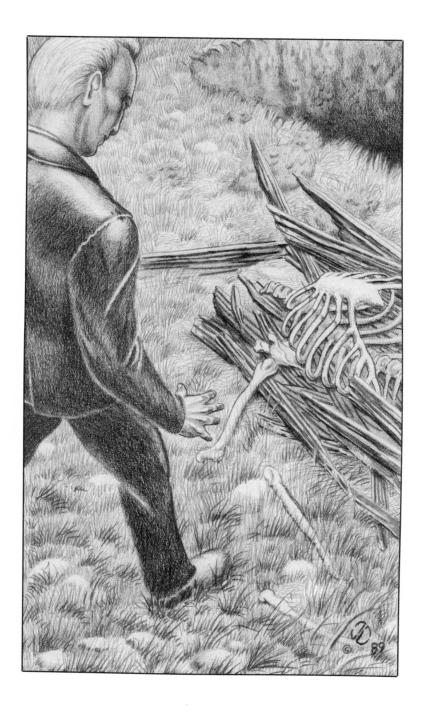

period of time except for you? . . .

What is that box that we found in your cellar, Pastor St. James? . . .

How long have you been a ghoul . . .

—I can barely bring myself to write that particular word in such a serious context. Its connotations are so far divorced from the things that I do that it is not only cruel, but inaccurate. The fear remains, however, the fear of exposure, of prison, of worse, and I cannot banish it even now, *especially* now, knowing what I must do.

A smile has just come to my face at a bizarre juxtaposition. I recall a recent law that states that whatever is put out in a person's garbabe is no longer theirs if someone else wishes to take it. I wonder if that could apply to my case if it were ever to be tried. For indeed, what is done to garbage? It is either used for land fill, or it is burned. And is that not what we do to our dead? They are discarded, useless shells wherein the spirit once dwelt, and now we either bury them (land fill) or cremate them (burning). The one method is a reduction to ash, the other a reduction to something quite unspeakable. Who would begrudge, then, a scavenger of human offal?

It sounds logical on the page, but they would laugh me out of court. I hope they will not laugh so hard after they read this (if indeed they ever do).

I must now tell of the first time, for it set the pattern for the others. I have said before how my mother left my father and me. My father died of a massive coronary while I was in my third and final year of seminary. He had never again heard from my mother after their divorce was final, but I received a letter from her every Easter and every Christmas. Her second husband was killed in a plane crash during the first year of my pastorate at Dunbarton Methodist, and the following year I received a telephone call from a hospital in Philadelphia informing me that my mother had died during exploratory surgery. Cancer had been devouring her for years, but her irrational fear of doctors (that I still remembered from my childhood) had prevented her from seeking help until it was far too late, and when she was opened up, the tissues were found to be in such a degenerative state that there was no way to put (and no point in putting) her back together again.

Her will (which left her limited possessions to me) dictated that she should be cremated, and I arranged for the body to be shipped to Jim Meinhart's funeral home, where it arrived only two days after her death. A short memorial service was held the next day (more people came than I expected, more out of deference to their pastor's loss than a respect for the deceased, whom no one even knew), and the body was taken to the crematory for a simple disposition. The ashes would be placed in the columbarium at Peace Haven, as Dunbarton Church has no columbarium of its own.

Jim and I were the only ones in the small chapel. His assistant had helped us set the simple wooden box on the catafalque, from which it would slide on a mechanically driven belt into the crema- tion chamber, and then left. Jim remained to do the honors, but I asked him if he would leave me alone for a few minutes with my mother, and he graciously acquiesced, telling me to just let him know when I was finished.

The feelings that went through me were indescribable. Up to that point, I had not looked at the body, as no embalming or other cosmetic work had been done. I did not even know if my mother was clothed or naked. The only thing I knew was that I had to see, for one last time, this woman who I had loved and who had deserted me. The box was not sealed, and I lifted the lid slowly, thinking that it had been four days since her death, and wondering how much decay could have set in in that period of time.

It was not nearly as bad as I had thought it might be. Jim had washed the body and dressed it in the white slumber gown it wore. The face, terribly gaunt, as was the rest of the body, was a yellow- gray, and the eye sockets had begun to sink in, but it was easily recognizable as my mother. The expression was peaceful (no doubt altered by Jim, who could not resist a challenge, even when no one but himself was there to see his work), and the hands were folded upon the chest.

Tears pooled in my eyes, and I blinked them away savagely, feeling loss and anger and regret and a dozen other emotions, and thinking most of all, *This is what you bring to me, this is how you come back to me,* wanting her to hold me again as she used to when I was a child, feeling like a child at that moment, needing love, needing to be fulfilled in some way that was (I thought) impossible now, and I reached out and grasped her hands.

The fingers were stiff, the flesh was cold, but the contact surged through me like an electric current, and it suddenly struck me how I could keep her with me, how I could cling to her despite her living desertion and the final desertion of death. I let my fingers trail gently over the flesh of her hands. It was still soft and pliant, and I remembered that evening in my bed and my first taste of flesh, remembered my mother's embraces, remembered the fulfillment that the taking of communion gave me, remembered the penknife that I carried in my pocket for opening letters. These disparate things coalesced in my mind into one logical, undeniable need that demanded to be transformed into action, and my next clear thought was from where I could take the flesh.

I would remain when Jim Meinhart set the crematory into operation and the box slid in, but how was I to know that he would not look into the box beforehand, prefatory to checking on some required form the line, "Body observed before cremation," or some such phrase? But even if he did such an unlikely thing, particularly in the presence of the bereaved, he would certainly not look beneath the slumber gown.

Praying to God to understand (if not *what* I did, then at least *why*), I took the hem of my mother's gown and slid it upward, unutterably relieved to find that she was wearing underwear. I think that if I had had to gaze upon her nakedness I should have had to abort my plan. But instead I drew the gown over her stomach, revealing the ragged line where the surgical incision had been stitched up. The stomach was (mercifully) not at all bloated, and I surmised that the doctors had removed the offending organs for autopsy before closing the rest. The thought occurred to me that Jim Meinhart may have performed some of his magic here as well, for when I made my first cut I felt certain that someone had drained most of the blood from the body.

It is painful to confess that I felt no remorse in incising my mother's flesh, but I did not. I felt, of course, the normal distaste that one would feel who is used only to applying a blade to cooked meat, but the queasiness did not delay me, for I knew that I had little time. So I cut straight across my mother's stomach—two long parallel lines which I joined with two shorter ones to make a rectangle an inch wide and perhaps six inches in length. I then put the blade of the knife beneath one end, and, my fingers wrapped with a handkerchief, pinched the end of the flap of skin and pulled upward, surprised at how easily the strip pulled away from the yellow tissue beneath. There was very little blood, as I said.

My first concern now was what to do with this fragment that symbolized so much to me. It seemed relatively free of fluid, so I decided to wrap it in my handkerchief and put it in my inner suit coat pocket. Having done so, I placed my mother's gown back over her body, and was just about to lower the lid when I noticed that the gown over the spot from which I had taken the flesh was darkening with some seepage from the open wound.

Panic raced through me, and I envisioned Jim Meinhart opening the box, noticing the mark, investigating further, realizing the truth, and exposing me to the world as a man who . . . what? Defiled the corpse of his own mother? It sounded like the most loathsome act imaginable, and the gravity of what I had just done burst upon me. I broke into a cold sweat, trembling with sudden fear, imagining even that my mother's corpse would push the lid aside, sit up in her thin pine box, and accuse me of that unspeakable crime, her cold fingers drawing her gown upward like some cadaverous ecdysiast, exposing not only the nakedness of her flesh, but the deeper nakedness where that flesh had been cut away.

At last I steeled myself, made certain the lid was closed and the pitiful evidence was safely tucked in my pocket before I opened the door and, without a word, beckoned Jim Meinhart inside once again. His face took on an instant attitude of sympathy, as I am certain he interpreted my fearful unease as the throes of grief, and he patted my shoulder, a surprisingly delicate gesture for a man with hands so large, and told me that he knew how hard it was to lose a mother, then asked me if I wanted to leave while he ushered the box into the cremation chamber.

I said that no, I would stay. I did so mostly to make sure that he would leave the box closed, and the ploy worked (or so I thought—I learned later that he never opens the boxes after they are placed on the catafalque). Jim disappeared into the small operator's closet, and in a moment the doors of the chamber opened, the box slid in, the doors closed, and I heard the dull roar of the flames. Jim reappeared and told me that it would take an hour before it was over. He would stay, and I could go back to the parsonage.

An overwhelming sense of freedom swept through me as I stepped outside. The leaves of the trees were bright green, and the day was crisp with the promise of oncoming autumn. What I had done was now being obliterated, save for the piece of flesh whose presence (so I sensed) beat against my chest like a second, external heart. It was with a great deal of effort that I put on a sober face for Mrs. Bunn, who was waiting in the kitchen with a pot of freshly brewed coffee and some hot rolls, which I declined, telling her that although I appreciated her sympathy, I wanted only to be alone. She took the hint and left in her car to shop for groceries, which gave me an opportunity to secrete the piece of flesh I had taken.

I dared not open the handkerchief to look at it, for I feared what I might do with it. To devour it was my intent, of course, but not immediately, not like a beast or some ghoul, but in reverence, at the proper time and the proper place (which I would come to decide later). I took a piece of aluminum foil and placed the handkerchief-wrapped treasure in it, folding the foil over and around, then put it in the freezer in the cellar, far beneath similarly wrapped cuts of beef, veal, pork, and chicken that Mrs. Bunn would not unearth for many weeks.

When I ascended, a half hour remained until my mother's body was reduced to ash, so I sat on the porch and watched the trees and the sky, into which the slightest wisp of white smoke was drifting from the crematory chimney, invisible to anyone who was not looking for it against the backdrop of dark green leaves. For a long time I spoke to God, asking for His guidance, for His assurance that these longings that I had were not evil, but good, some manifestation of His love. And I heard Him in my heart, felt His love and compassion and pity, and I knew then that this was only one way of worship, one way that I could feel His touch in my life, and I knew what I would have to do.

Of course I doubted at times. I wondered if this sensation of the Lord's presence was nothing but a rationalization of some psychological quirk. But God works in strange ways, and in *many* ways, and I do believe that this is one, that He is truly within me when I take this communion.

There are others who feel that their deeds, no matter how horrible, are blessed. But they are mad—those who kill people, who place bombs for "religion's" sake. They are sad and deluded, and only think they feel God's glory. I have felt and seen and heard and tasted.

Then there are those others who make not even a pretense of searching for God in their actions. There are those, whether we wish to believe it or not, who search for something totally opposite to God.

Two weeks after the grave was robbed, the church was broken into. I did not discover it until the morning when, after breakfast, I was planning to do some work in my office. As I unlocked the door to the narthex, I was struck with a foul smell, which I followed into the sanctuary. I am not easily shocked, but what I saw nearly made me vomit up my breakfast. It was not so much the things themselves, but the idea of the sanctuary violated in such a way, of the mind that could ignore all the laws of God and the most sacred rules of society.

The chancel had been transformed into the site of a Black Mass, but a Black Mass as designed by a mischievous child. The communion table had been taken from its storage closet and set in front of the altar. On it lay a dead cat. It had been decapitated, and its head was on the metal paten that held the bread at communion services. Much of its blood spattered the table, but most had been caught in the chalice. On the altar, the brass crucifix had been turned upside-down, and was stained with what I guessed was semen. The altar Bible, opened to the Sermon on the Mount, had been defecated and urinated upon.

I wept. The sight was so appalling that I could do nothing else. I wanted to cleanse and make right, but I knew that I should touch nothing, so it was unbearable to stay a moment longer. I ran to my office and called the police. They arrived shortly, two different young men this time, but just as kind and agreeable as the others had been. They took their pictures and samples once again, removed the Bible, the cat's body, the chalice and paten, the altar cloths. The perpetrator or perpetrators had entered, they learned, through one of the sanctuary windows. A pane had been broken in order to let them unfasten the latch, push up the sash, and enter. They had most likely, the policemen said, gone out the same way. After dusting for fingerprints, they left, telling me that I could set the place to rights again, which I did with Mrs. Bunn's help.

The poor lady was as shocked as I was, and there were tears in her eyes as we both scrubbed and washed the defiled sanctuary. She kept muttering, "Why?" as she worked. "Why'd anybody want to *do* such a thing. Awful . . . just awful . . ." From time to time I nodded, concurring. It was indeed awful, and, although I am a Christian and believe in loving the sinner while hating the sin, I did not know what to do in such a situation where the sinner *becomes* the sin. For such an act as was performed upon the altar that night seemed to put the perpetrator entirely outside the mercy of God. A man may steal or even commit murder and still receive God's grace for the asking, if he truly repents. But to spit in God's face . . . it is incomprehensible to me, outside the bounds of human behavior or psychology, and I knew that there was no way I could ever love this sinner, and envied God all the more for his miraculous ability to do so.

That afternoon a reporter came and questioned me about the vandalism. I told her that yes, the church had been defiled, but when she asked in what way, I said in an obscene way, and that I didn't want to go into any details, and I would appreciate it if no speculations appeared in the newspaper. This was, after all, a place of worship, and such rumors could only serve to draw people's minds away from reverent thoughts. She seemed to understand, and assured me that her paper would print only the general outline of the case. I thanked her and she left.

It was late that night in bed that I suspected I knew who was responsible. These nighttime depredations had not begun until the Holt family moved into the area. Now I knew that other families from the cities had come in as well, but when I remembered Keith Holt's gaze and words and attitude, it seemed extraordinary to me that I had not thought of him before.

First of all, I had no doubt that the same person who had robbed the grave had also defiled the church, and neither, I think, did the police. This kind of occurrence was so rare that the odds of it being the act of two separate individuals were too long to consider. Oh, there was an occasional beer party in a car on the lane that led back to the church, especially in May, when high school graduations neared. I would find empty cans strewn among the trees on either side. But never before was so much as a tombstone toppled. And now these two abominable acts in quick succession—well, there was no other conclusion to draw.

Secondly, the culprit must have been young, and (this was my conclusion, not that of the police) he must have been evil. The sheer audacity and senselessness of the acts spoke of youth. Now admittedly, at the age of fifteen, Keith Holt should not have been able to drive the car that I heard the night the grave was opened, but to a boy who would do such things as rob graves and defile a church, the additional transgression of taking his parents' car seemed relatively tame.

I wondered what to do next. Should I go to the police and tell them of my suspicions? No, for what did I have to base them on except for my own distaste toward the boy? I did resolve to watch him more closely in church and to attend next Sunday evening's Youth Fellowship to see if I might be able to derive any clues from his behavior or his words. It is difficult for young people to keep their offenses secret from their friends, for half the joy of wicked acts (so I have read) is being able to tell others about them later.

On the verge of sleep, I began to imagine what deed Keith (if it was Keith) might perform next. He had already violated the cemetery and the church, and the crematory was unassailable, having as it did no windows and only one door with a heavy lock. That left only the parsonage then, and fear suddenly ate through me so that I sat bolt upright in my bed. It was not the fear of confrontation, for I am a large man and would have been more than a match for such a youth as Keith Holt. My fear was that of exposure. I remembered the cellar windows and their pitifully fragile catches that might easily be pushed open, leaving the cellar easy access for a body slender enough to slip through the gap. I could see him sliding down, feet first, stepping on the freezer, then on the wooden box behind it, the box breaking, the boy investigating . . . oh dear God . . .

The box. How did I come to the box? I came to the box as I came to the taking of flesh. One is dependent upon the other.

Several years ago, when I proposed to take the communion of my mother's flesh in the way I did, I waited until one of the Tuesday evenings when Mrs. Bunn went off to visit her relatives in Baltimore. She always leaves on a Tuesday morning, and arrives back the following evening, as weekends are always too busy to permit her absence (indeed, she had never asked—she is a wise and knowing woman). Her trips come only once every two months or so, and I decided to use the solitude to perform the act that I had so looked forward to for several weeks. Every time Mrs. Bunn left the parsonage, I would go down to the cellar, open the freezer, and check to make sure that my treasure had not been disturbed. It never was.

That Tuesday evening, after the adult choir had all driven home following their weekly rehearsal, I took the foil-wrapped piece of flesh from the freezer, pulled the blinds, locked the doors of the parsonage, and unwrapped it to find that the handkerchief was clinging to it in several places. I did not want to pull it away too hastily for fear that the cloth would tear and adhere to the skin, so I rewrapped it in foil, put it in a plastic bag, boiled a pan of water, and tried to thaw it so that the handkerchief would pull away easily.

After several minutes of boiling, I withdrew it from the pan and unwrapped it once again. This time the handkerchief came away easily, and the flesh lay exposed to my view.

The freezing had certainly done nothing to make it more visually appealing, as I had not wrapped the foil tightly enough to prevent ice crystals from forming, thus causing freezer burn, and (I discovered in later reading) I had done nothing to help the situation by my impatient method of thawing. Still, there it was before me, that yellow strip of flesh, and I cut from it a morsel no bigger than a dime, washed it under running water, and prepared for the service.

It was everything I had expected, and so much more, and I praised God and blessed His name for allowing me to come so near Him.

The rest of the flesh, however, was impossible to keep, although I tried. It would have done no good to refreeze it, and too much deterioration had set in to attempt drying it, if I had even known anything about drying meat at that time. So I wrapped it in foil once more and deposited it in the very bottom of the garbage, praying as I did so.

A month went by before I felt the first pangs of that spiritual hunger that had been so satisfyingly fed by the tiniest bit of flesh. I felt as though God and Christ and the Holy Spirit were somehow drifting away from me, as though their presence, and the totally fulfilling love that is the greatest part of that presence, had been withdrawn. My sermons seemed flat, my prayers lifeless. My service to my congregation, my attempts to knit together deteriorating families, to comfort the sick and bereaved, continued as strongly as ever, but I did not feel the gratification I had before, and it very slowly began to dawn on me that once you have gazed upon Heaven, it is difficult to accept life on Earth. I knew then that my communion of a month before had to be repeated, in the same way that regular attendance at worship is necessary to nourish a Christian and sustain his joy in his faith.

A simple disposition was to take place at the crematory that week. A sixty-four year old member of the congregation had died of a stroke. His memorial service was scheduled for Wednesday, and the cremation was to follow, with none of the family in attendance at the crematory. It would be the perfect opportunity. But this time, I confirmed, I would have planned in advance precisely how I would keep whatever flesh I was able to take, so as to avoid the spoilage that had occurred with that of my mother.

I went into the county seat and withdrew from the library a book on the preserving of meat. It dealt with several different methods such as canning, freezing, and smoking, but since I would be working with rather small portions, I found the section on dry curing to be of the most interest. Basically, all that curing does is to extract the water from meat by applying salt to it, thus enabling one to keep it without refrigeration for a long period of time. Chilling (but not freezing) the meat beforehand to slow the growth of bacteria is advised, but I could not very easily store pieces of human skin in the refrigerator which was Mrs. Bunn's domain, so decided that I would have to brave the risk of bacteria, hoping that ingesting such small portions over a long period of time would cause no more than a slight stomach upset.

I took the long way home, visiting a farm supply shop in the southern end of the county and there buying with cash the smallest curing box in stock, along with a bag of coarse salt. The clerk told me that I should buy some maple syrup so that the salt taste would not be so strong, but I told him I had some at home. That much was true, but I had no intention of adding it to the meat. I could bear the salt taste, for that would eventually vanish, leaving only the naturally sweet taste of what it had preserved.

When I arrived home, I discovered that Mrs. Bunn was out, so I was able to take the box and the salt down into the cellar and store them behind some unused furniture, where Mrs. Bunn would never look. She made no secret of disliking the cellar, for it was poorly lit, rather damp, and claustrophobic, what with its only six and a half foot high ceiling. She went down there only when she needed to fetch something from the freezer.

On Wednesday, following the memorial service, I accompanied Jim Meinhart to the crematory, and asked (partly out of curiosity, for this was the first cremation I had observed except for my mother's, and partly from the desire to get further on the man's good side) if he might show me the operation of the machinery when the time came. He smiled as broadly as was possible for him, and said of course, he would be happy to.

The body was carried in, the assistant dismissed, and I turned to Jim. "Jim," I said, for we were on a first name basis, having shared a dozen funerals since my tenure began, "when my mother passed on, it meant a great deal to me to be alone here with her before her

145

body was cremated. I think I pray more deeply when I'm by myself." Then I chuckled. "Terrible thing for a pastor to say, isn't it?"

Jim shook his massive head. "Not at all, Brandon. I know what you mean—I say things when I'm praying by myself that I'd never think of when I'm in church. Say no more. Let me know when you're ready." And he walked out, leaving me alone.

I could scarcely believe my good fortune. I had not even had to finish the little speech I had so carefully prepared. He had not even questioned my desire to be alone with the quiet dead. And why should he after all? I was—and am—a minister of God, a man in whom my congregation can put their trust. And that is the truth, despite what follows, and because of what will come.

I knew I had little time, so I removed from my inner coat pocket a small matte knife whose razor sharp blade slid out and locked with a flick of my thumb. In another instant I had the wooden box open and the body of Mr. Collins rolled over on its side. I pulled up the gown to the top of the old man's back, cut a square roughly eight inches long on each side, and peeled back the piece of flesh. The edges were purple where, I suppose, some blood had settled, but there was no puddling of liquid after I made my incisions. I pressed the inner surface of the piece of skin against the gown to blot up any exudations of fat or other moisture, then rolled the section of flesh into a cylinder scarcely an inch thick, worked it into a plastic bag I had brought for the purpose, and placed it into my inner pocket, along with the matte knife whose blade I had wiped clean on the gown. Then I pulled down the gown, rolled the body onto its back, quietly lowered the lid, and said a deeply felt prayer for Mr. Collin's soul, while at the same time adding my own thanks to God for His gifts and His grace. Then, making sure that I had no telltale stains upon my hands or clothing, I opened the door and invited Jim Meinhart back in, the roll of flesh hot against my chest.

He opened the door to the control room, and I followed him inside. There was barely enough room for both of us to stand. I prayed that the flesh would give off no odor that Jim would notice, and tried to concentrate on the panel with several buttons and switches mounted on one of the narrow walls.

"Procedure's fairly simple," he said. "This switch turns on the mechanism that opens the doors, and this button slides the casket into the combustion chamber. That light goes on when it's inside. Then you close the doors behind it." He then proceeded to push the proper buttons and throw the proper switches. I heard the sound of gears like the rushing of deep and secret waters, then the closing of the door of the furnace. "The equipment's pretty old," Jim said. "That door closing is one reason why we try to discourage relatives from staying."

I remarked that the sound did have a certain degree of finality to it, and Jim nodded. "There's only one switch that turns on the furnace," he said. "This one here. On and off." He flicked the switch and I heard a dull whoosh. "Once it begins, it can be stopped any time, but it takes an hour and a half for the remains to be completely reduced to . . ." He paused.

"To ash?" I said.

"Well, we don't like to call it ash, although that's what it is. 'Cremains' is the proper word, though I've never used it. I generally just say the remains and let it go at that."

"There's really very little remains left," I said, remembering the pile of fine gray powder that I had peered at in my mother's urn, before it was placed in the columbarium at Peace Haven, where my father was buried in an earth grave.

Jim nodded. "It's oxidation. The water in the body evaporates, and whatever has carbon in it, like the soft tissues . . . say, I hope I'm not getting too graphic for you, Brandon."

"No no," I said quickly. "The body is simply the shell of the soul, that's all, something to be discarded." I smiled gently. "With all due respect to your profession, of course."

"Well, the soft tissues are incinerated, and all that's left is the inorganic ash of the bone structure. The pulverizer reduces that to powder."

"Pulverizer?" I said.

He gestured out the door. I left the tiny room and he followed, closing the door behind him. We sat together on one of the narrow pews. "Not many crematories have them in the U.S., but most of them do in England—you can thank Pastor Fletcher for ours. From all accounts he was a strong believer in strewing the remains. But they're a bit hard to strew when you have bone fragments in them. That's what the pulverizer's for."

I invited Jim to the parsonage then for a cup of coffee, but he declined, as I had hoped he would. "I've got to stay here until it's finished. Legalities. But you go ahead. It can get pretty oppressive here." He left it unfinished, but I could hear his thoughts—"knowing what's happening a few feet away."

I told him I would be back just before the cremation was complete, and went to the parsonage. Mrs. Bunn was away, and I went directly to the kitchen, took the piece of Mr. Collins's flesh from my pocket, and set it on the sink top. Then I ran downstairs, got the curing box and the bag of salt, and began the operation that I had read of.

I took the salt (foreswearing sugar, maple syrup, or spices, all of which were suggested by my book) and rubbed it thoroughly on both sides of the skin. Then I poured more salt over the bottom of the box, covering it. On that layer I put one of the two wooden racks that had come with the box, poured more salt over that, then put in the flesh (skin side down, as directed). More salt went over it then, all the way to the top, and I closed the lid. I carried it downstairs and put it behind the freezer on top of the second rack, being careful not to block any of the drainage holes in the bottom of the box. I did not truly expect the salt to draw much fluid out of the flesh, but neither did I want to take my chances, so I put newspaper under the rack as well.

There was nothing to do with the flesh now but wait, so I went back upstairs, washed my hands, and went out to the crematory, for I had found the process of cremation to be quite interesting, and had had no chance to learn anything about it during the only other one I had attended, that of my mother. It would also be prudent, since the crematory was to be my source of communion material, to learn as much as possible about its workings.

So Jim and I resumed our conversation, and he told me a bit about the history of cremation, and the initial efforts of the funeral industry in this country to thwart it. "I've never had a problem with it myself," he said, "except for the fact that it doesn't give me much of a chance to do what I've been trained for. Still, it seems a respectful way to . . . dispose of the dead."

Finally Jim looked at his watch. "Long enough," he said, and we went back into the small room, where he threw the switch to stop the flames.

"Why isn't there any smoke?" I asked. "I noticed . . . when my mother was . . ." I trailed off.

"The heat's so intense that it doesn't create much smoke to start with, and it's got a special draft control. The way the gasses recirculate you hardly get any smoke at all." Jim pushed a small black button on the panel I had not noticed before. "The pulverizer. Just a minute or two." I listened, and heard only the slightest grinding of machinery. Jim finally pushed the button a second time, and threw the switch that opened the door to the furnace. We looked inside and saw what appeared to be several pounds of white ash, punctuated here and there by what I took to be the metal that had held the wooden casket together.

"I'll have that coffee now," Jim said. "By the time we're finished, it should be cool enough to remove the remains."

Inside the parsonage, we chatted for another hour over coffee and tea cakes, then went to the crematory once again, where I watched while Jim withdrew the casket nails and fittings with a magnet, then carefully collected together the white ash, pouring it into what appeared to be a clay urn, which he sealed.

"That's about it," he said. "I'll vacuum out the residue and take the urn over to Mrs. Collins tomorrow. Her son is going to strew the ashes in the river."

I said goodbye then, and left Jim to finish up.

Four days later, alone in the parsonage, I opened the box and dug away the salt until I reached the piece of flesh. It had shrunk considerably in its curing, and the surface of the skin was no longer smooth, but shriveled, though still the pale yellow color it had been before. Not knowing whether I needed to or not, I "overhauled" it, which consisted of examining the meat for bare spots (there were none), rubbing it well with the salt again, and repacking it as before. This time I left it only overnight, and when I removed the salt the next day, it was (according to the book) fully cured. Although I looked it over carefully, I could detect no moisture at all, and was amazed that only five days could serve to produce the dry and parchment-like prize that I now held in my trembling hands. It was far smaller than it had been originally, but it would last for weeks, months, if everything I read was true, and if I had done all properly (and I had no reason to believe I had not).

I decided to cut the flesh into smaller segments and wrap each individually. When I had finished, I had twenty pieces each the size of a quarter, a size which, I learned later, was too large, providing a veritable surfeit of richness that nearly made me ill. After that first attempt I cut each of the remaining pieces in half, which left me thirty-eight. They lasted four months before they began to deteriorate. But instead of throwing them away, I burned them. It seemed suitable.

149

Within a few weeks there was another cremation, and I took the flesh of yet another parishioner. It was easier that time, and became easier as the years went by and my communions continued. They are more recent now, occurring once every two weeks, corresponding to Mrs. Bunn's absences. In the intervening years, she only once noticed the box. When she asked about it, I told her that it was rock salt for the pavement. Even if she would ever want to use it, the odds of it being on one of the perhaps ten days a year that the flesh is actually cured in the box is minimal. Besides, the flesh is always near the bottom.

Still I feared, perhaps irrationally, that Keith Holt, in some nocturnal invasion, would somehow find the box, deduce its purpose, and search for and find what it had held. He seemed to me to have some darker wisdom than the dear, gentle, trusting Mrs. Bunn, who would never think of poking into the storage area in the cellar where my suitcases were kept. I could not help but feel that Keith would know exactly where to go, would take the third suitcase from the bottom of the pile, the one with the perforations to let whatever was inside breathe, would break open the feeble locks, and would find the carefully wrapped and stored away pieces of flesh.

Flesh. I am growing tired of calling it that. Perhaps the Host would be a better term, for flesh sounds so *fleshy*. And it is indeed the Host, the Host of the Eucharist, the guide that takes me by the hand (or the tongue) and so leads me into God's glory. But it would not have been the Host to Keith Holt, nor to anyone else who would stumble across it in that way. It would be nothing but the trove of a butcher.

I saw Keith Holt in church that first Sunday after the sanctuary was violated. He sat there with his parents and his little sister Kimberly, his eyes fixed on mine throughout the service. Every time I looked at him he was looking at me. Of course everyone looks at the pastor during the service. But this was different. This Sunday everyone seemed ill at ease, knowing what had happened in their place of worship, and few eyes met mine. Most of the people were looking down at their laps, stealing a furtive glance now and again at the altar, then looking away quickly, as if they could see what had been there. The details had not been published in the papers, but what the imagination creates can be far worse than reality.

As in my own case, to prove the point. If you were told that there is a rural minister who is a cannibal and a ghoul, and nothing more than that, your mind, instead of seeing the tall, thin, ascetic-looking, mild mannered fortyish man I am, would summon up images of some slavering, white-haired madman in an ecclesiastical gown (no doubt splashed with gore). His basement (or bedroom, depending on the psychosexual motivations you might come up with) would be filled with moldering corpses hanging from beams or tall trees, large chunks of meat cut from them and perhaps simmering in this maniac's kitchen. History and the popular press is full of human monsters who really perpetrated such horrors, and such easy labelling would be sure to befall me were my acts discovered. Far better to tell the truth, such as I have done here, than to let imagination run wild.

I have digressed again. But I did not digress from my sermon that morning. I could not. I was locked to the outline, my mind unable to wander, my concentration fixed as it was upon that smirking boy, who would look at me and, having caught my eye, would glance quickly to the place on the altar where the paten with the cat's head had sat. I would look at him again, and his knowing eyes would dart now to the new Bible that had replaced the old, befouled one. A third time I would look at him, and he would lead his gaze and our mutual memory to the cross, now wiped clean, but for both of us eternally stained. As my anger grew I clung to my outline like an anchor, and forged ahead with all due haste, anxious to be finished, and so quit of the presence of this demon child.

It was the shortest sermon I have preached, and when I said Amen and turned toward my pew, the congregation seemed too amazed to be delighted, although I received several favorable comments on the message as the people filed out. My practical side made a mental note to reduce the length of my sermons from then on.

That evening after dinner I walked over to the church and went to the activities room where Youth Fellowship had just begun. Keith Holt was there, that knowing look etched firmly on his young, smooth face. I observed for a few minutes, noticing that he did not sing the songs with the others, did not even move his lips. When Randy Kornhauser began to break the young people up into groups, I went over to Keith and smiled at him.

"I'd like to speak with you, Keith. Just for a minute."

He looked at me for the longest time, as if sizing up an opponent, then nodded. "Fine," he said. "Where?"

"My office," I said, turning. "Just upstairs."

"Your ground, huh?"

I turned back and looked at him. "Pardon?"

He gave a quick shake of his head. "Nothing."

My office is small but comfortable, much more modern in appearance than the library in the parsonage where I do most of my work. The office is for counseling, conferences, and phone calls. It's my public headquarters, while the library is my private one. Keith sat in one of the two armchairs without being asked, and I sat down behind my desk, facing him. "Don't you want to close the door?" he said.

"Why would I do that?"

He shrugged, crossed his leags, and waited.

"I wanted to talk to you, Keith, about some of the things that have been happening here at the church in the past couple of weeks." I didn't know where I was going, or precisely what I was going to say. I hoped to draw him out, and thought that seeming mild and ineffectual might be the best way. The weaker he thought I was, the closer he might come to bragging about his exploits, or at least giving me enough of a hint that I would know without his admission of guilt.

"Like what? Bake sale? Choir practice?"

"No. Not good things like that. Not things that serve God. *Bad* things."

"If you don't like pies and singing, those are bad things."

"I'm not talking about pies and singing. I'm talking about vandalized graves, about the defilement of the altar."

"Oh, yeah." He grinned. "I read about that in the papers."

"And what did you think of it?"

"I thought it might be pretty rad."

The phrasing was odd. "You thought it might be . . ."

"For whoever did it."

"You thought it might be a . . . pleasurable thing to do?"

"Pleasure." He made the word last a long time. "Yeah, I guess it would give a person . . . pleasure."

"Are you wondering," I went on, "why I'm asking you about this?"

"I guess because you maybe think I did it."

"You *are* the only person I know," I said, "who has expressed an interest in Satanism."

152

"Boy," he said, shaking his head. "See where my big mouth gets me? I mean, that's the thing about churches—you guys always tell us to say what we think, that we got freedom of speech and all, and when we do it, it comes right back to us." He cocked his head at me. "You say anything to the cops about me?"

"No."

"How about my folks?"

"No."

"And why not?" He went on before I could answer. "You didn't go to the cops because you don't have any evidence, and if you go to my folks and tell them, they won't really give a damn. Excuse me. A *darn*."

"You don't think they would care about something like this?"

"They wouldn't believe you because they wouldn't want to. Besides, they know what I am, and they don't care."

"What you are? Do you mean a Satanist?"

"'Ye say that I am,'" he quoted.

It was what Christ said when the council asked if he was the Son of God. "You know the scriptures," I said, surprised.

"Hey, I go to church, and some of it rubs off. Besides, it's important to know how the enemy thinks."

"And Christ is the enemy?"

"Seems dumb, doesn't it? I mean, how can a mealy-mouthed wimp like that be the enemy? No offense."

There was a painful tightness in my stomach. I sat for a moment, watching him, but he seemed to have nothing more to say. "What did you do with the skull?" I asked quietly.

"What did *I* do with it? Well, I can tell you what *another* Satanist might do with it, and that's to use it in a Black Mass. You ever hear of those? You go in a church, flip the crosses, crap on the Bible, say the Lord's Prayer backwards, sacrifice a virgin on the altar—"

"A virgin?"

His eyes narrowed. "They're harder to find these days, so sometimes you have to use an animal."

"Like a cat," I said.

He nodded. "A cat'll do fine. For starters."

We sat there looking at each other for a long time. I knew what he was doing—it was a staredown—and I knew that the longer I looked at him, the longer I went along with this childish contest, the worse I would feel when I finally looked away. And eventually I *would* have to look away, for this was no fight between good and evil, but simply a deluded boy trying to prove his strength, to prove to himself that he did have some power. Let him win, then, I thought, but act as if you don't care.

So I pushed back my chair, interlocked my hands behind my head, looked up at the ceiling, and said, "Will your parents be picking you up after Youth Fellowship tonight?"

Finally he answered. "Yeah. That's right."

There was triumph in his voice, satisfaction that he had held the gaze while I had looked away. "Will they both be here?" I asked, still not looking at him.

"Yeah. They visited some friends. Kimberly's with them too. Think you'd like to discuss me with her?"

"No. I don't think that will be necessary." I stood up. "Suppose you go back to the others now, Keith." It was on my lips to thank him for talking to me, but I realized that I need thank him for nothing. He had done more, I felt, than he could ever atone for, if not in God's eyes, then in mine. But he, I learned, was far more gracious, even in mockery, than I.

"Well, Pastor," he said as he stood up, "thanks for this little chat. I feel a whole lot better now knowing that a man of God is looking out for my welfare. And I'm sure my folks will be interested in whatever it is you have to tell them. And hey, if you want me to do up a batch of cookies for the next bake sale, you can count on me. Okay?" He didn't wait for an answer, merely turned his back on me and walked out the door.

I sat down again and thought for a long time about the boy, praying to the Lord to show me a way to touch him, to make him understand that what he was doing and thinking was sin, was abomination, that a change must be made. But God gave me no answer. The boy was no boy, but a monster, implacable and adamant. In earlier times, a word from me and he would have been burned for heresy, and, God help me, I think I would have turned him over to the Inquisition. For he was foul. That is the most brief as well as the most accurate word I can use to describe him. Foul.

My office does not command a view of the parking lot, so I went across the hall to the adult Sunday school room and sat there in the dark, waiting for the Holts to come pick up their son. Just before 7:30 I saw their car, a new Saab, pull in to the lot. I went outside, walked up to it, and waved. Mr. Holt lowered the window, and I told him that I would like to have a word with him and his wife in my office. They got out and were about to come into the church with their little girl, when Keith and some of the other students came outside. The boy cast a twisted smile at me.

"Hey Mom, Dad. Leave Kimberly out here with me, it's cool."

His mother gave him a peck on the cheek, and I remember thinking that even monsters have mothers. Then I turned and led the way into the church.

As we sat down in my office, they seemed utterly calm and comfortable, as though they had not the slightest idea of the things their son was doing. Perhaps, I thought, the impression was an honest one. Perhaps this busy, upwardly mobile, double-income family truly didn't know.

"I wanted to talk to you today," I began, "about Keith."

They smiled and nodded, as if the thought that I could say anything negative about their son had never crossed their minds.

"Are you aware," I went on, "of his interest in . . . certain cults?"

Mr. Holt looked at me with a cocked head, for all the world like a bird examining a rather sad example of worm. "Cults?"

"Yes. In particular, Satanism."

Both of them chuckled. "Oh, that," said Mrs. Holt with a dismissive wave of her hand. "He's been interested in that silly stuff for years."

I felt a hard, cold lump deep in my throat and swallowed, but it remained. "Silly stuff," I repeated.

"He gets bored so easily," Mr. Holt explained. "Keith is very, very bright."

"Ninety-ninth percentile on all his achievement tests, always gets straight A's, and his I.Q., well . . ." She shrugged as if any further detailing of the boy's genius would be embarrassingly un-necessary.

"So whenever he finds any subjects outside of school that interest him," Mr. Holt said, "we try to support that. He was into computers for a while, but got bored. I think it got too simple for him. But he's always had a fascination for this horror stuff." The man smiled and shook his head. "A lot of these rock groups now are into that. That's where he first got interested, I guess. Then he started reading the books. He's told us a lot about it, and it seems harmless enough."

"Harmless?" I said. "Satanism?"

"Well, it's not like he's *practicing* it," Mrs. Holt said. "It's just a . . . a *study*, an *interest* of his."

"You really don't know?" I said.

"Know what?" Keith's father asked. There was a hint of irritation in his voice.

"Your son *is* practicing it," I said, as calmly as I knew how. "At least he believes it. He as much as admitted it to me."

"Oh, come on, Pastor," Mr. Holt said. "You must have misunderstood him or something."

"I don't think so. He truly believes in the goodness of Satan, and considers God the enemy. He *told* me that not an hour ago."

"Well, he may have *told* you that," Mrs. Holt said, "but I'm sure he doesn't really *believe* it."

"Then why would he tell me?"

Mr. Holt gave a great sigh, as if about to explain something to a dull child. "Pastor St. James, when you were growing up, didn't you ever want to do something to go against authority? It's only *natural* for kids to want to question and even shock their parents or teachers . . . *or* pastors, shake them up a little, rattle the cage. We don't see what's so terrible about that, and after all we *are* Keith's parents. And I can assure you that despite what he might say, or the things he has in his room, that it's only a—"

"Things he has?" I interrupted. "What things?"

Mrs. Holt chuckled. "Oh, just *things*, you know. Crazy things kids collect."

"Like . . . what in particular?"

Mr. Holt sighed again. "All right, Pastor, read into it what you want to, I know you will anyway. Keith collects a lot of . . . weird things. Like bones, and, and things in bottles . . ."

"What kind of bones?" I asked. "And what's in the bottles?"

"*Animal* bones," Mr. Holt answered. "Things he finds in the woods, in the fields. He makes little patterns out of them, stars and designs."

"Pentagrams?"

"I don't know, I guess that's what he calls them, but it doesn't *mean* anything—"

"And the bottles?"

"Specimens," Mr. Holt said. "Just natural specimens, that's all."

"I don't understand."

"You know," Mrs. Holt said. "Things in alcohol."

"Formaldehyde," Mr. Holt corrected.

"Whatever." She giggled. "They give me the creeps, I can tell you."

"What things?"

Mr. Holt tossed his hands in the air. "*Things.* Like, uh, dead baby birds he found, or sometimes he finds a dead animal and dissects it and keeps parts. That's because of a biology project he's planning for next year's science fair, Pastor. He's not going to *eat* the damn things, pardon my French." The phrase, *eat the damn things,* shot ice into my heart. "It's just the natural curiosity of a bright boy, that's all."

I shook my head slowly. "I'm not sure. But I think you're wrong. I think there's far more to it than a science fair project, or whatever else he might be telling you."

"I know what *you're* telling us," Mr. Holt said, and his voice was cold and angry. "You're telling us that we're not good parents, that's basically what you're saying."

"Listen, please, I don't mean to—"

"You think we don't pay attention to our son? You don't think we give him quality time?"

"It's hard with both of us working," said Mrs. Holt, "but we do very well with Keith. He knows he can talk to us. But we feel it's best to let him get these things out of his system, so we try not to be too judgmental, and if you don't think that's the proper way to raise children, well, I'm just sorry."

"You don't need to be defensive," I said. "I'm not criticizing you, I'm just trying to help."

"Well, I don't think we need your help," Mrs. Holt said. "And I certainly don't think we asked you for it, or for your opinion on how to raise children. Now being from this area you may see things differently than we do, but—"

"*Yes,*" I said, with more force than I wanted to use, but I had to stop them somehow. They had interpreted my concern about Keith as a criticism of their behavior as parents, proving themselves, in their own selfish way, to be just as evil as their son. "Yes," I repeated. "I do see it differently. I don't think you're willing to admit what's happening."

Like a malignant and living thing, a cruel smile twisted its way across Mr. Holt's face, seemed to pass through the air between the couple, and crossed the countenance of his wife as well. I knew then the source of Keith's evil grin, and suspected the source of so much else as well. "And you do, huh?" Mr. Holt said. "You in your God-given wisdom think our boy is a . . . a devil-worshipper."

It was time to tell them. "He was the one who robbed the grave. And he also defiled the sanctuary."

Mr. Holt's face turned red. His wife's turned white.

"It was a Black Mass," I went on. "A Satanist ritual."

"*Damn* you!" The force of Holt's words threw me back physically. "If I find that you've told anyone that—*anyone!*—I'm going to take you to court! That's slander, *Pastor*, and I'm not going to put up with that for a second!"

"Your son needs help—"

"He doesn't need any help! There's not a damn thing wrong with him! *You're* the one who needs help!" He shot to his feet, and his wife did the same. I have never seen such raw hate on faces in my life.

"I'm sorry," I said, fearing them, yet wanting them desperately to stay. "I only want—"

"Goodbye, Pastor," Mrs. Holt said. "You won't be seeing us in *your* church any more." As they swept out of my office, I could almost see steam in their wake.

I walked over to the Sunday school room to watch them make their way to their car. Their backs were set tautly, their limbs stiff. When Mr. Holt threw open his car door, I heard a wail from inside, saw him freeze for a moment, then heard him saying something I couldn't make out, while what I took to be Kimberly's crying continued. What had happened while the little girl was in the car alone with her brother? I thought I knew, but I didn't want to think about it. I didn't want to think about the Holts at all. I did not even have the goodness to pray for them, and may God forgive me for that, as he has for so many other things.

One week, then two went by with no further disturbances at Dunbarton Methodist. The Holts, true to their savage word, did not return to the church, nor did Keith come to Youth Fellowship on Sunday evenings. Slowly the thought of the Holts began to leave me, and I turned my attention to my private and solemn communions once more. In the furor over the break-in, I had actually missed one of my opportunities for my biweekly services when Mrs. Bunn went to Baltimore. Now she was off to see her relatives again, and Tuesday evening after choir practice the church and parsonage would be abandoned by all but myself.

Two months had passed since the last cremation, and I had seven pieces of the host remaining. It would be more than enough to see me through until the next one, which, I felt sadly certain, would be that of Mrs. Jackson Ginger, a thirty-eight year old mother of two who was wasting away of cancer. Mr. Ginder had, just a week before, pre-planned the disposition with Jim Meinhart, specifying cremation (his wife's choice) at the Dunbarton Methodist crematory. I am not the only one whose heart is wrenched by Cynthia Ginder's oncoming death. She sang in the choir and was also a Sunday school teacher, her marriage had been ideal and blessed with two charming children, now twelve and ten, and leukemia is feasting on her. She is in the final stages now, and I go to see her twice a week on my visits to St. Joseph's Hospital. In her case I have prayed only for God's will to be done, because she seems to suffer more every day. Still, she bears it with good grace, and her faith is strong.

Once again I digress. Cindy's strength and faith are so overwhelming that it is impossible not to think about her and marvel at her. That some people, so put upon by life, should be so good, while others, like the Holts, who have everything that is wanted should be sunk in a swamp of selfishness and evil . . . it is inexplicable. Only God can understand, and it is good that he does.

I dreaded making Cynthia Ginder the next source of the Communion host, though I knew that, were she to understand, she would not begrudge it of me. The ecstasy of nearness to God, the sweet sensation of Him filling all one's senses—after one experiences these things, they can only be marvelled at, not condemned.

It was on the day of my mother's cremation, of course, that my plan was set, and I have never altered from it. It had to be not merely eaten in an attitude of worship, but in an *atmosphere* of worship, consecrated, blessed, sacred. And I knew why past communions, though they satisfied my intellect, had never truly satisfied my soul. The pale, white, flavorless bread could never be Christ's body. It was a symbol, nothing more, and even the Catholics, try as they would to claim transubstantiation of their flat wafer, their dark and muddy wine, could never overcome the certainty that bread is bread, wine is wine.

But flesh is flesh, and the flesh of man is as close as one can come to the flesh of the *Son* of Man; the flesh of a Christian who

159

has become one with Christ has become, in a miraculous way, the flesh of Christ Himself.

That day my mother was cremated, that was the day this knowledge came to me. Tuesday night, when Mrs. Bunn was absent, I took a small piece of the chilled flesh into the sanctuary, locking the door of the church behind me. Nothing would be visible through the translucent windows. I set up the communion table, placed the piece of flesh upon the paten, and filled the chalice with wine, a fine French bordeaux, not the grape juice we usually use. Then I dressed in my vestments, lit the candles (my heart pounding all the while), and began to pray a prayer of consecration.

When I had finished, I said aloud the words of consecration, but with the wine first. I drank it, all of it (one of the few exceptions to my temperance, and one which I have repeated), then set down the chalice and turned to the paten.

My heart was beating wildly, and I must confess that I felt a priapic pressure as well. The inch square piece of host glimmered as yellow as the flame of the candles that were its sole source of illumination. I said the words automatically, and in the middle of them came the terrible fear that what I was doing was the worst kind of sin, that I blasphemed God and Christ and Man and motherhood and anything else that was good and pure and decent, and my voice broke, and I choked and coughed, while tears came to my eyes. But God brought me through those doubts, ushered me into the Truth, and I let His peace enter into me, and finished the words, and took the host from the paten, and—

ate.

I am no master of style, but I place that word separately (as I see fiction writers do) to try and express the importance of that moment, the *aqape*, the epiphany, the utter shock and realization that all I had believed was true, that God did live and reign, lived in the flesh and lived in me. It was a moment of the deepest knowledge, blinding truth, immeasurable joy.

Such was the spiritual impact born of the physical sensation, which was astounding in its own way. The flesh seemed at first to quiver on my tongue like a thing alive, and for a moment I feared that it was, that in revenge for being eaten my mother's skin would choke me. But the fear passed instantly as the taste of the flesh went through my body, a feeling physical yet spiritual enough so that my erection (caused by sheer excitement, of course) shrank immediately. I have no idea of how long it took, for time seemed both compressed and expanded, but the host—not dried this first time, but fresh and moist, you will recall—melted on my tongue into countless fragments, each as potent in its essence as the larger piece from which it sprang. I do not recall swallowing, but I do know that the host, in its numerous particles, entered my system, filling me with its power and holiness and love. It was not as though it descended through my esophagus and into my stomach, but as though it entered my very blood and nerves directly from my mouth, moving outward, downward, inward, as the word of God and the beauty of Christ comes upon all men and all nations.

It seemed to take an eternity, but an eternity that I wanted to last forever. Still, the sensation finally passed, and my mouth was empty. The feeling, though, lingered. The peace and love of God was within me, and would remain.

I recited the closing words then, to a congregation of myself— "For as often as ye eat this bread and drink this cup, ye do show the Lord's death till He come." Then I prayed once more, extinguished the candles, left the church, and slept the most peaceful sleep I can ever recall.

So the years have passed, the flesh has been removed and dried and consecrated and ingested—rather say *absorbed,* for it has become one with me, and when I partake of it I have become one with God. In no other place could I practice such communion, and so I remain at Dunbarton Methodist, even when other, finer, larger churches were offered me. They are offered no more. The diocese knows of my attachment to this place, and my congregation knows of my love for them.

And the second Tuesday comes, and I renew my strength, find more love, meet with God. It was time again, Tuesday night, but late now, as I had been to Daniel Hess's retirement dinner. I arrived back at the parsonage at 10:30 to find the choir long since gone from the church. I made myself sit down and have a cup of tea, and read from Galatians while I sipped. The anticipation had been present all day and all evening long, and now I decided it was finally time. I took a piece of the dried flesh from the small box in my parsonage desk, locked the parsonage, and went out to the church. No one would notice the lights on in the sanctuary at midnight, for the church was barely visible from the road. I had held my private services as late, or later, than this before. God seemed even closer in the stillness of the night.

I unlocked the church, donned my vestments, and prepared the communion table. I had no idea I was not alone. It had been a long time since I had locked the church door behind me. But halfway through my prayer I thought I heard a strange noise—the creak of a floorboard, or perhaps the slight groan of a pew as it was leaned upon. I froze, then turned around and looked back at the empty sanctuary. It was so dark that a figure would have had to have been in motion for me to observe it. I listened for a few seconds more, then, deciding that it must have been merely the sounds of wood expanding, turned back toward the altar and resumed my prayer.

". . . O gracious heavenly Father, I pray that you will sanctify these elements of wine and flesh . . ." (I had changed the phrasing to suit the reality. Perhaps I should not have done so, for once I nearly said flesh instead of bread at Sunday morning communion service) ". . . and by doing so bless this Thine Ordinance that we, in love, faith, and obedience—"

There. Something again, some slight noise, some presence glimpsed out of the corner of my eye. I jerked my head around, but saw nothing. It occurred to me to walk back through the pews, swiveling my head to look into each one, but I bit back the urge. Then a thought out of horror movies came to me—the people from whom I had taken the host had come back, returned to claim me at midnight, would fall upon me even as I was in the midst of my gruesome practices.

But fall upon me with what? I thought. They could not be reanimated corpses, as in the comic books of my youth, for there was no corpse left to reanimate. Ashes then? Ashes that formed together wetly into the consistency of papier-mache? Ashes that came together after being scattered in water, or on the winds? Absurd, ridiculous, impossible. No, there was nothing supernatural in the sanctuary except for the presence of God, and it was that presence, that comforting, reassuring presence that put my mind at ease, pushed back that clinging vestige of guilt. There was no reason for anything to avenge itself upon me, for there was nothing to avenge. They now lived with God, who had shown me how to use their flesh to see His face. I dismissed the bizarre fancy, and turned back to the altar.

". . . that we, in love and obedience and faith, may nourish our spirits and souls—"

"Upon this *worm food!*"

162

The end of the world had come.

I knew the voice instantly, without having to turn my head. Keith Holt. I could discern him now, a tall, thin figure standing near the front of the pews meant for the choir. When I looked at him, he smiled.

"A little private communion service, Pastor? Once a month not enough for God's munchies?"

He began to move then, coming around the side of the pew to which he must have crept in the semi-darkness. In another moment he would be by my side, and I thought of grabbing the host, stuffing it in my mouth, and swallowing it, but by the time I was able to put the thought into action, Keith had already lifted the paten, and was examining what lay on it.

"Flesh, you said." He sniffed at the host, then gingerly picked it up between two fingertips. "Not bread, but flesh." He turned it this way and that. I looked away, strangely ashamed, ashamed for my beliefs, and that made me even more ashamed, not to have the power of my convictions, not to stand up for what my God had had me do. Instead, I felt like a boy caught masturbating.

"It really is, isn't it?" Keith said, as if impressed. "Flesh. Skin. Dried human skin. Y'know, I saw some in a gris-gris shop in New Orleans when my folks took me there on vacation, but I always thought the old guy who ran it was jiving me. But no. No, it looked just like this." I looked at him then, and found that he was staring at me with disbelief and a touch of admiration that chilled me, as if he had discovered a brother. "Still waters sure as hell run deep, Pastor. I never would've thought it of you."

I cleared my throat roughly. "What . . . what do you want?"

"You mean originally?" The wolfish smile was there now. "I came out here tonight to do the real thing, shoot the works, do it right, y'know? No cat this time—the genuine article. Only I, uh . . ." He shook his head regretfully. "I came a little early, so to speak. But when I got out of the car—I parked up the lane—I saw the light in the church, that little candle glow? Looked just like a Christmas card. When I came in you were praying so loud you didn't hear me crawling up the aisle until I almost got where I wanted to be. I figured something weird was going down. I mean, you all dressed up and all? Actually, I thought maybe you were into the same thing as me, but you disappointed me. Still praying to God." He shook his head in mock resignation. "But you sure got a strange way of doing communion. Skin. Holy shit." I write his words, though I do not approve of them. "What were you gonna do with this?" His eyes narrowed. "You gonna eat it? Like the bread?"

I gave no reply, but he saw the answer in my face.

"I underestimated you, man. That is pretty radical." He weighed the piece of flesh in his hand, then put it into the pocket of his blue-jeans. "I think I'll just keep this. For insurance? And if you don't think anybody'll believe me, they will. I mean, you're at all these cremations, so who else could get human flesh around here beside the undertaker? Probably got some way to dry it too, huh? Got the whole operation going. How long you been doing this anyway?"

I didn't answer.

"Undertaker leaves you alone for a while with 'em? To pray or something? I bet the police asked him he'd tell 'em that's just what happens. And that's when old Pastor St. Ripper goes to work, huh?"

I had suspected before that the boy had some dark knowledge, some way of looking within people, and now I saw it clearly. He was a tool of the devil, to be pitied, perhaps, but a tool nontheless, whether he had chosen his destiny or had it dictated to him by his parents. Whatever the route, he now lived in hell. His mind worked like one of its citizens. He could not be brought back, not in this life. He was not the first insane person I had ever spoken to, nor the first evil one, but he was the only one who was, without God's prompt intervention, most certainly damned.

"It's amazing," he said in the silence. "I mean, a sacrifice is one thing, but to eat them afterward . . ."

One of his words struck a further note of alarm in my already chaotic soul. "Sacrifice?" I said, recalling his words about coming "a little early." In what sense? Surely not a sexual one. But what?

Then I remembered the cry his little sister had given, alone with Keith in the car. Suddenly everything came together, and I was blessed (or cursed) with knowledge myself, the knowledge of what Keith was doing here, the nature of his sacrifice, and the reason for his regret at what he had done "a little early."

I turned my back to him and ran down the aisle, through the door, down the lane in the dim light of a gibbous moon. The autumn leaves crunched beneath my feet like the bones of small animals . . .

Or small children.

Kimberly Holt lay dead in the front seat of the car. Her face was turned toward me, and through the window I could see her staring

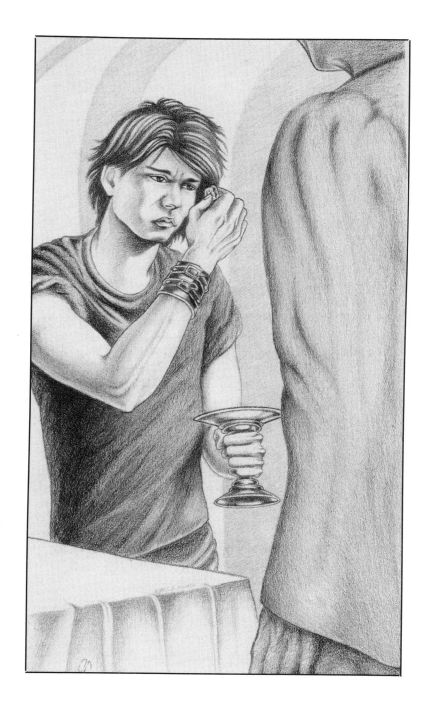

eyes, her tongue filling her mouth, blood still shining wetly at both flared nostrils. The head was at a right angle to the line of her shoulders.

"She didn't want to play any more," said Keith's cold voice behind me. I couldn't take my eyes off the girl, and whispered prayers for her soul while Keith went on. "I told her it was a game, that I had a big surprise for her at the church. She liked Sunday school a lot, and was pissed when Mom and Dad wouldn't take her any more, so when I mentioned the church, it was easy to get her in the car, even this late. But when we got here, she wouldn't get out. She was scared of it at night, scared of the graveyard."

He gave a deep sigh. I would like to have heard in it regret for his sister's death, but I heard only exasperation at the failure of his plans. "I wanted to get her into the church alive, and *then* do her. But the dumb little cunt wouldn't go. You wouldn't believe the things I offered her—candy and toys and dolls and all kinds of shit that I said was inside, but no way. So I grabbed her and she started to pull back and started yelling and I was afraid you were gonna hear and call the cops, so I started shaking her just to make her shut up, and put my hands on her neck so she'd stop yelling, you know, muffle her a little. But I guess I didn't know my own strength."

"Or the strength of Satan," I whispered, and he chuckled.

"Yeah, that's pretty good—the strength of Satan. I guess that's true."

"You don't *know* that it's true?" I asked him. "I thought you were so sure."

"I am," he said rather defensively. "I *am* sure."

"'I know that my redeemer liveth,'" I quoted from Job, "'and that he shall stand at the latter day upon the earth.'"

"Mine too, asshole," Keith said with a snarl. "And with both of them there the shit's really gonna hit the fan."

I looked at the little girl again, and then back at Keith. "What if you get caught, Keith?"

"You won't tell."

I didn't agree to that. "You're careless. Your sister disappears, you'll be investigated."

"I won't get caught, Pastor. I have faith. What did Jesus say about faith? That if you have as little as a grain of mustard seed, you can really kick some ass? Don't worry. The devil watches over me. He lets me know when things get too dangerous. He doesn't want me caught, 'cause then I couldn't serve him."

"What were you going to do with your sister?"

"Consecrate her, then leave her. According to my parents, I'd've been home all night."

"But your parents—they would know, they'd figure it out."

He shook his head and gave the same patronizing sigh that his father had given me. "Pastor, even if they *knew*, they wouldn't do anything about it. I mean, being the parents of a murder victim is one thing, but being the parents of a murderer? You've met them, you think they'd stand for that?"

With a shiver, I knew that what he said was true, and even as I hated him, I pitied him. "What will you do now?" I asked him softly.

"'Not my will, but thine.' The devil can quote scripture, huh? You're going to help me, Padre. I'm going to wipe the little bit of blood off this nice vinyl upholstery, drive this car back home, and we're all going to wake up tomorrow and wonder whatever became of my little sister. And you know what? Nobody's ever going to find out."

"Why not?" I didn't have to ask. I knew what he had in mind.

"You have a key to that crematorium, don't you?"

My hesitance told him I was lying. "No."

"Bullshit. Sure you do. And I know your pet nigger isn't in tonight, so we won't be disturbed. Get the kid." I stood there, not moving. "Come *on*, Pastor! Get that kid and let's get it done, or the tabloids are gonna have a fuckin' field day next week."

Dear God, I prayed, I put myself in your hands. Make me an instrument of your will.

And suddenly I felt peaceful, serene, and I somehow knew that God wanted me to do what Keith Holt told me to. I did not question His ways, I only obeyed.

Keith opened the car door and jerked his head toward the still form inside. I leaned over, took out my handkerchief, wiped the blood from the child's nose, then lifted her in my arms. Keith closed the car door, and I followed him as we walked down the lane to the church and the crematory. It was the first time I had ever carried a child in my arms. She was still warm, the limbs still supple, and I realized that adults' arms were meant to carry children, and I grieved that I had never had any of my own. I prayed for her soul as we walked, and by the time we arrived at the locked door of the crematory, I knew that she was with Christ in paradise, and knew too that this had been Christ's way of delivering her from the hands of her parents, under whose ministrations she would only have become as evil as they. It had not been Satan's strength, but God's that had entered Keith Holt's hands.

"You got the key on you?"

I did. Hoisting the little girl higher in my right arm, I reached with my left for the key ring that held those of the church and parsonage as well, and handed it to Keith. "The one on the right," I said.

He unlocked the door, pushed it open, fumbled for the light switch, found it. "Come on," he said, as the light from inside flooded over me and my soft burden. "Hurry it *up*." His voice shook.

I entered and walked up to the cremation chamber door, where I lay Kimberly, very gently, on the catafalque. When I straightened up, Keith was looking about warily. "Okay, now this thing . . . it just kind of dissolves her, right? So nothing's left?"

"It turns the body to ash. Except for some bone fragments. But there's a pulverizer for that."

"A pulverizer, huh? That's good. Not even any teeth left, huh?"

"No."

"Okay. Well, let's get to it then. That it there, where you put her?" He pointed toward the doors to the furnace, and I nodded. "Open it up, let's do it."

I opened the door to the control room, stepped inside, and pushed the switch that slid the doors open. When I came into the chapel again, Keith was leaning across his sister's body, staring into the cremation chamber.

"Not much room in there, huh?"

"No. There doesn't need to be."

Keith looked at the catafalque. "This thing slide her in?"

"Yes."

"Okay," he said, stepping back. "Do it then."

"Let me pray over her," I said.

"Uh-*uh*! No way. And I guess you'd like me to leave too, so you can cut off a steak for a souvenir." My cheeks burned at the words, not in shame, but in anger that I could never make him understand. "No. No prayers. Just do it."

Into thy hands I commend my spirit. Those are the words I thought and prayed as I went back into the control room. What happened next was His doing. My memories of it all are dim, as seen "through a glass darkly."

I know I pressed the button to set the belt into motion and slide the body on the catafalque into the chamber, but nothing happened, no whirring of machinery, no grinding of gears. I pressed it again—still nothing.

"What's going on?" I heard Keith Holt cry.

"It's not working," I called back.

"The hell it's not! *Do* it, or it's your ass!"

With a sob, I pressed the button again, but there was no response. I began to tap it rapidly, then hit it, over and over. When I looked up, Keith was in the doorway, his face bright with fury. "Fuck that," he shouted. "Just fuck it, I'll *push* her in!"

Shoulders slumped, my soul in turmoil, I stood at the control panel, listening to his footsteps cross the floor, a scuffling as he climbed onto the catafalque, the sliding noise of cloth as he pushed the body through the doorway—

—the sound of the machinery as it surged into life.

He yelled once, once only, as the belt pulled him into the combustion chamber, before the doors slammed shut behind him and his sister's corpse, and the red light went on. Then, whatever further cries he might have made were smothered by the roar of the furnace.

In panic I looked at the control panel, and, though I felt as if my hands were hanging useless by my side, I saw them on the buttons, my fingertips against the switches, and then saw only blackness.

*　　*　　*

When I opened my eyes again, I was lying at the base of the control panel. The crematory was silent, and the red light was dark. For a minute I remained where I was, breathing deeply, then I looked at my watch.

It was three o'clock in the morning. At least two hours had passed since I had lost consciousness. If the boy (and now that he was, I was certain, dead, I thought of him as *the boy*) had been truly trapped in the furnace, there would be nothing left. Had I done it? I asked myself. Had I thrown the switches, pushed the buttons to draw the boy into the furnace, close the door behind him and cremate him alive?

I had. I could not deny it. I had seen what my hands had done.

And yet I knew that I had not—I had been only God's instrument. It had not been *my* will that had done these things, but His, and I prayed that I could accept that and learn to live with it. How many others, I wondered, would have fallen prey to Keith Holt's hideous designs had he lived? Yet I had not judged and condemned him. God had.

Now there remained only the cleaning up. I steeled myself, pressed the button that brought the pulverizer into operation, and shuddered through the minutes I had to listen to its growl. Then it shut itself off, and in the silence I began to think of the things I had to do—clean out the chamber, scatter the ashes, drive the Holts' car back to their house or to some deserted place, and make my way back to the church again. Oh dear God, I asked Him, full of sorrow, what good can come of this?

I turned toward the open door, stepped through it into the chapel, and knew. I knew that God was righteous and wise and kind and good, and that all things came to pass through Him.

There on the catafalque lay the skins of Keith and Kimberly Holt. Side by side, they were whole and bloodless, the arms and legs neatly folded over onto the torso, which was itself folded once, the faces on top like masks.

I know that some would accuse me of having done this. They would say that while I thought I was unconscious, I turned off the furnace, pulled out the bodies (Keith would have died from the intense heat instantly), removed the skins, and put the bodies back into the furnace once more, my purported unconsciousness merely a self-delusion to protect myself from the truth others might find monstrous. But I tell you this would be a lie. My mind is not God's mind, and could not have worked as perfectly as His, could not have come to those realizations, conceived of those splendid resolutions, created *miracles*, for miracles they were, and miracles yet to be.

Keith Holt, instead of serving Satan as he wished, will serve God in a way he could never have imagined, and there is a true miracle—the miracle of God's love for Keith, one of His children. Even after all that Keith did and said against Him, God still loved him enough to make it possible for Keith to serve Him, and so, perhaps, enter His kingdom.

There is a second miracle, in that God in His wisdom has granted me the grace of keeping at least one family together, for the corporeal remains of Keith and Kimberly (the ashes I scattered among the fallen leaves in the lane) are in the box in the cellar, salted and curing, closer than siblings have ever been.

And the final miracle, the greatest of all, will take place next communion Sunday, when I plan to preach on how Christ multiplied the loaves and fishes, so that there was enough for all, and even some left over, and the plates with the host are passed, and I say the words, and my congregation comes closer to the heart of God than they could ever hope to in this world.

For such miracles were men once made saints.

Assurances of the Self-Extinction of Man

The land is the sea's cemetery.

When a sea creature dies, the sea throws up onto the land its empty shell.

Keeping this in mind, it is not too difficult to imagine that the sea, millions of years ago, had a reason for throwing life onto the land. "This new and particular creature," it said, "is already dead. It carries the seeds of its death in its mind."

And up we went.

After-Words

Chet Williamson is the only person I know who has been published in The New Yorker, The Magazine of Fantasy and Science Fiction, Playboy, and Twilight Zone Magazine. In other words, the four top short story markets in the country. When not writing superior short fiction, he also writes equally absorbing novels. To date, five have been published: *Soulstorm* (1986), *Ash Wednesday* (1987), *Lowland Rider* (1988), *McKain's Dilemma* (1988), and *Dreamthorp* (1989). To some critics he's still new on the scene, so he's occasionally been counted among the "splatterpunks," a loose-knit group of young writers who sometimes compare their style to "literary rock 'n' roll." In response to that charge, the ever rational Williamson has joked, "If these guys are writing the rock 'n' roll of horror, I'd like to be seen as the field's jazz writer." In his office, Williamson uses "an IBM clone" word processor, and does the major part of his writing in the morning.

*　　*　　*

SW: What was the inspiration for "Blue Notes?"
CW: I came to be interested in jazz while I was writing *Dreamthorp*. There's a character in there who's a serial killer and his father is a professional jazz musician. And in order to make this character sound believable, I went out and bought some jazz records. I bought the Smithsonian collection of classic jazz, which is a nice overview, and I just fell in love with this stuff! I just went crazy over it! So now, some two years later, I have a jazz collection of over 800 albums, I have a small library of books on the subject, and I'm playing the tenor saxophone. [laughs] It's like being a born-again Christian—you just go over the wall.

So I liked the idea of a blue note. And the concept that's behind a blue note. So I thought it would be kind of neat to write a story with a jazz setting, and use that theme, and open it up into an emotional and spiritual blue note as well. So that's how the story started.

174

SW: Your work is usually noted for its rich characterizations. Yet with "Blue Notes," it seemed vital that its philosophical impact took precedent over the eventual fate of the characters.

CW: You're absolutely right! [laughs] I liked those characters, but I think characters always look better in longer pieces. In short stories, I'm usually going for one effect—you can only go so far with a character in a short story, whereas in a novel you can really stretch out with a character and get into their skin . . .

SW: Which makes for a subtle segue into "Confessions of St. James."

CW: That was one of those stories which really seemed to write itself. There was very little rewriting on that that I had to do; once I had the basic idea, it just seemed to flow. The novella was a great length to write in, and I'd love to do it again, but there's just no market for it! When I try to think back about the original inspiration, I don't know what it was, but it may have been along the lines, "Okay, this is NIGHT VISIONS, let's get outrageous!" You know? [laughs] So I started to think about what's outrageous: religion, cannibalism . . .! So I started with that basic idea, and said, "Let's see what happens here."

And as I got into the character of St. James, he just absolutely fascinated me. For me, anyway, it became not a piece of sensationalistic writing, but a long character study of a person who is very much disturbed, yet in a way, very good. I really got to *like* the Reverend St. James. Because writing to me is kind of like acting; you take on the guise of a character, and you keep in that mind-set the whole way through the work: His innumerable asides, and all the times he says things that he puts in parentheses. I don't think you'll find this style in anything else I've written, because it was very much one particular character. And when you write like that, and you're relaxed, it does tend to flow a lot more smoothly than it might otherwise.

SW: What kind of research went into this story, or did you know some of it from first hand experience?

CW: Once I had the basic plot in my head, I wrote down a list of things I was going to have to do some research on. I went down to my library, at Elizabethtown, to get a few things on inter-library loan. So I turned in my list, and the librarian saw that I wanted books on: cremation, curing and drying meat, and careers in the ministry. So she looked at me and said, "This is going to be a *strange* one, isn't it?" [laughs]

As I said before, trying to get into the character is almost like method acting. I didn't work a day on this story without having a piece of jerky by my side. And I mean the real good jerky you get from a butcher shop, not those in the thin plastic containers. So when it came to these scenes, I would tear off a piece of jerky and let it just sit in my mouth. And I think that was a big influence on my work.

SW: Yet some people might think you are writing an anti-religious tract; that it's outrageous theme was purposely meant to shock and inflame certain groups of people.

CW: I really don't want to get into interpretations. But it's not meant to purposely upset anyone. In a way, it's saying that using religion or using whatever your spiritual belief may be—and we're currently in an immense search for spiritual values—that people can use religion to rationalize anything. And that's the big danger in it. Of course, it's been done since the birth of Christianity, and it's always been one of the dangers that true Christians have had to fight. So it's really not meant to incite, though there are some people who will read it and say this is just pornograpic, anti-religious material. But it's not. It's absolutely not.

SW: Tell us how long it took to write the novella?

CW: About three weeks. Which is fast, because generally when I'm in the process of writing, I do 1500 words a day, which works out to about six pages. And with this one, it was more like eight or nine, which for me is terrific.

SW: Finally, in 80 words or less, explain to us the "Assurances of the Self-extinction of Man."

CW: What is there to say? [laughs] I suppose if you had to call it anything, you could call it a prose poem. Or a fable. I mean, it's very depressing. I think it's the most depressing eighty words I've ever written. It seemed to me very profound at six o'clock in the morning when I was drunk when I wrote it—just kidding! [laughs] But I think it's a very succinct statement about the human situation. I don't know; I guess I must have been very depressed at the time! It would make for a hell of an epigraph for a novel. But I don't think anyone would ever read the novel; they'd slash their throat by the end of page ten.

We should just let that one stand as a dark thought. But it's a night vision, that's for sure.

Gary Brandner

1

Quinn Kirby's eyes snapped open. The bedroom was dark with only a pale glow reflected from the street lamp outside. Beside him Janice lay on her back, breathing gently in sleep. He sat up carefully holding the sheet and light thermal blanket against his bare chest. His hands shook. Fear sweat oozed out from under his arms and trickled down his rib cage. His heart was a drumbeat. Then, a block away, the dog barked. Kirby sat in the dark listening. Another bark. Still far away. He eased his head down onto the pillow, but he slept no more before the dawn. Again it was dogs. Always the dogs.

* * *

It was a bright and sunny day. Quinn Kirby's family sat with him at the breakfast table. Pert blond Janice, his talented wife, still looked like a college cheerleader at 31. His son Matthew had his mother's blond good looks and a quick mind that placed him well ahead of his class in school. A fine day, a fine family, and to top it off, the day after tomorrow was the start of a three-week vacation. But Kirby's mood was all wrong. He could not forget the dog in the

179

night, but he would not admit that was the cause. He searched for something else to lay the blame on.

"Did you have some trouble with the electric frying pan?" he said.

Janice looked at him quickly, surprised. Then she frowned. "No, I can manage the frying pan. Are you saying something is wrong with your breakfast?"

"Wrong? Heavens no, nothing's wrong. I just thought maybe the frying pan was overheating or something."

Janice made a piece of business out of leaning over the table to look at his plate. "Let me guess . . . the bacon's too crisp."

"Well, I do like it a little more tender than this."

Matthew looked up at his parents with the weary expression of a boy who has heard this kind of exchange too often. With a sigh he returned to his bowl of Sugar Frosted Flakes.

"Maybe you'd like to make breakfast yourself," Janice said with a smile that was in no way convincing. "That way you could do your bacon exactly the way you like it."

"I *do* make breakfast," he reminded her. "Every other weekend."

"Yes, of course you do," she admitted. "And on the alternate weekends you complain."

"Just a damn minute—" he began.

Janice glanced sharply toward Matthew. "Are you through eating?"

The boy spooned up a last mouthful of cereal. "I guess so."

"Then you're excused from the table."

Matthew got up with a heavy sigh and slouched out of the room. At the door he turned. "Okay if I watch cartoons?"

"No," Quinn said.

"How about when you guys are done fighting? Can I watch then?"

"Matthew . . ." his father said with a dangerous rising inflection.

The boy got the message and vanished.

Janice and Quinn finished their breakfast in silence. He made a point of pushing the overcrisped, uneaten bacon to the rim of the plate, wondering at the same time why he couldn't let it go. These sessions of petty bickering were his fault, initiated to avoid having to talk about the things that frightened him in the night. He helped himself to another cup of coffee and lit a cigarette, trying to frame some kind of compliment to smooth things over. Then Janice got up and opened the kitchen window.

Kirby's good intentions vanished. He held the cigarette aloft like a badge. "This is just about the last vice I have left. And not the surgeon general nor Dear Abby nor the Marching Mothers Against Tobacco nor you and your window banging are going to take it away from me." He inhaled noisily and blew smoke at the ceiling.

Janice faced him with the super-reasonable expression he hated. "Aren't we overreacting just a teensy bit? Nobody said a word about your messy habit. If I want to let a little fresh air into my space, I guess I have that right."

Quinn opened his mouth to reply, but a dog barked outside the window and he was instantly on his feet. He ground his teeth to keep them from chattering.

Janice dropped the combative posture. "It's all right," Janice said softly. "It's only Lady next door in the Coopers' back yard."

"She didn't jump the fence?" Quinn was unable to keep the anxiety out of his voice.

"Of course not. And if she did, Lady is the friendliest old dog you'd ever want to meet. She wouldn't bite anybody to save her life."

"I can't help it," Quinn said, feeling like a jackass. "You know about my thing with dogs."

"Don't I!" she said. "This dog neurosis of yours has caused us more trouble than anything else. Matthew can't even have a pet like other little boys."

"I said he could have a cat."

"A cat is no pet for a boy. He needs something he can rough-house with."

"Janice, we've been over this . . . how many times?"

"If you'd just see somebody about it . . ."

"I don't want to *see* anybody about it," he said through clenched teeth. "I'm fine. All we have to do is keep dogs away from me."

She turned toward the window and let the straight line of her back speak for her.

Quinn pulled in a lungful of smoke. He ground out the cigarette in a saucer. He said, "Janice, why are we doing this to each other?"

She shrugged without turning around. "You tell me."

"Because it's become a habit," he said. "A bad, bad habit. Did you see how Matt looked at us when he went out of here?"

"I saw. And you're right: Something has to change, Quinn. I

mean, here we are all ready to leave on a vacation trip to California and we're at each other's throat. We should be happy and planning our trip instead of fighting."

"I've been thinking about our trip," he said, "and I had an idea. What about instead of burning our skins on some beach and wandering around buying cheap souvenirs at Disneyland, we do something more substantial. Something that might help pull our family together." He did not add *Before it's too late.*

"You mean not go?" she said.

"I mean go somewhere else. Try to recapture the old traditional values that our parents and grandparents knew."

"Where do you have in mind?" Janice was guarded.

"Danziger."

"Danziger, Wisconsin? You're kidding."

"Why should I be kidding? It's where my father and my grandfather were born. It's small town heartland U.S.A. It's roots."

"Quinn, how would you know? You've never been there in your life. All we have is those old black and white photos from your father's album. You're never shown the slightest interest in going to Danziger. Why now?"

"Because we're in trouble now, our marriage, my family, and I'm trying to find something that might help. If we don't at least try, Janice, we're finished. You must feel that too."

"But why Danziger?"

"Because it's something completely outside our experience. It's an old way of living, but to us it will be new. I've always wondered what the town is like. Dad never talked much about it . . . I mean when he could still talk. We can drive up to see him today. Tell him we're going. It might just cheer him up." Kirby softened his tone. "Listen, Janice, maybe going to Danziger will be a complete bust, but we haven't got a lot to lose, have we?"

She nodded reluctantly. "Maybe you're right. I suppose it couldn't hurt. Besides, I've been to California. But I don't want to be the one to tell Matthew."

"I'll tell him," Quinn said.

He had a momentary impulse to get up from the table and take his wife into his arms. It had been a long time since he had acted on an impulse like that. But as happened so often, he waited too long. Janice stood up and started clearing away the breakfast dishes. The moment was lost.

Matthew did not take the news well.

"Are you saying no Disneyland?"

"I'm saying that instead of sitting in a cramped airplane for three hours or so, then schlepping around Los Angeles with a couple of million other tourists, you and I and your mother are going to drive across the western United States together as a family and see the town where your grandfather was born."

"Why?"

Kirby swallowed his growing anger. "Because it's a part of our country none of us have ever seen."

"Or ever wanted to," Matt added.

"It's decided, so I don't want to hear any more objections. Go wash your face and we'll drive up to see Grandpa."

"Do we have to?"

"Yes."

If the kid said, 'why?' one more time, Kirby was going to smack him. However, Matthew merely sighed and slouched off toward the bathroom.

2

The Lakeview Nursing Home was situated, appropriately enough, on the eastern shore of Lake Washington, from where that body of water was clearly in sight. It was less than an hour's drive from the Kirbys' home in suburban Seattle, but on this fine June morning it seemed much longer to Quinn Kirby.

The ride seemed to take longer because in essence, if not in fact, he was alone. Janice sat silently next to him being careful not to let their elbows touch across the arm rest that separated the seats. She gazed steadily out the window on her side of the Chrysler New Yorker, apparently absorbed in the view of new housing tracts going up and groves of Douglas fir coming down. Matthew sat in the back seat sulking and muttering under his breath. Kirby punched the radio to a station that played electronic rock music and drove grimly on, wondering whether he was doing the right thing, or if this was one more mistake in a lifetime of mistakes.

When his father was first stricken ten years ago Kirby had made it a point to drive over and see him at least once a week. As the years dragged by and the old man did not get any better, the frequency of his visits slipped to once a month, then less. He rationalized that his father probably wasn't even aware of his presence, but he could not be sure. As he drove through the well kept grounds and up to the pleasant main building, Kirby realized he had not seen his father since Christmas.

With Janice speaking to him only in monosyllables, and Matthew dragging along as though he were being taken to the dentist, Kirby led his family into the building down a pastel-painted hallway to the old man's room.

The room was small, neat, painted in neutral hospital beige. It had a high hospital bed and a window that looked out over well-tended grounds to the lake. There was a bathroom with stainless steel fixtures. On the wall hung a large print of a snow-capped mountain. A 15-inch color television set rested on a small table. The bureau top held a few personal effects—notebook, pen a wooden-handled spring device for strengthening the grip. All were arranged neatly and geometrically.

The feature that made Carl Kirby's room different from the others was his collection of books. A short shelf above his bed held a dozen volumes, all of them old and battered. They bore titles like *Tractatus de Maleficiis, Doemonum Investigatio, De Monstris et Monstrosis.* They were written in strange languages that Carl Kirby had no way of understanding. Yet he pored over them for endless hours when left alone in his room. Quinn had found them for his father over the years after the old men had scribbled down the titles for him. To the son it was just one more aberration of a declining old man—inexplicable but harmless.

When the Kirbys entered his room the old man sat in a metal and canvas wheelchair with his back to the window. He was only 68 years old, but his face bore the lines of a man fifteen years older.

Quinn turned the wheel chair so his father was facing into the room. Aside from the crippled left hand, which lay in his lap like a dead crab, Carl's body was not in bad shape. The stroke had robbed him of the power of speech and addled his mind. It had short-circuited the motor nerves that controlled his movements, but there were days when he got around quite capably. Regular therapy kept his muscles from atrophying. Some of the more cynical staff members at Lakeview thought the old man could get up and walk any time he really wanted to. They joked that he was searching his ancient occult books for a magic spell to let him fly out of there.

Carl looked now at his son, daughter-in-law, and grandson with veiled eyes. His face held no more expression than a potato.

"Hi, Dad," Kirby said with the false heartiness of a man who knows no one is listening. "How are you? They treating you okay?"

No answer was expected, and none was forthcoming.

"We just thought you'd like to know we're taking a trip back to your home town. Back to Danziger."

Did the old man's eyelid flutter? Did the withered old lips compress for a fractional second?

"Yes, well, we'll tell you all about it when we get back."

The potato was back.

Kirby gave conversation and a desultory shot for twenty minutes while Janice sat is a chair and gazed out the window and Matthew made hopeful gestures toward the television set.

"Well," Kirby said finally, bringing his hands together, "I guess we've taken enough of your time." *Jesus, what a dumb thing to say.* "So we'll be pushing along."

On an impulse he went over and squeezed his father's still solid shoulder, then was immediately embarrassed by this unaccustomed display of affection. He said, "Take care of yourself, Dad. I'll see you soon." That was a lie. Kirby did not plan on coming again before next Christmas. Looking into the veiled eyes he well remembered why he had let six months go by since the last visit.

Carl Kirby's head moved. For a moment his son thought he might be aware of the other people's presence in his room. But then the old man looked through him and beyond him toward his shelf of arcane books. Quinn Kirby took his wife and his son and went out, closing the door softly as he left.

185

3

Carl Kirby's eyes remained fixed on the door after Quinn and his family went out. There was a calendar Scotch-taped there with the daily activities at Lakeview written into the squares. Monday, backgammon lessons. Tuesday, a nature talk with slides. Wednesday, a Dixieland band from the University of Washington. Thursday, a pool tournament. Friday . . .

What difference did it make? Carl Kirby did not participate in any of the Lakeview's group activities. He could not pull together the concentration or the coordination required. He did not object when Miss Pierce wheeled him out to watch one event or another. He would sit placidly and watch whoever had come to entertain the inmates. But the scenes he saw were happening in other places, other times.

As he stared now the calendar with its stick-on happy faces and bright crayon doodles wavered and faded. The door behind it dimmed to a foggy outline. With powers that were buried deep in his blasted mind, Carl Kirby pulled together fragments of memory. Other places, other times.

Danziger, Wisconsin. A place name out of the past. Quinn, his only son, had said he was going back to Danziger. No, not *back to*. Quinn Kirby had never been to the town. Carl himself had never gone back. Not since the day he left it forever when he was twelve years old. There was no reason to go back. Plenty of reasons not to. It was a bad time. A bad town.

But not always. When Carl Kirby was about the age of little Matthew, back in—what? 1927, '28—times were good. The whole valley was prosperous, and the Kirby farm was one of the richest around Danziger. Carl was an only child, unusual among farm families, but his had been a difficult birth, and his mother was unable to bear more sons. Fortunately, Henry and Freya Kirby could afford hired hands to work on the place, doing the jobs that usually called for a large family.

Life was good back then, and his childhood, what Carl could remember of those early years, was an idyll.

Then everything went bad.

There was the Great Depression, of course. The Kirbys' money

186

disappeared, they had to let the hired hands go and could no longer work the land. The bank eventually took their farm. But things like that were happening to everybody all across the country, so at least you weren't alone. They could have survived.

But Danziger's misfortunes did not stop with the Depression. The spring rains did not come, and such crops as there were withered in the fields. A deadly strain of influenza, the worst since 1918, hit the town, striking down one person out of every five. The small glove factory went broke, costing many jobs. In closing the factory they dumped the tanning fluids, which seeped down into the water table and polluted the wells. People who were not sick with influenza were poisoned by the water.

So wretched was the plight of Danziger and its people that the surrounding towns, poor as they were, felt themselves lucky in comparison. They isolated their less fortunate neighbors, feeling somehow that the Danzigers could bring the town's misfortune with them if they resettled. They spoke of the wretched village in guarded voices, and they gave it a new name.

Damntown.

As the Depression wore on the town sunk deeper into its mire of despair. Half the people were sick, many were hungry, and all were wretchedly poor. There was not enough medicine, little to eat, and nothing to hope for. The Kirbys, with their farm gone, shared a falling-down frame house alongside the railroad tracks with two other families. By the time he was twelve, Carl had a wisdom beyond his years. Childhood was forever behind him. He was hungry and hurting all the time, like the town itself. Hungry and bitter and without hope.

Into this pit of gloom came the stranger. No one saw him arrive, no one knew from whence he came. One day he was simply there. There was even disagreement about exactly what he looked like. All you knew for sure was that wherever he went he commanded attention.

He moved right in as though he belonged there, and the way he carried himself, nobody was about to challenge him. He took the best room in the New Brandenburg Hotel and he made it his business to meet everybody in town who still had any respect from his neighbors.

The fate of Danziger was sealed the day the stranger gave these men his proposition.

187

*   *   *

Carl Kirby's memory shattered at that point, the fragments flying apart like an exploded jigsaw puzzle. He struggled to hold on as the pieces whirled away. Here was the black storm. There the town's bargain. The judgement. The break for freedom. The trees. The darkness. Running. Terror. Pain. Blood.

The broken pieces spun past him and away, out of reach, making no sense. He fought to pull the picture back together, but always in his path were the dogs. The terrible dogs.

Carl's good right hand worked fiercely—clenching, releasing, clenching. The coiled spring of the gripper creaked with each fist. The wooden handles clacked one against the other. His chest heaved, his throat hurt. Someone was shouting, screaming in his room.

Miss Pierce pushed open the door and hurried to the old man who sat squeezing the hand exerciser and shouting hoarsely at nothing. At fifty, she was eighteen years younger than Carl Kirby, but she spoke to him soothingly, as though to an agitated child.

"Carl, Carl, easy now. It's all right. Everything's all right. Here, give me that."

She took the hand gripper from his fingers. He continued to clench and unclench his fist.

"Now give me your arm."

The old man continued to shout, but he did not protest as Miss Pierce pushed up the loose sleeve of his flannel shirt, swabbed the inside of his elbow, and inserted the hollow-pointed needle.

"It's all right, Carl. Just take it easy. Rest now. Rest."

The sedating fluid entered his veins. The spinning memory fragments receded into a soft gray distance. The shouting voice quieted. Everything went away as a warmth stole over him. Everything but the dogs. The terrible dogs.

4

The drive across the northwestern United States turned out to be not as deadly as Quinn Kirby had feared. They took a leisurely five days to cover something less than 2,000 miles. He confined his cigarette breaks to rest stops, and Janice showed her appreciation by smiling at him now and then.

His main concern was Matthew. As was the case with his father, patience was not a strong suit with the boy under the best of conditions. Kirby feared that confinement in the back seat of the New Yorker might push him to violence. He kept the boy sedated with Slurpys and the lurid comic books he favored. Then on a one-day detour to Yellowstone Park the proximity of live bears made him forget, at least temporarily, that he was losing Disneyland.

By the time they reached the Badlands in South Dakota the Kirby family was traveling in comparative harmony. Matthew was lost in his grisly comic books and Janice seemed to take an honest interest in the spectacular scenery.

Stopping at motels was a welcome diversion. There was always a television set in the room, often a cocktail lounge nearby, and usually video games to keep Matt busy as long as his father's supply of quarters held out.

By the time they crossed the Mississippi River from Minnesota into Wisconsin, Kirby was feeling pretty pleased with himself. He had taken hold of the reins and made a decision that just might save his marriage and keep his family from disintegrating. Matthew had not mentioned Disneyland since Wyoming, Janice had actually put some verve into her lovemaking last night in the Holiday Inn, and Kirby himself was feeling a whole lot better. The strain of the recent days was lifting, and driving the New Yorker gave him something non-taxing to occupy his mind. Best of all, there had been no more of the dreams since they left home. No dogs.

They turned off the Interstate just beyond Tomah and headed north on the smaller state and county roads. Kirby made several wrong turns, and had to backtrack along rolling vistas of dairy farms and generous stands of timber.

"Darn map's all screwed up," he commented, trying yet another unmarked turnoff. Wisely, Janice did not suggest they stop to ask someone. In the time-honored tradition of men the world over, Kirby would fight strange roads and hidden byways forever before he would ask some stranger for directions.

Shortly before sundown his persistence was rewarded. A wooden sign at the side of the road, listing slightly to the left, read: *Danziger 5 Mi.*

Kirby flashed a smile of triumph at his wife and followed the bumpy road up a small grade to a crest that overlooked the valley below. There, under a layer of mist, spread out like a model town in somebody's basement, lay Danziger.

Kirby pulled the car over and stopped. He rolled down the window and drew a deep breath, as though he would inhale the moment. "How about that?" he said.

"It's . . . pretty," Janice said.

"Pretty? It's perfect. From up here it looks like something out of . . . out of . . ." he searched for a simile. "Norman Rockwell," he came up with.

He opened the door and got out of the car. "Come on out here and take a look."

Janice unbuckled her seat belt and climbed out.

"You too, Matt. Come on."

The boy followed without a lot of enthusiasm. Looking at scenery was not his idea of a great time.

The family walked together away from the road and through the ankle-high grass toward a thicket of gray birch. Kirby stopped at the highest point of the hill and gathered his family to him. He fairly glowed with a sense of togetherness—his wife on one side of him and his son on the other. At that moment, with the quiet, toylike town laid out below them, he felt confident that they were going to make it, and all be better people for this experience.

"It looks so peaceful," Janice said.

"Boring," Matthew translated, although his heart was not in the complaint.

"Just think," Kirby said, "no freeways, no air pollution, no street crime. It will be like spending a week in a different country. We'll have a chance to think about who we are and where we want to go with our lives."

"Well," Janice said after a short hesitation, "it's worth a try."

There was no warning for what happened next. No sense of

foreboding, no uneasiness, no tingling of Kirby's nerves. Just the sudden explosion from the birch grove of three huge, black dogs.

They loped, unnaturally silent, across the field toward the three people standing at the edge of the knoll. Teeth flashed, droplets of saliva sprayed as the dogs came on.

Matthew saw them first. "Hey!"

Kirby turned to look and his blood froze. The three dogs charged directly toward them. There was no mistaking their hostile intent. Had Janice not seized his arm Kirby would have stood rooted to the spot until the dogs were upon him.

"Quinn!" she cried. "Come on!"

Freed from his paralysis, Kirby ran with his wife and son toward the car. The dogs veered to head them off.

It was the old nightmare again, only this time it was real. Kirby's feet pounded the ground, the breath ripped from his lungs as he ran for his life. He was incapable of giving a thought to his family. The three ravenous dogs, coming at him, horribly silent filled his mind, leaving no room for anything else.

He hit the side of the New Yorker and scrabbled the door open. Only then did he remember Janice and Matthew. He shouted incoherently for them to hurry, holding the door open while every instinct screamed at him to jump inside and lock it.

Janice, half-carrying, half-dragging Matthew, stumbled past him and into the car, clambering past the steering wheel, pulling the boy with her. Kirby dived in after them, slamming the door as the first of the dogs hit the metal with a resounding thump. In an instant the other two animals were at the car. Their claws raking the door, their dreadful teeth bit at the safety glass of the window.

Shaking like a man with palsy, Kirby fumbled the key into the ignition lock and fired the engine to life. The dogs backed away, their eyes burned with a hatred no animal should know. Then, as though on a signal from an unseen handler, they turned and trotted back to the birch thicket and disappeared among the darkening trees.

Sitting in the locked car, his hands frozen to the steering wheel, Quinn Kirby did not hear what his wife was saying to him. He was staring at the greasy streaks left on the window glass by the dogs' teeth.

5

Kirby eased the New Yorker to the curb on the main street of Danziger, which was called, what else, Main Street. He leaned back against the head rest and breathed slowly in and slowly out, letting his pulse subside gradually to normal.

Janice sat next to him, saying nothing, watching him carefully.

Matthew leaned forward in the back seat. "What was the *matter* with them, anyway? Those dogs?"

Kirby shuddered, both hands still gripping the steering wheel.

Janice turned in her seat and spoke to the boy in a soft, controlled voice. "They were probably abandoned out in the woods by their people. Dogs can go back to the wild state then, and run in packs."

"Wow. They really looked like they wanted to rip us up, huh, Dad?"

Kirby swallowed. His throat felt like it had been caught in a noose. He said, "It's over now. They're gone. Let's forget about it."

"What were they," the boy persisted, "Dobermans? They looked bigger. And meaner. Pit Bulls?"

"Matthew, please . . ."

"You heard your father," Janice said. "Let's drop the dogs, okay?"

Kirby shot his wife a grateful look. Beneath the light jacket he wore for driving his shirt was soaked through with sweat and pasted to his flesh. He shivered, then sat up and took a good look around at the town for the first time.

Danziger at sunset was not a busy place. No more than half a dozen cars were visible, moving or parked, along the three blocks of Main Street. The visible cars were very old. Relics. Maybe there was a classic car convention in town or something, he thought.

Pedestrians were as scarce as motor vehicles. A few people strolled the sidewalks. They glanced curiously at the New Yorker and its occupants, but did not linger. The people were of all ages from young children to the elderly. They acted normally enough, yet there was something just a shade off key about them. Something wrong.

"Look at the way these people dress," Janice said. "It looks like a Hard Times party."

"Probably not many of them take *Vogue* or *Gentlemen's Quarterly*," Kirby said. He regretted the sarcastic remark as soon as it came out of his mouth, but it was too late. He excused it on the grounds that his mind was still jittery from the confrontation up on the hill with the dogs.

He groped for something to change the subject. A sign on a building across the street caught his eye. It was the tallest building on the block—three stories. The sign was printed in black letters on the end of a marquee that overhung the sidewalk. *New Brandenburg Hotel.*

"We're in luck," he said. "We came to a stop right across from the hotel."

"That place looks yucky," said Matthew. "Can't we find a Holiday Inn?"

"No," said Kirby in a tone that ended the discussion. "We are staying right here at the New Brandenburg Hotel." More gently he added, "We can stay at a Holiday Inn anywhere."

"What time do you have?" Janice asked. She was squinting at her dime-size wristwatch and tapping it with a fingertip. "My watch seems to have stopped."

Kirby checked the face of his quartz-crystal Seiko. The LCD rectangle was blank. "Mine too. I must need a new battery. This one didn't last long."

Leaving the car where it was, the Kirby family crossed the street to the hotel. With so little traffic there was no need to look for a crosswalk. The other people on the street gave them mildly interested glances, but continued on their unhurried way.

The lobby of the New Brandenburg Hotel would never be mistaken for a Holiday Inn. The ceiling was way up there in semi-darkness. Marble pillars grew like stone trees from the tiled floor. Couches and overstuffed chairs of dark brown leather were positioned along the walls and around the pillars. No one sat in any of them. No one, nothing, moved in the lobby.

The registration desk was heavy dark oak. The man behind the desk was so motionless that at first he looked like a wax figure. His face was round, pale and smooth, the eyes small and dark, like raisins pushed into a dough ball. As the Kirbys approached he became animated. His face split into a welcoming smile. He placed two pudgy hands on the counter and cocked his head to one side.

The wall behind it was sectioned into pigeon holes, each one

193

labeled with a room number. On the desk was an open registration book with an old pen and inkwell beside it. A silver call bell rested beside the pen.

"Talk about state of the art," Janice said under her breath.

"Isn't it great," said Kirby, his enthusiasm returning. "Like stepping into another time."

"I hope they at least got a Coke machine?" Matthew piped.

"I'm sure they do," Kirby told him. "Let's get checked in first."

They stopped at the desk and the round-faced man regarded each of them in turn with a benevolent smile. He wore a dark suit with pin stripes, a maroon tie, and a pearl gray vest.

"Hello there, folks, and welcome to the New Brandenburg. You *will* be staying with us, I hope?"

"That's why we're here," said Kirby, trying to match the man's joviality.

"That's wonderful. Wonderful," the man said with what Kirby thought was an excess of good cheer. "I'm Armand Esterhaus. I manage the place here. Anything you want, anything at all, call on me."

"Well . . . thank you. My name's Kirby. This is my wife and son." Why, he wondered, was he introducing himself to a hotel manager. Maybe it was just small town, middle west friendliness. "Right now, we'd like a room. Something with an extra bed for Matthew here."

Esterhaus leaned across the desk and beamed at Matt. "A fine looking young man. We'll be glad to accommodate you. A nice room on the third floor, right in front. Three-sixteen. Nice double bed for the grownups and a day bed for the boy. Has its own private bath too."

Janice shot him a look, which Kirby ignored. "That sounds fine. Uh, what's the rate?"

"That's seven dollars a night."

"You said seven dollars?"

"I can give you one for five, but it's in the rear . . ."

"No, no, that's fine. It's just that seven dollars . . . well . . ."

Esterhaus's heavy lips stretched into a smile, showing small, very white teeth. "I know, I'll bet your from the city."

"Well, Seattle, actually."

"Way out there. My, my. I dare say you'll find quite a few things different here in Danziger from what you're used to."

"That's what we're hoping," Kirby said.

The manager turned the registration book around and handed Kirby the pen. "Got a fresh new page all ready for you," he said.

Kirby looked at the old pen and turned it over in his hand. He smiled at Janice and dipped the point in the inkwell. He signed, *Mr. & Mrs. Quinn Kirby, Seattle, Wash.*

Esterhaus reversed the book and read the name. He looked up at Kirby with very dark eyes sunk deep below heavy black brows. "Kirby . . . Kirby. The name has a familiar ring. You ever live in Danziger?"

"No, but my father was born here."

The round-faced man rubbed his hands together. The fingers were thick and smooth. "Then this is something of a homecoming, is it?"

"In a way, I guess," Kirby said.

"If there's anything I can help you with while you're in town, just say the word. I've been here long enough to know my way around Danziger." He laughed, a rumble from deep in the barrel chest. "Not that you have to be here all that long to know the place."

Matthew tugged at his father's coat sleeve. "My boy wants to know if you have a Coke machine?" Kirby said.

"There's a cooler back by the stairs. You need a nickel to get the lid open."

"A nickel?" Matt said.

"Thanks," Kirby cut in. "These kids have to have their soda pop."

"I know how it is," said Esterhaus. He plucked a key, attached to a fiberboard number tag, from one of the pigeonholes and handed it to Kirby. "Hope you can manage your own luggage. I have a boy usually handles that, but he didn't show up today."

"No problem. We're parked across the street. Will it be all right there?"

"Why don't you just pull her around in front. There's never a parking problem in Danziger."

While Janice and Matthew waited inside Kirby crossed the street and brought the Chrysler around in front of the hotel. As Esterhaus had promised, there was plenty of space to park at the curb, and no inhibiting signs.

As the sun set the street lights came on along Main. They were old fashioned metal poles with incandescent bulbs that cast small yellow pools of light at regular intervals along the sidewalk. No need here for the bright sodium vapor lights used in high-crime areas.

Kirby was liking the town better all the time.

He carried two suitcases into the hotel, noting that most of the businesses along Main Street were dark. An early to bed town. Well, they had not come here for the night life.

Esterhaus beamed and nodded as Kirby reentered the lobby. The man was certainly friendly enough. And he seemed sincerely to want to be helpful. And yet, there was something about him . . . something that made the hair prickle at the back of Kirby's neck. He would try to get over his city-bred suspicion.

Janice and Matthew were standing at the rear of the lobby waiting for him. Matt held a Coca-Cola bottle in his hand and was staring at it.

"They didn't have any cans," the boy said. "Just these funny green bottles."

Kirby took a look at it. "That's the way Coke used to come," he said. "Maybe it still does around here."

"And it really did cost a nickel," Janice said.

"So, enjoy."

"Did you happen to notice what time it is when you came in?"

"I don't think I saw a clock in the lobby."

"That's funny."

"It's sunset, that ought to be close enough. We're not catching a plane. Where's the elevator?"

"That's another thing. There isn't any."

"No elevator?" Kirby frowned momentarily, then relaxed. "But why should there be. It's only three floors. We can manage two flights of stairs. If we wanted elevators we could have gone to—"

"Disneyland," Matthew supplied.

"Come on," Kirby said, and led the way up the stairs.

Down at the registration desk Armand Esterhaus looked toward the stairs as the Kirbys climbed up and out of sight. The dark little eyes were hidden in their deep sockets. The smile he wore now was not a smile Quinn Kirby would have found inviting.

6

While night dropped its curtain over the Wisconsin town of Danziger, the sun had not yet set in California. Carl Kirby lay on his side in bed and stared out the window at a grove of Douglas fir that stood at the edge of Lake Washington. The pill they gave him after lunch had worn off, and the veil that closed off a part of his mind fluttered and almost lifted. He knew . . . somehow he just *knew* that he had to remember . . . to think about when he was a boy. His parents. And the town. And the stranger. It was important now. Deathly important.

Danziger was a dying town in 1933 when the stranger came. The people were like separate cells of a doomed body, each of them slowly wasting until at last the town itself must perish. They sat in their cold, decaying homes and stared at the walls. Or they trudged the grimy streets like walking dead with no direction, no destination. The glove factory was closed. The bank was busted. The five-and-ten had quit. The feed and supply store was open only three days a week. The New Brandenburg Hotel had only one floor open. The Graphic was boarded up and had not shown a picture since *Hell's Angels* two years before.

The people of the town were silent. They had little left to say. They averted their gaze from one another on the street, not wanting to read new sorrows in the eyes of old friends. Their present was bleak, and the future was nonexistent. Then the stranger came.

All of a sudden, the people had something to talk about. The stranger attracted attention because he was so healthy, so prosperous looking . . . so alive. Funny thing, but no two people agreed on exactly what he looked like. Henry Kirby, Carl's father, thought he was a man of the soil like himself, who had done well and somehow escaped the ravages of the Depression. His mother, Freya, saw him as a debonair man of the world. Carl's gullible friend and classmate Wally Mayer thought the newcomer looked a little like Santa Claus. Mr. Isham, the postmaster, told people he resembled Uncle Sam. The disparate impressions of the stranger did not seriously trouble anyone. They all agreed he was an imposing figure, and they all had a distinct feeling that his presence in Danziger was important.

Young Carl Kirby's impression of the stranger was different from anyone's else's. He saw a tall, lean man with dark snapping eyes, a pointed beard, and teeth that were too white and too sharp. A dangerous man. Nobody wanted to hear that, so Carl didn't talk about it.

The stranger called himself Bachman. He traveled alone, and did not invite conversation about his past. Whoever he was, whatever he had been, everyone in town had the feeling they should know him. And his appearance was unquestionably that of a man of substance. Not that he was high-hat or anything, just sort of . . . kingly.

In a week's time he made it his business to meet all the important people in Danziger, the men who had been the leaders of the town in better days, and still commanded respect from their neighbors. Bachman got to know them all, and he talked with each of them about the plight of the town. He had a plan, he said, that just might deliver them from their misery. He would be ready to reveal it shortly, he told them, at a public meeting in the park. He told the men who were the town's leaders he would appreciate it if they could turn out the citizens for the announcement.

Getting the people of Danziger to show up was no problem. Any kind of event to distract them from their troubles was welcome, and everybody was crazy curious about the stranger anyhow. So when the day came—a hot, bright, Saturday in June, the square patch of park in front of the old band shell was filled with the people of Danziger. Henry Kirby, still considered one of the town's leading citizens, had a place in the front row with Freya and young Carl. The chatter of crowd was almost cheerful, harking back to the picnics held there in happier times.

When everyone was assembled, and it did seem like everyone who was not too old or too sick was present, Bachman arrived. He strode across the brown grass wearing a black cloak and a soft black hat with a brim that turned down to shadow his eyes. He was an impressive figure, flashing his smile this way and that as he marched toward the bandstand. A wake of silence followed the stranger as he passed, so that when he reached the front and stepped up on the little stage where the band had played, the crowd was still.

Bachman did not use any kind of microphone or loudspeaker, yet his words carried clearly to the people standing on the very edge of the crowd. His voice was deep and powerful, and he spoke with a mighty conviction.

"I am gratified to see so many citizens of Danziger here today," he said. "I know that coming here was not easy for some of you, and I appreciate your effort. I believe that when you hear what I have to say you will all agree that the trip was worthwhile."

He paused and looked around at the assembled people, many of them sickly, shabby, dispirited. Every person there would swear later that Bachman had looked directly into his eyes.

"Danziger is not a happy town," he continued. "I don't have to tell you of the many misfortunes that have been visited on your community. Most unfairly so, I would add. While your neighbors in Riverton, Johnsburg, Three Forks, and Mortonville ride out the hard times in comparative comfort, Danziger must suffer unspeakable hardships."

A murmur of assent rippled through the listeners as they turned to one another and agreed that they had been most unjustly singled out for punishment.

"There is no rain for your crops, no medicine for your sick, no work for your men, no money to buy food . . . if there were food to buy. People of Danziger, you have been sentenced and punished without even a trial."

The sound of the crowd turned indignant as the truth of the stranger's words sank in. He paused long enough to let each of his listeners build up a healthy resentment.

"My friends, I am here to change that."

Dramatic pause while the people stared and wondered what was coming next.

"I am here to offer you . . . *deliverance*." Bachman made the word ring in the still air.

The stranger scanned the weathered faces of the people standing before him. "Can he do it?' you are asking yourselves. A fair question. You are not simple folk to be taken in by a medicine show charlatan. You have heard miraculous promises before. In fact, you can hear them every Sunday spoken by men who I see here today. Men who tell you they have a private pipeline to the Power." The stranger's next words thundered like a cannon shot. "*They lie!*"

There was a stirring in the crowd as the people turned to seek out Reverend Steiner on one side and Father Gunnigan on the other. The clergymen shifted uncomfortably in their seats.

More quietly, almost in a whisper, the stranger said, "And you know they lie. You need only look at your lives to see what 'miracles' they have wrought." The volume of his voice began to rise again. "I have not come to you with empty promises. You have had enough of promises. I am prepared to give you proof. Proof that I can do what I say I can. *Watch!*"

Bachman thrust a forefinger dramatically upward. The faces of the crowd followed his gesture. As they stared strange, dirt-colored clouds streaked in from nowhere to darken the blue June sky. They roiled and churned like the surface of a murky cauldron. Cool, fat drops of rain began to fall.

The people of Danziger shouted with joy at the first rain of the spring. They held their faces and their upturned palms to it, reveling in the wetness.

And then, as suddenly as it started, the rain stopped. The heavy clouds dissolved and sifted away to nothing. The people groaned with disappointment. Their eyes returned to the stranger on the bandstand.

"A sample," he said, "of deliverance. Rain for your fields, renewed health for your sick, all the money any of you will need. Comfort, contentment, freedom from all your problems. All this can be yours."

It was Carl's father Henry Kirby who rose from his chair in the front row and spoke the question they were all thinking. "What is the price?"

The stranger smiled. "A good and fair question. An intelligent question. Of course there is a price. Not an exorbitant one, but surely a price. My . . . let us call it my *organization* requires a head-quarters from which to operate. We have selected Danziger. In return for all we are prepared to give you, we ask in return only that we be given control." He spaced the next words out slowly. "Complete . . . control . . . of . . . your . . . town."

"Wait!" The cry came from Rev. Steiner. He began to move forward, as did Father Gunnigan from the other side of the crowd.

"Don't listen to him," called the priest.

"He will cheat you," cried the minister.

Bachman extended his arm with his hand palm-out, traffic cop fashion. "Hold."

The two churchmen stopped in their tracks.

"You two men have had months, years to present your case, to make your feeble pleas and mouth your impotent promises. You have delivered nothing but more misery. Here today it is my turn.

Let the people of Danziger decide who has made them the better offer." He spread his arms to encompass all present. "Is that not fair?"

Nodding heads and mumbled approval.

With a flashing smile of triumph at the clergymen, Bachman turned his attention to Henry Kirby and the other leaders of the town who sat in the first row.

"You men have been designated to speak for your neighbors. Your word is trusted, your judgment respected. Now . . . what is it to be?"

The men conferred quietly for a minute, then Henry spoke to the stranger. "We'd like to talk it over. We think we ought to hear from Rev. Steiner and Father Gunnigan too before we make a decision."

"By all means, talk it over," said Bachman. "And if you must, go ahead and listen to more pious platitudes from your two unctuous friends. But I must have your decision quickly."

The stranger pointed off behind them. "Look!"

The people turned and gasped. Just outside of town, twisting and writhing like a live thing, was the angry funnel of a tornado. Such a storm was unheard of in Wisconsin, but there was no mistaking what it was.

"I don't have to describe to you people the terrible destruction a twister can bring." Bachman's voice rang over the sudden hollow roar of the storm. "It can level this town and kill everyone in it in seconds."

The tornado moved sinuously from side to side, an enormous deadly snake.

"I can banish that storm as easily as I brought the rain. Or I can let it come."

As though cued by his words, the dark funnel moved closer. There was the bang of an explosion. Splinters and chunks of debris spiraled upward in the whirling cloud.

"Joe Ziegler's barn!" someone cried.

The crowd shifted and there was a babble of voices.

"Too bad," said Bachman from the bandstand. The power of his presence silenced them all. "But unless it is stopped, your town is doomed."

"All right," said Henry Kirby. "We'll meet your price."

"Good," said the stranger. "There is only one more thing."

201

The people standing before him murmured, but their attention was on the tornado, which continued its deadly dance, seemingly eager to pounce.

"No one," said Bachman, pausing to look around and let his words sink in, "no living person must ever leave Danziger." His lips twisted into a parody of a smile. "But then, with the benefits I can guarantee—health, wealth, security for all time—who in his right mind would want to leave?"

The smile faded slowly. Bachman looked into the eyes of each of the men in the front row. "Agreed?"

One by one, the men nodded their assent, but averted their eyes from one another.

"Your leaders have spoken," said Bachman, "but since each of you in the town of Danziger is a part of the bargain, there must be no question that you all agree. There must be no single voice raised in opposition."

Fearfully, out of the sides of their eyes, the people of Danziger looked for Rev. Steiner and Father Gunnigan. The churchmen were nowhere to be seen.

"They are gone," said Bachman. "Along with their meaningless sermons. If there is no one else to oppose our will, then let the bargain be—"

"No!" The piping voice of 12-year-old Carl Kirby cut through the air like a knife. His parents and the others in the first row stared at him. Those farther back craned to see who had spoken out.

Carl stared straight up at Bachman. "I know who you are. I don't want you here."

The stranger seemed to swell where he stood. He glowered down at the boy. "Will someone silence this child? His parents?"

The angry funnel writhed and rumbled behind the people.

Henry Kirby put a hand on Carl's shoulder. He stood straight and looked up at the scowling stranger. "My boy is right. To bargain with you would be a terrible mistake. I change my vote to stand with my son."

On Carl's other side his mother, pale with her illness, moved closer. "I too," she said.

The tornado roared like a ravening beast. Bachman swept the crowd with eyes of fire.

"*It is now up to the rest of you to Choose. Silence this family or die.*"

202

*　　*　　*

Carl Kirby twisted and groaned in his bed in the Lakeview Nursing Home. The curse of Danziger was closing in on him again. He had to do something. He had to . . . to . . .

The blackness seeped in from the edges of the old man's mind and blotted out everything. He slept. But he did not rest.

7

The Kirby family climbed the two flights of carpeted stairs to their floor in the New Brandenburg Hotel. Quinn went first, carrying the two suitcases, trying to pump up enthusiasm in his wife and son. Janice followed, looking around with distaste at the flower-patterned wallpaper, the closed, silent doors up and down the halls, the little dust balls that hid in the corners. Matthew brought up the rear, taking the steps reluctantly, one at a time like a boy on his way to the gallows.

The hallway on the third floor was a duplicate of the hallway on the second. Quiet, empty, musty, dimly lit by low-wattage bulbs spaced at regular intervals. Kirby stopped at the top and waited for his wife and son.

"Exciting place," said Janice.

"What is it, haunted?" chimed Matthew.

"Let's give it a chance, shall we?" said Kirby. "So it's quiet, and maybe not as modern as the Holiday Inns. Just because something is different doesn't make it bad."

They walked down the hall, watching the room numbers. Kirby stopped suddenly and turned to grin at his family. "Come here and check this out."

Janice and Matt came over to the alcove where Kirby was stand-ing. Mounted on the wall was an old telephone with a hornlike mouthpiece and separate receiver hanging from a hook on the side.

"Is it real?" Janice asked.

"Where's the dial?" Matt wondered.

Kirby lifted the earpiece from the black prongs and listened.

"*Number, please*," said a filtered female voice.

"Just testing," Kirby said, and replaced the receiver. "How about that? An old-fashioned real live operator asked me for a number."

"How can you get a number without dialing?" Matt said.

Janice looked weary. "That's fascinating, but do you think we could find our room?"

"Don't you think it's kind of romantic?"

"Sure," Janice said. "I just hope we've got an indoor toilet."

Kirby blew out an exasperated breath through his nose and con-tinued down the hallway. He found number 316, shoved the key into the lock, and pushed open the door.

The room was dark. He felt around on the wall next to the door until he found a pushbutton lightswitch. He depressed the top button and a shaded overhead light came on.

The room that greeted the Kirbys was not promising. It had a double bed with a frayed chenille spread, a metal day bed, two thinly padded arm chairs, a bureau, and a writing table. There was a floor lamp between the chairs. A folding screen stood against one wall. A forest scene was amateurishly painted across the screen's three panels.

Kirby pulled out the drawer in the table to find several sheets of Stationary with an idealized drawing of the New Brandenburg, a pen and inkwell, a penny, and a crumpled Baby Ruth wrapper.

"No Bible," he said. "The Gideon Society must be slipping."

He walked across the room to the tiny closet and rattled the coat hangers. Nothing there. He tried the door opposite the closet. It opened into the bathroom.

Janice wrinkled her nose. "The room smells like it's been closed for years. I don't suppose we have air conditioning?"

"Better than that," Kirby said with forced joviality. "We have a real window that opens." He shoved the window up in its frame and looked down on Main Street. All the store fronts were dark now. Nothing moved. The pale circles of light from the street lamps fell on empty sidewalks.

"Hey, there's no television set," Matthew complained.

"It won't hurt any of us to do without the boob tube for a few days," Kirby told him. He turned away from the window and walked to the bureau where an old wooden cathedral Philco stood. "At least there's a radio."

"That's a *radio?*"

Kirby stroked the varnished wood surface. "This is what they used to look like before they all went digital and high tech."

Matthew wrinkled his nose, unconvinced.

Janice turned down the spread and blankets on the bed. "At least the sheets are clean. I hope the bathroom's big enough." She walked through the door and snapped on the light. "Quinn, there's no shower in here."

He joined her and looked around at the porcelain sink, toilet, and old bathtub that stood on four clawed legs. He flushed the toilet, then tried the faucets, hot and cold.

"The plumbing works. What do you need with a shower?"

"I always take showers. I hate sitting in my own used bath water."

"Rough it," he said.

He left her frowning at the bath tub and went back out into the other room. Matthew was standing at the bureau fiddling with the knobs on the old radio. "I can't get anything," he complained.

"Let me try," Kirby said, moving the boy aside. He adjusted the volume and slowly turned the dial. All that came through the speaker was static until he found a faint station with some tinny sounding music. "There," he proclaimed.

"What's that supposed to be?"

A voice cut in on the music. *"From the beautiful Mayfair Room of the fabulous Bedford Hotel in the heart of downtown Milwaukee the Mutual Broadcasting Company brings you the listenable, danceable rhythms of Hal Kemp and his orchestra . . ."*

Kirby leaned closer to the speaker as the voice faded into static. "I'll be damned, a big band remote broadcast. I didn't think they did things like that any more."

"Sheesh!" said Matthew.

"Go brush your teeth and get ready for bed," said his mother.

The music of Hal Kemp and his orchestra faded in and out for the next fifteen minutes, finally giving way to a crackling hiss of static. Kirby snapped off the old Philco.

"I guess that's it for the night."

"Why would we only get one station?"

"Beats me. Maybe the hotel doesn't have much of an antenna."

"You need an antenna for radio?"

"Hell, I don't know. I'm no engineer."

"You don't have to bite my head off."

Matthew came out of the bathroom wearing his Spiderman pajamas. Kirby and Janice cut off the burgeoning argument.

Once Matthew was tucked into the day bed Quinn and Janice sat for a while making desultory conversation. He tried the radio again without success.

"Might as well turn in," he said, faking a yawn.

Janice took a long slow look around the room. "Might as well," she agreed.

They climbed into their own sides of the soft double bed where they lay for a long time before falling asleep.

Kirby was intensely aware of the breathing of each of them. Janice's came in exasperated little puffs. Matt produced a series of heavy sighs and half-stifled groans. Kirby kept his own breath controlled and shallow, so he could listen. Their breathing, he realized, was so noticeable because there was not another earthly sound to be heard inside the hotel or out.

No radios. No plumbing. No loud voices from other rooms. No footsteps. No traffic. No dogs barking. Nothing. Only the breathing of the three people in Room 316. A crushing, suffocating silence settled in. A silence with an unsettling undercurrent beyond normal sensory range. The silence kept Quinn Kirby awake deep into the night.

8

Kirby awoke poorly rested and on edge the next morning. The bedclothes were in a tangle. Janice was not in bed with him. He sat up as she came back from the bathroom. She did not look happy.

A cool breeze blowing in through the open window chilled the room.

"I'm hungry," Matt announced.

"We're all hungry," Kirby said. "Get dressed and we'll find some-place to have breakfast."

They dressed with a minimum of conversation and headed downstairs.

The huge lobby was as empty of other guests as it had been the night before. Outside the morning sun brightened Main Street, but the lobby still held deep shadows in the corners. Armand Esterhaus smiled at them from behind the registration desk, looking exactly as fresh as he had the night before.

"Doesn't that man ever sleep?" Janice muttered under her breath.

After the Good Mornings were exchanged Kirby asked the manager, "Can you recommend a good place for breakfast? We're all famished."

"We used to have an excellent dining room right here in the New Brandenburg. Unfortunately, it is closed for renovation. However, the Royal Badger, right across the Main Street, has about the best food in town."

Kirby thanked him and led his family out of the hotel and across the quiet street. Traffic again was at a minimum, and the only vehicles in sight were older than Kirby. There was again the scattering of oddly dressed strollers on the sidewalk. No one in town seemed in a hurry to get anywhere.

The name of the Royal Badger Restaurant was lettered in gilt script across a plate glass window. A green velvet curtain was drawn across the lower half of the window. Nothing of the interior could be seen.

"I wonder if it's listed in the Michelin Guide," Janice said.

"I hope they've got pancakes," Matthew put in.

"Whatever they've got, you'll eat it and like it," Kirby told them both. "Let's go in."

The interior of the Royal Badger was divided into two sections. The first, nearest the entrance, had a counter along one wall, and square tables with red and white checkered cloths. The tables were unoccupied. Beyond an arch at the rear of the restaurant was another room, dark now, that was apparently used for the dinner hour. Booths and an unoccupied bar could be seen through the archway.

There was no one sitting at the tables. Two men at the counter looked from their coffee and followed the Kirbys with their eyes.

"Rush hour," Janice muttered.

A woman with marcelled hair, wearing a blue and white uniform dress, smiled at them from behind the cash register. "Just sit any-where, folks. Menus are on the tables. I'll be with you in a minute."

Kirby selected a table and they sat. There was a chromed napkin holder, tall glass salt and pepper shakers, a sugar dispenser, mustard and ketchup pots, and a menu. Kirby picked up the card and glanced at the entries. His jaw dropped.

"Jesus, look at these prices." He passed the menu to Janice.

"I can't believe this. Stack of Pancakes fifteen cents. Ham and eggs fifty cents. Steak and eggs sixty cents. Is it a joke?"

The girl from the cash register came to the table. She placed thick mugs before the adults and poured coffee without being asked.

"Do you have Sweet 'n' Low?" Janice said.

The girl blinked at her. "Excuse me?"

"Never mind. I'll use sugar this time."

The girl gave her a puzzled smile and blinked again. She licked the point of a stubby pencil and poised it over her check pad. "What'll it be for breakfast, Mr. Kirby?"

"You know my name?"

"Sure. Small town, not many visitors. Welcome to Danziger."

"Well . . . thank you." He tapped the card with a forefinger. "Is this the real menu?"

"Sure. Anything wrong with it?"

"The prices seem kind of . . . low."

"I suppose we are, compared to the city. I guess you won't complain about that, though, huh?"

"No complaints," said Kirby. He ordered steak and eggs for himself and Janice, pancakes with a side of sausage (fifteen cents) for Matt.

"I'm going to get a newspaper," he said, and walked to the counter where there were a stack of *Milwaukee Journals*. He dropped a quarter on the glass and started back to his table.

"Mr. Kirby," the girl called, "you forgot your change."

"Change?"

The girl bonged the cash register, took out two dimes and two pennies, and dropped them into his palm.

Kirby was still staring at the coins when he got back to the table. "You won't believe what a newspaper costs here."

Janice was staring at the folded *Journal*. She took it from under his arm. "Never mind what it costs, look at what it says."

She spread out the newspaper on the table and they both read the headlines: *Dry Era End Approaches as Two More States Ratify 21st, Italy Threatens to Quit League of Nations, Roosevelt Urges Global Non-Aggression Pacts.*

The Kirbys looked at each other.

"Prohitition?"

"League of Nations?"

"Roosevelt?"

"Look at the date," Janice said.

It read *June 17, 1933.*

Kirby forced a grin. "I've heard of towns being behind the times, but this is a little extreme."

"I don't like it," Janice said. "Gives me the creeps."

"Well, here comes your sixty-cent steak and eggs. Maybe that will help you adjust."

They finished their breakfast in uneasy silence. Janice even forgot to fan the air when Kirby lit his after breakfast cigarette. When Kirby paid the bill he was assured that it did indeed come to $1.65, including the two coffees and a glass of milk for Matt. He left a fifty cent tip on the table and felt a little giddy when they walked out into the sunshine.

Up the street, in what seemed to be the center of the town was a small square park. The grass was lush and green, tall shade trees provided shelter. At one end was a statue of a World War I dough-boy, at the other a white painted wooden bandstand.

"Look at that," said Kirby. "Band concerts in the park. You won't find that many places today."

"I believe it," Janice said.

They strolled on up Main Street, looking into the store windows as they went.

"Those clothes," Janice said. "They're years and years out of date. But, they're *new*. What's going on, Quinn?"

"I don't know. Look at the signs in that barbarshop. Fitch Shampoo. Lucky Tiger Hair Tonic. I don't think they even make that stuff any more."

The Graphic Theater had a sign in the box office: *Open 6:45 P.M.*

"Look what's playing," Janice said.

"Yeah. *Hell's Angels.*"

"And not a remake."

Kirby studied the posters featuring Ben Lyon and Jean Harlow. "Nope," he said, "it's the original."

"I don't like it, Quinn. There's something wrong about this place. Let's go back to the hotel."

"Are we going to leave?" Matthew asked hopefully.

"No," said Kirby. "We're going to enjoy ourselves right here in Danziger if it kills us."

*   *   *

Armand Esterhaus was in his customary position behind the desk when the Kirbys returned.

"So. Have a little look around our town, did you? What do you think of Danziger?"

"I'm confused," Kirby said. "We had breakfast for a price too low to believe. There are nothing but old cars on the street. All the clothes in the stores, and on the people for that matter, are long out of date. The theater's playing a movie that's more than fifty years old. What's going on?"

Esterhaus chuckled. "I suppose I should have told you about it before. It's Deliverance."

"Deliverance?" Janice repeated. "What's that?"

"Most little towns in the Midwest like Danziger have an annual celebration. They may call it Homecoming or Field Day or Reunion. In Danziger we call ours Deliverance."

"Peculiar choice," Kirby observed.

"We think it fits. On June 17, 1933, a freak tornado threatened to wipe out the town but it was averted at the last minute. Deliverance."

Kirby stared at him. "You celebrate a storm that didn't happen?"

"Well, it was a pretty big thing here. So once a year we try to restore the town back to the way it was back then. The event doesn't draw many tourists, I'll admit, but we're happy you folks came to celebrate with us."

"Yeah, celebrate," Kirby said doubtfully.

"Can we go up to the room?" Janice said.

"Why isn't there any TV?" Matt complained.

"Deliverance," Kirby told him. "Quit complaining and tonight maybe we'll go to a movie."

"Oh, yay," Matt grumbled. "We get to see some old piece of junk that's not even colorized."

"Come on," said Kirby through clenched teeth, and led his disgruntled family to the stairway.

9

They did not, after all, go to the movies that night. Kirby had seen *Hell's Angels* on the classic film channel, Janice had never heard of Ben Lyon, and thought he looked like a wimp, and Matthew was uninterested in anything that was not *Nightmare on Elm Street* or *Police Academy*. Instead, they strolled around the little town, marveling at the authenticity of the 1930s disguise.

The people they met in their wanderings were friendly, but cool. They politely evaded Kirby's attempts to question them about the Deliverance celebration or the event itself.

"Tomorrow's the big day," they said. "You'll get the whole story then."

"Are you sure we want to stay for this thing?" Janice asked as they crossed Main Street for a look into another store window.

"Hey, we're here. We might as well see what their big day is all about."

"It seems kind of morbid to me, dressing up like people long gone and picking, of all times, one of the gloomiest years in the nation's history."

"It's no goofier than, say, celebrating the Day of the Dead in Mexico. They eat candy skulls."

"Yeah?" Matt showed a flicker of interest.

Janice shuddered. "Thanks a lot, Quinn."

"Or what about Mardi Gras? People dress up weird and get drunk out of their minds in honor of a crucifixion."

"It's not the same thing, and you know it."

"I'm just saying that Deliverance in Danziger is not all that outlandish."

"Maybe."

They strolled on up Main and turned onto a silent street of big old houses and sturdy shade trees that closed in overhead to form a kind of dark green cave in the twilight. Kirby grew increasingly uneasy as they walked farther away from the minimal traffic of Main Street. If it would not be admitting defeat, he would have agreed to packing up and getting the hell out of this creepy town.

The street ended at a graceful old brick building that backed up to a grassy slope. At the top of the embankment was the forest. The dark growth of trees unsettled Kirby's nerves.

"Nothing much happening down this way," he said, trying to sound cheerful. "We might as well head back to town where the action is."

"Some action," Matt grumbled.

"Another queer thing," Janice said, "Nobody seems to have any pets in this town. We haven't seen or heard a single cat or dog." She squeezed Kirby's hand when he shivered. "Except for those three vicious things on the way in."

"That was plenty for me," he said.

"Matter of fact, I haven't even seen any birds. Have you?"

"I haven't been looking for birds," he said.

"No, but usually they're just around."

"So maybe the pesticides have finally done them in. Maybe they've gone north for the summer." Kirby did not want to talk about birds, or cats, or, especially, dogs.

Janice stopped suddenly and looked around. "Where's Matt?"

An icy finger touched the base of Kirby's neck. He turned, peering into the gathering gloom around them. "I thought he was right behind us."

"Matthew!" Janice called. There was the fragile, crystal note of panic in her voice.

The old houses, the shade trees, the forest seemed to inch closer, listening.

"*Matthew!*" Kirby's masculine bellow demanded a response if the boy was anywhere within earshot.

"*What?*" The response came from back at the end of the street where the brick building stood.

"What are you doing?" Kirby demanded, the sudden relief he felt making his tone harsher than he intended.

"Just looking at something."

Kirby walked back and climbed the four stone steps leading to a weed-grown path to the vestibule. There he saw Matt fooling around the entrance. The building was old but solidly built. There was no visible damage, except to the gothic arched windows, which were completely broken out. Thick boards were nailed across the double-width front door.

Matthew was rubbing at the tarnished bronze of a plaque at one side of the door. When Kirby leaned close he could read:

St. Paul's First Lutheran Church
1906

Janice came up behind him. "Matthew, don't run off from us that way."

"I didn't run off," the boy said truculently.

Janice was peering over Kirby's shoulder. "What is it?"

"A church. At least it was."

Janice ran her fingers over the boarded-up door. "Why would they close it up?"

"Who knows? Move to a new building, maybe."

"That doesn't seem probable." She stepped back and pointed at the wall above the doorway. "Look at that."

Even in the twilight they could see outlined on the dark weathered brick a lighter patch in the shape of a cross.

"They took down the crucifix," she said.

"What of it?"

"I don't like it, Quinn. This is the only church we've seen, and it's boarded up. I don't like anything about this town. I want to leave."

"When are we going to eat?" Matt demanded.

"Right now," Kirby said, seizing the chance to avoid a show-down with Janice. He herded them down onto the sidewalk and back toward Main Street.

As they turned the corner where at Woolworth's five-and-ten, the street lights blinked on, dropping their pale pools of light onto the sidewalk. Kirby was marching his family grimly toward the Royal Badger restaurant when he heard the small voice behind him.

"Mr. Kirby."

He turned and looked down to see a thin, somber-faced boy of about twelve dressed in an argyle sweater, knickers, a zipper jacket, and cloth cap.

"Yes?"

"I'm Wally Mayer," the boy said.

Kirby shook his head. Was the name supposed to mean something to him?"

"I knew your father."

"You mean your father knew my father."

"No, I did. Carl Kirby and me were best friends."

Kirby decided to humor the kid. "Oh, really?"

"I shouldn't be saying this, but I will because your father was my friend. You've got to get out of Danziger. You and your wife and your little boy."

"What are you talking about?"

Janice and Matthew moved up to stand close to Kirby, family disputes forgotten for the moment.

"Get out while you can." The boy looked nervously over his shoulder. "I hope it's not already too late."

"Just a minute, son—" Kirby began. He was interrupted by two men who hurried across the street.

"Wally," one of the men called. "You were warned about this."

The boy threw one frightened look at the men and took off running up the dark street the Kirby's had just come down.

"Sorry about that, Mr. Kirby," one of the men said. He was a balding, burly man in a leather jacket. "I hope Wally didn't bother you."

"Not really. But he did say some awfully strange things." Kirby looked off after the thin, dark haired man who ran after the boy.

"That's Roy Mayer, the boy's uncle," the first man explained. "I'm Ben Oliphant. Town constable. It's a real shame about young Wally." He tapped the side of his head. "The boy's not right up here. He makes things up. People in town understand, but sometimes he scares visitors. Please don't take anything he said seriously."

"No problem," Kirby said.

Oliphant looked off toward the trees at the end of the street.

"I'd better go help Roy round him up. Nice to meet you folks." He touched his hat brim and hurried off after the others.

"What do you suppose that was all about," Kirby muttered.

"Weird kid," Matthew observed.

Janice hugged herself as though caught by a sudden chill. "We shouldn't be here. We don't belong."

"You sound as nutty as that kid," Kirby said. "Let's go eat. We can talk about it over dinner."

The Royal Badger dining room was as empty as the outer room had been that morning. As far as Kirby could tell in the dim light, only one other couple was present in one of the booths. The same young woman who had brought their breakfast waited on them for dinner.

Kirby and Janice ordered pot roast, a specialty of the Royal Badger, according to the menu. The prices again were unbelievably low. Matthew ordered a hamburger which, to his disgust, was served on plain bread without so much as a lettuce leaf for garnish.

"They call this a hamburger?" he complained.

"Shut up and eat," Kirby said.

"You don't have to shout at the boy," Janice said, her voice infuriatingly soft.

"I did not shout," Kirby said, smiling with clamped jaws.

"I hate this hamburger."

"Matthew!" Kirby's rising inflection was a warning.

"Listen to us," Janice said. "This town is poisoning us."

"Let's not blame it on the town, shall we?"

Janice started to answer, then changed her expression to speak to the boy. "Matt, why don't you take your hamburger and run on back to the hotel room."

"And do what?"

"I don't care. Play the radio. Read your comics."

"I've read all my comics."

Kirby went into his Parental Authority mode. "Matthew, do what your mother tells you. Here's the room key. Now get going, and no more argument."

Matt swallowed his next complaint, took the key. He wrapped the offending hamburger in a napkin and carried it out of the restaurant.

Janice looked after him worriedly. "I didn't want him to have to listen to us argue. Do you think he'll be all right?"

"The hotel's right across the street. Anyway, what could happen to him in this town?"

"I don't *like* this town," she said. "I want to get out of here."

"Tomorrow's their big celebration. Deliverance."

"I don't care. I hate it."

Kirby took his time lighting a cigarette. He blew out the smoke in a long stream. He spoke slowly and distinctly. "We will leave when I am ready."

"Excuse me?"

The Kirbys' heads snapped up in unison at the sudden soft voice close to their ears. A young man with square-faced good looks and a shag of healthy blond hair smiled down at them. His eyes were deep set and blue. They sparkled with good health.

"I'm Marcus Diamond. Hey, I hope I didn't interrupt anything."

Neither of the Kirbys spoke.

"You're Mr. and Mrs. Kirby, aren't you?"

"That seems to be pretty well-known," Kirby said.

"Well, we're a small town—"

"And don't get many visitors," Janice finished for him.

Marcus Diamond laughed. "You've got that right. I understand Mr. Kirby's father was born here."

"And *his* father," Kirby said.

"So it's kind of a homecoming for you."

"In a way, I guess."

"The thing is, my sister and I, we're over there in the booth, wondered if we could buy you a drink."

"I don't think—" Janice began.

"That's good of you," Kirby said, cutting her off. "Why don't you join us."

"Great," Marcus said. "I'll get my sister."

Janice glared at her husband as Marcus Diamond crossed the room to the other occupied booth. "What do you think you're doing?"

"I am being friendly to the natives and trying to liven up our vacation a little. Isn't that what you wanted?"

"What I wanted was to get the hell away from here."

Janice pasted on a smile as Marcus returned with a dark, willowy young woman with glossy black eyelashes and a flawless complexion.

"My sister, Aurelia," Marcus said.

The Diamonds sat across from the Kirbys, and Marcus ordered

a round of drinks from the all-purpose waitress, who relayed the message to the bar.

Kirby had a scotch on the rocks, Janice took white wine. The Diamonds each had something pale pink in a tall glass.

Conversation was fitful, carried largely by the young brother and sister team. Kirby put in an occasional comment while Janice maintained a chilly silence. The scotch had a heavier taste than he was used to, but not unpleasant. In a few minutes he began to feel more social.

"I guess you folks are finding Danziger pretty quiet," Marcus said.

"It is a little short on night life," Kirby agreed.

"Have you heard of the Purple Cow?" Aurelia asked. She looked up at Kirby through those long moist lashes, and he felt a stirring in his groin.

"I don't think so." He made it casual. "What's the Purple Cow?"

"A roadhouse, sort of. It's out at the edge of town, not far from where Marcus and I live. They have a band and dancing, and they serve a stronger drink than they do here."

"I'm a little tired," Janice said.

"How can you be tired? We haven't done anything. I'd like to see this Purple Cow." Kirby laughed self-consciously. "I know I'd rather see than be one."

"I'm getting a little headache too."

"A headache?"

"Why not? People get headaches."

Kirby turned to the younger couple with a see-what-I-have-to-put-up-with expression.

"You go ahead," she snapped. "Go see this Purple whatever-it-is."

"But if you really don't feel well . . ."

"I'll be fine. You go ahead and have fun." It was a challenge.

Marcus Diamond leaned toward her. His tanned young face showed genuine regret. "You're sure you don't want to come? Not even for a little while?"

Janice's voice softened. "No, really, thank you. My husband is more adventurous than I am."

The gauntlet was down. "I'll just look in, have one drink," Kirby said.

"Fine." Janice rose from the table. "Nice to have met you. Have a good time, Quinn."

As she walked away stiff-backed, Marcus said, "Seems like a real nice lady. Too bad she's tired."

Kirby suddenly felt awkward. Part of him wanted to back out, to hurry after Janice. The rebellious part said to hell with her. He was going to have some fun. This was the part that won.

He said, "How do we get to this Purple Cow?"

Aurelia's dark eyes stroked his face. "I can show you the way. I'd really like a ride in that car of yours. It's nicer than anything around here."

"Sure, we can all go in my car," Kirby said. His face felt hot. The drinks? The stuffy room?

"I better follow you in mine," Marcus said. "We live out that way and there's no sense me making a trip back to town to pick up the Ford."

As they walked out of the restaurant together onto the dark street Aurelia Diamond's long sleek thigh brushed against Kirby. He looked at her quickly to see if it had been an accident. Her eyes told him what he wanted to know.

10

Wally Mayer had always been a good runner. He knew how to pump his arms in rhythm with his legs, and how to control his breathing to get the most oxygen into his lungs. He could outrun anyone his age, and there were few adults in the town of Danziger who could catch him. Wally ran now for his life.

Behind him on the dark street he could hear the pounding feet of his uncle. He knew that in a moment Ben Oliphant, the constable, would join the chase. If they caught him he was dead. They had heard him talking to the Kirbys, trying to warn them. That had been a dangerous thing to do. Wally knew that. He knew the risk he was taking, but he felt he owed it to his boyhood friend. A long time ago, when he might have spoken up and helped Carl Kirby, he had remained silent. With a chance to help Carl's son and his family, he felt he could not hold back.

But once again he had failed. And now they were coming for him. Wally glanced over his shoulder and saw his uncle and the stocky constable running, running. They kept a steady pace, but they were not gaining any ground. Wally knew he could stay ahead of them. But could he escape? No one ever had.

He ran past the hulk that had been the Lutheran church and scrambled up the grassy slope to the trees. It was forbidden ground. What lay beyond the trees? Freedom? Safety? No one ever talked about it.

Down on the street his Uncle Roy and Ben Oliphant thudded grimly closer. Wally could hear the *huff-huff* of their ragged breathing.

He turned away from the town and dived into the trees. The high branches closed overhead, shutting out any glimmer of moonlight. The boy had to slow his flight as he strained to see the trees before him. He kept his hands stretched protectively before his face. Still the branches lashed him painfully.

For many minutes he made his way deeper into the forbidden forest. He paused to listen. There were the night sounds of scurrying small animals, the *chirr* of crickets, the rustle of the branches overhead. No sound of running men behind him.

Wally relaxed just a little and went on more cautiously. He began to think it was maybe just possible he was going to make it through the woods and away. Away from the men who followed. Away from Damntown.

There was no warning. Just a sudden searing, cramping pain in his right calf muscle. With his leg held fast, Wally crashed headlong to the forest floor. His face mashed down into the dead and rotting leaves. He struggled onto his side, fighting vainly to pull his leg free. He looked down and saw what had him.

The dogs.

The demonic black dogs that guarded the perimeter of Damntown. One of them had Wally's lower leg clamped in his powerful jaws. The boy could hear the gritty sound of the animal's teeth grinding on bone.

The other two dogs moved in swiftly on silent feet. Wally

screamed in pain and terror. He held up his arms, crossed before his face in a pathetic attempt at keeping them off.

One of the dogs caught him at the elbow and cracked it like a chicken wing. The other went for his face.

Wally Mayer's last sensation was the smell of the animal's hot, sour breath as its teeth ripped at his flesh.

11

While Wally Mayer lay helpless under the jaws of the Damntown Dogs, Carl Kirby shivered in his narrow bed in the Lakeview Nursing Home and stared up through the darkness at the ceiling. There were little flecks of mica embedded in the plaster. They picked up fragments of reflected light from the dim night lamp and were supposed to represent twinkling stars. To Carl Kirby, the sparkling bits were memories, images, faces, voices that whirled in his mind. He concentrated fiercely, trying to bring the bits together into a coherent whole.

Sensations began to coalesce. There was the chill of danger. He could feel it. Danger to his family. Now, and in the past. He had to do something; take some action. The last time he had been unable to help. Now Fate, God, Kismet, whatever was out there, was giving him another chance. This time he must not fail.

The door whispered open. The night nurse came in. Her name was Tina. Carl knew that because it was written over her breast pocket in script with blue thread. Like a mechanic working in a garage. She was much younger than Miss Pierce, the day nurse. The night staff was all younger people.

Tina leaned over and looked into Carl's face in the dim orange night light. She smiled at him. They all smiled at him a lot. He could not imagine why. He never responded. It must have been like smiling at statue. Or a dead man.

"Time to go night-night, Carl."

That was another thing they all did. Talked to him like he was an idiot child. Carl did not resent it. They meant no harm. If he was ever to be treated like a whole man again, he would have to recover the power to act like one. He stared up at the young woman, unmoving.

Nurse Tina filled a little plastic cup with water from the plastic pitcher on his bedside table. She held out a red and white capsule in her antiseptic pink palm. With her other hand she gently touched his chin and drew his jaw down. "Time for the pill so we can sleep without bad dreams, Carl."

We. It was always *we* with these people. *Time for our bath. Let's eat all our breakfast this morning. Did we move our bowels today?*

Carl allowed the young nurse to open his mouth and place the Dalmane capsule on his tongue. When she looked away for a moment he shifted the capsule underneath, holding it with the bottom of his tongue against his lower teeth. She helped him raise his head and held the cup to his lips. He drank, being careful not to dislodge the capsule.

"That's good," Tina said, easing his head back down onto the pillow. "Now you'll have a nice quiet sleep right through until morning."

That's what you think. Carl let his eyes flicker a goodnight to Tina. She smiled at him again and left the room. He rolled his head to one side and spat the capsule out into his hand. Tonight he did not want sleep, he wanted to remember.

Slowly, slowly the mental picture shifted into focus. The small square park in the center of Danziger, the statue of the soldier behind, the bandstand in front. The stranger glaring down at him, the people of the town stunned and silent, staring at him. And just outside the town, the twister, gray-brown and ugly, writhing like an enormous serpent on a leash.

What had made him speak out as he had against Bachman and the terrible bargain he wanted to strike with the town? Carl had always been an honest, obedient boy. He was attentive at school and industrious at home, where he worked with his father alongside the hired hands. Never, ever, had he contradicted his elders. Never until now.

When his worn-out father and his sickly mother had moved on either side of him and spoken up for him, Carl knew he could never take back his outburst. Most important, he knew he was right. Bachman was Evil. He would lead the town to its doom, surely as he stood there. Carl knew this. How he knew, the boy could not have said. But he knew. Others in the square that long ago June day must have known it too. They knew who the stranger was and where he would lead them. But they had suffered so much they could not imagine how things could be any worse. They had no will left to resist. Only a 12-year-old boy, only Carl Kirby was willing to stand against the stranger. And only Carl's parents stood with him.

"Bring the dissenters," the stranger thundered from the bandstand. "All three of them."

Bachman stepped off the bandstand and started out of the park. The crowd shifted uneasily, but no one moved to obey him. Seeing this, the stranger raised a powerful right arm, the fingers pointed clawlike at the storm. The roiling funnel moved closer. With a muffled explosion, a house was sucked into the maelstrom. Debris whirled through the sky. A terrified horse flailed its hooves high in the air high above them before the tornado dropped the beast to its death.

"Choose," ordered the stranger to the crowd. "Bring the three dissenters, or all of you die."

With a sound from many mouths that sounded like the moan of a giant, the Kirbys' neighbors closed around Henry, Freya, and Carl and bore them along in the wake of the stranger.

The procession headed up the short dark street that ended at the edge of the forest. They slowed for a moment, cowed by the bulk of the Lutheran church, but Bachman urged them on.

On the steps he paused, pointing at the arch over the heavy oak door. There a bronze crucifix was affixed to the brick wall.

"Someone tear down that abomination," he ordered. "We have no more need for superstitious symbols."

There was a shuffling of feet among the crowd, but when the wail of the waiting storm grew louder a boy of about 18 stepped forward. Using the carved frame of the heavy door for steps and handholds, he climbed above the entrance and chipped with his pocket knife at the cement around the cross until it broke loose and clanged to the sidewalk. Someone else picked it up and flung it toward the woods.

"Now," said Bachman, "we can continue." He led the townspeople, with the Kirbys firmly in their grasp, through the door and into the church.

Rev. Steiner was, of course, nowhere to be seen. The interior of the building had been stripped of all religious symbols. The sanctuary was smashed into rubble. Hymnals and prayer books were ripped to bits and strewn over the floor. Paintings of the saints had been torn from the walls and slashed beyond recognition. The stained glass windows had been smashed to tiny glittering fragments. The dark, high ceiling, the empty pews and the denuded altar gave the place a cold, cavernous feeling.

Bachman marched down the center aisle and took his place on the bare pulpit. The Kirby family was marched in after him and brought to stand before the chancery rail.

"I want three men to step forward now. Three men to take these malcontents into the forest and silence them."

After a stunned moment Peter Mayer, the father of Carl's friend Wally, spoke up. "You mean . . . kill them?"

"Kill them!" Bachman said, his voice booming and echoing in the defiled church.

Deadly silence as the people of Danziger held their breaths.

"This then is your choice?" Bachman raised an arm toward a broken window through which the hungry funnel of the storm could be seen weaving, waiting. It's roar filled the room, blasting the ears of the people.

"No," cried an angular man in torn overalls.

"You have something to say, Joe Ziegler?" Bachman waited, his arm poised.

"I lost my barn and my stock with it. All I have left is my wife and my two little girls. They're layin' sick and helpless in my house right over where that twister is. I'll do whatever I have to save them."

"Good. Now I want two more," said the stranger. "Two more men who are willing to do this simple job. Two more volunteers, or the town and every living thing in it will die."

"I'll go." Eldon Isham, the postmaster, his bald spot gleaming with sweat moved over to stand with Ziegler.

"One more," said Bachman. His eyes ranged over the crowd, settled on Peter Mayer. "You."

"Don't ask me to do that," said the farmer.

"I ask nothing. The choice is yours to make. Go with the others and do what you must, or the blood of this town will flow in its streets."

Carl's mother began to cough. Henry Kirby put an arm around her thin shoulders and held her against him. His other hand gripped the shoulder of his son.

"All right," Mayer said. His voice was barely above a whisper, yet it echoed through the barren interior of the church like a trumpet blast.

Carl Kirby could not believe that this thing was happening to him and to his parents. He wanted to do something—strike out, run, shout. He wanted to cry, but he was 12 years old and helpless.

Bachman reached down behind the lectern for something. Freya Kirby tried to shield young Carl, but he saw. Three heavy-bladed knives, gleaming softly in the gloomy church. Bachman passed them to the three executioners. They took the weapons silently, guiltily. But they took them.

While their neighbors bound their hands, Carl's father looked down at him and smiled sadly. "This is not your fault, son. You did the right thing."

His mother coughed once more, then straightened her back and moved close to her husband as her hands were bound.

The three of them were tied together with short lengths of rope and marched out of the church. Peter Mayer, Joe Ziegler, and Eldon Isham followed the Kirbys out. Young Wally Mayer looked as though he wanted to say something as his friend passed him in the aisle, but his mother and his uncle, Peter's brother, pulled the boy back from the aisle. The rest of the people turned away as the little procession passed.

There was no conversation as the six people clumsily climbed the grassy bank behind the church. There they stopped for a moment at the edge of the forest, the condemned and the executioners, and looked back toward Danziger. The gutted church loomed dark and forbidding. The sky above it was an ugly bronze color with the deadly tornado doing its weaving dance on other side of town. After a moment one of the men motioned with his knife and they walked on into the woods.

12

Janice slammed the door of the hotel room and stood with her shoulder blades pressed against it, breathing slowly and deeply.

Matthew jumped up from the day bed, a well-worn comic book in one hand. "What's the matter? Where's Dad?"

"Nothing is the matter," Janice said. "Your father will be up later."

"But where is he?"

"Why aren't you in bed?"

"I was."

"I mean in your pajamas and asleep."

"It's too early."

"Well . . . find something to do then."

"Can I go down and get a Coke?"

"Oh, I suppose so." She found her change purse in a bureau drawer dresser and dug through it. "Let me see if I have any quarters."

"Coke only costs a nickel here."

"Here's a dime. Keep the change."

Matthew took the coin from her and scurried out the door. It banged shut behind him, making Janice wince. She walked over and sat in a chair by the window. Down in the street she could see Quinn standing on the sidewalk while that girl, that Aurelia What-ever-her-name-was, walked around the Chrysler.

Something strange about that girl. She was attractive in kind of a dark, too thin way, but her eyes always seemed to be laughing at you. Apparently it did not bother Quinn. He practically leaped at the chance to go off with her. It was a good thing, Janice thought, that she was not a jealous woman.

A knock at the door.

"It's not locked, Matt," she called.

After a moment the door opened and the blond handsome head of Marcus Diamond peered in at her. He smiled, the even white teeth a contrast in his tanned face.

Janice stood up quickly and smoothed her skirt. "I thought you were my son."

"Not by quite a few years," he said. He came on into the room without waiting for an invitation, and eased the door closed behind him. All the while he continued to smile at Janice.

Her body tingled with the scary thrill of being alone in a hotel room with a strange man. He certainly did not look threatening, but you never knew. "Was there . . . something?"

"You forgot this." He held up her shoulder bag by the strap. It was buttery soft wallaby leather from Frederick & Nelson's.

Relief washed over her, tinged with just a hint of disappointment. "Thank you. Boy, that was careless of me."

Marcus walked to the center of the room, still holding her bag. "No harm done. Nobody in Danziger was likely to steal it." He took a look around. "Nice room."

"I . . . I suppose so."

"Is your headache better?"

"Headache?"

"You said down in the restaurant . . ."

"Oh, right. Yes, it's better, thanks. I think all it is is I'm tired."

"I'm not keeping you from going to bed, am I?"

Janice felt her face growing warmer. "As a matter of fact, I thought I'd stay up and read for a while."

He watched her, still smiling. He *was* a good looking young man. Strong. Wholesome. And yet, in some odd way, disturbing.

"My little boy will be back any minute," she said, hating the giddy sound of her voice. "He went downstairs for a Coke."

"I'm sorry you didn't feel like going with us tonight."

"We couldn't have left Matthew here alone anyway."

"That didn't seem to bother your husband."

It sure as hell didn't, she thought. Her eyes were drawn toward the window.

"They just drove off," Marcus said, reading her mind. "I saw them as I was coming up."

"Yes, well, I'm sure they'll have a good time." *God, where did she get that sneer in her voice?*

"My sister can be a lot of fun."

"I'll bet."

They stood facing each other, without speaking, for what seemed to Janice like a painfully long time. Marcus's eyes stayed on her face. He showed no embarrassment at all.

"Too bad you have to spend the evening all by yourself."

Janice was saved from answering when Matthew opened the

227

door with his Coke bottle in his hand. Janice swooped across the room to seize his arm. The boy looked up at her, startled.

"This is my son, Matthew."

"Hi." Marcus grinned down at him.

Matthew looked at the young man and back at his mother.

"I left my bag in the restaurant. Marcus . . . Mr. Diamond brought it to me."

"Oh." The boy was not appeased. Why did she feel she had to explain to him?

"I guess I'll be on my way," Marcus said.

"Thanks for bringing the bag."

"Don't mention it." He showed the fine white teeth. "I hope I'll be seeing you around. You are staying for Deliverance, aren't you?"

"I don't know. We were thinking of leaving in the morning."

"That would be a shame. Well, maybe you'll stay longer than you planned. Folks often do. Goodnight." He reached down to rumple Matt's hair. The boy pulled his head away. Marcus went out and softly closed the door.

"Who is that guy?" Matt said.

"Just somebody we met in the restaurant."

"I don't like him. His mouth smiles at you but his eyes say something else."

"You shouldn't be in a hurry to judge people."

"I'm not in a hurry. I just don't like him."

"Drink your Coke and get ready for bed."

"We're not going to, are we?" Matt said. "Stay here longer?"

"We'll see."

"I hate it when you say 'we'll see.' It means you don't want to tell me."

"Get ready for bed, Matt."

Janice walked back to the window and looked down at the street. Marcus Diamond crossed to an old Ford pickup. He had a confident, wide-shouldered gait. At the door of the pickup he paused and looked up at her window. Their eyes met for just a moment, then Janice stepped back feeling unaccountably light headed. Damned if she wasn't moist between her legs.

* * *

"God, I love this car!"

Aurelia Diamond squirmed in the seat next to Kirby. She rubbed her back and buttocks against the fine Corinthian leather. She petted the dash panel, running her fingertips over the lighted displays. "It's like a rocket ship or something."

Kirby drove slowly down Main Street past the empty sidewalks and silent store fronts. "How far is this Purple Cow?"

"I'll tell you when we get there."

Her hand left the dash panel and rested lightly on his thigh. A shock of guilty pleasure pulsed through his body from the warm spot where the girl's hand lay.

He looked up into the rearview mirror. "I don't see your brother behind us."

"Don't worry about Marcus. He knows the way."

The interior of the car swam with her perfume. Some spice Kirby could not identify. He buzzed down the window on his side. The cool night air did not help. He felt more than half-drunk, although he had downed only a couple of scotches.

"How far is it?" he asked, then had to clear his throat of the huskiness.

"Not far."

What the hell am I doing? Am I going to fuck this girl? God knows I want to. I haven't wanted to do anything so bad in years. Am I going crazy?

He drove on past where the buildings of the town ended and dark, rolling fields stretched away from the road on both sides. Beyond the fields, faintly lit by the three-quarter moon, he could see the black tangled wall of the forest.

Aurelia's hand slipped between his legs and stroked him gently, insistently.

In the nine years of his marriage Quinn Kirby had been unfaithful to his wife only twice. The first was a meaningless one-night stand. A business trip to San Francisco, a night out with a couple of men from the local office. Three party girls in a North Beach bar, some kidding-around sex talk with a good-natured redhead named Connie who had an enormous pair of breasts. Then back to the hotel for a half-drunken roll in the hay. Never heard from Connie again; never wanted to. He brought home an especially fine pair of earrings for Janice that time.

The second time was more serious. A woman in the accounting

department of the aerospace firm where Kirby worked. Her name was Vera. Tall, brilliant, twice married, she brought Kirby a combination of sex, sophistication and companionship that he was not getting at home. It went so far that Kirby suggested to her that he leave his wife. A mistake. Vera slammed the relationship shut so fast his ears rang. The affair lasted just over three months and ended four years ago. That one was good for a diamond necklace.

Now here he was about to do it again. With his wife and son waiting for him in a hotel room back in town he was creeping along a nighttime country road letting this dark, sensuous girl play with his cock. And he was loving it.

"Stop here," said Aurelia.

Kirby pulled to the shoulder and braked. "I don't see any Purple Cow roadhouse."

"There isn't any Purple Cow." Her hands were at his belt now, deftly undoing the buckle, sliding the zipper down.

"This might not be a good idea," he said.

Aurelia freed his penis from the jockey shorts, milking it gently with her hand. "Do you want me to stop? I will if you want me to."

"You know I don't."

"Mm-hmm. I know."

Without taking her hand away she shifted around in the seat so she could dip her head down under the steering wheel. She planted a wet kiss on the head of his cock, then took it in her mouth. Her lips were soft and hot as they enveloped the shaft. He felt the gentle rasp of her tongue as she tasted him. Kirby reached down to the back of her head. He lay his hand on the cool black hair and watched it move as Aurelia expertly sucked his brains out.

Slowly she drew her mouth away, kissing him again on the swollen head as she left him.

"I want you in me now," she said.

"There's not much room in here."

"We'll manage."

Moving with compact grace in the confined space of the Chrysler, Aurelia skinned off the black sweater. Her small perky breasts bobbled in the moonlight. With another smooth motion she was out of her skirt and pale panties. She knelt on the leather seat and thrust her pelvis toward Kirby. She pulled his head forward into the velvety black patch of pubic hair. He tasted the pungent moisture of her.

230

"See, I'm as ready as you are," she said, pulling back. "Now you just slide over this way a little bit and I'll do the rest."

While she raised her naked body over him, Kirby eased over the arm rest to the passenger seat. He was acutely aware of his erection waving in the moonlight.

"That's good," the girl said. She positioned herself over him, reached down to take his cock, and slid it into her.

Kirby gasped as she settled onto him, taking his full length inside.

"You just sit there, honey," she said, "and let me make you happy."

Her dark, mischievous eyes never left his as she rocked on him. Her naked body rose and fell, rose and fell, bringing him at last to a wild explosion. At the moment of his climax Aurelia leaned forward and fastened her lips on his. He felt her tongue, still salty with the taste of him, probe deep into his mouth.

The eruption went on and on until he felt his body must be drained of every fluid. When at last Aurelia lifted herself and let his flaccid member drop free, she smiled at him.

"Now wasn't that a lot better than a Purple Cow?"

13

Kirby had no idea what time it was when he pulled to a stop in front of the New Brandenburg Hotel. His wristwatch still showed a blank face. He should have tried to buy a new battery today. If you could find such a thing in this time-warped town. More trouble— the dash clock in the Chrysler was malfunctioning now too. It blinked repeatedly: *12:00.* Forever midnight.

Main Street was empty. Nothing stirred. No breath of breeze even rustled the candy wrappers in the gutter. The moon was gone.

The blank storefronts had a melancholy, long-abandoned look.

Kirby sat for a moment behind the wheel of the New Yorker. He leaned back on the fine Corinthian leather and asked himself what the hell he was doing here. More specifically, what the hell was he thinking of tonight? The gut-twisting ache of guilt was mingled with the carnal memory of Aurelia Diamond and the wild, sweet, intoxicating things she had done to him.

The car reeked of sex. He had mopped it out as best he could, using the last of the Kleenex box they kept under the dash, but the animal scent was still powerful. Kirby resolved to get up early tomorrow, find a car wash if there was such a thing in this forlorn town, and get the Chrysler douched out.

He stepped out onto the curb. The slam of the car door was like a gunshot on the silent street. Kirby half expected lights to go on up and down the block and people to spill from the doorways to investigate the commotion. Nothing of the sort happened of course. It was merely the sound of a car door closing.

The lobby of the New Brandenburg Hotel was dimly lit, the marble pillars standing like giant ghostly travelers, frozen forever on their way to check in or check out. Behind the desk, in the light of a brown gooseneck lamp, he could see Armand Esterhaus. Janice's question came back to him, *Doesn't the man ever sleep?*

The manager's eyes were in shadow, but Kirby could feel them follow him across the lobby. His lips were stretched in a smile that said *I know what you did.* Patently absurd. How could he? Kirby kept his own eyes resolutely to the front as he crossed to the stairway and started up.

*   *   *

In Room 316 Janice Kirby sat in one of the straight-back chairs under the lamp. In her lap was an ancient copy of *Saturday Evening Post* she had found in one of the bureau drawers. The magazine was filled with ads for long-gone brands of cigarettes like Black Cat and Old Gold, Hupmobiles, Lux Toilet Soap *"9 out of 10 screen stars keep their skin lovely with Lux . . ."* Movies like *Dinner at Eight,* and *King Kong.* There was an article about the shooting of Chicago Mayor Cermak, and interview with Clara Bow, pictures of the dirigible *Akron* before its final disastrous flight. The short stories, as

232

much as Janice could read of them, were insipid to the point of nausea. She found it impossible to concentrate on anything in the magazine.

She had unfolded the screen and placed it to shield Matthew from the light. Behind it on the daybed the boy slept the innocent sleep of childhood. Janice felt a tightening of her throat as she listened to her son's regular breathing.

Quinn's key rattled in the door. Janice immediately became absorbed in an ad for Camel Cigarettes. *"Blow some my way!"*

Kirby entered the room, dropped his key on the bureau and immediately began emptying his pockets. "Still up?"

She knew at once. A wife always knew. It was in his too casual posture, the counterfeit note in his voice, the way his eyes bounced around without ever directly looking at her. And if that were not enough, there was the smell of him. He stank of another woman's lust.

"Have a good time?" she said.

"So-so." He yawned and stretched elaborately. "I'm bushed."

I'll bet you are. "Yes, it's late."

"Think I'll take a bath and hit the sack."

Too late. I already got a whiff of you, you philandering sonofabitch. "Go ahead. I think I'll sit up a while."

For once, Janice noticed, her husband hung up his clothes carefully instead of just dropping them where he stood. He wadded his shorts and shoved them into the plastic bag they used for laundry. Well, sure. He didn't want her going over his things, finding the stuck-on pubic hairs, the telltale crusty stains of semen.

He padded into the bathroom, holding a towel modestly around his waist. Janice she could hear him urinating, then the sound of the tub filling. When he came out after twenty minutes she offered a cheek for his perfunctory goodnight kiss, then turned away while he piled into the bed and was almost instantly asleep.

So much for conscience, she thought.

Janice put aside the magazine and stood for a minute looking down at her husband. He lay on his side, knees bent, one hand, palm up, tucked under his cheek. They always looked so innocent asleep, men and other carnivores. She searched her heart for any remnant of the love she might still feel for this man. Only traces remained. A shadow of remembered tenderness, an echo of some small joy they had shared. It was not enough.

She pulled the smaller of the suitcases from the closet and began to pack her things and Matt's. She made no special effort to be quiet. If Quinn woke up, he woke up. Maybe he would try to talk her out of this. Maybe he would succeed. Janice found she did not much care one way or the other.

She woke up Matthew, whose complaints died in his throat when he saw the look on her face.

"Get dressed," she said, "we're leaving."

"What about Dad?"

"He isn't coming." The absolute finality in her tone cut off any more questions.

The boy did as he was told, blinking sleepily as he got into his Wrangler jeans, *Fangoria* T-shirt, junior Nikes, and Seahawks jacket. In less than twenty minutes both he and Janice were packed.

Quinn Kirby slept on. At the door Janice turned once more to look at her husband. It seemed as though she should say something, leave a note. But there were no words. She boosted Matt gently out of the room, followed him into the hallway, and closed the door behind them.

Downstairs Armand Esterhaus regarded them blandly from behind the desk, as though there were nothing unusual about a wife and son leaving the hotel, suitcase in hand, while the husband remained upstairs asleep. He watched them with a meager smile all the way across the lobby and out the door.

The night air hit them and Janice shivered. She pulled Matt to the curb where the Chrysler was parked and let him in the passenger side. As she started around to get in, two men approached along the otherwise deserted sidewalk. One of them carried something in his arms. A child? Janice hesitated.

As the men drew near she recognized them as the town constable and his friend who had spoken to them earlier.

Constable Oliphant touched his hat brim. "'Evening, Miz Kirby."

Janice did not respond. She was staring at the burden the other man carried. It was the little boy who had given them the cryptic warning. The one who claimed irrationally to be a friend of Quinn's father. He was now recognizable only by the clothes he wore. His face and throat were ripped savagely to the bone. The zipper jacket was shredded, the sweater soaked with blood.

"Dogs got him," the other man said. "There's a pack of 'em runs in the woods."

234

"I'm sorry," Janice said.

"Maybe he's better off," said the man carrying the body.

Janice remembered he was supposed to be the boy's uncle. Pretty damned cool about his nephew's ugly death, she thought. The men continued along the street, and she quickly locked herself in the car.

The Chrysler stank of the rutting couple. Janice lowered both windows despite the chill of the air outside. Off to the east the sky was growing lighter. God, had she sat up all night? It did not seem that long. No way to tell for sure without a working clock in the whole stinking town.

With the suitcase tossed in back and Matthew belted in beside her Janice keyed the engine to life. She hit the headlights, knocked the shift lever to *Drive* and took off down the empty, silent street. Goodbye, Danziger. Goodbye Quinn.

In less than a minute they were beyond the dark Esso station that was the last building of town. After another mile Janice breathed deeply and slowed the car. The headlights picked out a sign up ahead: *You are now leaving Danziger, Wisconsin. Please come back.*

"Fat chance," Janice said through her teeth.

Matt looked at her.

"Don't mind me," she told him. "I'm just talking to the road sign."

Then the engine died.

"Oh damn damn damn!" Janice pounded the steering wheel as the New Yorker rolled to a stop.

The gas gauge registered more than half-full. The headlights continued to beam on the mocking sign. She twisted the ignition key and tromped on the gas pedal. Nothing.

"Damn damn damn!" she said again. "Shit!" she added for good measure.

She became aware of Matthew staring at her. She stretched her lips into a ghastly smile. "Looks like we're going to have to hoof it, partner."

"Walk?" the boy said.

"We won't get anywhere sitting here. Come on."

They got out of the car. Janice pulled the suitcase from the back seat. It seemed to have grown heavier now that there was a possibility she might have to carry it for some distance. The ugly color of the horizon had not lightened enough for her to see much. Only a short stretch of road was visible in both directions. Off to the sides were fields, and beyond them the black shadow of the forest. Janice helfted the suitcase. This was definitely not going to be fun.

Before they started walking there was the sound of an engine behind them. Janice turned with renewed hope to see approaching headlights. She faced the oncoming lights with Matt at her side, waved her hand, and put on a helpless look. Who would fail to stop for a woman and child in obvious distress?

An old Ford pickup truck braked to a stop. The square, blond face of Marcus Diamond grinned at them from the window of the cab.

"Got a problem?"

So glad was Janice to see the friendly All-American face that she forgot about the strange urges she had felt with him in the hotel.

She said, "Our car died. Could you possibly give us a lift at least to the nearest town?"

"Hop in." Marcus's square white teeth gleamed in the reflected light of the headlights.

While the engine idled, Marcus jumped out of the cab and effortlessly tossed Janice's suitcase into the truck bed. He boosted Matt into the cab and helped Janice up beside him, then went around again and climbed in behind the wheel.

"Kind of a late hour for you to be taking a drive," he said, releasing the handbrake. "Lucky I came by."

"It's a long story," Janice said.

Marcus rammed the gear shift into low and turned the pickup hard to the right. Then he cranked the wheels and shoved it into reverse.

"What are you doing?"

"Taking you to the nearest town."

"I didn't mean that. I don't want to go back to Danziger."

"I'm afraid you're going to have to."

Janice stared at the young man. The warmth was gone from his voice. In the dim light the fine All-American features had thickened into a hostile mask. Marcus kept his eyes on the road as he headed back toward Danziger.

"You have an appointment back here," he said. "It's Deliverance Day."

14

Carl Kirby lay awake, alert, and unsedated in his bed at Lakeview Nursing Home. He was acutely aware of the night sounds. The gentle waves of Lake Washington spanking the shore. The unison tenor song of the tree frogs. Soft rattle of the Douglas fir adjusting their limbs. And inside, the pad of rubber-soled feet passing in the hall, the muted warble of a telephone at the nurse's station. These were sounds normally screened off from him by the nightly pill, the one he had hidden under his tongue and which now was jammd under the mattress. Tonight each of the sounds was clear and isolated in his mind like the bowing of a single violin string.

For the past two hours, since the night orderly looked in on him, Carl had lain in the narrow bed concentrating his will on recovering the mental and physical strength that had drained out of him over the past ten years. He repeated silently, over and over, phrases and passages he had memorized from the books on the shelf behind his bed. How he knew even their titles, let alone understood the languages, Carl Kirby could not have explained. He knew he drew strength from the words, and he knew that somehow the knowledge had been implanted in his brain more than fifty years ago. It was on the night three of their friends and neighbors led Carl, his father, and his mother into the woods outside Danziger to kill them. He was a boy then, without the knowledge to prevent the tragedy. He was a man now, he had studied. He was as ready as he was ever going to be.

There had been no conversation that long ago night when the Kirby family, their hands bound, were marched into the forest. Behind them came the three executioners carrying the heavy bladed knives the stranger had pressed into their hands back at the church. It was Joe Ziegler who finally broke the silence.

"This is far enough."

Carl Kirby, twelve years old and not yet comprehending what was happening to them, looked to his father. Henry Kirby, thinned and weakened by three years of the Great Depression, seemed to regain some of his former stature in the dire circumstances. He smiled down at his son and gave him a reassuring nod. Freya stood close to her husband so their bodies could touch.

"You men aren't really going to do this, are you?" Carl's father said.

"Don't waste your breath, Henry," said Ziegler. "You'll just make it harder for everybody."

Carl's father looked to Eldon Isham. The postmaster could not meet his eye. "You're a government man. Are you gonna be a part of this?"

"We got no choice. You heard what Bachman said. Either it's you folks, or the whole town dies."

"And you, Peter Mayer. We were neighbors before we both lost our farms. Your boy Wally is my Carl's best friend. What are you gonna tell your son?"

Mayer seemed on the verge of tears. "Henry, I'd rather cut my own throat than do this. So help me, I'd do it if it would help. If only your boy hadn't spoke up the way he did."

"I'll take it back," Carl said. "I'll say I'm sorry."

"No you won't," said his father. "You were the only one there with the guts to say out loud what we all knew about the stranger. It's the rest of the people in town who should be sorry for the way they acted. No, son, you'll take nothing back."

"It's too late anyway," Ziegler said. "We gotta do it, Henry. We'll make it quick."

Freya and Carl Kirby moved in closer on either side of Henry. Freya began to sob. Henry reached over with his bound hands and touched her arm.

The three executioners stood for a moment. Each looked at the others.

"How we gonna do it?" Isham asked. "One at a time or all together?"

"Take me," Henry said. "Let Freya and young Carl go. I know you men, you couldn't kill a woman and a little boy anyway. It ain't in you."

"We got to," Joe Ziegler said, his voice near breaking. "You saw what that man could do with the storm. There ain't no other way."

"Maybe there is," said Peter Mayer.

The others, victims and executioners, looked at him, their eyes eager for some way out.

"If we bloody up the knives and our hands and tell Bachman we done it . . . and if you Kirbys run like the devil and never ever come near Danziger again, maybe we can pull it off."

"I don't know," Ziegler said. "That Bachman ain't no fool. What happens if he figures out we didn't do the job?"

"Then he figures it out," Mayer said. "But if you're afraid to try it, Joe, then you go ahead and kill 'em. I ain't gonna help."

Ziegler looked to the postmaster. "Eldon?"

"I can't. It's wrong."

Joe Ziegler's shoulders drooped. "I know. I can't do it neither. God help us if Bachman finds out." He looked up at the others. "Where we gonna get the blood?"

Carl's father turned sideways and offered his bound hands. "Here. Take it out of me. All you need."

After a moment's hesitation Ziegler stepped forward. He severed the rope that bound Henry's hands.

Henry massaged his wrists for a moment. "Let them loose too," he said, nodding toward Freya and Carl.

Peter Mayer motioned for them to turn around, and cut their hands free.

Henry then pushed up his sleeve to bare his left arm and held it out. "Don't watch," he told his wife and son.

Freya looked away, but Carl could not pull his eyes from his father's bared arm and the knife blade.

Ziegler placed the point on the meaty part of Henry's forearm and drew it down toward the wrist. The skin parted smoothly behind the blade and bright red blood spilled out and down to Henry's clenched fist.

Ziegler drew back. For a moment the three men stood transfixed by the blood flowing from the three inch wound.

"Come on," Henry said. He pumped his fist to make the blood flow. "Do what you gotta do."

First Joe Ziegler, then Isham, then Peter Mayer cupped their hands under Henry's wound and let the blood run into their palms. They smeared both hands and the blades of their knives. When they were through Freya took a kerchief from her throat and tied it around her husband's arm.

"Get outta here now, Henry," Peter Mayer said. "Run fast and run far. Don't never come back. Any of you."

As though to punctuate his words a cold blast of wind hit the trees around them, and the boughs began to thrash wildly. The three men turned and fled into the night.

"Follow me!" Henry shouted above the rush of the wind. "Don't fall behind."

He started away, deeper into the forest. Freya stayed close behind her husband, reaching forward repeatedly to touch him.

Carl hurried to keep up. The thrashing of the branches across his face made it difficult. The thorny underbrush clutched at him with cruel little fingers.

A heavy root seemed to snake up out of the ground and seize the boy's foot. He fell heavily on his face, knocking the breath out of him for a moment. When he recovered and struggled to his knees, his father and mother were not in sight. All he could see were the dark thrashing branches that reached for him like demon claws.

The boy lurched to his feet, terror squeezing his insides. Where were they? Which way had they gone? He called out for his father, but his shout was snatched away by the wind.

Run! The only message his panicky brain could get through to his taut muscles. *Run!*

And he ran. Blindly stumbling, falling, fighting off the branches, banging into trees, he ran. Time and distance had no meaning. The universe consisted of the dark thrashing trees and the terrible wind. Nothing else.

Then there was a light. Only a glimmer at first, glimpsed through the black branches. Flickering, pale, but a light. Blindly Carl ran toward it. Then, with no warning, he burst out of the forest. He slipped on wet grass and fell rolling and tumbling down the slope until he fetched up against a brick wall. The church.

He had run right back to where he had started. The light he had seen came from one of the broken-out windows directly above the patch of grass where he lay. Carl picked himself up, raised on tiptoe, and peered in over the splinters of stained glass that lay on the sill.

Bachman stood on the bare altar looking taller, darker, more sinister than ever. Before him, proffering their bloodied hands, stood Joe Ziegler, Eldon Isham, and Peter Mayer. Watching from the shadows of the nave were the townspeople of Danziger. A terrible silence hung over the scene.

At last Bachman spoke. "So you have fulfilled the task, have you?"

The three executioners mumbled their assent.

Bachman burned each of them in turn with his eyes. He continued in a voice of deadly calm. "Which of the three died first?"

"Henry."

"The boy."

Ziegler and Isham's words tumbled upon each other. They exchanged a stricken look.

"Which?" snapped Bachman. "Was it the father? Or the son?" He paused. "Or maybe it was the woman?"

"We did them all at once," said Peter Mayer, talking rapidly.

"Oh. I see. All at once." The Stranger let the silence drag on painfully as the three men shifted where they stood, their gore-smeared hands dangling before them. When Bachman next spoke his voice was like the crack of a whip.

"Or maybe none of them died?!"

The men seemed unable to respond. They stood dumb and shifty-eyed. Caught.

"So you allowed your friends to live. At a terrible, terrible cost, you spared the lives of three people who broke the bargain. By your misguided act of mercy you have doomed this town and everyone in it. And for you three . . . a special punishment."

The mouths of the three men opened and closed, but no words came.

"A *very special punishment!*" Bachman seemed to grow and grow until he towered over the executioners.

The boy standing outside the church window bit his tongue to keep from crying out. While the scene he watched branded itself on his young mind, his fingers closed convulsively on the window sill and bits of colored glass sliced through the skin.

15

The first thing that occurred to Quinn Kirby was that the light in the room was all wrong. It was dull and coppery, and somehow unhealthy. Kirby rolled over and buried his head in the pillow so he would not have to look at the room in the sickly light.

241

His head hurt. His mouth was dry. His body ached. What had he done last night?

Oh, *shit*. Aurelia. And doing it in the car, for God's sake. He must have been crazy. What was he going to say to Janice? Wait a minute . . . she was awake when he came in. What did he say then? Did he give himself away? Did she know? How was he ever going to get out of this one?

With his face still in the pillow he reached over tentatively for his wife. If she responded to his touch, maybe everything would be all right. Maybe she didn't know. Or if she knew, maybe she forgave him. But if her body was stiff, or she moved away from him, he was in for big trouble.

His hand crept across the bed. His fingers found the sheet, the other pillow, the far edge of the mattress. No Janice. She must be already up. Bad sign. Cautiously he rolled his head to one side and peeked. In the coppery light the room looked empty. The bathroom door was ajar—nobody in there.

Then he saw that the screen had been folded and leaned back against the wall. The blankets and sheet on the daybed were rumpled. The bed was empty. Matt was gone too. What the hell?

Kirby threw back the covers and swung his feet to the floor. He stood up and swayed for a moment, light-headed. He closed his eyes and reopened them. The room wavered for five seconds, then steadied. Kirby was alone. His wife and his son must have gone down to breakfast. That was what his hopeful mind told him, but his gut knew better.

A brisk check of the bureau drawers revealed that most of Janice's clothes and personal things were missing. Matt's clothes were gone too. Her suitcase had been taken from the closet. Very bad news. Worse than he thought.

He crossed the room to the window. Above him the sky was the color of a bruise. The street below was empty of life. Bits of paper skittered along the gutters before a feeble wind.

Kirby dressed rapidly. He did not bother to shave. What time could it be? The damned useless watch was no help. The low, heavy clouds outside gave no hint of where the sun was.

He hurried down the two flights of stairs to the lobby. Armand Esterhaus stood as always at his post behind the registration desk. Kirby hesitated as he crossed the lobby and met the other man's eye for a moment. Something was different about Esterhaus today. He seemed younger, darker, leaner than he had been. His pale face remained impassive as he returned Kirby's gaze.

Suddenly uncomfortable, Kirby turned away from the hotel manager and pushed on out through the glass doors to the street.

The Chrysler was gone from the curb where he had left it last night. He halfway expected it to be gone, but it gave him a jolt all the same. He looked up and down Main Street. Not a thing moved. No cars, no pedestrians. No stores seemed to be open for business. Shades were drawn across the windows of the Royal Badger Cafe.

Kirby whirled and ran back into the hotel. He pulled up at the desk facing Armand Esterhaus. A faint smile quirked the lips of the manager.

"Hello, Mr. Kirby."

"Did you see my wife and my son come downstairs?"

"Yes, I did."

"What time was that?"

"Not long ago."

"Did you see which direction they went?"

"They got in your car and left . . ." his arm shot out with a suddenness that startled Kirby, ". . . going that way."

Dumbly Kirby turned and foolishly stared at the lobby wall where Esterhaus was pointing.

"Outside, of course," the manager explained.

"You mean they left town?"

"They drove off . . ." he pointed again, ". . . that way."

"And you say it was not long ago?"

"Not long."

"What time is it now?"

"It doesn't matter."

Kirby looked at him sharply.

"In Danziger time is not relevant."

Kirby was not about to stand here trying to figure out what the man was talking about. With a snort of impatience he spun away from the desk and hurried back outside.

The angry sky pressed closer over the town. A chill wind cut through Kirby's light poplin jacket. He had a sweater upstairs in the room, a warm bulky thing. But there was no time now to go back and get it. Kirby turned up the collar of his jacket and started to walk in the direction his wife and son had taken.

Paper scraps scampered along at his feet like small animals, as the wind picked up. The blue-black sky pressed down on him. Something rumbled far away. Thunder?

He met no one. He saw no one. Stores were shuttered, windows empty. Kirby began to walk faster. His footsteps clacking on the sidewalk were the only sound, save for the whisper of the wind.

Faster and faster he walked until he was jogging, then trotting, then running. The blank storefronts of Danziger seemed to lean in on him like claustrophobic images from a dream. In the soft rush of the wind past his ears he began to hear voices. Mocking, taunting voices. The cold seeped through his clothing and his skin into his vitals.

He was running full out now, pounding down the middle of the street, his breath rasping. Perspiration soaked throught his T-shirt, the wind chilled it and turned it clammy against his skin. On past the Esso station at the edge of town he ran, on between the overgrown fields, along the hard black strip of the road. He was beyond rational thought now. Sheer reflexes kept his arms pumping, his legs scissoring as he ran mindless on and on, trying to escape from . . . from *what?*

Up ahead he spied something in the road. A car. He pounded on, sweat stinging his eyes. It was the Chrysler. His car.

With an intense effort of will, Kirby slowed his pace. By the time he reached the car he was walking. He gulped in great draughts of the chill air, his aching lungs pumping like bellows. He leaned against the familiar metallic finish of the New Yorker. He stroked it like a favorite steed. There was no one inside. At least, not sitting upright. He pulled open the door and looked in front, then in back. No sign of Janice or Matt. The interior still smelled of stale sex. It was strong enough to make him gag.

The key, Janice's key, was still in the ignition. On the end of its chain dangled a coin struck with her astrological sign—Scorpio. Kirby slid in behind the wheel and twisted the key. Nothing. Not even the *click-click-click* of a moribund battery. He tried the horn. Nothing. Forget it.

He stepped back out of the car and the icy wind lanced into him. He looked back toward Danziger. There the angry clouds seemed to have lowered almost to the ground. Ahead of him, more of the same. A storm was brewing, but a storm unlike any he had ever seen. On either side of him were the fields that ended in thick stands of trees.

The trees seemed much closer. Were they moving? Ridiculous. Birnham Forest coming to Dunsinane? He was beginning to hallucinate.

Kirby arranged his thinking into a logical pattern. Janice and Matt had left the hotel in the Chrysler. They had got this far, then for some reason abandoned the car. Why? He had no answer for that. It was his job now to find them. Nothing would be gained by standing here asking himself riddles. Returning to Danziger was not an appealing thought. Crossing the weedy fields on either side of the road to reach the trees made no sense. That left only one path open to him—straight ahead in the direction the Chrysler was pointed.

He started to walk. A sign at the side of the road caught his eye. *You are now leaving Danziger, Wisconsin. Please come back.*

As he approached the sign, Kirby saw something moving up ahead on the road. Coming toward him. Something dark and bulky, low to the ground, moving fast.

"Ah, Jesus!" Kirby felt the clutch of fear at his bowels as he recognized it. He looked off over the fields. Another was plowing through the weeds. Coming at him. On the other side. Still another. They were closing on him from three sides.

Dogs.

Step by step he backed away, making soft whimpering sounds as the dog up ahead in the road loped closer. He could see it clearly now, mostly black with brown markings on the broad chest and around the muzzle. The teeth, great cruel teeth, showed between the black lips.

The other two burst from the fields to join the third just yards in front of him. There they stopped and stood for a moment, huge animals, their legs braced, neck for bristling. Their red-rimmed eyes glared deadly menace. The heavy jaws opened and closed, opened and closed, showing him their yellow killer teeth.

From the throat of one of the beasts came a rumbling growl. It was the most terrifying evil sound Quinn Kirby had ever heard. It pierced his brain and squeezed his testicles. For a long ghastly moment he was paralyzed where he stood. His muscles were frozen, his feet implanted in the asphalt of the road. His heart seemed unable to pump blood into his arteries.

The dogs, as though on signal, lunged toward him. A second before they would have hit him, Kirby regained the power of motion. He whirled and leaped back in the direction of Danziger. He could hear the easy *huff huff* of their breathing as they followed.

Only minutes before Kirby had leaned against the car, exhausted to the point of collapse. He would have said it was impossible for him to run another ten yards. Now he sprinted along the asphalt, wind roaring in his ears, as though the hounds of hell were behind him. The jarring impact of his feet on the road sent jolts all the way up his legs, along his spinal column, to his skull. His breath came in ragged snorts and gasps. Tears blurred his vision until all he could see was the patch of road dead ahead of him. Everything else was darkness.

Close behind he could hear the soft, insistent pad of the dogs' paws, the click of their claws on the asphalt. Whenever he lagged he felt a sharp tug as one or another of the beasts nipped at his pant legs.

In Kirby's fear-numbed brain the thought registered vaguely that the dogs should have been able easily to overtake him. Their power and stamina so far exceeded his that he was finished whenever the dogs wanted him. But instead of attacking, they remained always just behind, following, ready to tear the flesh from his bones if he faltered.

After an endless, pain-wracked run he passed again the Esso station that marked the edge of town and flung himself on into Danziger. The streets were still empty and dead, the stores shuttered, the sky darker and lower than ever. Nothing in the world mattered to Kirby, except that he escape the terrible teeth snapping at his heels. He bolted past the curtained Woolworth, the dark Graphic Theater, the closed Royal Badger Cafe. With the last ounce of his energy he fell against the door to the New Brandenburg Hotel, pushed it open, staggered inside, and dropped to the cold tile floor.

On the other side of the glass door the three huge dogs stopped and stood and . . . looked at him. And in their terrible eyes an unreadable look—triumph? Regret?

It was several minutes before Kirby could summon the strength to rise. He looked again at the door, and the dogs were gone. He felt . . . he *knew* they had not gone far. A million dollars could not have persuaded him to walk out that door.

He staggered toward the registration desk. Behind it Armand Esterhaus waited, watching him coolly. The man had made no move to help, showed no concern now for Kirby's condition. When Kirby fell against the desk, supporting himself on the counter, Esterhaus smiled.

"Welcome back, Mr. Kirby. Welcome home . . . to Damntown."

16

Home to Damntown.

It was a possibility Carl Kirby had never allowed himself to think about. For the first twelve years of his life Danziger *was* his home. After the stranger came, it would never be the same.

His life, his world changed on the terrible day of the twister, the gathering in the park, the blasphemy in the gutted church, and the executioners' walk into the woods. Once he had escaped, Carl thought no power on earth could drag him back to Damntown. Until his stroke ten years ago, the entire episode had been locked away in the deep recesses of his mind. With the sudden curtailment of his activities, the memory of the horror solidified. All the despair and pain of the Great Depression paled after the stranger came. Bachman, he called himself, but there were other names he could have used.

The ugliest parts had remained in darkness, but Carl always knew that someday he would have bring it out into the light and remember. The confrontation was always there in the indistinct future. It was against that time that he had devoured the ancient volumes of the occult and the mystical. He had read, studied, reread when he did not understand, until he had absorbed as much arcane knowledge as possible. Soon it would be time to bring it into play. It was necessary now that he remember. To stiffen his resolve he had to relive the scene in the defiled church . . . and what came afterward . . .

The twelve-year-old Carl had shivered with the chill of the night as he stretched up to the window and watched in horror the thing that happened to Joe Ziegler, Eldon Isham, and Peter Mayer. All sturdy men in the prime of their years, they had cowered like children when confronted by the black anger of Bachman. The knives they had carried, stained with the blood of Henry Kirby's wound, dropped from their palsied fingers and clattered to the floor.

Standing above them on the naked altar Bachman seemed to swell to twice normal size. His anger crackled around him like an electrical storm. He leveled an arm at the three men. The outstretched fingers twitched as though each has a life of its own.

"Not only have you whimpering specimens failed in the task I gave you," he thundered, "you have compounded your failure. You have lied to me! The price of your treachery will be greater than any of you can imagine. What you are about to suffer is only the first payment."

The three men dropped suddenly to their hands and knees as though stunned by simultaneous hammer blows to the back of the head. They tried to rise, but their limbs would not respond as some unseen force pinned them down. The men made grunting sounds that were not words. Their fearful eyes looked up at Bachman, and they began to whine.

Standing on tiptoe outside the church, watching the scene, young Carl Kirby fought down the impulse to cry out. Inside on the floor the men's limbs jerked and twisted into unnatural positions. Their faces were pulled into grotesque distortions. They tore at their clothing with hands that crumpled into nonhuman shapes.

The townspeople who filled the interior of the church shrank back, but could not pull their eyes from the agonized trio before the altar. Under the outspread fingers of Bachman the executioners writhed and screamed in voices that were not their own. Their clothes were soon shredded and flung aside. Wiry black hair sprouted over their bodies as the bones twisted and cracked and reformed under the skin. Their faces pushed forward in distorted muzzles, strong yellow teeth pushed out through black gums while bloody foam spilled from their lips.

At least they stood on all fours, the short black fur still wet as though from the act of birth. They growled from deep in the powerful chests, bloody eyes upturned to their master.

Dogs.

The full transformation took no more than three minutes, but it seemed to the horrified boy to stretch over hours. When his young mind could stand no more Carl pushed himself back from the window, scrambled up the grassy bank, and ran blindly into the forest. He crashed on heedless of the thorns that ripped his flesh and the tree branches that lashed him like whips. He ran without thinking, without feeling, trying to flee from the sight of the terrible dogs.

He fell repeatedly, painfully banging his knees, scraping the skin from his hands and from his face, but fear had numbed him to small hurts. Each time he fell he scrambled at once to his feet to continue his headlong rush. His only goal was to get as far away as he could from the dreadful things back there in the church.

Something caught him from behind.

The air blasted from Carl's lungs in a prolonged squeal of terror. He struggled and thrashed, fighting for his life, but he was held fast.

With his strength finally exhausted Carl collapsed, limp and helpless, to accept his fate. He tensed for the attack to come, but instead of the ripping teeth he expected, the grip on his shoulders eased. When after a minute nothing had struck at him the boy slowly opened his eyes. The anxious face of his father looked down at him. And beside him stood his mother, hands pressed to her mouth, watching him with eyes brimming with love and fear.

All the terror and the pain burst forth then as Carl Kirby held onto his father and cried as he had not cried in years. The sobs were wrenched up from deep in his soul, the tears streamed unchecked down his face.

Henry Kirby held Carl to him, stroking his matted hair, saying nothing. He let the boy cry out his agony until finally, gradually, the terrible sobs diminished and he was quiet.

"We thought we'd lost you son," Henry said when at last Carl stood back and faced him. "We must never separate like that again."

Carl tried to speak, but the words came faster than his tongue could handle. "The church . . . dogs . . . Bachman . . . the men . . . dogs . . ."

"Don't try to talk now," his father said. "Later, when we're safe, you can tell us all about it."

With Henry leading the way, the family again started through the woods. This time Henry made sure he kept his wife and son in sight at all times.

"Once we're on the other side of the woods," he said, "away from Danziger, we'll be safe. He'll never be able to reach us." Henry did not have to explain who "he" was.

It was Carl who heard it first—maybe because his ears were younger and sharper, maybe because he was listening for it.

The barking of the dogs.

He seized his father's arm and held him. Henry cocked an ear and listened.

"It's only dogs," he said.

"No," the boy insisted. "It's them. It's Joe Ziegler and the others. He's sent them after us."

Henry and Freya Kirby exchanged a look. "Don't worry, son," said Henry. "They won't hurt us."

Carl's brain screamed with the warning he could not put into words. He could only follow as his father and mother hurried along the path through the wind-lashed trees that would take them to safety.

Behind them the dogs gained steadily.

After several minutes the trees began to thin out, and Carl began to think they might actually escape. He believed his father when he said that once out of the trees and away from Danziger they would be out of reach. Then, from the underbrush just ahead of them, the dogs exploded onto the trail.

They were huge, each big as a bull calf. Standing shoulder to shoulder they blocked the path. Their eyes were small and mean, their ears laid back for battle. Saliva dripped from their open mouths while the powerful jaws worked.

No word was spoken, no warning was sounded before the dogs attacked. Henry Kirby barely had time to thrust his son into the brush before the animals bore him and his wife to the ground. Carl, panicked to the point of madness, leaped forward as he saw one of the dogs lunge for his mother's face. He struck at the beast's head distracting it for a moment. The dog clamped Carl's hand between its mighty teeth until the bones crunched. While the boy reeled back in agony the dog turned back and tore out his mother's throat.

Her death scream brought a last surge of strength to Carl's father. Momentarily he threw back the two dogs that were ripping at his flesh. One of his eyes was gone, a thumb dangled by its tendon.

"Run, Carl!" he shouted. When the boy hesitated, cradling his ruined hand, his father called up the commanding voice Carl had learned in infancy must be obeyed. "Run, boy! Run, and don't look back!"

As he had throughout his boyhood on the farm, Carl did as he was told. While his father vainly battled the three monstrous dogs, he sprinted on along the path and out of the woods. With his left hand flopping uselessly he ran across the fields, over train tracks, along strange roads until he could run no more. Honoring his father's last words, he had not looked back, but he heard. The sounds of what the dogs were doing to his father and mother would stay with him the rest of his life.

*   *   *

The name of the night orderly on Carl Kirby's floor in the Lakeview Home was Lyle. He was a plump, smiling young man who always seemed happy, no matter what unpleasant job he was given. Carl felt a twinge of regret at what he was going to do, but he could not afford compassion now.

He pressed the call button, then slipped down from the bed and crossed quickly to the door. His muscles responded with a snap that belied his years as a semi-invalid. His brain was clear and functioning without a hitch. He knew it was a false vitality, a cosmic booster shot of adrenaline, and it would not last. He prayed he could hold onto the rush long enough to do what he had to.

Carl flattened himself against the wall next to the door. After a minute he heard the muted footsteps outside and the door opened. Lyle entered and took two steps into the room. There he stopped, puzzled, looking at the empty bed. Carl took one long stride forward and hit the orderly hard with his fist right at the base of the neck. In his boyhood he had seen his father club a hog at that spot to stun him before butchering. The orderly grunted and went limp. Carl caught him around the chest as he fell and lowered him gently to the floor.

From Lyle's pockets he took forty dollars in cash and a Visa card. Together those would get him where he had to go. The time consumed in travel would make no difference. Time, he knew, stood still in Damntown. But he knew he must go now.

He took a pillow from the bed and placed it under the head of the unconscious orderly. "Sorry, Lyle. You'll have a little headache in a couple of hours, but you'll be all right."

He went to the tiny closet, dressed quickly in the clothes that were loose now on his body. He walked to the shelf at the head of the bed and ran his hand across the spines of the books there. Whatever knowledge he had distilled from them over the years would have to carry him now. Carl spread a blanket over the fallen orderly, and started home.

17

Quinn Kirby gripped the edge of the registration desk as his labored breathing and heartbeat gradually returned to normal. He stared across the counter at Armand Esterhaus, or the man he had known as Armand Esterhaus. There was very little left as a reminder of the genial innkeeper. The man was taller now, taller than Kirby. He was lean and hard looking. His hair was black and thick, his age unknowable. Only the eyes, small, dark, shadowed in deep hollows, were the same. The expression on the dark face was one of pure malevolence.

Kirby became aware of a soft rustling behind him. He turned to see the lobby filling with people—the people of Danziger. They came from the shadows, from the corners, from beyond the marble pillars to stand silently and without expression, forming a semicircle. Kirby recognized the waitress from the Royal Badger Cafe, the bartender, Ben Oliphant the constable, Roy Mayer, the strange boy's uncle. Many of the other faces were those of people he had passed on the street, or had seen driving the antique cars. Now there was no sign of the restrained friendliness they had shown him. The faces were cold and empty. He saw Marcus Diamond standing in the front row, and next to him his sister Aurelia. No more friendly drinking partner. No wild and sensuous lover. Just a deadly serious stare from both of them.

He turned back to the man he knew as Esterhaus. "What's going on? Where are my wife and my boy?"

"They are here, Mr. Kirby, you may be sure of that. No one is going anywhere." His eyes flicked toward the rear of the watching people. "Bring the woman and the boy."

The silent crowd parted to make way for two rangy young men in rough denim clothing who pushed Janice and Matthew forward into the light. Janice's eyes darted about like those of a trapped animal. Matt's young face was set in grim lines. Kirby knew the boy was fighting hard not to cry.

"What have they done to you?" he said.

"Nothing has been done to them, Mr. Kirby," said Esterhaus. "Your wife and son tried to leave Danziger. They were brought back. As you were."

"But why?" Kirby whirled on the man behind the desk. "I want to know what's happening here. What's the matter with this town? Who the hell are you?"

The other man's lip quirked in the suggestion of a smile. "Please control yourself and I will make it clear to you." He placed both hands flat on the altar and spoke in a deep, sonorous voice. "Fifty-six years ago the people of this town made a bargain."

"What are you talking about?" Kirby demanded. "What kind of a bargain? And with whom?"

"They made the bargain with a stranger who had much to offer them. That stranger was I. They knew me then as Bachman. I have been called other things. But what is in a name after all, eh, Mr. Kirby?"

"What has this to do with me and my family?"

"Three people violated that bargain, Mr. Kirby. A family much like yours . . . a man, woman, a boy. Very much like yours, even to the name. Kirby."

"Are you talking about my father?" Kirby's mind raced back, searching for anything his father had told him about Danziger or his grandparents. He realized with a jolt that he knew nothing. The old man had spoken only in the vaguest of terms about his past. He had evaded any direct questions and switched the subject whenever it came up.

"Your father," Esterhaus confirmed. "Along with his father and his mother, tried to leave Danziger fifty-six years ago today. This was a direct violation of the agreement the town had made. And after your grandfather had been a party to the agreement. A judgement was made against them and a punishment ordered."

254

"You're crazy," Kirby said. "Or I am."

Esterhaus continued as though there had been no interruption. "Those other Kirbys foolishly thought, even as did your own wife and yourself, that they could run. They tried. Two of them were caught and were dealt with. Your father, by some fluke, got away. Because of his betrayal the town has suffered grievously. Because of him I have suffered. My . . . connection does not accept failure. For fifty-three years Danziger has hung in limbo, apart and untouched by the world. The town has been neither alive nor dead, existing only as a stopped clock exists, without logic or purpose." Esterhaus' face darkened, his voice dropped to an ominous rumble. "This town owes me, Mr. Kirby. Your family owes me."

"You're talking nonsense!" Kirby turned to the silent watchers. He scanned the empty faces. "What's the matter with all of you? Can't any of you see that this man is raving? He's dangerous. How can you just stand there? Have you no minds of your own? Have you no feelings?"

Before he was halfway through his speech Kirby could see from the frozen faces that he was wasting his breath. His voice faded to a whisper as he finished.

"As you see," Esterhaus said, "you can expect no help from these people. They stand with me now. We have you. And we have your wife, and your little boy. The three of you can now pay the debt owed by your father, and the people of Danziger will be free at last. *I* will be free."

At a signal from Esterhaus the men holding Janice and Matt released them. The woman and the boy ran forward to join Kirby.

"What is this, Quinn?" Janice said. "What are they going to do?"

"Can we go, Dad?" Matt said. "Can we get out of here?"

Kirby put an arm around Janice, feeling her shake under his touch. He rubbed Matt's head with his other hand. "It'll be all right," he told them.

What a chickenshit meaningless cliche! *Nothing* was going to be all right. Eveything was as rotten wrong, and it would get worse. Kirby hated himself for the lie. Nevertheless, his words had an effect. Janice gradually stopped shivering. Matthew looked up at him with a trust that tore his heart.

"Don't even think of running," Esterhaus said, spacing the words carefully. "I was guilty of a lapse in judgement last time. I made the mistake of turning the task over to others. We have all paid for that. This time, as I should have done before, I myself will do what must be done."

He raised his hand slightly in a signal and half a dozen men stepped forward and seized Quinn Kirby, Janice, and Matthew. Kirby struggled for a second or two, but quickly realized it was useless. The men holding him had muscles like steel bands.

"Bring them," Esterhaus ordered, and stepped out from behind the registration desk. He crossed the lobby, his heels clacking on the tiled floor. No longer the plump little hotel manager, he was a tall, menacing figure.

With escape impossible, at least for the moment, Kirby let himself be pulled along in Esterhaus's wake. He wanted to somehow reassure Janice and Matt, who were being carried along beside him, but what could he say?

They left the hotel and stepped out onto Main Street. The cold wind knifed through their clothing. The heavy sky allowed only a dull coppery light to come through. Off to the west, above the roofs, an ugly gray-brown funnel twisted and writhed to a muted roar. Tornado? Kirby had seen them before in movies, but never one like this. It seemed to hover just above their heads, yet it did not seem to be moving in any one direction. As though it were waiting.

Kirby had no time for contemplation of the eerie phenomenon. He was pushed and pulled along Main Street, past the shuttered stores, the old cars parked at the curb, the long-dead Graphic Theater where the faces of Ben Lyon and Jean Harlow were frozen for all time. Around the same corner that he, Janice, and Matt had strolled . . . how long ago was it? Time did not exist in Danziger.

On up past the silent old houses with their neglected lawns, under the thick umbrella of shade trees, to the old brick building at the end of the street. The church that was no more.

Esterhaus paused at the entrance. He looked up at the lighter patch of brick where a crucifix had once hung. His teeth glinted in a smile. Then he entered.

The silent townspeople followed, bearing the Kirbys with them. A film of dust rose from the floor, stirred by their shuffling feet. Through one of the smashed-out windows Kirby could see the twister moving sinuously back and forth, back and forth.

Esterhaus mounted the altar, the dried-out boards of the steps creaking under his weight. He turned to face his morbid congregation. He seemed to look into each face before he spoke. Kirby, held fast by the two men who had brought him, felt the power of the man's gaze.

"It was here," said Esterhaus, "that the bargain was betrayed more than fifty years ago. Here that the family named Kirby did break their word to me and did abandon their responsibility to you, their friends and neighbors. Because of that betrayal the town of Danziger, instead of enjoying the eternal comfort and prosperity I promised, was damned to the shadow life you and I have suffered through the decades."

He paused and once again looked around the interior of the church. A low, ominous muttering came from the crowd, a restless shuffling of feet.

"So it is fitting," he gestured toward the window and the twister, "with our constant guardian at hand, that it be here that the betrayal is wiped out. Here that the debt is paid. Here that the bargain at last is sealed." His hand dropped below the altar. "Here that the family named Kirby should make final payment."

He raised his hand. It gripped the ornate hilt of a long, heavy-bladed knife.

Janice made a little whimpering sound and sagged against the men holding her.

"Dad!" Matt was looking at his father, pleading with him to do something.

All Quinn Kirby could do was shake his head. He twisted in the grip of his captors, searching for a face, just one sympathetic face in the gathering of zombies.

"There is no help for you here," Esterhaus said. "These are not your people. They are mine."

He stepped down from the altar carrying the knife before him like a torch.

"Who shall be the first to die?" he asked.

Kirby strained forward, the power of his rage almost, but not quite, breaking him free. "You bastard!" he snarled.

Esterhaus looked at him with a slow, terrible smile. "Thank you for helping me decide. It will be the boy first, then the woman. I will do it slowly so you can watch."

Janice tried futilely to wrestle her arms free.

Matthew looked to his father with terror-filled eyes.

Esterhaus moved toward the boy.

18

The knife touched the soft skin just below Matthew's eye. An impressive man in overalls stood behind the boy and pinned his arms while Esterhaus wielded the knife. A bright drop of blood popped out at the point of the blade. Matt's knees sagged; his eyes rolled wildly, searching vainly for help.

Kirby strained forward, his muscles screamed at the tension. A callused hand clamped over his mouth to stifle his shouts. Tendons popped in his neck as he fought to break free from the sturdy men holding him back.

Esterhaus looked over at him, savoring the moment. "You see now you are not strong enough to stop me. I wonder if you are strong enough to watch."

"Stop where you are you hellborn sonofabitch!" The bellow came from the rear of the church. Esterhaus looked up, teeth bared in his dark face. The watching people turned. Kirby craned his neck to find the source of the thundering voice that echoed with a strange familiarity.

The intruder strode down the center aisle with the confidence of an avenging angel. No one dared move to impede him. Esterhaus took a step back from Matthew, drawing the knife blade away from the boy's face. Kirby breathed a silent prayer for the interruption, however brief. Then the intruder stalked into his line of vision. Kirby's heart lurched in his chest as he recognized . . . his father.

The Carl Kirby who marched through the somnambulistic citizens of Danziger to the front of the ruined church was in shocking contrast to the near helpless old man Kirby had left lying in the nursing home. The hair was still gray, the face deeply lined, but his jaw jutted forward with determination and his eyes were clear and full of purpose. He walked straight and tall, with no hint of a limp, his arms swinging powerfully. Only the twisted left hand was a reminder of his infirmities.

"I am the one you want," he said, his eyes steady on Esterhaus. "These people have nothing to do with what happened here fifty years ago."

Esterhaus recovered some of his control. He gripped the hilt of the hunting knife in his right hand and lay the blade across his left palm. He tested the point with the ball of his thumb.

"Are you now offering yourself in their place?" he said. The smile spread across his dark face.

"If you can take me," Carl Kirby answered.

Esterhaus beckoned him on. "Come forward. Let us find out."

With every step he took down the aisle the old man seemed to grow younger, stronger, more determined. A murmur rose from the townspeople. They stayed well back out of his path. The hand fell away from Quinn Kirby's mouth. He felt the grip on his arms loosen. Janice sought his eyes. He saw that she too was not so securely held.

"I knew one day you would return," Esterhaus said as Carl Kirby continued to stride toward him. "Your father never left a debt unpaid. It's in the blood."

"Let my son and his family go."

Esterhaus began to laugh. A greasy, gutteral laugh dragged up from his bowels. The laughter echoed through the cavernous interior of the church.

"Let them go?" he boomed. "You, Carl Kirby, should know better than anyone on earth . . . No one leaves Damntown. No one!"

Matthew was watching wide-eyed as his grandfather advanced toward the man with the knife. Kirby caught his son's attention, and with a small movement of his head beckoned the boy to him. No one tried to hold Matt as he walked to join his parents.

Carl Kirby came to a stop facing Esterhaus from an arm's length away. "I knew you fifty-six years ago," he said. "I know you now. Spawn of hell, Demon-seed, in the name of Moloch and Adramelech, show your true face!"

As Quinn Kirby, his family, and the people of Danziger gaped, Armand Esterhaus changed into something else. His head flattened out, lizardlike, the smooth mouth opened and closed, emitting a hissing sound over a thick black tongue. The arms lengthened, the legs grew thick, the feet dug horny claws into the floorboards. A scaly, taloned hand clutched the cruel knife. Carl Kirby never faltered in his advance.

In a blur of motion the demonic creature that had been Esterhaus thrust the knife in a lethal arc toward Carl's lower abdomen. Almost as swiftly, the gray-haired man dropped his left hand for protection.

The gleaming blade pierced the back of the old man's twisted hand and thrust out through the palm. Carl Kirby's lips parted in a grim smile. With a twisting motion that popped the knuckle bones he jerked his arm away with his hand still impaled by the knife.

The reptilian creature roared out its fury. Carl Kirby did not flinch. Something between a sob and a groan came from the crowd of watchers. The hands holding Quinn dropped away.

Still wearing the terrible smile, and never taking his eyes from the demon thing, Carl Kirby grasped the hilt of the hunting knife and drew the blade out of his hand. Dark blood oozed from the wound and dripped to the floor at his feet.

"You can't hurt me there," he said. "Not any more."

The mouth of the demon thing gaped, baring rows of small, spiky teeth. It leaped at him. Carl raised the knife, but the sweep of a scaly arm knocked it away. Carl staggered back under the force of the assault.

"Dad!" Quinn Kirby, acting on long-dead instinct, started forward to help his father.

The old man caught his balance and braced for the next attack. He cut his eyes toward his son.

"Don't do it!"

"But, Dad—"

"Run, Quinn!" the old man barked in an echo of the order shouted by his own father fifty-odd years before.

Still Quinn hesitated.

Keeping his eyes on the lizard-like demon, Carl spoke to his son. "This is my fight, Quinn. You can't help me. Your job is to save your family. Go with them now. And son . . . don't look back!"

The demon lunged with astonishing swiftness. Carl turned to meet the charge and the two bodies collided. They grappled for a long moment, a nightmarish pair of Greco-Roman wrestlers. Then the demon creature's greater strength began to tell as step by painful step he forced Carl Kirby back.

Quinn Kirby hesitated a moment longer. It was clear that this was a fight his father could not win. If he obeyed now and ran, leaving the old man to his fate, would he ever be at peace with himself? But if he joined his father in the hopeless battle, what would happen to his wife and his son?

Quinn Kirby made his decision. He gathered Janice and Matthew to him, steered them to the center aisle, and sent them running out of the church. He followed, watching as he ran the

260

people on both sides of the aisle. The people eyed him, swiveling their heads as he went by, but made no move to stop him.

When they were outside Kirby paused. Parked at the curb a short distance up the street from the church was a familiar old Ford pickup. Marcus Diamond's. A glance through the window showed him the key was in the ignition.

"Come on!" Kirby boosted wife and son into the cab, then ran around and climbed in on the driver's side.

It took him a minute to find the starter button on the floorboard under the clutch pedal. He tromped on it, giving silent thanks as the engine fired. Before pulling away from the curb he took a last look at the church. Under the angry sky the brick building loomed dark and massive. There was no sound from inside, but through the broken windows he could see flashes of strange blue-white light. What manner of unearthly combat was taking place in there?

"Quinn." Janice's voice brought his mind back. He levered the Ford into gear and pulled away.

Main Street was again deserted. Overhead the dirty looking clouds roiled like a stewpot. Behind them the eerie tornado continued its weaving dance. Kirby kept his eyes grimly on the black ribbon of asphalt that would lead them to safety.

He passed the Esso station and the fields beyond, and soon recognized the Chrysler dead in the road ahead. He looked over at Janice and allowed himself a tight grin.

"Almost out," he said.

He swung the pickup over onto the shoulder of the road to ease past the stalled car, and the engine died. He pumped the accelerator pedal vainly as the gears brought the pickup to a jerking stop.

"Oh, God, no," Janice cried. "This is what happened to me."

"Don't go to pieces," Kirby said. "That sign up the road marks the limits of Danziger. All we have to do is walk past it. Once we're over the line, we'll be all right."

"How can you be sure?"

"I'm not. But let's find out."

He went around and helped Janice and Matt out of the pickup. A probing wind swirled and eddied around the three people as they walked between the two dead automobiles toward the sign: *You are now leaving Danziger, Wisconsin. Please come back.*

They were just thirty feet away now. Twenty-five. Twenty. Quinn could smell the fresh air of freedom. He could taste it. His mind raced with promises—all the ways in which he would be a better husband and father once they were out of here. Everything would be different as soon as they crossed the invisible line that marked the boundary of Danziger. It was so close now. So close. Just a few more steps.

He froze. There, ranged across the road blocking their way, stood the dogs.

Quinn Kirby felt his insides shrivel. His throat tightened up, the beating of his heart hammered against his ribs. The nightmare of so many years had come true at last. Vomit rose in his throat and for a moment he thought he might faint.

Janice was crying. Matt was tugging at his hand calling, "Dad, Dad!"

The dogs came toward them, stiff-legged, neck fur bristling. Their growls were deep and manacing. The powerful teeth glistened with saliva. There was no mistaking the animals' purpose. Three pairs of red eyes bored into Kirby's skull.

With a violent shudder, he shook off the paralysis that held him to the spot. He pushed Matt to one side of the road and held Janice for a moment until he saw that the dogs were ignoring the boy.

"Get out," he said to Janice between clenched teeth. "Take Matt, get across the line with him and run like hell."

"Quinn . . . you can't . . . the dogs . . ."

He squeezed her shoulder, putting into the caress all the things he had left unsaid over the years. Then he pushed her gently after their son. "Run, Janice," he said again. And repeating the admonishment of his father and his grandfather, he added, "Don't look back."

The three dogs had him surrounded now, and were moving closer. He released Janice and started her across the road with a little shove. On the other side she grasped Matthew's hand. Together they ran to the sign.

As Quinn had directed, Janice did not look back. As she and Matt crossed the line he heard a shout from her husband. Triumph? Pain? A battle cry? She could not tell. Then came the snarling, growling, gobbling sounds.

The wind rose and a curtain of dry brown dust closed over the scene.

19

The first thing Janice saw was the wallpaper. It was awful. Little baskets of lavender flowers intertwined with a leafy vine. Rosebuds spaced along the vine like overripe birds on a telephone wire. The wallpaper first, then the clock.

A clock! An old-fashioned wall clock in a wooden frame with a brass pendulum encased in glass beneath the face. The marvelous thing about it was the pendulum swinging back and forth, back and forth. It was the first working clock she had seen in . . . in how long? She couldn't say.

She was lying on a couch in a small, cozy room with a clean blanket thrown over her and a pillow under her head. There was an open window through which bright sunlight streamed. In the corner of the room a television set was on with the volume turned low. Cartoons. Matthew sat cross-legged in front of the screen, enthralled.

A man and woman entered. Middle-aged, healthy, concerned. The man wore a blue work shirt and jeans. The woman had on a flowered dress.

"Well, our guest is awake," the man said. "How you feeling, Mrs. Kirby?"

"You know me?"

"We looked through your purse," said the woman. "Found your driver's license. Hope you don't mind."

"No, of course not." Janice rubbed her eyes. "I'm still kind of whacked out." She looked around at her surroundings. "uh . . . uh . . ."

"'Where am I?' Isn't that what you're supposed to say?" the woman asked with a smile. "They always do on TV."

Janice felt herself smile. "All right, where am I?"

"Riverton, Wisconsin," the woman said. "Just outside, actually. I'm Wilma Verrick. The big guy here is my husband Frank. This is our farm. Frank found you and your boy out on the road about an hour ago. You have an accident or something?"

"I . . . No, no accident." Her memory was cloudy. She tried to pull her thoughts into lucid form. "My husband . . . did you see him?"

GARY BRANDNER

A wary look flashed between the farm couple.

"There wasn't anybody else," Frank Verrick said. "Just you and the boy."

"You're sure?"

"I wouldn't likely miss a full grown man in broad daylight. Where'd you leave him?"

"He was just the other side of the line."

"Line?" The Verricks showed their puzzlement.

"In Danziger."

Frank Verrick took a step toward the couch. "Danziger? Where did you hear about Danziger? You must have read it somewhere."

"We were just there," Janice insisted. "My husband, my little boy and I."

"That isn't possible," Wilma said gently. "You must have taken a bump on the head."

Janice pushed away the blanket and sat up. "No. We were all there in the town." She studied their faces, tried to read the looks she saw there. "What is it? What's wrong?"

Verrick spoke softly in a tone meant to be calming. "Mrs. Kirby, there isn't any Danziger. Hasn't been for a long time."

Janice could only stare. "I don't understand."

"Back in the Thirties, during the Depression, a freak storm touched down over there. A twister. Never been anything like it around here before or since. Wiped out the town right down to the last stick of kindling wood. They say nobody got out of town alive. Most likely that's an exaggeration, but you couldn't prove it by me. They never built it up again. Danziger's nothing but a dead place on the road."

Janice began to shiver violently. Wilma Verrick pulled the blanket back up around her shoulders.

"There, there," she said. "You mustn't take a chill."

Still shaking, Janice looked toward the window. It was not the cold that had seized her.

"What's wrong?" Wilma asked.

"Don't you hear that?"

The Verricks cocked their heads and listened.

Frank Verrick smiled. "It's nothing to worry about," he said. "Just the dogs."

Like his colleague Robert *(Psycho)* Bloch, fellow California author Gary Brandner will no doubt eventually be given a middle "name" due to the film adaptations of his first—and most famous—novel. This of course is *The Howling,* which was made into a successful film by director Joe Dante in 1981. Since then, no less than three "sequels" have appeared on the silver screen, even though Brandner has in fact written novels of only *Howling II* and *Howling III.* Nevertheless, even more movie sequels are planned. Like Bloch, he takes the movie series in stride, as it has enabled him to do screenplays of his own. Not surprisingly—even though he has published nearly two dozen novels—he is best known for the movies produced from his work. These include *Cameron's Closet* and last Spring's television mini-series *From the Dead of Night,* which was based on his *Walkers.* A native of Sault Sainte Marie, Michigan, Brandner works every day "from nine to five" on his word processor, either writing novels such as *Floater, Carrion,* or *Quintana Roo,* or adapting them into screenplays.

*　　*　　*

SW: When you're in the midst of a story, do you have to be actually frightened by what you're writing to make it truly successful?
GB: Yes, it works best if I can scare myself. When I was writing *Cameron's Closet,* for example, I used the closet right across from my office room here as a model. And I kept looking over there when I was writing the scarier parts, and would hear these strange noises from in there! And if I can do *that* to myself, then I figure the writing is going well.
SW: Do you have any belief in the occult or the supernatural, or is all purely academic research to you?

GB: I'd have to say it's mostly research, though when I'm really involved in a story, then I really *believe* in the subject while I'm writing. If I'm writing about werewolves, then I believe at the time in werewolves. I would have to say I can't absolutely deny the possibility of anything.

SW: Could you give us then the origins of "Damntown."

GB: The genesis of the story goes back to 1981, when I first had the idea of it as a novel. I worked on it, but it just didn't seem to fit as a novel. I tried it again in 1983, then put it away in a folder. Then came your novella offer for NIGHT VISIONS, and it was just the right length. And a novella is a beautiful length for horror, I think. So I reshaped it, dropped some unnecessary characters and sub-plots, and rewrote it as a novella. It took about two months.

SW: Since it's difficult to calculate the number of drafts when so many writers use word processors, do you recall how many versions of "Damntown" you went through before you were satisfied? Or do you print out drafts and edit them as you go along?

GB: I do it all in the word processor, but it still winds up as three drafts. I do the first draft as fast as I can—I don't slow down so that I can put everything in. Then I clean it up somewhat and correct any errors in the second draft, and then the third draft is where I really polish it up. I don't print it out until I'm ready to mail it.

SW: Are there any autobiographical elements in "Damntown"? The town certainly had the feel that you were bringing it forth out of memory as much as your imagination.

GB: Yes, small mid-western towns are my roots. Both of my parents were born in towns very much like Danziger. I did use a lot of my memories, and I have been back to the area where I grew up. In a lot of my books, I use a small mid-western town in some way or the other. I really *like* these kinds of communities—not that they all have problems like Danziger!—but I don't think I could live in one for more than a couple of weeks without going crazy. [laughs]

I could also say that the key idea to the story is that I sometimes write about the flip-side of a situation. Like the flip-side to "Brigadoon" which is about a town that's frozen in time. And when it comes back, it's such a lovely place that everyone is happy and wants to stay there. I thought, "What if a town was frozen in time, and then came back to the present. Only it wasn't such a nice place, and it would be hell to get out of there . . ."

SW: You're known for your powerful portrayals of demons and supernatural creatures. The dogs in "Damntown" are as memorable as any of the human characters. Do you recall why you made them almost an underlying theme of fear?

GB: At the time I was working on the first draft in 1981, I was living in a kind of seedy Los Angeles neighborhood. And there was this pack of loose dogs running around, terrorizing people. If I had somebody over to my apartment, I would have to walk them back to their car with a stick in my hand. They were on the mind at the time I started to write the story, so I wrote them into it. I personally am very fond of dogs, but this pack of apparently abandoned dogs were simply *mean*.

SW: Even the tornado seemed an unusual, yet oddly familiar menace.

GB: Well, referring back to my flip-side idea finding, I thought of the tornado from *The Wizard of Oz*, which at first appears to be quite menacing, but turns out to be kind of friendly in that it deposits Dorothy in the land of Oz. But I wanted a tornado to hang around that would be like a tornado from hell. So thinking "flip-side" that way has given me a lot of kick-off points for stories.

After-Words

Okay, so Charles Lang just may be the proverbial "new kid on the block." Born in Beverly, Massachusettes in 1959, Lang currently —and perhaps quite appropriately—resides in the world famous town of Salem. As to why he became an artist in the horror/fantasy/ science fiction genres, he admits that it took but a single look at a Frank Frazetta painting to make him realize where his destiny lay. Although he has had some formal art school training, he claims to be mostly self-taught. His lovely wife Wendy is also an artist, and together and separately they have been responsible for some of the most memorable TOR book covers of the past few years. Few years indeed—since Lang has only been a professional illustrator since 1986, his work first appearing in that classy periodical, *Aboriginal SF*. He has also illustrated Fritz Leiber's *The Big Time* for Franklin Press, and done a back cover for Stephen Bissette's controversial *Taboo*. For now, he is best known for the stunning work executed for Dark Harvest's edition of *Swan Song* by Robert R. McCammon, Judging from the work seen in progress for this volume, it appears that Lang is going to be increasingly sought after as a dark star rising.

*   *   *

SW: Any special research required for this project?
CL: Well, for Richard Laymon's "Mop Up," I had to find some good photos of some flamethrowers, and for Gary Brandner's story I needed some of tornadoes. So I went down to our local library and spent about four hours looking for photos of flamethrowers and tornadoes. But I really couldn't find anything. But at home I have about 200 National Geographics, so I poured through those until I

269

found an article on tornadoes. Still no luck on flamethrowers. Then I remembered we had John Carpenter's *The Thing* on tape. So I ran it through, and whenever there was a scene with a flamethrower in it, I paused the VCR, and sketched from the still on the TV screen. So that's how I went about getting my reference material just for the flamethrowers.

SW: You told me you admire realistic artists. From your work it's obvious you're a stickler for detail.

CL: If I can find something specific that's mentioned in a story—like if a character is wearing such-and-such a ring—I'll try and find a photo or an actual facsimile of that ring to work from. Within the time limit I have to do a project, I try and be as accurate as possible. With human figures, I use models. Why I do that is because it helps me with getting the proportions a little more correctly, and sometimes helps me with the lighting. Also the photo reference gives me something to fall back on while I'm actually doing the painting. First I do a rough sketch, as you've seen. Then I do tighter, final sketches on tracing paper. When I do those, I also do my lights and my shadows. So that when I paint it, all I have to figure out then is color.

SW: The cover is especially striking—it reminds me of a mural.

CL: I'm personally real happy with that, because I've never had a chance to do it before. I think of it as sort of a montage style. Over a reddish, nightmare sky, I've put images from all the short stories. I hadn't seen that done before. At least, I hadn't seen it done on any of the previous NIGHT VISIONS anthologies. For even though these books are collections of short stories, all I've ever seen on the cover is an illustration from *one* of the stories. From my own point of view, if this is a collection, it should be multiple images of what's going on in the book.

Everybody should be represented. The only reason some figures are larger than others is because I felt it looked better compositionally. It wasn't that I felt this story was better than that one; what I tried to do was to put on enough main characters or images to make a good cover.

SW: How realistic do you plan to make some of these images? The sketch for the scene in ''Bad News'' with the man biting into the rat-thing is unsettling enough as it is.

CL: I am working from a photograph. And I'm just trying to get it to look as real as possible. Even the pose of the arms, I try to get as accurate as I can. I work from Polaroids that I use later for photographic reference. I'll be photographing a close-up of my hand against my face as if I was biting into the rat-thing. And what I might do is get a small ketchup tube and squeeze it open—just so I can get a sense of how the blood will fly onto the cheeks. [laughs] I'll do just about anything to get the final illustration more accurate.

SW: This is your first opportunity to work with several different authors and stories, rather than on a single novel. Any difference in your approach?

CL: Personally, I'm more of a short story reader than I am a reader of novels. I think it takes a lot more effort to put across the essence of a short story than it does a novel. The challenge in the short story —and the novellas—is to find the *exact* scene which will best show off what the author is trying to get across. Or at least enhance the story without hurting it. The problem is there were more Richard Laymon stories than I could illustrate, while there was only one Gary Brandner story. With the Laymon stories, it was a choice of picking what I thought were the strongest stories. While with Brandner's "Damntown," I found a ball-park range of pages between illustrations, so that the reader would get a treat, and wouldn't have to wait another hundred pages before seeing another illustration. So as to break up the novella and try and give it an easy rhythm.

SW: So you're looking forward to people recognizing you as someone who consciously wants to specialize in horror and fantasy illustration?

CL: Oh, definitely! I'm having a blast doing this. With NIGHT VISIONS 7 I've had more freedom than any other project to date. I get to do the scenes that *I* want to do! And the very first time the public is going to see a visualization for this book, it's going to be my work. That in itself makes a difference. Hopefully, I can carry it off, and people are going to say, "My God—that *is* what it should look like!!"